The Ways of Magic

The Ways of Magic

Nameless Magery
Of Swords and Spells

DELIA MARSHALL TURNER

FANTASY

NAMELESS MAGERY Copyright © 1998 by Delia
    Marshall Turner
    Publishing History: Del Rey paperback July 1998
OF SWORDS AND SPELLS Copyright © 1999 by Delia
    Marshall Turner
    Publishing History: Del Rey paperback January 1999

First SFBC Fantasy Printing: April 1999

Published by arrangement with:
The Ballantine Publishing Group
201 East 50th Street
New York, NY 10022

Visit us online at *http://www.sfbc.com*
Visit Del Rey's website at *http://www.randomhouse.com/delrey/*

ISBN 0-7394-0192-0

PRINTED IN THE UNITED STATES OF AMERICA

Contents

NAMELESS MAGERY

1

In Which I Don't Eat a Rat

It was winter. I was half-starved and so wet my armpits were starting to mildew. My father's finger bone hanging on a thin metal chain was the only thing left of my life—all seventeen years of it, but that was forever to me then—and it seemed my future was going to end shortly in a dismal pile of my own bones.

I knelt down in the slush of half-frozen mud. Stretching as far as I could to avoid leaving a scent, I spread my awkwardly constructed snare next to the hole in the tree. I placed the tiny lump of rotting meat that I'd kept back from the last meal in the center of the snare. Paying out the trip-line, I backed up on my knees through the mud until I was out of sight behind a bush. I settled myself to wait. The bush was leafless and gave no shelter from the relentless rain, but I was already so wet and cold it made no difference. Sooner or later the ratlike thing that lived in the tree would let its hunger overcome its caution and come out, and I would have something to eat for today.

I tried to meditate, but I couldn't separate my mind from the slithery feeling of the wetness between my skin and the tattered old robe I wore. Meditation was meant to be sung aloud, on a sunny day, with friends and family singing with you, and food set out warm and smelling good at the worship table. My Voices, muttering in the caverns at the back of my mind, had no prophecies to give and were reduced to nonsense, mostly speculations on the spiritual significance of the number four.

My nose was running, the eye I had injured the week before was beginning to water again, my feet were falling asleep, and the rain felt like it was getting colder, but I didn't move. Food was too hard to get in the cold season, and I was hungry. At least the Enforcers' casual blows had finally taught me what my Guardian couldn't, how to keep quiet when it was necessary. The Living God never had to be cold or hungry or even in pain, except at the end of the year. The rain fell, and I waited, watched, and listened to the hiss and crash of water on the tree branches.

Later, some time after I lost sensation in the fingers holding the trip-line, I heard a sound that was not caused by the winter rains. Something big was crashing up the hill from the stream, something with four feet, that didn't care about the underbrush. I snatched the snare back to me with a quick motion and rolled it up. There had been no large animals in the forest in the year I had been hiding there. Were there things that ate flesh here? It was very heavy, whatever it was. The ground thumped beneath me to the heavy steps. I peered through the stems of the bush, crouched and ready to run if my numbed limbs would let me.

When the source of the noise surged through the underbrush on the other side of the clearing, it was the last thing I expected to see on this god-lost planet: an ordinary big bay horse with a whiskered nose and furry fetlocks, and a tall man riding on it. He was wet and grouchy with a dripping nose and sodden leathers, not looking where he was going and not particularly caring. He could have been an ordinary traveler in any backcountry on Mennenkaltenei, except for the wispy streaks of blue flame I could see trailing from his head and questing about him.

I almost stood, almost ran to intercept his horse as it plodded wearily by, almost shouted to him to stop and help me. I didn't. I held my breath and stayed crouched behind the bush, watching him go and cursing myself. How many times had I promised myself that if anybody found me I would grab them by the knees and beg them to adopt me? I had thought I would even welcome Enforcers, endure their dead cruelty for the sake of food and warmth and human company, however hateful that company had been. But I couldn't do it.

When the horse had passed behind the nearer trees, and the sound of its steps receded toward the top of the hill and the narrow path there, I stood painfully and followed after. I had to know where he was going. I had seen no people since I'd sacrilegiously escaped the Enforcers, stranding myself on this strange world. I looked up at the top of the hill, and saw distant flickers of the man's cold flame disappearing into the darkening sky, and found myself hurrying. I moved as silently as I could, though. If he turned out to be an enemy, I could always fade back into the forest. The woods were not always against me, only in winter, and spring might come again.

The walking horse and its weary rider were unaware of me as I stole along, always a few trees behind in the gathering dusk. I watched him as closely as I could. The horse, if shaggy, was well fed, unlike most servants of the Enforcers. The man was not dressed like an Enforcer, either. He had obviously been traveling for some time; his leathers were well worn and cracked in places, and the boots on his long legs were creased and coming apart at the seams. Though he kept his head down to keep the rain out of his eyes, his shoulders were strong. He was neither a starving ascetic nor an overfed parasite. He did not treat the horse badly. He never struck her in the hours that followed, and though she must have been terribly tired and cold, she kept on willingly.

After a time I followed them only by the blue wisps of light, the fire that only a few spirit-born Mennenkalts could see. Lle fluttered and flicked about his face, veining and forking, looping and whirling, never still, always seeking, but he paid ller no mind. If lle was so attached to him, he could only be an Adept himself. Why, then, was he dressed so? My mind was not working very well by now, what with pain and tiredness and water running down my face. I'd forgotten the Adepts were all dead.

Puzzling woodenly over the problem he posed, I nearly ran into the back end of the horse when she came to a halt at a fork in the path. With a gasp of fear, I took a step backward, but the rider wheeled the horse around at the sound and, startled, stared at me in the light of his spirit-fire.

In that moment, before I lurched away, I saw his face clearly. Then I bolted off the path, through the whiplash switchings of the wet bushes, hearing a tired baritone chuckle behind me. I kept running for a long time, longer than I needed to, until the pain in my chest and my hoarse breathing forced me to stop. For the rest of the long cold night, as I crouched inside a rotten stump far from the path, I saw behind my closed eyes the straight nose, the wide arrogant mouth, the high cheekbones, and the dark lock of hair falling slantwise across a high forehead. It would have been an attractive face, the first face I'd seen in two years, if the amused and astonished eyes had not glowed a ghastly, cold, phosphorescent green. I'd seen the like only once before, in the face of a possessed woman being ritually exorcised. Toward dawn, exhausted and half-hallucinating, I fell asleep in a crouching position, braced against the rotting wood.

There were no birds in this winter-shriveled forest to sing the approach of morning, and what insects there were didn't buzz or whine, but crawled about their business silently. The weak winter sun, rising high enough to glance through the top of the hollow trunk, finally woke me from my dismal and uneasy slumber. When I opened my eyes, I could see the sad true sunlight, but my spirit sight drowned it out with a sulfurous, pulsating glow. Gentle languid streamers of luminescent yellow, as insubstantial as a rainbow, were slowly circling my shelter, interweaving llerselves in a lattice as though to capture me in a cage of light. More yellow ropes of glowing plasm, insubstantial but lazily purposeful, wound toward me across bushes and around trees like intoxicated snakes.

I scrambled over the top of the stump and dangled myself down to the ground, sliding cautiously between the circling shell of light and the skin of the dead tree. With my back to the stump, sucking at a splinter in the heel of my hand, I considered the opalescent blaze inches from my face.

It was the wrong color for Enforcer fire. The hard sad dead fire the Enforcers used was a metallic blue like reflections in steel. On the Enforcer ship, they hauled themselves through space with claws of glittering cold spirit fire, spreading death in endless fractal patterns, and it had always been blue. So this was familiar ller, not Enforcer fire. I knew how to deal with ller, though I'd preferred not to since my improper, irregular theft of the lifeboat.

Clasping the finger bone dangling from my neck, I closed my eyes briefly, aimed my will, made my desire clear, then opened my eyes and raised my hands, saying, "May I pass?" As I gestured, the lattice of light unwove itself politely and curled away from me. I stepped composedly through the opening. I jumped and ran like a rabbit, spoiling the effect, when a startled voice cried out from somewhere very near me. As I ran, I heard footsteps behind me and a deep, exasperated voice shouting in a language I didn't know.

My rotting soles picked that particular time to finally rip free of my shoes, and I was running painfully, prancing almost, and flapping my robes like a chicken with the effort of keeping my balance, when I slammed face first into a tree I'd thought I was avoiding. I wasn't sure who I was for a second, and when I finally figured that out, my head hurt, and somebody was tying my thumbs together behind my back while I had my nose ground firmly into the tree. As soon as my thumbs were tied, my captor said something incomprehensible in an admirable voice, put his hands on my shoulders, swung me around, and firmly propelled me back the way we'd come. As I staggered ahead of him, guided by brisk but not unkind shoves, I reflected that there was nothing like complete calamity to take one's mind off the daily grind of starving to death in an inadequately rat-infested wilderness.

We came back to the trail, where the shaggy bay horse was calmly scratching her massive side against a young tree. My abductor, when I finally got a look at him, turned out to be the unexpected wraith of the night before, though his eyes were no longer glowing chartreuse. Now they were an ordinary gray. He seemed exhausted, dirty, irritated, and surprisingly normal. He confirmed that impression by flopping down on the ground with a heartfelt groan. I followed suit, my hands still bound, and we examined each other with suspicion.

Finally, he said something to me with an inquiring lilt, and when I didn't answer, he sighed and dug through his pockets, unearthing some solid and greasy bread, which he broke in half and shared with me. It was probably the best meal I'd ever had, hard and chewy and stale as it was, shoved in my mouth piece by piece with his grimy fingers. It had been a long time since I'd had bread of any kind.

Once we were fed, he bundled me unceremoniously onto the back of the horse, swung up in front of me, and continued his interrupted journey southeast on the half-cleared trail. It was a clear pale day in the last dregs of winter. The dead leaves on the forest floor were shabby gray, the hardy scaled beetles had shredded the weedy undergrowth that hung on from last fall, and the endless trees were purple, stark, and sad. But the sun, though pale, filtered through to the ground in delicate patterns, the horse's rolling motion was soothing, and the man's back before me was stolid and warm. Eventually, in spite of the burning in my bound arms, I fell asleep with my cheek between his shoulder blades.

I awoke with a jerk at noonday to find him sliding nimbly off the horse. He hoisted me down, untied my thumbs, spoke to me briefly in his incomprehensible language, and walked aside to relieve himself matter-of-factly against a tree. I stood there in my filthy and tattered robes, with my bony feet, absurdly adorned by the remnants of my shoes sticking gracelessly out at the bottom. My chopped-off hair was matted and greasy, and I felt a ridiculous pang of injured vanity. Even though I was supposed to be above such things, I'd always enjoyed young men's appreciation, but this creature obviously didn't even realize that I was female.

Actually, I hadn't had much occasion lately to think about my gender either, but in spite of the road dirt and worn leather clothing, he was a very attractive man, well put together and supple with enough heft on his bones to give a woman something to hold on to. I would have crooked my finger at him any day on Mennenkaltenei, and maybe even tumbled him if I was somebody else. He turned, lacing up his flies, saw me watching him like a skinny dog at a duck roast, and grinned one-sidedly, motioning me to sit down and relax. I had no more doubts now. Whatever this weary wayfarer might be, he was no Enforcer slug.

I learned over a dry noon meal that my abductor's name was Simon; I am, though I didn't tell him then, called Lisane, meaning "Nameless." It's more of a title than a name, but it's not an appropriate title anymore, since I vacated the office it describes. On Mennenkaltenei, if I was named at all, I was called Kaltenhelsterdeimennet, meaning roughly "did a pretty good job of picking her parents." The Enforcers never knew me by any name, but the mages nowadays call me the "damnable foreign witch," which should give an idea of how few real foreigners showed up before on this planet.

Over the next few days, I kept my mouth shut and never understood a word Simon said. He didn't tie me after the first day, seeming confident that I wouldn't try to get away.

Did he have more up his sleeve than the luminous, yellow, spirit-fire net and the eerie glowing green eyes? If not, he had no reason for confidence. I was more capable than most of playing that kind of trickery, though it was rankest heresy. I wasn't supposed to handle ller that way, but I was less rigid about matters of religion than I'd once been.

Simon showed he was, like me, a pragmatic practitioner of elemental manipulation when the first night of our joint travel he summoned some tendrils of air spirit with a spoken word and a flick of his finger to start a campfire. It seemed presumptuous to harness spiritual energy to cook dinner, but a lot more practical and not nearly as heretical as the Enforcers' way of killing ller to ram their warships through the universe.

I'd always known that lle was good for other things than worship service, anyway. When I'd been a cheeky ten-year-old on Mennenkaltenei, confident that no one would dare scold the Unnamed whelp of the Year-King, I'd called up some elemental energy on my own and found a way to put it to a more prosaic use than the usual ecstatic communal ritual. Before my sister's mother discovered me and, to my injured surprise, whacked me in the head for my perverse materialism, I had managed to conjure disembodied arms to steal fruit pies from the local harvest-wife.

Those elongated arms had shone eerily, just as Simon's conjurations, only half-visible to me as if shining with something other than light. My sister's mother couldn't see them at all, but she could see the pies floating, so she smacked me again and took me to my tutor, Jenneservet, for extra training. Jenneservet got the petty vandalism out of my system fast, but I tucked away the information that elemental energy was good for more mundane purposes than the glory of the spirit. It had come in handy when I'd escaped the Enforcer, though I still felt guilty about that.

Now I was glad of the fire at night, however it was started, and of the fat tree-rats and swamp-swimmers he caught and cooked over his fires during the next few evenings. I would sit picking the last shreds of meat off fragile bones in the warmth of the campfire, and he would sit with his long arms around his knees, contemplating me seriously. He was growing more and more puzzled by me. He'd obviously made some kind of assumption originally about who I was and where I'd come from, because he'd been more amused than dismayed by my sudden appearance in the middle of wilderness where there had been no other human for over a year. I'd given him pause when I broke free of his yellow spirit-net so swiftly, but he didn't stop to marvel at my skill, just took advantage of my clumsiness, whomped me, and cheerfully dragged me along on his trip.

Now, though, something was beginning to itch at him. For one thing, I wouldn't talk to him, and I obviously didn't take in a word he said. He tried all kinds of conversation on me, from lectures to questions, to creeping up on me and yelling, but nothing he did got through. Well, it did get through in one way; he had a lovely deep voice with an agreeable huskiness to it, and if he'd offered me barley sugar with that voice, I would have sat on his knee, or any other part of his body, immediately. He didn't offer, though, not that I could tell.

For another thing, I was dressed funny and I acted funny. He couldn't place the once orange draperies that were my legacy from the Enforcer lifeboat, and he couldn't fathom why, every break I got, I wandered off into the underbrush and squatted down with my robe spread out around me, staring into space. He was beginning to act as if he thought I had severe brain damage, and for myself I was beginning to wonder if this delectable creature had ever watched any woman pee, including his mother, from a distance of closer than a mile.

The only thing that kept me from opening my mouth and shattering his illusions was that I didn't know where he was taking me, and I didn't know if I was going to like his friends nearly as much as I did him. It went against my grain to mistrust him. On Mennenkaltenei, we welcomed strangers as much as friends. But when the Enforcers came along, and we welcomed them as amiably as any other tourist group, they disemboweled us. They killed the Year-King before the spring had even started, they incinerated my Mother, they murdered my sisters, they slew the Year-King's postulants, and they killed any Elders and Adepts they could identify. They would have killed me too if they'd known what I was, future llerKalten, earth's blood, and Mother's mouth to the whole planet. Jenneservet told me to lie to them when they came, but I never lie. I just didn't say anything. They shoved my tutor and me in with the rest of the hostages they took until that greasy dolt took a liking to me.

So now I sat enigmatically by the fire, keeping my counsel and picking my teeth while Simon puzzled away at the conundrum I posed. By day I rode behind him on the tree-legged horse, trying not to press my chest too firmly against Simon's back, although at my age and weight my feminine attributes there weren't too evident, and enjoyed the ride. Then one day we emerged from the forest to find ourselves at the foot of a steep precipice topped by an appalling erection of masonry and rock, as huge as a minor mountain, riddled with windows and bedizened with architectural embellishments like a hat with fruit.

Simon dropped the reins, raised his cupped hands, and shouted something up at the top of the cliff. From above, a disembodied voice intoned a substantial and sonorous incantation. Thick cords of half-visible spirit plasma writhed down to wrap around and beneath us. The horse, the man, and I began to float grandly up the cliff face. It was certainly an elevating spiritual experience, but I couldn't help thinking, as we rose amidst evanescent fields of force, that it was missing some kind of point to harness fire elements for a job that could be done just as well and more permanently with stout rope and some lumber. Or even, in a pinch, with some of those little tools it wasn't polite to use.

It was the most appalling building I'd ever seen, and it kept getting uglier the closer I got. Warty towers stuck up everywhere, balconies sprouted on blind walls, gargoyles belched rudely under and over and behind every arbitrary outgrowth of builder's whimsy, and none of the hundreds of windows were the same shape. Fat brown birds fluttered and squawked on the highest ledges, dropping the occasional bomb on the vast array of shabby laundry that draped various windowsills. I don't like big buildings on principle. They just put a lot of people in one big box and make them useless. You have to haul food in to feed them, pipe the sewage out, hire middlemen to deal with the rest of the world. Before you know it, you have to have money and accounting and bureaucracy, and you don't know what's real anymore. The only thing a big building is good for is a temple or a jail, in both cases because it keeps troublemakers out of circulation. It turned out that this pile of building was both of those things, as well as an exclusive boys' school and one of the seats of planetary government.

Once we reached the top of the cliff, Simon sketched a salute to the stolid individual who'd apparently brought us up, and led the horse and me through a dismal dripping archway leading to a courtyard and stables. The horse stalls, at least, were well kept. Simon shouted out, and a wary teenage boy trotted out to take the horse. Without looking back at me, Simon headed briskly for a broad stair. I swung hastily off the horse and trotted after him, clutching my disintegrating robes. The seams were almost completely gone by now.

Simon was looking for somebody. He stopped and questioned a heavy-browed boy of eight or so, who pointed, gave him brief directions, and shot me a poisonous look after Simon passed him. I smirked back. He spat venomously at my feet. I stuck closer to Simon after that.

After several more inquiries from equally surly male people under the age of seventeen, Simon finally tracked down his quarry, a gray-haired, broad-chested man in scarlet knee pants, who had cornered two twelve-year-olds at the end of a corridor and was cursing them with his hands on his hips. I wished I spoke the language, because he sounded brilliant, never repeating himself once. His words leapt out like hammer blows, sharp and bright and perfectly placed. The two boys were backed up against the wall, still and expressionless, until he finished in a blaze of vituperation and turned his back on them. Then they split up and dashed past him on either side, yammering unrepentantly.

The gray-haired man ignored them, looking astonished and pleased to see Simon. They embraced each other and spoke for a moment, and then Simon turned and gestured me forward, gripping my shoulder sharply as I came to stand beside him. The man examined me with puzzled protruding blue eyes, and shook his head "no" to Simon. I wasn't sure what was happening, but from their expressions, they weren't sure either. Simon began to argue, the gray-headed one kept shaking his head, and finally Simon hauled me around to face him. He demanded something in a pleading tone, and since he was turning out to be a lot nicer than anybody else I'd seen so far, I nearly talked to him.

Before I could open my mouth, he blew his breath out in exasperation, stepped back from me, pointed at me, and shouted something dire. A hideous pink not-really-there blast of spirit-fire streamed slowly from his fingertip toward me. I wasn't about to hang around and find out if lle smelled as bad as lle looked, so I dropped and rolled under the stream, losing the rest of the rags of my robe in the process. The elongated blob of fire flowed around in a curve, following me. I panicked, rose to my knees, pointed my own finger at it, and yelled, "Aspect of ller! Lose this form and go back to where you came from!"

Now, that was an unpardonable contraction of a simple but elegant exorcism ritual I'd learned as a child, and in its extended form it was designed to reduce a curse to infinitely small particles of ectoplasm and send ller spiraling back in a flaming cloud to purify the soul of the misguided one who'd set the spell in the first place. The Adept who had taught it to me would have slapped me silly and made me perform it all over again if I'd tried to cut corners like that on Mennenkaltenei. Sloppy as it was, it worked, though not the way it was usually supposed to. The pink plasma snapped into a nervous glob, quivered in the air, and rushed back into Simon's fingertip. He jumped as if he'd been bitten, and snapped out something that made the glob disappear before it ate his finger.

Then the two of them just stood there gawking at me like cornered rabbits at a weasel. I looked down and realized I'd blown my cover in every possible way, down to and including my so-called clothes. I sat back on my naked scrawny haunches, laced my hands demurely in my lap, smiled at them innocently, and said, "Well, boys, great party so far. You want to dance now or shall we get something to eat?" When I spoke, they flinched. I'm lucky they didn't understand Wirdenish, because it turned out later their idea of a party with girls resembled my idea of guerrilla warfare. Of course, my idea of guerrilla warfare hadn't worked very well against the Enforcers. Sarcasm and sullenness have their limits as weapons when the opposition has flamethrowers and disruptors.

Simon, particularly, was staring at me in complete horror. I was certainly not in the best shape to be flaunting my body, a diet of roots and rats and very little of both having made me bumpy where I should have been bouncy, but I didn't think that called for such an appalled look.

The gray-haired man turned to Simon. Simon wrenched his gaze from my anatomy, and they conferred worriedly. With nothing else to occupy my attention, I noticed that Simon's friend wore a necklace made of two cords wrapped in a spiral, one black like his shirt and one the same cherry red as his knickers. Where he showed skin, it was thatched with thick gray hair, so the costume jewelry had a jarringly juvenile effect. Simon wore a coffee-brown choker that matched his leather and homespun just as neatly. His was less affected-looking, though.

They came to some decision and I found myself being rushed down the hall between them, Simon snatching the rags of my robe up from the floor and flinging them over my shoulders. I was getting hungry, and I hoped there was some food where we were going.

Up stairs and down ramps, around curving corridors and through connecting rooms, we scurried past the occasional slovenly boy, until we arrived at a set of ornately carved wooden doors. Gray-hair gabbled an incantation, the doors swung open of themselves, and we entered a dim, cool library. At the other end, a dark man, perhaps fifty years old, sat casually on a low stool reading a leather-bound book. He paid no attention to us, though we stood before him panting and fidgeting, until he finished the page he was reading.

Then he closed the book, sliding a silken marker neatly into it. He leaned gracefully and placed it where it belonged on the shelf. His square hands were strong, sure, and swift. Though he was tonsured, his neatly turned skull made me wonder why other men bothered having hair. He wore a neckring like the other two, though his had three cords that were black on black on black. The plain shirt and loose trousers on his pared-down body were black as wet winter trees at home. Then he looked up, looked at me, and all I could see were his black, glittering, fathomless eyes. He was a well of power, dark, deep, utterly controlled but with wildness in the depths.

He held me transfixed like that for a long moment. Then Simon at my side jerked my tattered covering away again. The dark man raised his eyebrows, turned up the corners of his generous mouth, and surveyed my naked body minutely, with amusement, before turning to Simon to ask him a question. Even his voice was black and smooth as funeral velvet. It made all my exposed skin tingle.

He listened at length to the explanations of my two companions, then sat gravely thinking, his knuckle to his lips. We were silent, waiting. The room creaked occasionally with footsteps from beyond the walls, and a breeze scurried in and scurried out. Then he dropped his fist, extended the fingers of his hand to me, and spoke one word. I heard only the beginning of the word, and then the room, all the books, the air, the sky outside, and the earth itself drowned him out, roaring, "Understand . . ." and I understood.

For at least a minute I had a working knowledge of the secret of the universe, of which I only remember that it was hilarious. Then enlightenment fled, but I had voices in my head, talking very fast and with great detail, even more insistent than my own Voices. I put my hands to my temples and bent over in pain.

Dimly, below the shrill gabble in my brain, I heard him saying, "No, she's real enough, even if she is female; and she's very strong, or what I just did would have killed her. I'm afraid she'll be quite vivid when she's healthy. Look at those green eyes and the black hair, and I believe the skin would be particularly fine if it wasn't so grubby." He hesitated. "No, there's no help for it, and she's strong enough to defend herself. Put her with the older students. If she survives for a year, Council will figure out what to do with her then. She's your responsibility, boy," he added to Simon. "You will have to teach her as well as teaching the student you've already been assigned. I don't want to see her; I don't even want to hear about her again until Council judges her." He turned away from us, looking out the window as if we no longer existed.

Simon and the gray-head said, "Sir," gravely and in unison, and led me, still naked and doubled over, my head spinning, out of the room. Simon paused outside the door to fling those wretched rags over me again, and I looked dizzily under my arm to find the man in black looking back at me past the slowly closing door. That was how I first met Kaihan, King and Wizard, Eldest and Master.

2

In Which I Don't Learn
the Rules

It seems odd to me now that I didn't realize I now spoke their language. I understood everything Simon and his friend said as they steered me to the senior Student rooms, but I was so confused and sick with migraine, and the new tongue was so much part of me now, that I couldn't take it in until I lay tucked into a small bed in a narrow cold room. All I remember of their talk was that Simon was upset and aggrieved, his friend thought the dark man senile, and they argued over whether I could possibly be attractive. It didn't help that the mages don't have any word for their own language—either you can talk or you can't talk, as far as they're concerned. So now I could "talk," and it seemed as if Wirdenish was an imaginary language. My head was soggy as a swamp inside my skull and alive with chittering creatures. My Voices were sulking.

How much of thought came from words! "Lle," for instance. Everything I called "ller" was "magic" to these people. Have you any idea how blind, malicious, and dangerous the universe looks when everything is caused by a thing called magic? No wonder they summoned the spirit to do their mechanical work, and lit campfires with elemental plasm. It was all self-defense, mastery of the wilderness, putting things in order. Very admirable, really. At the same time, in another language, it was blind materialistic pigheaded atheism.

I lay, sick, tired, and limp, wishing I could sleep. Every stray thought I had ran bang into incongruity and split into fountains of jarring contradiction. "Sick and tired," for instance, sounded like "defenseless and defeated." I couldn't find any words in my new language that would make it sound all right to relax. Everything had hard edges and ominous overtones. "Sleep" defined in my new language had more in common with a dangerous ship voyage than a safe haven.

The tiny white-plastered room had a very high ceiling. Near the top was an open stone-framed window shaped like an arrowhead. Late winter afternoon sun cast an arrow-shape of light crazily across the wall and ceiling. A dim blotch of shadow fluttered into the sunny shape, and I saw that one of the plump brown birds had come to perch on the sill. It preened each wing feather carefully, extending and resetting its pinions with a shake as it worked. Finally, it shifted its claws, puffed its chest out with a wriggle, and dove its brown-eyed ball of a head beneath a wing, matter-of-factly and with finality. I followed its example by curling into a ball and hiding my head beneath the thin coverlet, carefully not thinking in words, just holding the picture of the sleeping bird in my mind.

When I opened my eyes, the patch of sun and the bird were gone, and the sky was a pale cold rose color. The coverlet was wound about me and the room was morning chilled. I was so hungry I felt as if my guts had been scooped out and thrown away, but the inside of my head was quiet now. A dark blue cotton shirt and drawstring pants were flung over the end of the bed. They were baggy but long enough. I would have to gain some weight before they looked like anything but a couple of sacks on a pole. Clothed but barefooted on the cold floor, I tried the door and peered out cautiously. It opened onto a big common room full of shabby leather divans and armchairs, low heavy tables, and half-empty bookshelves, with closed doors spaced along the walls. No people, though. It must have been just after dawn.

I padded out, closing the door silently behind me and marking its location. Closer up, the furniture was furred with dust in its corners and the wood was interlaced with roughly carved names and crude pictures. A blooming purple iris grew from the leather back of one of the chairs, its leaves pinched and torn, and from the center of a table sprouted a fist making a rude gesture. Someone had wound a wilted sprig of parsley around the upthrust finger, giving it a festive air. The scattered books on the shelves were torn and beaten up. I took one down. It fell open to a dryly illustrated technical discussion dealing with extracting groundwater from arid ground by supernatural means. Several hands had scribbled irrelevant messages in the margin. I shut it back up and laid it on the dusty shelf. From the combination of dust, vandalism, and disorder around me, it seemed I was in some kind of boarding school. The students must be sleeping behind the doors that surrounded me.

I could smell porridge cooking somewhere in the distance past the archway at the end of the common room. The hollow space inside me expanded further, and I stole out with my nose lifted, searching.

The kitchen, when I found it, was a vast cavern designed to feed an army. Only a corner of it was in use, by a puffy-eyed gaggle of juvenile cooks, supervised by a lanky young man with a purple necklace, arms folded, who looked profoundly bored and remarkably dissipated. When he saw me, he looked even more so, and flapped a languid hand at a line of carts, each loaded with a vat of gray porridge, chipped earthenware bowls, and wooden spoons. I took a cart and trundled it out as if I knew what I was doing. It shook and swayed and rumbled, and my stomach rumbled louder, so after I was out of earshot I stopped, served myself a bowl, and gulped that and a second one down scalding hot.

It was lucky I did, because as newest student in the senior hall I would have had to fight for my food. The moment I shoved the cart back into the common room, doors flung open with a series of crashes and a horde of half-clothed young men raced out, elbowing each other to get at the food. I stood by the door watching them warily, and they paid me no mind until each was firmly settled in a chair with his precious breakfast. One long-nosed lad was left forlornly scraping and licking the vat.

Then a grizzled veteran of perhaps seventeen, sporting a precocious and inadequate beard, looked up from his next-to-last spoonful and spotted me.

"Ho! New boy!" he shouted. The others watched me sidewise and continued to eat. I didn't correct him, and he repeated, "New boy! I'm talking to you. Get your hindquarters over here." I decided not to. He slammed his bowl down, stood up, and shouted, "*Now,* pie-faced mongrel!" Little sparks began to pop into existence around his head, so I guessed what was going to come next. I shook my head at him gently, bending my knees so I'd be ready to jump or roll if he threw some mechanistic conjuration at me. It seemed to be a habit with these people.

His eyes watered with anticipation. The whole room was watching us openly now, grinning with malice. Sure enough, he clapped his graceless hands together, and when he drew them apart there was an orange-sized glimmer of spirit wavering between them, which slowly flowed through the air at me like a frog swimming upstream. It was the silliest thing I'd seen in a while. I straightened my legs back up, put my hands on my hips, and addressed the floating spell directly. "Lle zhattern begtevogen hals bekmelter," I said. How odd. Wirdenish as a second language. The spell stopped in midair and flattened slowly as if it had hit a wall. "Kop mesmikken rhee ver, loselt," I said firmly. Lle snapped gladly into a pea-sized ball, zoomed back to the bearded boy, and the next thing the unlovely worm knew, the hairs were pulling themselves out of his chin one by one. It was handy I could still speak Wirdenish, because the language of my new home didn't have the proper declension for speaking to ller fire directly—the practitioners call ller "it" or sometimes "you," but lle doesn't listen real hard to that. I don't blame ller.

There was dead silence in the room, except for the strangled grunts from the one being unbearded. The grins had melted away. I looked around. There were fifteen closemouthed, hard-eyed, half-naked juvenile criminal types staring at me. I figured if I ran for it they could bring me down easily, so the only hope for it was to show no fear. I walked, as calmly as I could, through them toward my room. I had to pass particularly close to one blond blue-eyed angel with a sculpted pink-nippled chest who lay across his armchair with his eyes narrowed thoughtfully. The rosy tip of his tongue showed between his rounded lips, his delectable hand caressed his smooth belly, and he looked capable of any number of disgusting things. As I passed by him, he said languidly, "You have an odd voice, child, though you're pretty enough. Are you younger than you look, or are you by some unfortunate accident missing something between your legs?"

I looked at him, puzzled for a moment, and then realized he also thought me a boy, and was trying to be insulting. I'd never met so many males over the age of three who couldn't tell a woman when they saw her. I wasn't that skinny. "You are all sadly lacking in experience," I said to the room in general. I walked haughtily past him, went into my room, shut the door, and climbed back into bed. I could still feel the weight of that sinister angel's gaze between my shoulder blades, but two bowls of breakfast went a long way toward easing the burden.

At mid-morning Simon slammed the door open, yanked me out of bed, and hustled me off. It turned out that I had to go to lessons every day, as did all the rest of the half-baked monsters who called themselves students, and Simon was my teacher. He wasn't anywhere near as nice when he was playing teacher. He could also turn a better spell than I'd thought, as I learned after he stuck me to the ceiling for an hour for arguing with him. I usually spent the mornings with him, and every afternoon I had to work like the rest, in my case digging up the fields that lay beyond the monstrous conglomeration of towers. The building, I found, stood not on the edge of a cliff but on a towering mesa that stood in complete geologic impossibility in the center of the rolling forest.

Except for the field foreman, who only spoke when I made a mistake, nobody besides Simon talked to me much. Simon was busy catching me up on the basics I'd missed by showing up at school ten years over-age. The pimply noodlebrains who grudgingly shared the senior student hall with me had come to the school as young children, though most not as young as I was when I had my name taken away, and had spent the intervening years mastering magic. I didn't think it had done them much good, but I tried to keep my opinion to myself. That's something I'm not very good at.

According to Simon, the practice of magic followed complicated rules, which had to be followed rigidly, and which he vainly tried to teach me. There was a graded scale of difficulty in spells, ranging from simple illusion, which any student could master, to the creation of new self-reproducing life, which was barely possible but explicitly forbidden. He was disappointed to find that I couldn't do illusions at all, because I couldn't see them as illusions. They just looked like oddly shaped balls of spirit-fire to me. I'd always been able to see the spiritual elements, being godling born and bred. Most Mennenkalts have to work blind, by feel, smell, hearing, or guesswork. Simon would create some glamorous apparition or another, and I would stare at it blankly and guess until he dissolved it in disgust. I said, "All I can see is magic."

He couldn't believe for a long time that I saw it. Finally, suspiciously, he said, "What does it look like?"

I said, "Well, when I first saw you, you had snakes of blue fire flicking around your head. And your eyes glowed green, too. It's why I ran away from you."

He was puzzled for a while, and then he remembered. "I was using a locator spell because I didn't want to get lost, and a spell for night-sight because it was getting dark. No wonder you looked so terrified. I thought at first it was because you were a student on your ring-Quest who had been abandoned by your guide, and you were frightened because you thought you'd be punished. Then, when you wouldn't speak, I thought you might be a renegade mage." He considered, looking troubled. "Perhaps you are one. No, if Master Kaihan didn't bring it up . . ."

"What's a renegade?"

"It's probably better not to discuss it." And that was that.

As for the so-called forbidden task of making living creatures, both physical and spiritual, I had done that myself many times before, both alone and with worship groups. All you had to do was explain what you wanted clearly enough, and lle was happy to please, though you had to be willing to live with the results and maintain the proper reverence.

Simon didn't like it when I tried to explain my attitude toward what he called magic and I called ller. It made him nervous and edgy. When he glued me to the ceiling, it was because I told him I wasn't going to act like some solemn technician. I said, "Magic likes you to enjoy yourself and be creative. Where's the fun in following procedures and rules?"

He said, "That's a good way to get yourself or somebody else killed. Magic is very dangerous." I hated it when he talked like that, as if he were the Year-King and I were some farmgirl caught praying to the crops all alone.

"Yes, I'll bet it's dangerous, the way you manipulative bug-suckers treat it. I'd be dangerous, too, if someone tried to shove me around like a machine all the time."

"Stop trying to make magic human. It's not human. It's pure energy, and it can fry you."

"It surely isn't human, you've got that right. But it's not just energy. It's . . . you don't have the word. Listen, it's important to respect magic, but you have to love it too, because it deserves that from you." In retrospect, I suppose I sounded like an Adept dressing down a shamefaced smith. He didn't like that tone of voice any better from me than I liked it from him.

He snapped, "Woman, your so-called mind is an emotional morass. You'll have to learn to fear and mistrust magic, or it will eat you alive. Let me give you a mild demonstration."

I found myself bobbing up to the ceiling, my gravity reversed. I lay looking up at him, or maybe he was hanging by his feet from the floor. He continued, "Think about this until I decide to let you down. Every last student is here because the first thing he did when his Power awoke was hurt somebody. Uncontrolled magic can cause terrible damage, and the whole purpose of our brotherhood is to control magic and keep it out of the grasp of individuals. I won't even go into what a fully developed renegade mage can do when there are so many examples close to hand. There are boys in your own hall who have killed their whole families with magic. One destroyed an entire village of people when he was only five." He turned on his heel grandly and left the room, presumably leaving me to meditate on my foolishness. I rearranged the magic so I hung more comfortably, and settled myself for a short nap.

So these miserable children had all awakened to uncontrolled Power, and had hurt someone with it. Little ones have tempers, just like grownups, but they don't know how to handle getting angry. It went a long way toward explaining why every child in this bollixed barn of a building looked hostile or hunted. Why had nobody stopped them before they hurt someone? It's easy enough, if adult Adepts are in the community, to pick out which babies have Power and train them properly.

I had an idea which lad had blitzed a village. The blue-eyed blond creature was very dangerous. He had no scruples, and he knew when force was the wrong approach and when it was the right one. The other boys in the hall where I lived feared him and avoided him.

They feared and avoided me as well, especially when they realized I was female. It seemed I was impossible. They didn't believe women could have Power. In my turn, I didn't believe it was possible, what with the elementary rules of genetics I wasn't supposed to know, that males could be born with Power and females without it. Whether or not they believed in me, they left me alone during the day, but at night they practiced every nasty trick they knew and a few they weren't sure of yet. Every night before I went to bed I checked my room and set a ward spell on the door, and every morning I defused an assortment of trivial and painful traps they'd set. They only got me once, though, and it wasn't with sorcery. Fat Ommo and Benoit, the newly beardless one, balanced a bucket of water on the ledge over my door, tied with a rope to the knob, and when I came out it poured all over me. I shrieked loudly and then laughed myself silly, sitting on the floor with the bucket in my lap and water everywhere. The whole lot of them were confused and offended by my laughter, which was a shame. The direct simplicity of the trick was so refreshing after the torturous manipulations of their earlier efforts, I almost liked the boys then.

The blue-eyed boy always sat watching, expressionless, his elegant legs flung over the arm of his chair, cleaning his nails with a slim knife. He was prettier than a male animal should be, with rose-petal cheeks, long blond lashes, and wheels always turning inside his sleek head.

The end of the first week, Blue-eyes walked right up to me and introduced himself. Everybody by then knew I was a woman. "Mistress

Green-eyes," he said, "allow me to introduce myself. My name is Deteras Anhand, and I must apologize for speaking so boorishly before." He held out his hand, and pearly teeth glinted graciously. He reminded me of my sister's uncle Willemheed, who was all please-and-thank-you until, whoops, he had his fist up your ass.

I ignored the hand and said shortly, "Deteras Anhand, I am Lisane." I felt like a bumptious rube next to this glossy creature.

"Call me Detter, sweetness," he said gently, bringing his hand closer. I swayed away from it and barely avoided being hit with a poisonous lump of spell that had been behind his fingers. It had scarlet tentacles and a mouth, and if I hadn't ducked behind the hapless long-nosed youth it would have gotten me. Long-nose, whose name was Peselin, got all glassy-eyed when it hit him, and tried to embrace Detter intimately. Detter had to fend him off while canceling the spell, and I sat on top of a chair and chuckled.

Detter gave me a mature and reproving look, and sauntered serenely to the other end of the common room. A war had begun, and I knew my enemy.

The other boys only wanted to humiliate and hurt me, partly because it was what they did to each other and partly for my offense of being female and stronger than they. Detter did not do me the compliment of hating or fearing me. He saw me as a thing, a potential possession, a handy tool he wanted to add to his collection, and quite a collection it was. In addition to a corps of pale, frightened children who ran all his errands, he had a string of well-formed underclassmen who took turns attending to his physical needs. They left his room at odd hours, blank-eyed, rumpled, and sometimes bruised. He avoided such entanglements with the senior students mostly, I think, because they were at the late stage of adolescence when they were coarse and half-finished, neither boys nor men. I certainly found them unattractive enough.

Detter's conjurations against me were subtle, well crafted, and just infrequent enough to take me by surprise. They usually involved mental rather than physical assaults, which meant according to Simon's scale of difficulty that he was skilled and accomplished.

One afternoon in summer, for instance, as I weeded in the sun-baked glare of the potato bed, I suddenly looked forward to spending the evening manicuring Detter's toes. I straightened up to stretch my back, rubbed my ribs as well, and ruminated on the real elegance of his delicate feet. Funny I'd overlooked that before. I wondered how they tasted. I thought of sticking my tongue between his toes and cleaning out the crevices. I felt a mounting impatience to get started. The field foreman saw me gazing idly into the drifting clouds and said sarcastically, "You see potatoes in the sky that need weeding, Lisane?"

"No, just feet," I answered absentmindedly. That didn't sound right, so I tried again in Wirdenish, "sheppenborter," which sounded even stupider. The spell was already inside my head, so it took me fifteen minutes to coax it out while I pretended to dig. Detter didn't even look disappointed when I showed no interest in his nether extremities that night, so I put a rot spell on his dinner. He threw it up on my favorite chair.

I asked Simon about him at lesson the next morning. Simon said only, "Avoid him."

"But Simon, I can't avoid him. He's determined to control me somehow, and he's a really good magician."

"Lisane, get it straight. He is, like everyone else here, a mage, but he is not yet a Magician. He is only a student. He may never become a Magician, if there is any justice."

"I can't keep track of the ranks. Why is it so important to you to have titles?"

"They are not mere birth-titles," he said impatiently as if inherited rank were the lowest of the low. "They are earned titles, and earned with great pain and trial. A student is only a young mage who is learning how to practice magic. A Magician has had to learn when magic is not appropriate, and how to ignore his own desires. Detter has not learned that, and he may never learn that. By all means defend yourself against him, but don't make the mistake of taking him too seriously."

"Don't take him too seriously? But he's incredibly powerful and subtle. He's better than any other student I know. If he's not going to make it, where does that leave the rest of them? They're unbelievably incompetent, and they're almost as malicious as he is."

"We are not here to discuss your classmates. We are here to pound some elementary knowledge into your thick skull. Stop trying to distract me." Simon took his job seriously, and anything I said that didn't fit was a distraction.

Our mornings together were pleasant, though much of what he was teaching me seemed arbitrary and upside down. Simon would sit with me at the table in his study, impatiently going over and over the rules and regulations governing correct magical behavior, his clear gray eyes crackling with intensity. He was always shoving his shining dark hair back when it fell stubbornly over his forehead. When I got bored with our studies, I would tune out his voice and admire his body, imagining myself crawling over the paper-strewn table between us to straddle his lap and shove his head between my breasts. I had no excuse, except he was the only soul in the place who talked to me. He always caught me out just when the daydream was getting good, I guess because my expression gave me away.

"Lisane," he'd bark, and I'd jump guiltily. "Pay attention, rot you, this is important," and he'd go through the whole rigmarole again. As far as I was concerned, he had his priorities reversed. I'd have loved to show him what was really important, if he hadn't been such a blind dunderheaded lump of a pedagogue, and if I weren't a professional virgin princess. In spite of his handsomeness, though, I supposed he was probably what every other male in this monastic prison seemed to be, a flaming gravedigger. He was certainly very careful to avoid touching me, though it seemed more like caution than distaste.

If you take a bunch of little boys away from their mothers, shut them in the middle of wilderness with a lot of nasty bigger boys, and make them grow up that way, that's what you get. It's fine for little boys to play fiddle-the-latch-hooks in between playing priest and kiss-the-muffin with little girls, but for almost-grown men to spend *all* their time in that activity struck me as a waste of good material. Not to mention what it would do to the fertility after spring rites, though I supposed they didn't have them here.

Summer passed slowly, and fall, and then the winter rains hammered the fields flat again. Somewhere in there, I turned eighteen and grew two inches taller. I acquired hips, finally, something I'd given up hoping for. I sparred with Ommo and Peselin, Benoit and Pick, and the other vermin in my quarters, establishing a sullen truce of sorts. Detter's legs got longer, but his skin was still as creamy as a baby's, and the hexes he threw at me grew more viciously subtle. Three of the older boys disappeared one by one, and were replaced by truculent but swiftly subdued junior students.

In early winter, we had our only excitement. The older neckringed men who ran the place started talking in furtive twos and threes, falling silent when the students came near, though I overheard the words "animals" and "were-beasts." Then for several days they disappeared on an expedition, leaving only the younger men to supervise us. When the expedition returned, the students found out somehow and we were all waiting on the broad stair to watch their arrival.

It was a miserable group that levitated to the plateau. The men with rings were wet, grimy, tired, and sour, but they had an unringed prisoner with them who must have been even unhappier. He was blindfolded and gagged, his hands and feet were bound with cloth and wire, and he was in a sling carried by four men who seemed intent on not touching him.

The gray-haired man I met on my first day brought up the rear of the procession. I only recognized him because of the scarlet knee-pants. His hair was still gray, but now it covered every visible patch of skin in a thick pelt like a dog's. His upper lip was furry and split down the center, black whiskers jutted out from his muzzle, and the teeth that showed on either side of his long pink tongue were yellow and pointed. The end of his nose was black and shiny, and he was looking away from everybody's eyes.

"I wish I was a renegade. I'd give anything to be able to make the old geezers dance to my tune. Even if they caught me in the end," breathed Benoit to me. Then he realized I wasn't the person he'd thought he was talking to, and he moved away hastily.

From the entrance they went straight to Kaihan's chambers, and didn't come out for the rest of the day. When they came out, their prisoner wasn't with them, Gray-hair was back to normal, and nothing was said. That was it for the excitement.

Gray-hair had a new student a week or two later, one who didn't live with the other students. He was an older man who looked as if he'd been badly beaten; he was undoubtedly the renegade, and he followed Gray-hair around like a bewildered shadow.

Nobody explained it to me. Nobody except Simon ever really talked to me anyway, and the older neck-ringed men who ran the place looked right through me as if I didn't exist. It still all seemed better than trapping rats in the forest.

Simon's lessons grew more intense, as if he were racing against time. He kept discovering another important gap in my information, getting more upset each time.

One dreary late winter day, with rain and wind spraying sidewise through his study window, I asked him, "Simon, what are those necklaces you and the other men wear? The students don't have them. Do they stand for something, or are they just decoration?"

His face fell, and his hair fell too, into his eyes as usual. "You don't know? Haven't I told you that?" he demanded.

I shook my head dumbly. He took a deep breath and shoved the books away from him. He leaned forward, hooking his thumbs under his brown neckring to show it to me.

"This is a badge of rank, and also a permanent warning. It was placed on me when I became a Magician, and it cannot be removed except at my death, even if I should acquire the rank of Sorcerer, when another would be added."

"So you *are* a Magician, then. I wondered," I interrupted.

He drew his imperious brows together and demanded, "How can you not know that? Don't you even listen when your classmates talk?"

"They don't talk much when I'm around. They treat me like a contagious disease."

He blew his lips out frustratedly. "Oh, all right. A single ring is a Magician, of whatever grade. A double ring is a Sorcerer. A triple ring is a Wizard. We don't completely understand the significance of the colors, but they have something to do with individual skills and ability."

"How do you get them? Who puts them on? Who makes them?" I said. "And why don't you understand the colors?"

Simon let the ring drop back on his collarbones. It looked as if it were made of some kind of semiprecious stone or translucent ceramic. "You'll find out if you ever need to know," he said dismissively. I hate it when people do that. They've been doing it to me all my life.

I tried another avenue. "So the skin-headed old goat in black you took me to when you brought me here must be a Wizard. He has a triple ring."

Simon slapped his hands down on the table with a sharp crack. I jumped. "You will speak with respect," he said. He seemed truly angry now, not just stuffy. "He is Master, and he did you a great favor by allowing you to live at all. He is older and wiser than any mage in the world, and he could crush you and me both, or the entire school for that matter, with only a single word."

I knew it was a mistake, but I said anyway, "So he's in charge here. Does he have a name? Or do you just call him 'Sir' or 'Oh, Great Bald of Head'?" I really wanted to know. That sinuous dark man in the quiet library kept creeping into my thoughts and dreams at odd moments, and I wanted to hang a label on him.

But Simon said only, "This lesson is over. I'm tired of this. No other teacher has to deal with two students at once. I don't know if I can stand to face my other student this afternoon. You are both making it incredibly hard for me as well as for yourselves." He did look tired, and despairing. I knew I gave him a hard time, and he was so earnest and well meaning. I left him massaging his forehead.

The next time we met he drilled me dryly on the different types of transmutation, refusing to be sidetracked. A week later the rains finally broke, and the buds began to swell open on the trees that clung on the plateau. I had been in the school for a year, and Mennenkaltenei seemed even farther away, something I had dreamed. But then of course I always take my dreams seriously.

3

In Which I Don't Behave Myself Correctly

I was sitting on a windowsill in the lazy spring sunlight, half a mile above the world, making kissing noises to a doubtful brown bird and trying to coax it to me with the rest of my supper from the night before. My room was temporarily uninhabitable; Detter had somehow infested its walls with slimy chittering bugs that started to eat me when I went to sleep. I'd been too tired to deal with it last night, so I'd found a useless tower room toward the top of the building and bundled there. I had spring fever. I decided not to go to Simon's study that morning. Simon had been unbearable this week, nervous, tense, and angry.

Something was bothering him. I had asked him, but he wouldn't tell me what it was, just cursed me sharply for prying. "If you'd just do your own work instead of poking your pointy nose into my business," he said, "my life would be a whole lot simpler." Later on, over a minor matter of setting his chair on fire when I'd meant to light the candles, he called me a moronic bitch, and said if I didn't blow my incompetent self up before the week was out he'd have to kill me himself to keep the world safe. When I left him, he was slumped red-eyed at his table, his hair rumpled and greasy. He looked as if he was about to cry. So let him mope, I thought, let him snivel until he dissolved, see if I cared. My nose was not pointy, just pleasantly assertive.

The shabby brown bird cocked its head at me and scrabbled a few steps closer to my hand. Like everything else about this place, it was a little worse for wear, missing a few feathers and a chunk of its beak. It chirped at me scratchily, and when I didn't stir it pecked the bread from my hand, getting some into its mouth while the rest fell swirling down the side of the building. It fluttered its wings, hopped back to the other side of the window, and chirped again, a dull, dirty sound.

I heard voices calling from below, indistinctly. My own Voices were saying something scratchy and unpleasant about duty, honor, and powers of two in the back of my head. I tucked my legs back into the corner of the window, hoping nobody would find me. The last time I'd been caught playing hooky, the gray-haired gent in the crimson knee-pants— Memmipeg, the school Warden—had given me a command performance with his wretched renegade student as sole audience. He was as good at verbal abuse as I'd suspected, but it was hard to listen appreciatively when I was the one being called a slatternly, dawdling, second-rate, pig-humping streetwalker.

A flicking blue search spell trolled up the outside wall toward me. Some mage, probably Simon, was looking for me. I told it halfheartedly, "Lle benteren eckesterverter," but lle merely dimmed politely and kept coming. Oh well, so much for my holiday.

The tower room door behind me crashed open and, sure enough, Simon came stomping through, all dressed up in brown satin robes and curl-toed slippers, and mad as a polecat. He reached out the window and pulled me in by my hair. I admit I did scream, something I normally disapprove of, but he just gritted his teeth and kept pulling. I crashed to my back on the floor and barely got my feet under me as he charged out the door, his fist entwined in my hair. He kept banging me into the walls, and I was busy grabbing at his hand so I fell over a lot. He went up some spiral stairs that way, and I managed to trip him halfway. We both fell down the stairs, tangled up, but at least he had to let go of my hair to keep from sliding through the banister. I jerked my leg out from between his chest and an unforgiving chiseled stone step, and kicked him. He grabbed my ankle and we both slid through the banister, falling heavily to the landing below. I got to my hands and knees and stood up, my chest heaving, but he just lay there on his back, groaning over and over, "Why today? Why of all days today?" He had a deep cut on his chin from the steps, and his finery was block-printed all over with dust and stair grime. I nudged him with my toe cautiously and said, "What's today? Why the fancy dress?"

He rolled a wild eye at me. "What's today? Why, nothing at all. Completely unimportant, you misbegotten slut." He dragged himself up, trying to slap the dust off his robe. "Who cares whether you live or die? Why should I be so sentimental? I don't want to drag you with me half the way around the world anyway, you monstrous abortion. I'll have enough trouble as it is if my other student survives." He gave up dusting himself and headed for the stairs again, not looking back. I trailed after him, asking, "What's going on, Simon? What do you mean, whether I live or die? You never tell me anything, Simon, how am I supposed to know you needed me today? Hey, Simon . . ." up the stairs and through a passageway, up some broader stairs and across a grand hall, until finally he came to a stop at the bottom of a ramp leading to a pair of enormous ebony doors. He kept his back to me as I trotted up, still nagging, and he said, "Just shut up for *one minute*, Lisane."

I waited, nearly bursting, shifting from one bare foot to the other. Finally, he turned around and faced me. He was absolutely hollow-eyed with rage barely kept in check. It frightened even me.

"Listen to me for once," he said. "Lisane, the Master made me keep you here and train you, sky's blood knows why, but not without conditions. You've had as much schooling as I can force into your head in a year, and my other student is as finished as he'll ever be. So school's Council summoned you both and me as well this morning, to pass judgment on us all. The worst that can happen to me is that I'll have to stay here another year with a new student. My other student should be killed outright if the Council has any sense at all, and it would be small loss. But you, you're the only woman with Power this Council has ever seen, and you seem to be horribly strong. It doesn't matter how innocent you are. If they don't think you're safe, they'll kill you today without a second thought. I don't know why that bothers me, but it does," he finished forlornly. His forelock fell into his eyes again, and he brushed it back impatiently, leaving a smear of dust on his forehead.

"Simon, if you'd told me before," I started, and Simon said, roughly, "I was not allowed to," so I fell silent again, my eyes smarting. I had been under sentence of death one way or another all my life, so I wasn't as disturbed as I suppose I should have been, but I was sorry to see Simon so distraught.

"We'd better go in now," he said gruffly. I said, "Wait a minute," and wiped the smear off his face with my sleeve. He looked angry, tore himself from me, and went up the ramp. I threw a little dust-catcher spell after him hastily, so at least his pretty clothes would look all right.

We reached the doors. Though they were two stories high, they swung open silently at Simon's touch, revealing a shallow anteroom ending in slightly smaller doors of inlaid enamel. Detter, my nemesis, was standing there before the inner doors, his peach-fuzz face flushed unhealthily. He saw me, but I wasn't important. He said to Simon, "They didn't do it. They didn't kill me. I'm going with you, after all." His lovely pink lips twisted up in a dreadful victorious grimace. "I knew they were going to kill me in the end, and I didn't care. But they didn't do it." Between his clenched and grinning teeth his breath came in an audible hiss, and his glassy blue eyes were triumphant.

Simon embraced me and pushed me toward the inner doors, saying hastily, "Whatever you do, tell the truth. The chamber is spelled to destroy you if you lie." I backed toward the door, watching as Simon turned exhaustedly to face the grinning figure of my enemy.

I emerged, unsteady on my feet as I turned around, into a great high-ceilinged chamber like an amphitheater, where fifty mages glared flintily down at me from the benches. I must have looked like a scared stray cat as I padded on bare feet to the center of the floor, but their expressions didn't soften. I was still wearing the blue cotton pajamas I'd lived in and worked in for a year, now far too short in the legs. My scraped ankle was bleeding and matted with dust. My hair felt half torn out and was probably standing on end. Simon had probably wanted me perfectly clean and properly dressed for this event.

I stood in the center and surveyed them all, swiveling around. They were a grim bunch. They looked as worthless as the Enforcers and a lot healthier. Every neckring was at least a double, and there were seven triples, including the choker on the neck of the Master. He sat in the center of the curve on a black granite throne that swept from the alabaster stone steps in chiseled sweeps as if it had grown there like a giant tulip. The Master was leaning forward, his chin resting on his hand. The other hand was splayed neatly on his thigh. I was willing to bet he knew exactly where every cell in his body was and what it was doing. He was dressed entirely in deep dull black, and the throne framed him with granite sparkles that matched his living eyes. I hadn't seen him for a year, yet he was exactly as I remembered him. And I had remembered him often.

A voice came from one side, making me jump. I'd already forgotten anybody but the Master was in the room with me. "You are late. Is there a reason?" The voice came from a young man, or maybe not so young once I saw his eyes, who was wearing green and maroon and holding a carved ebony staff.

"Not a good one," I said, but my voice wasn't there. I cleared my throat and said, "Not a good one, sir." He waited, but I didn't have anything to add.

Green-and-maroon consulted a sheet of paper. He had a dark toothbrush mustache and a mobile upper lip, so the mustache jumped up and down as he spoke. "Your teacher, Magician Simon, says you are opinionated, egotistical, stubborn, and argumentative. You are unable or unwilling to perform the simplest of spells, while you perform complex and dangerous ones with no caution whatever. You are at odds with the entire senior student hall, you are utterly undiplomatic in all situations, you repeatedly question authority, and it is your teacher's opinion that you have frequent hallucinations." He looked up. "Have you anything to add to your list of defects?"

Well, thank you, Simon. I never hallucinate. Everything I see and hear is quite real, thank you. The rest of it sounded about right. I just shook my head no.

He looked at the paper again and his mustache started jumping again. "He also says you are honest, terrifyingly bright, hardworking, considerate when it occurs to you, and passionately idealistic. If given an alternative, you prefer not to use magic at all, even if it means physical labor or pain to you, despite your remarkable command of the Power of magic. Again, have you anything you wish to add to your list of assets?"

That list was even more insulting than the defects. Idealistic? Me? I consider myself coldhearted and pragmatic. I just shook my head again. No use contradicting these people. The mages were shifting in their seats and muttering to each other.

Green-and-maroon put the paper down, pounded the staff on the floor with a startling crack, and intoned, "Colleagues of the Council, your attention, please. The candidate stands before you. From the preliminary investigation two things must be considered. First, she is the first woman to come before this Council and is therefore unpredictable. Second, her origin is unclear, and some have suggested she is not naturally born, but a trap, an abomination constructed by a renegade wizard seeking to disrupt the Order. The candidate is free to be questioned." He waited, and there was silence for a moment. My heart was thumping. My palms were sweating. How odd. If I let go my control for a second, I felt as if my rigid muscles would shove me squawking and twitching into the ceiling. Somewhere in there since I'd sauntered into the chamber, I had become terrified.

Finally, a lean mage in an ornate tunic hunched forward and addressed me, with a tired and condescending air. "I understand you were found starving in the forest by young Simon. How did you come to be there?"

Now they ask, I thought bemusedly. No one had even wanted to know until now. "Self-absorbed" doesn't begin to describe this bunch.

"My . . . my . . . boat . . . landed there a year before. I was running away from enemies, and I ended up on this world by accident." That sounded just great. The mages stirred and grumbled.

The lean one said, disbelievingly, "Your *boat* landed in the *woods*? What is that supposed to mean? And what do you mean by 'on this world'? Did you live in the clouds, then, or behind the sun?"

Oh, great balls of geneventner dung. He wanted me of all people to explain astronautics and cosmology, in a language that didn't even have those impolite concepts. "Sir. It was a kind of a sky boat, a boat that flies between the stars. And, umm, the Sun is a star like the ones you see in the night sky. I came from a world like this one, whose sun is a different star." This came out very confused and self-contradictory in their language, and I blushed furiously at actually admitting that the Lisane could know of such ideas. They discussed it between them heatedly, except for the Master, who still sat poised, unmoving, on his massive throne. He was exquisite. I still remember how he looked.

My interrogator started to say something further, but the Master broke his trance and interrupted. His voice projected through the babble like a battering ram. "You were running from enemies. Who were they?"

I had to think for a moment, to translate it into his language. "They were called Enforcers."

"Why were they your enemies? Had you done something to harm them?"

I was outraged. "They came to my world, a good place, full of love and life, and they killed us. They killed my family, they destroyed every other ruler or priest, they took us as hostages and dumped useless, bewildered strangers on our planet. The only reason I was not killed with my family was that I was so young they did not know my Power." I stood up straight and proud to address the Master, as llerKalten would have. I've been told I looked like a monkey standing on its hind legs and babbling, but if I didn't look as good as I thought, at least I wasn't paralyzed with fear anymore. The Master looked relaxed and genuinely interested, unlike his fellows, who chuckled sarcastically and looked aside at each other.

I continued, "They are utterly evil. They hate themselves and all other human beings. They hate life itself, and they believe their way is a truth all others must obey even if it means the end of life. They don't believe in what you call 'magic,' though they wield and consume it with powerful machines."

"This is fantastic nonsense, Kaihan," said a plump grumpy Sorcerer in ice-blue and white to the Master. "Let's get it over with and have lunch."

The Master ignored him and asked, "This was one of their ships that you landed in the wood?"

"Oh, no, that was just a little lifeboat, a raft kind of thing. One of the Enforcer ships is as big as this building." The mages began to laugh, a nasty jeering roar.

Master Kaihan said low, cutting through the noise, "Silence," and they froze, affronted but cautious. "Something very strong and strange certainly occurred in the wilderness west of here two years ago. Student, what happened to your 'little boat' after you landed in the forest?"

"I set it on fire, sir. I didn't want the Enforcers to find it or me. The fire was hotter than I expected, and it burnt up a good deal of the trees. I barely escaped." I still felt guilty about asking spirit-fire to consume the boat, though I should have gotten over that after a year with the mages.

"There was such a fire, hot and fierce," he said.

"Kaihan, what are you trying to prove? This abomination is obviously making it up as it goes along. It has no history to tell. It's circumventing the truth spell somehow," said a triple-ringed Wizard with ferocious red eyebrows.

Kaihan said gently to me, as if the man hadn't spoken, "You mentioned machines. These Enforcers control magic, you say?"

I nodded. "They use it, and in using it, they destroy it."

"How powerful are they? Could they defeat a mage of full Power, say?"

I nodded again, vehemently. "From what I've seen, they could defeat a thousand such, Master. My world was full of wielders of magic, yet the Enforcers shriveled our spells like tissue in a bonfire." He looked me in the eyes a long moment, and parted his lips as if to ask something further, then leaned back instead, placing his arms on the throne's sides and relinquishing his command of the floor.

The others tore into my story promptly and sarcastically. I rapidly became too angry with them to behave myself. The debate raged on, my judges enjoying my torture too much to kill me just yet. I half believed by the end that Mennenkaltenei was a figment of my imagination and the Enforcers a nightmare. I was red in the face, spluttering incoherently, when Kaihan came back to life, negligently waving the others back. They fell silent, settling complacently in anticipation. I supposed it was judgment time, and I'd half decided the fools had no jurisdiction over me after all. It could have been very ugly.

"Supplicant," said Kaihan. "This building has been erected over millennia by small individual acts of magic. Would you consent to add to it?"

The mages leapt to their feet in unison, turning to Kaihan and shrieking with rage. What with neck-cords standing out, fists waving, and raised voices, I couldn't make anything out. I put my hands over my ears. Kaihan raised a finger and said the same thing over and over until enough of them ran out of breath for his voice to be heard: "Humor me. What harm can it do? The Beast will eat her if my judgment is poor."

Green-and-maroon snarled, "She's here as a student, and a strange one at that, not a full-fledged Sorcerer asking for final search. Are you finally losing your mind? It is our job to prevent monsters like this from entering the world." Kaihan smiled at him warmly, as if he were murmuring endearments.

I was still furious and I didn't care anymore what I said in front of these idiots. I interrupted, my high voice falling thinly in the still echoing hall. "Excuse me, Master, but this building needs another addition like a fish needs hair. It's already the ugliest mess I've ever seen." They all goggled at me as if I had blown flame out my ears, but Kaihan laughed, the skin tightening about his eyes.

"I agree," he said, "but you must do something if you wish to leave here. Would you care to rearrange the whole thing, wipe the slate clean?" There was an intake of breath from the outraged men around us.

I thought about it, but shook my head. "I could make it look good, but somebody would be bound to come along after me and stick another lousy turret in the middle of the wall." To the accompaniment of hostile jibes from the benches and solemn advice from my Voices, I looked around the room, trying to think something up. I raised my eyes to the windows that ringed the top of the wall, and saw a pair of fluttering brown forms perched on a sill. I smiled, and said, "I've got it. It's not a change in the architecture, but it will change the building permanently."

"Then go ahead," he said.

It was going to be a complicated and difficult piece of work, since so many parts were involved and each part must give permission. I braced my legs apart on the floor, stretched my arms, and called as much of ller as I could get from the room. A mage fell off his bench as a spell-mended leg failed. It wasn't enough of ller, so I called harder, and flaming swoops of spirit poured into the room from the sky and earth— chartreuse, cinnamon, crimson, every color I knew and others I couldn't name. The room filled, and filled again, until I couldn't see anything but coruscating swirls. I spoke and shaped ller, until a deep hum began to rise in volume and tone. When it sounded like a crystal mountain struck by storms, I asked the roomful of ller to do me this small favor. Abruptly the room was empty again except for mages.

They looked old and shaken, even Kaihan, whose head lay back canted against the high back of the granite throne, his eyes blinking. I felt just fine, the best I'd felt in weeks.

"It's done," I said. "It's only a small change, but it should cheer things up."

"Show me," said Kaihan with a rasp in his voice. I looked up toward the fluttering forms still perched in the window, and chirped, calling one to me. The bird came gladly now, no longer brown, but a graceful glide of brilliant color. It perched on my finger lightly, cocking its crested head at me. Its emerald eye gleamed, the iridescent feathers with the cerise tips fluttered, and the long trailing royal blue tail switched and flipped like a silken cord. I looked up at Kaihan and said, "All those ugly brown birds are like this now, and so will be their children and their children's children. Forever." The bird opened its throat and a glorious music like golden hammers on hanging chimes struck out in the still air. Its mate sounded from the high window, weaving a duet of exquisite sadness and joy that finally fell to silence like a promise. I lifted my hand, and the bird flew back up and out, into the midday sky, starting to sing again. I could hear echoes, other songs, in the distance. I was pretty pleased with myself. I'd done a good job. My Voices murmured appreciatively.

"Oh, yes," I said. "They taste terrible. In case the students get any bright ideas."

Kaihan looked around him. The others avoided his eyes. "It is solely the Master's right and responsibility to declare a Supplicant ready for

Final Search. I do so now." He added to me, "May the Beast be merciful to you—and may you be merciful to the Beast."

I didn't know what that meant. Kaihan said to me, "Go on, girl, get out of here," and I turned to leave. He called after me, "Tell Simon to come back this afternoon," over a mounting babble of strenuous objections from my erstwhile judges. That was my second meeting with Kaihan.

When I came back through the curtains, Detter was no longer there, and Simon was stretched out on the floor with his arm over his eyes. "So Detter's your mysterious other student, hmm?" I said. He flung his arm out wildly and jerked upright, his eyes bulging at me. "I think I just got the Master in trouble. What's a final search, Simon? And what's a beast?" He was suddenly all over me, clutching me to his chest and pounding my back. I tried to keep talking, but my face was buried in his chest and he was quivering, whether with laughter or tears I couldn't tell. I forced my chin up to look at him. "So what happens now?" I said.

He looked down at me with bright eyes and kissed my nose. Then he backed away from me as if I had attacked him, looking upset and shy. It was a shame. He had a nice, firm body, just as I remembered from our time in the forest.

I never went back to the senior student hall. I had nothing left in my room, anyway. Simon led me down to the ground-floor caverns where the stables and storerooms lay. He refused to answer any of my questions, saying only, "You don't have any choice in the matter. You don't need to know anything, just do what I tell you." He rapidly regained his normal color and his maddening air of avuncular condescension. I followed his broad shoulders down the stairs, talking to the stiff back of his head and dancing with impatience. We walked through the stable, the horses nodding their heads at us from the musky dark, and passed through the dim tackle room into a large clean room filled with lockers, chests of drawers, and wardrobes. Detter was standing before an open cabinet, a large jumbled pile of clothes and tools lying on a blanket spread out behind him. Simon looked annoyed at that, his mouth compressed to a thin line, but he didn't say anything to Detter, just introduced me to the contents of the room.

Everything a traveler could desire was there, light and heavy clothing, fishing rods, cookstoves, climbing tools, spears, swords, and tents. Simon told me, "You may take anything you think you might need for a long, arduous journey through all kinds of country and every extreme of weather. You will be traveling *on foot*," he said, but Detter didn't take the hint, just threw another gewgaw on his pile.

I went over to the knife drawer as Simon left the room, saying he would return in a couple of hours. I knew just what I needed, having spent a year in the woods dreaming of such a wish list. First, a knife, light but strong, not too short. I found one at the back with a roughened bone handle and a tempered straight blade, sharp and true but sturdy. Then a leather harness. It had clips in front for the knife scabbard, for small game, and for the medium-sized waterskin I chose after checking the seams. The harness had strong hooks at the shoulders for an oiled fabric backpack, not too large. Detter was admiring a curved ornamental sword that flashed and glimmered in the lamplight, but finally decided against it, thank goodness.

I moved to the drawers of woven goods. A woolen blanket, an oiled rain cape, a light cotton all-over robe with a hood and a face mask. They all folded neatly into small bundles and went into the pack. Detter added a carved wooden staff to the jumbled heap on the floor.

I agonized over a slender, beautifully twisted fifty-foot length of linen rope, and finally added it to the pack, which left room for gloves, a small iron cookpot, a spoon, and a bowl. Detter was rummaging through a trunkful of tents.

Now for clothing. It didn't take long for me to find some cotton knickers, a long-sleeved undershirt, a soft hat, and a capacious high-buttoned dark green wool shirt with sleeves that could be rolled up. Trousers were a different matter. I really did have hips now, and either the waistband stood out from my belly like a rain gutter or the pants were so snug in the thighs I couldn't raise them high enough to button the fly. I finally settled with a grimace on a serviceable but worn brown wool pair, sized somewhere in between. I shoved five pairs of socks into the crevices of the pack, and tried on boots for nearly an hour until I found a heavy pair that fit without pinching or sliding.

Detter, expressionless, had found a mirror in the corner, and was modeling a series of embroidered cloaks that made him look like an elvish prince. Never in my life would I be as beautiful as he was, I thought, and the thought made me feel obscurely pleased. I avoided the mirror myself, out of habit, though I supposed there was no real reason anymore not to look.

Finally, I was set. I bit my lower lip and glanced at Detter under my lashes. He was oblivious to me, lost in his vanity, so I quickly shucked off all my broken-down ill-fitting student clothes and slid quickly into the new ones. I tried on the harness, adjusted it, clipped on the knife and waterskin, and slung the pack on my harness hooks. I bounced up and down, testing, and breathed a sigh of relief. It was light, well balanced.

I took the pack off and sat on the floor with my arms around my knees. Detter sorted through his pile, trying to decide. He couldn't seem to abandon anything, though he hadn't picked anything that wasn't either useless, heavy, or more easily made on the trail. It was obvious he'd never even been on a day's hike.

It was puzzling. The way these students were raised you would have thought their masters were trying to make sure they were as unpleasant, incompetent, miserable, and self-destructive as possible. What earthly use could they be to themselves or anyone else that way?

I was beginning to understand that Mennenkaltenei had been a fool's paradise, but there had been much good in the way I was brought up. As an infant, I was dirty, into everything, taken everywhere. My milk-mother gave me suck until I couldn't spare the time from my play. When I was two, it was clear how closely I lived with ller, so I was Chosen by llerKalten, even though llerKalten was also my true mother. The priest called a blessing on me that protected me from my Power until I was five, when I was considered wise enough to take on some responsibility for my gift. When I was not running and learning worship with the other children, I was being trained in my life's work. I was loved, indulged, trained, protected, and disciplined by every adult I knew, though every Mennenkalt child was raised so to some degree.

I *was* treated differently, for I was the future fount of the spirit as well as the Power-blessed daughter of the Mother and a Year-King. A Year-King so adored that at the end of his reign they saved his finger bones from the spring feast and made them into pendants for his babies. It was an idolatrous act, not polite at all, but I cherished my token, the worn bone still dangling between my breasts. I slid my hand into my shirt and fondled it now, dreaming idly. It was the only thing that made my life before the Enforcers real, and it had given me courage to escape them.

The room faded out as I drifted into my favorite well-worn fantasy. I had been initiated as Mother after all, and I stood before the Celebrants, facing the newly crowned, naked Year-King, his hands red with his predecessor's blood, and the joy and fury of the Living God glowing in his face. I raised my hands gracefully to the catch of my golden cape. My head was raised proudly, and as the heavy fabric slithered down my body the assembled throng began to cry out gladly in one ecstatic voice. . . .

"Wake up, girl, we have to get moving," said Simon, standing in the doorway, and to Detter, "What is this cretinous explosion of garbage supposed to be?"

I hauled my mind reluctantly back to the gear-littered room. Detter's face was as calm as ever as he stood up. He did not answer. He did not seem to care when Simon kicked his heap apart with a scornful toe. He acquired a restrained and superior smile as Simon grabbed plain and useful things from the drawers and threw them at him. Graciously, Detter condescended to pack according to Simon's orders, as though he were the master and Simon an amusing, bumptious pet. If I had not seen his performance that morning, I would have been content to hate him. Now I also feared him. His pride and desire for victory at any cost would have made him a worthy enemy were he not consumed entirely by the effort of denying his terror. A man who will not permit himself even the thought of cowardice is a vicious and unworthy opponent.

Simon made me dump out my pack. He grunted approvingly. I put it back together, even better this time.

"You know the rules," he said to Detter, who nodded, bored. To me, he said, "No matter what status Kaihan gave you, I am in charge. I am your guide. You are my apprentices, and you travel where I lead. These are the rules. From now until I tell you otherwise, no spells, no conjurations, no use of magic whatsoever under any and all circumstances, or I will destroy you utterly. Obey me in all things, or I will kill you without a second thought." He paused, and said, "And since I have been cursed with two incredible monsters instead of the usual single incompetent fool, my first order is that you both leave each other strictly alone. No fighting, no sniping. Don't even talk to each other. Understand?"

I nodded mutely, but Detter didn't budge. Simon flicked out a hand and struck him in the mouth. "I said, do you understand?" Something shone incongruously in Detter's heavenly blue eyes, and he breathed, "Yes." It looked like I was in for a lot of fun.

"We are leaving *now*," said Simon. Picking up his own pack where it lay outside the door, he strode out. We headed for the edge of the plateau, but this time there was no bay mare, and we didn't take the magical express elevator. We walked down a goat-sized path the whole interminable way. The sun was already half set when we reached the bottom. Detter had already tripped me twice.

4

In Which I Don't Kill
Either of Them

Three battered travelers stood peering from under a massive copper-tinted tree, looking out at a voluptuous green prairie with faint blue mountains beyond it. Nearly a month after we started, we had finally come out of the forest. Simon looked wonderful, lean and regal, his eyes creased at the corners. I had not fared so well. My worn trousers were loose on me and torn at the knee, and my arms and hands were scratched. I had an especially long scabbed stripe running diagonally down my face; Detter had released a bent-back thorn branch as I walked behind him on an overgrown path. Walking behind him was only slightly safer than walking in front of him.

Detter was the worst off of the three. He had been unused to exercise, relying on his sophisticated use of Power so much, and he had lost too much weight on the trip. His face was badly roughened and wind-burned. His hands were scorched, bruised, scarred, and chapped. Worst of all, he walked with exaggerated care, hobbling, for his feet were a mass of oozing, infected blisters. Every night Simon made him boil water and cleanse his feet. Afterward Detter sat, hands clenched at his sides, and stared expressionlessly at the flames until it was time to sleep. He was almost too miserable to torment me, but he managed somehow. He had not cast a single spell I could see since we left the school, but he was ingenious and persistent with his petty cruelties nonetheless.

He had tripped me, pelted me with rotten fruit, led me through briar patches, mud holes, and spiderwebs, and burnt me with stray coals. He had poured water on me (by accident), urinated on my blanket (by accident), dropped my food in the dirt (again by accident). He never spoke to me. He never spoke of me. He never acknowledged my existence. It was like traveling with an enormous eight-year-old boy in a permanent snit.

Simon was remote, pleasant, considerate, but firm to both of us. I no longer found him attractive in the least. I didn't even like him. I hated him. I hoped he would fall headfirst down a hole and die. Then I would kill Detter. After that I would sit down and cry for a week. I was very tired.

The flat plain lay before us now, full of rushing grasses. The sky was overcast but blinding white, the air was dry and smelled like singed bread, and it was hot. Simon said, unhitching his thumbs from his pack straps, "Midday's a bad time to travel across the plain in summer. Let's rest here awhile."

It was pleasant under the tree. I waited until Detter sat down, then sat far enough away from him. Simon squatted at the edge of the shade, chewing a grass stalk and peering at the dim mountains. "There's a good pass between those two peaks," he said, pointing. "We should be able to reach it in less than a week if we walk fast."

Out of the corner of my eye I saw Detter's face grow pinched. He could barely walk now. Fast walking in hot sun would kill him. I sucked my teeth, listening to the quiet Voices in the back of my head, which were making sense for a change. Detter kept silent, of course. He would walk through a desert on the bloody stumps of his ankles with a bored smirk on his face if the alternative was any kind of surrender. I would be happy if the fool died, but the Voices were firm.

"Simon," I said. Simon grunted inattentively. I threw a clod of earth at him and he looked at me, startled. I said, "Explain something to me. If a person wants to kill himself and you help him do it, does that make you an altruist or a murderer?" Simon narrowed his eyes with scorn and turned away again. That was all I felt moved to say, so after a while I lay back and stared up at the inky leaves.

I woke from a doze to find everybody in the same place, though Detter had removed his boots. I couldn't tell where the sun was in the hazy white sky. I turned to my side and went back to sleep. Simon woke me in the late afternoon, saying, "Go catch us something for dinner." I rolled to my feet still groggy and sweating, and stumbled off. When I returned at dusk with two fat birds, he had gathered wood and dug a deep fire pit. Detter still sat under the tree, not looking at anything, his suppurating feet sticking out before him.

This trip was apparently something every student mage had to endure before he became a Magician, and Simon, to become Sorcerer as he wished, must take his students on the journey he'd already once taken himself. What was the point? If they wanted mages to learn how to behave themselves in the real world, they should raise them in the real world, not walled away in that elevated dungeon they called a school. If the point was to kill us off, they should have done it before we left. My Voices disagreed with me, and also pointed something out about prime numbers I hadn't known before. I supposed they were bored. They never used to be interested in numbers.

Though Simon never actually said we were waiting for Detter's feet to heal, we stayed there four more days. When we started out again across the plain, we only traveled for half a day at a time. Detter's feet slowly got better. He didn't even speak to Simon anymore, he didn't play any more tricks on me, he just walked, mechanically, until it was time to stop.

Walking on the plain was deceptively easy. You simply swung your legs forward from the hip, parting the blades below with the foot and above with the hands. But after a time, our clothes were covered with burrs and clinging, bloodsucking insects, our pockets and folds were full of seeds and chaff, our hands burned from the constant strokes of the sharp edges of the blades. Our eyes swelled and watered with the pollen and the sun. Our backs began to hurt from the goose-step gait, mine in particular since I was shortest. When we finally gave up for the day, we would sit in a circle below the tops of the grass, sneezing and picking off parasites. At night, the wind blew across the surface of the grass, and the land hissed and sighed above us where we lay in a calm still pocket beneath the wind waves.

I finally got Simon to talk to me a bit, by asking why there were no large wild animals.

"Large wild animals? You mean like lost cows or sheep?" he chuckled.

"No, big cats, lizards, wild dogs. Meat eaters. In wild country like this I'd expect to meet up with some dangerous animals."

He was scornful, disbelieving. "Those are things to frighten children with, dragons and such. There are no large animals that are not tame."

"Maybe not here, but where I come from they're common. Master Kaihan mentioned a beast. Isn't that some sort of wild animal?"

"The Beast is dangerous enough, but he's not an animal at all." I could hear the capital letter in his voice.

"What is he, then?"

"Different things to different people." He changed the subject. "Kaihan did say you came from a different world. It seems that must be true. Is this very strange country to you?"

"Not so strange. All worlds have forests, plains, and mountains. I'm used to seeing more people, though. And why was the school stuck way in the middle of a dense forest on top of a rock, miles away from anywhere?"

Simon said, "There was a time when there were small kingdoms dividing up the whole center of the Lesser Shore—that's the continent we're on now—but a few centuries ago, the Sassevin Council, the ruling council, moved all the people to the coasts, created the forest around the school, and thrust up the plateau beneath it."

"Why? What were they afraid would happen to the students?"

"*To* the students? Nothing. They were afraid *of* the students."

"Oh, come on. Frightened of a handful of incompetent brats?"

Simon said, reprovingly, "You know nothing of the past, and you continue to underestimate the danger of magic. Your ignorance will end up destroying you." So pompous already at his age.

"Simon, my ignorance is enormous. If you like, I'll shut up. But how can I know anything of the past? I'm from another world with another history."

He remained silent. But next morning, as we waded hip deep in the wild grasses, Detter trudging doggedly behind us, Simon began to talk as if telling a fairy tale.

"In the childhood of the world," he said, "when every father's son was heir to a kingdom, magic rolled across the land in waves like an invisible ocean. To plow a field, the farmer had only to speak, and the earth turned itself over and sprouted grain. To sire only sons, the farmer had only to speak, and his wife's womb was filled with healthy life. A child's laugh made the sky rain flowers, and flowers rained down day and night. All men were mages then, and the life was sweet and golden.

"Yet rich as each man was, there were always some who wished more wealth. Misers gathered magic to themselves as a jackdaw gathers river stones, and to less purpose. They envied one another, and quarreled, and drew apart, each to his own land, the better to guard his store of magic.

"There came a time when, to cast a simple spell, a lesser man must go and beg his fellow to release some from his stores, for magic no longer flowed free, but sat in stagnant pools, puddled around this greedy one or that. As one man grew richer and more powerful, hundreds were bereft of power, and had to till the land by the poor strength of their arms. Savage wars of spells broke out. Neighbor no longer welcomed neighbor, and one hand was raised against another.

"Humanity was now two kinds, those without Power and their masters, who feared losing it. Children starved, and no one cared. The farmers in the valley feared the herders in the hills, the horsemen in the plains fought the hunters in the forest. Each man spoke only the words of his master, and no two masters shared their words. Chaos ruled, and brutal fear, and the blasted land became scorched and barren. Across the wreckage of the world, the mages fought sorcerous battles, conjuring demons and dragons and djinns. Only the innocent died, in numbers too great to be told, while the evil ones lived and thrived. Darkness fell across the world, broken only by wavering witchlight and the blaze of burning mountains. To our twilight was added the blight of vengeful invaders from the sky, the people of the sunset, who seared us with their terrible judgment.

"Then from nowhere came a stranger with no name, the first true mage, who wandered the world in its days of desperation. He sought joy and pleasure, tenderness and love, yet found only filth and fear. After untold years, the mage with no name rested on lost Mount Erichelah in the heart of the Greater Shore, and decided to leave this world and, leaving, mend what was broken.

"He stretched up his arms and drew down magic from the stars, where none before him had been able to reach, until the mountain itself began to loosen from its roots and float in the air. With Erichelah bearing him, he drifted into the heavens, paying with his earthly life for the Power he must wield. As he entered the night behind the blazing stars, he called down his curse on the world, and the world changed forever and for good. Each man turned in wonder to another, and spoke, and was understood, for all spoke the same words now. Where Erichelah had lain, Sassevin city of mages now rose, and at its heart was the Beast in his Room. The Beast called out, with the voice that commands, to each master of magic from all parts of the world. Each mage in turn must face the Beast alone, to prove beast himself and die, or true man and live, but as slave to those he would have ruled. And as the sign of slavery, the Beast bound those who lived with a collar, and sent them out to wander all their long lives, landless, alone, and unloved."

Simon fell silent, looking solemn. I had managed not to laugh. What a grim and self-important fable. Where were the gods and spirits for these people? Where did women figure in their stories? And how bizarre to even think of owning magic.

I said, "So your ancient ancestors are supposed to have screwed things up and you're still paying for it thousands of years later? That doesn't seem fair. You shouldn't take on so much guilt and pain for something you didn't do."

Simon said harshly, "Oh, something we didn't do? Do you really believe I would spend my life doing penance for someone else's crimes? You must think me a virtuous fool. Thank you very much, but I must disappoint you. I have committed cold and bloody murder like every other mage, and you'd better get it through that piece of moldy cheese you call a head." He pushed ahead of me coldly, soon leaving me far behind as I struggled through the grass.

Some time later, a cool and elegant voice wafted from just behind me, saying, "I am curious. Please enlighten me. Have you never tried to kill anybody or are you just being deliberately naive?" I was so surprised, I felt like my entire chest had just tried to shove itself up my throat. I hadn't really expected Detter ever to speak again, and certainly not to me.

I said warily, "I hit somebody once as hard as I could with a piece of pipe, but that was self-defense. He was trying to rape me."

"No, no," he said reasonably, coming up even with me. "Have you never used your Power to destroy someone? You are as inhibited now as priggish Simon is, but surely when you were a child you must have been angry enough to kill? Come now, be honest."

I felt like I was talking to a ghost, though the sun cast a real enough shadow behind him. Detter was wading along through the grass beside me, swinging his arms, as if we were continuing an ongoing chat instead of having our first conversation ever.

"Detter, I've been mad enough to murder as recently as last week, but if I did, I'd do it with a rock or knife, something with some heft, not with magic. It wouldn't be any fun if I couldn't do it with my own hands. I was the same way when I was little. Besides, if I'd tried anything, the closest grown-up would have spanked me raw and told my mother."

"What could your mother do to stop you? You have Power, you could make her do your will as well," he said. "Or is it just that you are female, and thus more submissive to authority?" He seemed to be genuinely trying to understand, so I didn't belt him just then.

"When have you seen me ever submitting to authority? Dog eggs, Detter, my mother was bigger and meaner and stronger than—than Master Kaihan. She had more Power than anybody I've ever met. I did what she told me."

"Your mother had Power, and yet bore a child?"

"Well, sure. Fifteen children. And every one of them by a man of great Power himself. It was her job, kind of. Weren't your parents mages?"

He said remotely, as if commenting on the terrain, "My parents were ordinary, normal. When I was five years old, I set my mother on fire like a torch with my very first spell, and I watched her burn, because I was tired of her beating me." His blue eyes were calm. "Then I did the same to my father, because he tried to hit me, and my sisters because they were screaming and it hurt my ears. And after that, I set everybody else in my village on fire because I thought they would tell on me, and then I sat down and waited to die myself. When the mages came to get me I was nearly dead of starvation and thirst."

We walked in silence together a few minutes. Moths and jumping insects leapt out of the stalks we thrust aside.

I said, "I think you did die. You've been dead a long time. Why don't you lie down, have a nice funeral, and get it over with?"

"I thank the gracious lady for her kind advice. It's good of you to condescend," he said with no perceptible sign of offense, but he too forged ahead of me, to my great gratitude. My two companions were even leakier in their upper stories than I'd dared believe.

I turned and looked back, with no great hope of escape. A wavering trail, smudged and bruised, blurred back across the surface of the high grass toward the horizon, disappearing in the middle distance. In another day there would be no sign we had passed this way.

After three weeks we were across the grasslands and hiking in the foothills below the sedate mountains. Up close the range was a worn and ancient one, eroded and rounded, great organic swells of rock mostly covered with greenery.

Detter kept popping up at my side periodically to chat of death and deviltry. Simon said nothing after all to stop our conversations, probably relieved we were keeping each other busy. Simon was growing more and more silent, staring into the distance when he walked and when he rested. He looked happy, and I left him alone, but I wasn't sure I could stand being Detter's confidante.

Detter told me candidly of all the petty tortures he had practiced and of prolonged revenges he'd taken for minor slights, seeming neither to gloat nor to confess. When I could bear it no more, I would say something cold and cutting. He would call me a hypocrite and wander away, relaxed, leaving me shuddering. Was this some elaborate punishment? Had he found my weak spot and concentrated his efforts there to break me down? Or was this all he knew to talk about if he wanted to converse? I couldn't tell. There were times I wished I could match him bloody tale for bloody tale. I felt so innocent and naive.

Yet one time, as we wound among low flowers in a valley between two ridges, I managed to shock him. He was rambling on about his sexual practices with the junior students, in elaborate and unpleasant detail, and I was passing my thumb absentmindedly over and over the well-worn bit of bone hanging from my neck.

Detter, seeing I wasn't paying attention, lost interest in his tale of power, terror, and petty cruelty. "What's that you're fiddling with?" he said. "Let me see it."

"It's just a little worry-stone," I said casually, folding my hand over it to hide it.

"Nonsense. You get an expression on your face like you're seeing things when you touch it. What is it, a magic talisman? That's breaking the rules."

"It's not a talisman. There's no spirit in it at all. It's a keepsake, that's all. It reminds me of home." He had me on the defensive, and he was starting to get that considering expression that meant he was seeing a weak spot. I was surprised to find it *was* a weak spot with me, just where I'd thought I had only strength and comfort. I opened my hand and looked at it, gray and porous and grubby on my palm. I lifted the chain over my head and handed it to him, which was not what he'd expected.

I said, "It's a human bone, the tip of a finger. My father's finger. Someone gave it to me when I was a baby, after his death."

Detter's eyes widened. I had finally managed to startle him. "How ghoulish. So part of him didn't get buried."

"Oh, none of him got buried. He was llerMennet, the Year-King; he was special. We cooked him and ate him and burned the leftovers. Well, I didn't really eat any, I was too young for meat yet."

Detter's lips were pulled back in an involuntary grimace of disgust, or possibly pleasure. "Was he alive when he was cooked?" He stared at the bone in fascination.

"Oh, no, no, no." What a horrifying thought. "His successor, the new Year-King, slit his throat first. *Then* we cooked him."

"What had the man done that you had to execute him in such a gruesome way?"

I was puzzled and a bit taken aback by Detter's reaction. "He was the Year-King. He ruled the world for a year, he chose a successor, the new King killed him, and we ate him. That was his job. There wasn't anything gruesome about it."

"Why would anybody take a 'job' that was going to last only a year and end with death?"

"That's like asking why be born if you're only going to die eventually. It was a short but glorious life, and a lot of men wanted it."

Detter's blue eyes blazed from his sun-reddened, road-weathered face. "What good is a glorious life if it's cut short?"

"It's better than a miserable life that lasts forever."

He seemed to take that personally. He flung the pendant back at me and strode ahead, looking like a straw-headed scarecrow. He wasn't such a limpid porcelain youth anymore, not after going without a hat all that time.

I considered the bone again for a few moments, turning it over and over again in my hands. Then I tossed it into the underbrush, leaving it and the past behind. It was the best thing I could have done, and I regretted it immediately. Detter didn't talk to me again for a long while, to my great pleasure.

We made it through the pass easily, not even needing my rope. On the way down, we came across a mountain spring and followed it from its source until we came to a twenty-foot waterfall with a turbulent pool beneath, the first water deeper than a puddle we'd seen in weeks. Simon and Detter immediately started stripping their clothes off by the pool to do their laundry and wash themselves. I retreated swiftly up the bank to the top of the waterfall and took my own bath. I lay down face-up in the shallow rapids and let the water run cold slithery fingers through my hair and over my skin for a long time, until my breasts, my face, and the tops of my thighs were the only parts of my body that weren't numb and shriveled. I didn't feel completely clean even then, but I had to get out.

I sat on a flat rock in the hot sun, waiting for my clothes to dry. Idly I peered over the top of the fall, to see Detter and Simon lying naked near each other, dozing on a rock shelf.

They looked funny, with tanned faces and pale bodies, and they looked beautiful, too. Detter was pink and white, with golden hair only at his groin, and his muscles were firm, round, and young. Simon's skin was more opaque, richly furred, and he was all nerves, tendons, and bones. Like all naked men, they looked surprisingly vulnerable, soft, and delicate. I leaned back so I couldn't see them anymore. They were very irritating people.

I felt languid, relaxed, and clean in the sun. I lay on my back and closed my eyes, seeing only a red glow, and thought sleepily about the paradoxical nature of desire. If I'd never cared for Detter, I could at least appreciate him as an art object. I couldn't imagine coupling with him, even though he obviously could imagine coupling with me. Simon, on the other hand, I could have desired and admired. He had the fervency of the young Postulants who encircled my mother. But like them he seemed to be retreating further and further from his own humanity, seeking solace in his rules and ideals and the voyage itself. Unlike them, he had no hope of redemption by Possession. Perhaps he was just going to get grayer and grayer until he turned into mist.

I tried to summon up my favorite dream of the Year-King, but since I'd thrown my pendant away there was no longer any passion there for me. I had seen nothing but indifferent males on this benighted world, and I was beginning to feel like some genderless lump of flesh, but the sun felt good on my chilled skin so I didn't care. I dozed off.

I was in that library. My Enforcer rags had peeled from me like an onion skin, and Master Kaihan's bleak, humorous eyes were flickering over every inch of me like invisible tongues. The smooth skin of his head rippled as he began to smile, and he looked up again at my face. My skin was tingling again. He leaned back, and I sauntered closer to him. I saw a woman reflected in his eyes as I approached, and I did not know who she was. On the sides of his head, close-cropped salt-and-pepper hair glinted subtly in the light as he moved. What did his head feel like? Was the skin as smooth and warm as it looked? How did that chiseled, considerate mouth taste? I was standing bent over him, my hands framing but not touching his face, and his face was full as a clear glass

*brimming with the dark-flavored liquid of eager desire. But who was
that woman I saw in his eyes?*

I awoke with a foul taste in my mouth. My clothes were dry, my
companions were calling me, and we moved on. I was annoyed with my
dream all the rest of the day. It hadn't felt like a false dream, but I didn't
accept it. Jenneservet had raised me better than that, that I should think
lustfully about old men with Power.

Two weeks later, we encountered a real road, with horse carts traveling it, and hitched a ride with an obliging farmer all the way to the
port city of Deistel Dom, capital and royal seat of the country of Emsadorn. All Simon would tell us was that we would be visiting someone
there.

On this road, I finally saw some other women. Though they dressed,
spoke, and acted differently from the men, and seemed not to associate
with them, at least they were identifiably members of the same species.
Though I stared at everyone we passed on the road, none stared back at
me when I could see them. It was as if I should not exist, and they were
politely ignoring me.

My first view of the city was uninspiring. We were entering the
gate nearest the market, at dawn. The air smelled of rotting garbage, the
stones of the street were slippery and dark, and the warehouse buildings
were patched and tumbledown. The farmer dropped us off when he came
to his broker's station, and Simon led us around the back of the building
and up a steep narrow street. As we walked, the sun rose above the low
buildings and clear light shone on the scarred walls, vagrant dewdrops
sparkling on scattered weeds. By the time we reached the castle park at
the height and heart of the city, the sun was high and hot, the streets
were dry, and the citizens were in full display. Detter was gawking as
much as I at the bright costumes and the bewildering variety of goods
for sale. After all, he had spent most of his life imprisoned in the school.
He must be nearly as naive as I about the outside world, though that
didn't seem possible.

Simon knew his way and spared no attention to sight-seeing. He
said, "Follow me closely and do not speak," and led us to the entrance
gate, where several well-fed soldiers lounged. One of them stood up as
Simon approached, and the others eyed us lazily.

Simon said, as he approached, "Good day. My name is Magician
Simon, and I am guide to these two, student mages both. The King
issued me an invitation—" He stopped, perplexed. The guard was grinning and waving him through.

"—the King's old apprentice," said one of the loungers aside to another. Simon's ears were turning red as he led us in. The soldiers eyed us all frankly, but with goodwill. Simon was walking too fast, and I stumbled to catch up. It was nice to see Simon being human again, even if I didn't know what the joke was.

We arrived at a grand entrance completely overgrown by a vine with drowsy-smelling white flowers. A spectacular color guard stood ranged on either side of it, with crimson and orange diagonal striped uniforms and glossy steel pikes. Simon stopped before them, looking, with his wayward black hair, brown neckring, and dusty brown clothes, like a pirate compared to the gaudy soldiers. He began, "My name is Simon—"

And the lead guard interrupted, "—to the life! Welcome, sir! I'll tell His Majesty." Simon rolled his eyes resignedly and the entire guard laughed in a friendly way, beckoning us into the entrance hall.

A few minutes later an enormous man barreled into the hall, trailing ginger-colored spirit-fire like the wake of a boat, and slammed Simon against the wall, kissing him full on the lips. Simon squirmed helplessly and shoved at him. He was taller than Simon and would have made two of him.

He pulled his head back and laughed at my crimson-faced teacher delightedly. "You solemn, pompous duckling! So you're still alive, are you? You look just the same, only stuffier." He released Simon, whose mouth was twisted wryly, and turned to us, saying, "Introduce me to these darling playthings. A matched set, I see, boy and girl, how handy." He was massively fat, with a large head, florid and jovial, but he judged us both shrewdly while Simon introduced us. He was the King himself, of course, and his name was Jens, and we were to call him by it. He wore a double saffron neckring half-concealed by the magnificent ruff around his neck. I made a mental note to ask Simon how it was that a mage could be a king—from the fable he'd told me on the road I'd thought mages were sworn to renounce possessions and power.

Jens was particularly interested in Detter, prowling around the boy while Detter tried to pretend he was made of ice. The King turned to Simon, and said, "Bet you've been utterly polite and correct with this animal. Looks like he's been driven right to the edge. Lucky he hasn't murdered you in your sleep, you sanctimonious prig. May I borrow him for a few days?"

Simon raised his eyebrows and gave him the faintest of nods, whereupon Jens slapped Detter on the side of his head with a meaty hand, so hard that Detter fell to his knees. "Come on, boy, let's get you cleaned up. Don't want my sheets getting dirty," he said, and he dragged Detter out of the room by the back of his shirt.

I looked at Simon, half-appalled and half-tickled, and Simon said, "Detter will have the time of his life. Don't worry." His mouth was still twisted ruefully and his eyes were sparkling with amused embarrassment. "Jens is full Sorcerer, and a match for Detter on his worst day. He was my guide when I was student, and my master when I was apprentice. In case you hadn't guessed." Simon looked much younger with his cheeks flushed like that.

Now a young woman of infinite unreality and fragility floated into the hall with a rustle of full skirts. "The King instructed me to see to your wardrobe for the reception this afternoon," she said brightly to me. "Come this way, please." I trailed after her dubiously, feeling like a hoyden in my worn boots and dusty trousers. Simon stood behind in the hall, rocking on his heels and whistling.

5

In Which I Don't Take Care of My Clothes

I was standing at bay behind a chair, wearing only a few ludicrous scraps of silk. The three laughing women who were encircling me had already managed to force me into slippery stockings that were clipped to a bizarre contraption slung around my hips, and beguiled me into donning a breastband and a worthless pair of knickers that clung snakily to my various crevices and swells. But the condescending and amused ladies who had me cornered in the dressing room were not going to make me wear the thing they were brandishing. It was made of sticks and wire and whipcord, it was ugly and painful-looking, and it was designed for someone whose internal organs were distributed differently from mine.

"Oh, come, child," said one of them entreatingly. "Don't you want to look like a woman? I promise this will do wonders for you. Just try it. Come on."

"I *am* a woman. I don't have to try to look like one. Don't come near me with that thing. If I even tried to wear it, I'd throw up and then I'd pass out." While my attention was on her, the other two darted at me from the sides, trying to wrap the thing around me and lace it up. I sat down on the floor, pulled my knees up and my head down, and resisted the attack. They were laughing, but I had given up trying to keep my sense of humor. It seemed to me that I was getting the same kind of treatment as Detter, though it was less obvious.

"What is going on in here?" A stout young woman in her twenties with flaming red hair swept into the room in a spectacular purple gown. She obviously wasn't wearing any sticks or wire under her dress, because she rippled and bounced as she moved.

One of the woman wrestling with me, red in the face with amusement and effort, said, "She's some kind of a female student mage, visiting for the reception with her guide. She was wearing man's clothing and looked a sight. Jens told us to dress her up and make her look presentable for the reception."

I still had my jaw set and my arms wrapped around me. The redhead, her hands on her hips, said to me, "You don't want to wear the corset?" I shook my head grimly. "Will you let them dress you up if you don't have to wear the corset?" I nodded. I was being spoken to as if I were a three-year-old having a tantrum. The redhead said to my erstwhile adversaries, "Go ask Mistress Jessie for the loan of her green gown. It will fit her just fine without the corset." They left the room laughing and I relaxed cautiously.

The redhead still stood there, chubby hands on ample hips, looking at me appraisingly. "So you're a woman mage. Why didn't you just cast a spell on the girls instead of letting them pick on you like that? Or are you just a high-flown herb-wife?"

I grinned up at her. She had blue eyes and freckles, and she looked wonderful. "I'm a mage, but I'm on my student Quest. That means I'm not allowed to use magic at all. I'm Lisane. Who are you?"

"My name's Annesil. Come on—if Jens insists on having you dressed up, we'd better get going. The reception starts in half an hour." Annesil helped me into some petticoats, found some low shoes for me, and started brushing my hair. The dress arrived, a cool mint green with white piping and lace, and it took all four giggling women to slide it over me while I awkwardly tried to help them. I wasn't used to fitted clothes, and I wasn't sure I was going to be able to move once I got the dress on, but I was pleasantly surprised. They sat me down, threw a drape over me, and trimmed and arranged my hair. Except for Annesil, they made me feel like the unfortunate beggar girl in the fairy tale, being made up to play the doomed princess—or like a cat being dressed up in doll clothes. They thought it was terribly funny.

Finally, they finished. Annesil said, "Go take a look at yourself before you go downstairs." She pointed to a standing full-length mirror.

"I never look in mirrors," I said uncomfortably, slightly revolted at the idea but not wanting to offend. To my horror, Annesil took me by the shoulders and shoved me forcibly over to the mirror. I tried to close my eyes, but she tipped my chin up, and suddenly I thought, Why not?

I opened my eyes and saw a tall black-haired young woman with flushed cheeks and cool green eyes, whose black eyebrows tilted sardonically. Her wedge-shaped face was lightly tanned, but her arms were milk white. In the mint green dress her high soft breasts, wide shoulders, and firm waist were displayed with shocking audacity and exaggerated femininity. If I were to meet her in the street I would hide from her. She looked like my mother, and like the woman reflected in Kaihan's eyes in my dream. My heart ached for her. She seemed to be all display and no defense.

Annesil hooked her arm through mine, drew me away from the mirror, and we set off down the stairs, her confederates chattering along behind us.

She said, "Honey, we're going to be the only two real women down there. The rest of them are all sealed up like sausages in their corsets." I felt dizzy, and held on to her arm like a lifeline, though she had been the one who had done this to me.

We rounded a corner and everyone looked up, a whole ballroom full of dressed-up aristocrats of every shape and size, all turning their heads to look at me. Or no, they were looking at her.

Annesil felt my arm tighten in panic, leaned to my ear and muttered, "Sorry. Forgot to tell you. I'm the Queen." I started to laugh. I couldn't help it. She said, "Oh, good. I do like you. Let's get something to eat," as we paraded grandly down the rest of the sweeping stairs.

We came upon Jens and Detter halfway through the crowd. Detter was much cleaner, was dressed all in white, and looked as confused as I felt. Jens had his arm linked through Detter's and was whispering in his ear. Annesil waltzed up to Jens from behind, tickled him under the armpits, and danced away when he made a grab for her, nearly knocking Detter over again in the process. She coyly let him catch and caress her intimately, while Detter looked offended and fascinated. When Jens let Annesil go, she said, "Have you been officially introduced to Lisane?"

The enormous man looked at me, looked at me again, and roared, "Stop me! I can't help myself! I must have her!" waving his arms like windmills. It was funny, appalling, and almost serious.

Detter, taken aback, was also staring at me as if I had grown a tail and scales. He said, looking me up and down insultingly, "I hardly know you without your trousers on." I made a face at them both and slipped back into the crowd, aiming for the refreshment table I'd seen from the stairs. I felt silly and wild, bold and frightened, not like myself at all and nothing like a Mennenkalt Mother. Did I really have green eyes? I wanted to run upstairs again and check the mirror. The noise and crush of the red-faced, cheerful crowd was overwhelming. Someone's hand ran over my backside as I forced my way through, and I could feel eyes looking at me.

Annesil joined me at the table. She seemed to have adopted me for the afternoon. We ate some of everything, and Annesil watched as I inexpertly fended off several propositions both verbal and nonverbal. She thought it was funny, but she didn't have to put up with it herself, as no one seemed to dare flirt with the King's wife. After I managed to thoroughly insult one waggishly gallant old man, she said, "Don't you get any practice at this?"

I said, helplessly, "Back home no one would have dared, and since I left home no one has noticed I was female."

She looked puzzled, and was about to say something, but trumpets sounded a fanfare across the room. The people around us turned and began to shuffle in one direction, and Annesil said, "Oh, kitchen slops. I have to go be gracious. See you later." She sailed off in another direction, rippling and bouncing majestically.

It seemed everybody was drifting into line. I squeezed between a young and spotty scholar and a painted lady of an older vintage, and wondered what was going on. I saw Simon wandering alongside the line, looking for somebody. Maybe he knew. As he came up, he looked right through me and kept walking until I grabbed his arm and hissed, "Simon!"

He started violently and stared at me, his mouth open.

"Are you all right?" I said testily, forgetting for the moment how I was dressed. He did look simple gaping like that.

"Yesss. I'm fine. Yes," he said awkwardly. "Lisane, listen, when you get to him, don't curtsey like the rest. Kneel down on both knees, and stay down until he tells you to rise."

"Get to whom? The King?"

"No, no. Curtsey to the King, that's fine, just watch out because he's likely to tickle you. Lisane, you look wonderful," he said, sounding like no Simon I'd ever known. His eyes drifted downward. "I didn't recognize you."

I said, "Kindly remove your nose from my cleavage," more sharply than I'd intended.

He recoiled, said, "Sorry," and went back up the line. I still didn't know who it was I was supposed to kneel to. I couldn't get any clues from the conversation of the people in line near me. All I heard was things like "historic occasion," and "once in a lifetime," which could have described anything from snow in the summer to a naked gulay band playing ducks-and-buckets.

The line wobbled forward solemnly, and finally the scholar ahead of me was bowing formally to the honored guest standing beside the King and Queen. An honored guest whom I already knew. An elegant, amused, clear-eyed dark man in black with a triple neckring, standing like a column of smoke in the gaudy fire of the crowd.

Then I was standing before him in my turn, frozen for a moment looking at his face before he recognized me, and I sank slowly down to my knees, watching his expression change and thinking, oh my, oh dear, I don't want to know that. I stayed on my knees with my head down, my skirts spread around me, until I felt a warm dry hand gently lifting my chin.

Kaihan's face was expressionless again, and he said, "You may rise, Student Lisane. Well met on the path." I was now curtseying to Annesil, who looked at me with round eyes, saying, "And I thought I was the big shot around here. You know the Master?" I sidled past her, my face hot. Jens grabbed me and tried to kiss my neck when I curtseyed to him. I escaped and went back up the stairs at the other end of the ballroom, and sat down on a step around the corner out of sight.

My heart was pounding. I was out of control, too silly, too wild. It was this damned dress, it wasn't me. I would go back upstairs and find my clothes, go back to being invisible and unimportant. That blackhaired, green-eyed woman I'd seen in the mirror was dangerous for me when she was dressed like this. I was riding a runaway donkey in heat, and there was no safety here.

Simon's reaction had been bad enough. He had looked stunned and confused. Kaihan had been just the other way around. As he recognized me, in that moment before I knelt to him, his eyes had narrowed, his nostrils flared, and his lips had parted. He looked like a predator about to spring, like the avid, lustful man in my dream that day above the waterfall. Now I knew the dream hadn't come from nowhere, and I was even more afraid. It had indeed been a true dream, and I didn't know what it meant. I needed some kind of protection from myself.

Someone was sitting down on the step beside me. I looked up, and it was Simon. He said, "Sorry about my rudeness earlier."

"Simon," I said, "what is Master Kaihan doing here? He took me completely by surprise." I wished Simon weren't sitting quite so near to me.

Simon stared. "Don't you know? Didn't anyone tell you?"

"May your brains be fried, Simon, get this straight. Nobody tells me anything, ever. I am eternally and unremittingly ignorant. I ask you questions because I hope you will answer them, not because I like to make myself and you crazy." I took a slow breath. "What is Kaihan doing here?"

Simon still wasn't paying proper attention to the question, but he answered. "The Master of the Sassevin Council, the leader of the prime council of the order of mages, died in a freak dueling accident. Kaihan was named to take his place and is traveling there now. Since he had to pass through Deistel Dom, he paid a state visit. It's pretty rare for any Master of Sassevin Council to travel outside Sassevin, so every boot-licker in the country is here to smell his shoe leather. All right? Enough information, ignoramus?"

"Yes, thank you, wisest of teachers," I said demurely. Apparently the Master of Sassevin Council ranked with dead kings and disasters of nature as a sight that must be seen. Simon was looking intense and purposeful. He had a peculiar smile on his face. He slid his arm around my waist and, leaning over, kissed me firmly. Half of me suddenly wanted to drag him off to bed and the other half wanted to run screaming from the castle. Both urges being equal, I spent the next hour behaving disgracefully, teasing Simon and then biting his head off while he followed me around through the jovial crowd.

We ended up out on a balcony. I didn't know what to say to him, so I leaned on the balustrade, staring out into the late afternoon sunlight. Simon stood behind me, his hands on my shoulders. He said, dropping his hands to my hips and turning me indecently to face him, "Lisane, I don't know what to do. I don't know what you want. I'm helpless. Tell me to leave you alone, or let me make love to you, but please don't torture me." He looked terribly sincere and upset, but his hips were moving against mine, slowly and deliberately. It was crude and offensive, and I felt an almost painful sensation like a fist clenching in my belly below the navel.

We found a vacant dressing room with a couch. Simon had never been with a woman before, as I'd half suspected. Though I'd had plenty of theoretical training, I'd never had any direct experience—llerKalten having to be a virgin at her initiation. We managed all right, considering, though it was probably the silliest single event in my life, frustrating, painful, and driven.

Afterward, Simon wanted to ease me and I had to show him how, and while he was doing that he got interested again. While we were going at it a second time, Simon groaning and thrusting blindly, I started to get a glimmer of what it was all about. My first clue was that something was trying to knock the top of my head off from inside, and I wanted to help it along, primarily by moaning and hitting Simon. This inspired Simon to complete insanity, and we nearly fell off the couch. He got offended when I started to laugh, but it didn't stop him.

Afterward we lay in blank silence for a while, then helped each other dress. Simon's eyes were heavy-lidded, and he touched my skin all over as he dressed me. We drifted back out to the tail end of the party, and Jens waved Simon over as we entered the room. I went to get some more food. My hair had fallen down. I felt like I hadn't been introduced to myself. I was a stranger. I had looked in my first mirror, seen the blind mad god in the rational priestlike eyes of Kaihan, and lost my virginity in the same day. I wanted to go to sleep for a week. I sat down at a table and ate as much as I could hold.

Kaihan sat down next to me, straddling the tiny chair backward with his arms folded on the back of it. I looked at him warily, but the detached, amused expression was back. I felt as if I wore Simon like an amulet, to protect me against this man. He said nothing. I looked back across the room at Jens talking animatedly to my guide, and my earlier question came back to me.

"Master Kaihan," I said, "how is it that Jens can be King if he is a mage? And how can he be married to Annesil? I thought mages had to renounce all offices and attachments."

He raised his eyebrows, and his dark eyes sparkled like a child's with obscure delight. "On some rare occasions, we must take away the only son of a king. If the king continues to have no heirs, and the child survives school and his Quest and is willing to reign, then the son is returned to him, to serve as heir and King, and sire heirs in his turn, until his successor is of age."

He was perfectly poised on his delicate chair, his face glinting with unspoken pleasure, his mouth curving secretively. I asked, "Why are you so pleased I asked that particular question?"

I will swear he looked startled for an instant. I had only met him three times now, but I was willing to wager very few people ever surprised him. I wondered what I was doing right, or what I was doing wrong. Twice in one day I'd taken this man unawares.

He sat unmoving for a moment, and then said, "Did you know that I am the great-grandfather of your guide's great-grandfather? I am a trifle older than I look." It was my turn to be surprised. Somehow, I had assumed he must be in his fifties. The non sequitur distracted me from my previous question, which might have been its intention, while I tried to figure out how old his claimed relationship made him.

"Your guide, on the other hand," he said, "is younger than he looks and far too serious for his age. Would you watch over him for me? He will have some hard decisions, and you will be traveling together for a while yet." He appeared to be completely serious.

"I could no more look after Simon than I could look after . . . after you," I said severely. "I can barely look after myself." He was still watching me, his chin resting on his arms and his eyebrows raised.

"You are not an utter fool, my dear," he said in his velvet voice. "You won't get to be a total idiot until you are at least my age. So don't try to weasel out of this. I put him in your care." I turned away from him in exasperation, in time to see a haphazard group approaching.

Simon, the Queen, and the King, with Detter following closely behind, processed across the floor to us through the thinning crowd, zigzagging slightly as Simon attempted to loose himself from Jens' left arm and Annesil, similarly restrained, bumped her ample hip exaggeratedly against Jens' right side. The Emsadorn royalty, as manipulative, capricious, and arbitrary as they were, reminded me a little of home.

The King released his captives, and the Queen reached me before Simon could, cutting him out neatly and leaving him to Kaihan's mercies. Jens slipped his arm through Detter's again, turned, and led him away. Detter's golden head gleamed in the streaks of sunlight from the high windows. He was dwarfed next to the King's huge bulk.

Annesil and I went upstairs to change our clothes for dinner and submit to the exasperated but hilarious ministrations of her ladies. Annesil raised her ginger eyebrows at the condition of my borrowed gown, and apparently I blushed, for they all began to tease me without mercy.

Now I was wearing a rose-colored gown with about a hundred buttons down the front, which, though high-collared, was somehow even more suggestive than the green dress. I checked the mirror again, guiltily.

I still had green eyes, and they stared back at me shadowed and tired. I came down to a more intimate dinner, only fifty or so at a long table. Annesil was wearing an incredible bouquet of a dress in cream and burgundy. Jens kissed her hand, then started kissing his way up her freckled arm. Simon was staring at me with smoky eyes, his forelock flopping down, and I stared back at him across the table.

If he was younger than he looked, he must only be in his twenties. I looked at his intense gray eyes and the wide, confident mouth, and thought, I bet he's no more than twenty-five. A great physical rush of tenderness and amusement poured over me. His solemnity, and his inexperience, and what we'd been doing that afternoon made me feel much more kindly toward him.

Toward the end of dinner, Kaihan leaned over and spoke in Simon's ear. Simon reacted as if he'd been slapped. "Sir!" he said, outraged. "That's not fair to me or to my students! We're most of the way there already. If we turn back on the western road, it will take twice as long." Kaihan looked unmoved.

Simon tried again, "My lord, I'd have to pass through Betzindahl. You know what happens to any mage who's fool enough to venture there. You know I am forbidden its borders."

Kaihan looked back at Simon like a weasel at a rabbit hole, calm, cheerful, and utterly focused. "It's not open to discussion," he said. "Detter needs the time, Lisane needs the time, and you need the time. Do it." He turned his implacable gaze away. Simon, dismissed, looked wounded and frightened, but he collected himself with an effort. I didn't know where we were headed in the first place, though I figured it had something to do with Sassevin, wherever that was, and the Beast, whatever it was. So I didn't know enough to care whether we went the long way or the short. I could have done with a little less of Detter's company on the way, though Detter at the moment was looking stupefied, harmless, and oblivious while the King stroked his downy neck with a free hand.

After dinner, the King escorted Detter off, and Simon, watching them leave, said to me, "Do you know what my reputation is here, why the guards knew my name?" I shook my head, and he said, "Jens was my guide, when he was on his Sorcerer's Search and I was questing for my ring. I wouldn't sleep with him at all. It drove him crazy. He's still talking about it and still pretending to try to seduce me."

I said, "Why did you turn him down?"

Simon said, "I was very young, and I was in love with another

Student. I was going to be faithful." He looked morose and romantic, but spoiled it by saying, "Besides, Jens isn't to my taste. I like them smaller." I laughed. I pulled him upstairs, and made him unbutton my one hundred buttons, one by one. When I asked him, he told me reluctantly that he was indeed twenty-five. This time we didn't come close to falling off the bed, but I got my head banged against the wall and Simon was very contrite about it later.

Simon fell asleep, and I sat and wondered for a while how I did feel about him. Then I wondered if I knew how he felt about me. I poked him with my foot to wake him up and ask him, but he just grunted and turned over. I managed to button myself up again, and went exploring, though I was utterly groggy with tiredness and unexpected experience.

The palace was smaller than I'd thought, but a wonderful little place, all back stairs, extra rooms, attics, and closets. Most of the people who'd been at the reception must have lived somewhere else, and had now all gone home. I found the entrance hall again. The color guard was down to three men, who flirted amiably with me.

I poked around some more, found the steps down to the kitchens, and encountered Jens there, without Detter, taking ungracious lessons from a chef on how to make vanity cakes. I found a high stool and enjoyed the entertainment. He had an incredibly colorful vocabulary, which he used freely on the chef, the cakes, the cookstove, and all the utensils. I didn't think he noticed me in the shadows, but when the last batch of hollow cakes was pulled sizzling from the oil, the King wiped his greasy hands on his thighs, turned, and offered his arm gravely. I slipped off the stool and accompanied him silently back up the stairs and outside to a lamplit terrace.

It was quiet and hot, a slow humid breeze barely stirring the air. I could see that we were at the top of the city; lantern light flickered dimly all below us. The King settled his enormous bulk on a wooden bench, and I sat down in what space remained. I was feeling blank, drained, and only half conscious. My Voices were whispering sibilantly.

"The boy's in a bad way," he said, as if continuing a conversation.

"Which one?" I said dimly.

"Ah. I meant young Deteras. Simon is bad enough, but he's more cautious than anything else. Deteras is practically baying at the moon. My usual methods don't seem to have much of an effect."

I wondered what his "usual methods" were and what purpose they served. "The students all seem to learn only to hate one another, to fear their masters, and to despise themselves. How did you manage to survive the school? You still seem to like people and enjoy yourself."

He sighed gustily. "I was bigger than anybody, I'm a powerful mage, and I wasn't taken to the school until I was nearly ten. Nobody noticed my Power until then. Simon was brought when he was seven and Deteras was only five. The younger they start, the crazier they are. Kaihan tells me you spent only a year there, so that makes you a paragon of sanity. Advise me, paragon. What should I do with your young friend?"

What was I, everybody's all-purpose aunt? I didn't want to even think about Detter. I was silent. The King waited. My thoughts drifted, and the Voices muttered half-audibly in the back of my head. To my surprise, I heard myself eventually saying, in the flat voice of guided speech, "There is nothing that needs be done with him. He is as he is, and as he should be. He can master his pain, and it comforts him. He loves and he follows his truth. Let him be." It was probably the looniest thing I'd ever heard come out of my mouth, and I've issued some peculiar pronouncements at the prodding of my Voices. The massive shadow beside me didn't move. Maybe he wasn't listening. Maybe he was asleep. No, maybe I was asleep, and dreaming.

I was asleep. The King half woke me picking me up to take me inside, but by the time he got me to the guest chamber that had been prepared for me I must have gone under again. I awoke in the morning to muffled voices in a courtyard below my window, and looked out to find Master Kaihan, well-groomed, on a glossy black horse, taking his leave of Jens. I didn't make any noise, but they both turned and stared up at me for a long minute, with enigmatic expressions. Then Kaihan cantered out and the King turned and went back inside. I felt as if I'd been struck in the face; I wasn't sure why.

I looked down and found I was still in my rumpled dress. I seemed to be making a habit of ruining other people's clothes. With a tinkle and a crash two maidservants bustled into my room with breakfast, and I put off any thinking until after I ate.

Annesil, red hair flying loose, came in wearing a dressing gown as I was finishing. She laughed herself into hiccups at the condition of my costume, and summoned one of her ladies to undo me. I had red welts from sleeping on seams and buttons. I missed my traveling clothes. She wouldn't let me have them again, but dug up a comfortable dress for me, not too fancy this time. She made me look in the mirror again. I was fascinated that the exotic stranger in the glass remained the same, with black hair and green eyes, eyebrows tilted wryly as if what she saw amused her and saddened her at the same time. I guessed the image wasn't going to change.

We sat and talked for a long time, and then went outside and walked around the grounds. She told me that her marriage had been arranged; that when Jens returned to the court two years ago, just before his father's death, his father had held a dance for eligible girls and her mother had made her go. "I didn't want to," she said, "but my mother said she would never make me go to court again if I went this once." She stayed by the refreshments all night, stuffing herself and flirting with the steward. Jens spent the evening dancing with, stepping on, pawing, and offending every young woman in the hall except Annesil. He never even talked to her that night.

Two weeks later the old King began negotiating with Annesil's older brother for Annesil's hand, "which drove my mother nearly insane," said Annesil. "She was so used to being disappointed in me she didn't know how to handle it. She hasn't talked to me for two years."

She didn't really meet her husband until the wedding. "He'd never been with a woman before that," she said, and shook with remembered amusement, "because mages aren't supposed to sire children or indeed to lie with the Powerless at all. He wasn't incompetent, but it was an extremely odd experience." I could see why Jens had married her. She was candid, unaffected but not innocent, and she seemed to have little desire for power. I wondered why the old King had negotiated with Annesil's older brother for her hand, if she had a living mother. It didn't seem proper to let men get involved with the business of marriage, but nobody did things right on this world.

"How do they expect to get more mages if they forbid them to breed?" I asked.

"Oh, mages just pop up here and there like toadstools," she said vaguely. "You don't need to encourage them. There are too many of them as it is."

I knew, though I wasn't supposed to know, that on Mennenkaltenei the inheritance of Power depended on a complex pattern born to the body, a pattern that had little chance of appearing by accident. If they didn't breed for Power, either the potential was dormant somehow in most of the people of this fierce little world, men and women alike, or things worked differently here.

There were so many things I wasn't supposed to know, like the sciences and other things people only discussed in hushed voices when

I was near. Mennenkalts keep their deities far from the dirty business of technology.

No, Jens would have fat Powerful babies with Annesil. Suddenly, I remembered something Kaihan had said. "Annesil," I said, "if a mage tells you he's somebody's great-grandfather, what does that mean?"

"It means he's a liar, a cheat, or a king," she said promptly. I tucked the information away in my head. Kaihan might be any one of the three, but I'd put my money on the third.

We lazed about in the sunshine until lunchtime. She was the first woman I had talked to in four years, so I was grateful that she seemed to be as attached to me as I was to her. Other people joined us now and then, all seeming jovial and cheerful as their King, dressed grandly and gaudily. Though all the other women I met were underweight, and were trussed up and bound in yards of fabric like ovenbirds, they could laugh loudly enough, and they were friendly to me. The men, broad in the cheekbones and with twinkling eyes, tended to be fat and avuncular. I didn't trust them completely. All too often, the people who seem most hearty and kindly are those who don't admit even to themselves that they have impure motives.

Simon, looking handsome, peeved, and possessive, found us in early afternoon but I ignored him. I doubted that ignoring him would help me figure out how I felt about him, but it made him so uncomfortable I couldn't resist. Besides, I had begun to suspect it was not only the unlikely sight of the Lisane in a dress that had spurred him to action. He finally got angry and left.

Annesil said, "Are you afraid of him or was that just an exercise in meanness?"

I considered and said, "Both," and she grinned at me. Later in the afternoon I tried to apologize to Simon but he was being mature and obtuse. After dinner he followed me out to the garden as if by accident. We sat on a stone bench and kissed and quarreled and hugged and fought. He tried to tell me what I should do, and I told him he could either be my guide or my bed-cozy but not both in the same breath. He tried to be stuffy and self-sacrificing. I started unbuttoning his flies. We ended up on a patch of grass behind an ornamental bush. I ruined yet another dress that belonged to somebody else.

Afterward, lying beneath him, I grabbed his ears and said, "And just who told you yesterday it was all right to fool around with a woman if the woman's a mage too?"

His face closed up and he tried to pull away, but I dug my fingernails in and said again, "Who told you? It wasn't your idea and it wasn't just the overwhelming effect of my new dress." He reached up and pried my fingers loose, but I wrapped my legs around him. He propped himself up on stiff arms above me, looking dim and far away in the dusk.

I said, "It doesn't matter. I don't care," and let him go.

He hung there and said quietly, "Master Kaihan told me it was permissible after the reception line was over, and immediately I went to find you. I had desired you for a long time, but above all I am obedient to my order's rules. Are you angry with me?"

I laughed, though I felt bewildered. "Every time I run into Kaihan he sticks a spoon into my life and stirs." I pushed against the insides of his arms and he fell on top of me with a startled grunt. I wasn't going to think about Kaihan or the myriad plans he seemed to be pursuing.

That night I dreamed a true dream. I was flying the ancient and peculiar Master Kaihan like a kite. He was floating black-clad and still in a blue sky with no wind, looking down at me. I let go of the string and he swooped and eddied away into the depths of the sky, but I could still see him, and he felt close by. I woke up feeling oddly reassured, though I could find no reason why the presence of Kaihan could do anything but disturb me.

It was time to leave. I persuaded Annesil to give me my clothes back, and found that they had been repaired and embroidered with flowers that coiled around the sleeves of the shirt and the legs of the trousers. It made me feel terribly festive to wear them. I went down to the entry hall, where our small stack of equipment and supplies sat in a pathetic heap in the middle of the floor. Simon was dressed and ready to go, but Detter wasn't there yet. I occupied myself with repacking my supplies, while Simon paced back and forth.

He was impatient to get going, though he looked very gloomy about the route he'd been ordered to take. "We'll have to go north along the coast, then west across the mountains and through the hills of Betzindahl to the far coast, and take ship there. We'll be hitting the mountains at the worst time of the year, and even if we survive the mountains, Betzindahl is unfriendly to mages."

"Do you do everything Kaihan tells you to do? What's the point of going this way instead of that way?" I asked.

Simon said patiently, "I do as the Master tells me, because it is my duty and my responsibility. If you would learn to stop questioning everything, you would have far less trouble." So he was going back to being a prig now that we were heading back to the road.

Jens and Detter wandered into the hall, looking sleepy and content. The King had somehow managed to get Detter to look as pleased with himself as when he had managed to thoroughly humiliate two or three younger boys. I doubted that the King would submit to such treatment, and wondered for the first time what magical powers Jens wielded. The King embraced each of us thoroughly and enthusiastically, saving his last and best for a struggling Simon, and ushered us out into the morning sunlight. He stood in the flowered archway watching us go, genial and relaxed, and just before we reached the perimeter I looked back and saw Annesil slip up beside him and lean against him. An odd arrangement, but they seemed comfortable.

We left the city by a different route, exiting through a high gate in a mighty wall as the morning traffic of coaches and commercial wagons streamed in. The smell in the air was of spices and horses, dust and perfume, the aromas of power and success. We headed north on a road that paralleled the coast. People hailed us in friendly fashion, and I felt optimistic and happy. It was good to be traveling again, good to be free. I thought I could handle everything. It's good to feel that way once in a while, even if it's not true.

6

In Which I Don't Prevent
an Accident

Simon sank back into abstraction as we headed away from the city. He walked through the crowds of people and animals as if he were alone on a wilderness path, his long legs swinging out rhythmically and his gray eyes looking toward the horizon. Detter was similarly distracted, though his thoughts were turned inward. He smiled faintly to himself as he walked, and his blue eyes flickered back and forth as if he were listening to a conversation inside his head. The traffic parted amiably enough around us, some of the passersby saluting Simon's neckring with perfunctory bows and eyeing us, particularly me, with curiosity.

I stared frankly back. Though the day was hot, all the women wore full skirts and shawls, and their heads were covered. The men wore baggy pants and long loose overshirts. The colors of their voluminous garments were achingly bright, and the mixed stripes and patterns produced a vibrating, eye-straining effect in the brilliant sunlight. Simon, Detter, and I, in our drab walking clothes, looked like field animals in comparison.

We stopped at midday to rest beside the road and eat a bit of the provisions we'd been given at the castle. The road was less crowded now that we were farther away from Deistel Dom, but there were several small groups like ours taking shelter from the noon sun under the trees.

From one such group a man came over to us and patiently stood before Simon until Simon noticed his presence with a start, as if called from sleep. Simon said, "Yes? How can I help you?"

The man, dressed in a road-grimed but spectacular purple and green overshirt, grinned uneasily, showing two missing teeth. He said deferentially, "Lord, you are a Magician by your ring." Simon nodded. "My wife is at her time and having trouble. Could you help her?"

Simon said, puzzled, "Is there no herb-wife handy?" The man shook his head, and Simon grumpily stood up, dusting off his pants and muttering, "This is not my proper work." He prepared to leave but turned to us first. "I may be a while. Both of you morons stay where you are until I come back. And remember the rules."

Detter seemed not to hear him, but I was highly offended. Yesterday he had called me his heart's jewel, today I was a moron. "I'll promise I'll only *think* about turning you into a legless frog," I said snippily as they walked away.

The man with the missing teeth looked back in surprise and said to Simon, "They are both your students? I thought the girl a servant. She is a witch? Has she any knowledge of childbirth?" Simon just kept walking, and the man hastened after him, looking back at me over his shoulder. What a screwball question. Why should I be a servant if I were dressed exactly the same as my companions? Perhaps it was because women were not mages here, though the thought was worrisome. How could men have Power and women not? And what was a witch, and what was an herb-wife?

Detter sat cross-legged on a protruding root, meditatively chewing. A couple of days out of the sun had taken most of the boiled look from his face. He'd gotten a hat somewhere and was wearing it, so his skin would probably recover. He was still lovely and looked utterly innocent and fresh. He swallowed his mouthful and focused abruptly on me. "What did you say to the King about me? He said he talked to you."

So I had indeed spoken aloud to Jens. "I don't really remember, Detter. I wasn't listening to what I said to him." I often didn't listen to my guided speech, especially if it ran counter to common sense.

An expression of impatience crossed his face. "You needn't fear insulting me."

"Honestly, Detter, I really don't remember. I think I told him he should stay away from you." I was beginning to recall what I'd said, but I didn't feel like sharing it with Detter.

"If you won't tell me, it doesn't matter." He started unbuttoning his shirt. "He gave me a message for you, though. He said to show you this and tell you he took the easy way out." He pulled his shirt open with a nasty gleam in his eye. His white chest was covered with fading red welts, as from an enthusiastic whipping. The skin was broken and scabbed in spots. He watched me with detached amusement as I flinched, then he pulled the shirt down his arms to reveal his delectable shoulders mottled with gray-blue bruises. I looked away. I could not believe that grand, jolly, lusty man could have done this to anyone, even Detter.

Detter said, with a peculiar lift to his voice, "He said he left the hard road to you. What's the hard road?" I looked back at him. He was buttoning up his shirt casually but his eyes were dilated. "What's he want you to do, Lise, kill me?"

I didn't know. There was no possible way of answering Detter's question so I sat staring at him blankly, my thoughts revolving. I was an ignorant castaway, dragged by accident into the perverse and long-lived conspiracies of these mages. They were all pursuing their arcane goals, their grand strategies, and I was straggling along blind and witless behind them.

Yet they seemed to think me capable of all kinds of wondrous acts. Kaihan had thought nothing of asking me to take care of Simon, Simon who understood and obeyed all the rules of this world and moved in it with assurance and purpose, if without imagination. And now Jens was asking that I find some way to deal with this impossible blond demon.

Detter was leaning forward, obviously enjoying my discomfiture. I said abstractedly, "Oh, don't worry, Detter. I couldn't possibly do what he wants me to do, whatever it is." But I sat and stared at him, ignoring everything he said, until Simon came back from playing midwife.

He had refused payment, and the new father was following and timidly expostulating with him. Simon whirled on him and said, "I have no need of your money or your food. Accept my services as freely given and leave me alone."

"He'll just come and take the baby back in a few years," said a jeering voice from a group farther down the road. The man backed away from Simon and walked hurriedly back to his family. Simon glared in the direction of the voice. All of the groups of people within earshot began to pack up and return to the road, not looking at us.

Simon said to me, "There's a folk myth that we take children not to educate them as mages, but to kill them in some kind of mystical ritual." He sat down heavily between us. "It's pathetic. Some people even try to conceal their Talented brats from us. It's where most of the renegades come from. Some fool of a village is always raising a boy unguided by the Order, and then they beg us to rescue him when he's grown—if he hasn't already drawn our attention by trying to assassinate us."

Detter said blithely, "Well, don't we kill them? After all, how many boys actually live through school and Quest?" Simon ignored him. Detter said, "The little ones kill themselves off, the older ones murder each other, and most of the rest die from the Quest or the Beast. And then what?"

Simon got up again and shouldered his pack without speaking. I scrambled up to follow, and Detter sat on the tree root smiling cherubically. He continued, "The ones who survive get to travel around homeless looking for more children to condemn, or else they stay forever in Sassevin sucking up to more powerful mages, or they are glorified servants to this petty prince or that, or hated captive sires breeding more princes. We should just kill most of the children off to begin with; it would mean less time, less expense, less trouble . . ." We were out of range of the mocking voice.

Simon said to me bitterly, "Detter thinks he had such a hard time. At least he was leaving no one behind when he went with the mages. My father wept when the mages took me, even though I had killed his trusted friend with my first exercise of Power. He pleaded with them and argued, and when they wouldn't yield he cursed them and said he'd never offer welcome to mages again. He kissed me and told me I was no longer his son, that he had no son. Then he acted as if I wasn't there anymore." He sounded far more sorry for himself than Detter ever did.

I glanced back. Detter was strolling along well behind us, his hat pushed back on his ethereal head. What Jens had said intrigued and repelled me, for I had begun to realize what the "hard road" was with Detter. The easiest thing to do was to strike him when provoked, the hardest to hold back. No, the hardest would be to care for him as for a friend. I wondered if I could ever bring myself to feel anything but irritation and loathing for Deteras Anhand. It would be an interesting exercise of my childhood training, and it would certainly drive Detter crazy.

We walked comfortably for the rest of the afternoon, Detter strolling far behind. Simon and I chatted desultorily, on matters of general interest, and I wondered what would happen between us tonight. He would probably be embarrassed to share my blankets in front of Detter. Or maybe he wouldn't. Maybe I would be.

"Simon," I said, a thought forcing itself forward, "how can you aid a woman in childbirth? I'd swear you didn't know how a woman was put together until a couple of days ago."

He looked offended. "I don't have to stare at someone's private parts to cast a birthing spell."

"Why not? There could have been any number of different things wrong. Didn't you teach me the spell must be specific to the situation? What did you do, then, just rip the baby out whole with one spell and heal them both with another?" He nodded. "That's really sloppy," I said.

He was silent. After a moment he said stiffly, "You're right. It's how I was taught to do it, but you're right. I suppose the herb-wives do it differently."

Well, well, I thought, give yourself a medal, Lisane. You're right for once. I didn't push the topic any more. Detter caught up with us around dusk.

We'd passed through two small villages during the day, and gone past several small homes in between, but Simon decided to stop in the middle of a long desolate stretch of road with no signs of human occupation. We walked off the road to a level spot among some trees, well sheltered and dry, and unrolled our blankets. Simon put his bedroll apart from mine and from Detter's. I cocked an eyebrow at him and he pretended not to notice. He sent Detter off to gather some wood, and cleared a patch of ground for a fire, since with darkness the air had suddenly chilled. We all sat around the small crackling blaze and stared into it, our faces hot and our backs chilled, until we couldn't stay awake any longer. I wrapped myself up in my blanket all alone, and fell asleep almost immediately to the flickering glow of the banked fire.

Some time later somebody was nudging my shoulder. I opened my eyes to complete blackness. The fire must have gone out. A voice hissed gently next to my ear, "Lisane," and I realized it must be Simon. I extricated an arm from my blanket and gave him a firm shove. With a startled exhalation he rolled back. I snarled at him, "I won't pretend I only know you in the dark." A light chuckle sounded from the direction of Detter's blanket, and Simon went away. I heard no more of him that night. I wouldn't skulk around Detter as if he were a children's chaperon.

Simon looked gray and grouchy in the morning. Detter hummed to himself irritatingly. I set my jaw and decided to detest them both after all. We set off again on the road north. It took three days, during which I ignored Simon, Simon ignored me, and Detter strutted along behind us cheerfully, before Simon would condescend to lay his blanket next to mine at night. And two more days before I forgave him enough to enjoy myself.

Soon after that we crossed the border between Emsadorn and the next small country to the north. I thought at first it must be Betzindahl, because the people there obviously cared less for mages, but Simon said it was a minor kingdom called Telique. We were left strictly alone on the road and off it. People stared at us from the corners of their eyes, muttering to themselves and occasionally spitting not quite at us. They were dressed less colorfully than the Emsadorn peasants, and the whole countryside seemed less prosperous and confident. In our plain clothing, we might have stood out much less in this country were it not for Simon's plain brown neckring, but that was apparently enough difference for the locals.

When we camped for the night, Simon said, "If it's this bad in Telique, it will be impossible for us to travel openly in Betzindahl."

Detter laughed and said, "Why not just set a few of them on fire or turn them into animals? That would make the rest of these filthy peasants respect us."

Simon looked at him with a bitter light in his eye. "Why do you think they detest mages on sight? Some fool probably has done something like that to them already. Once you start trying to frighten people, you must keep on your guard forever."

Detter answered unrepentantly, "It's just because there aren't enough mages to keep the normals in line."

"How many mages are there altogether?" I asked, idly flipping a glowing coal over with a stick and watching bits of bark shrivel up in smoke. When I didn't get an answer, I looked up to see Detter smiling at Simon and Simon's face closed and still. I had asked an unfair question again, obviously.

Detter drawled, "There are a lot less than there used to be, aren't there, Simon?"

Simon didn't reply.

Detter said, "Didn't you say there were mages on your world, Lise? How many did you have?"

"They weren't mages, Detter. They were just people. Some had more Power than others, but I guess about half the population had Talent of some kind. None of them used it the way you people do, though. It would be considered rude."

Simon's lip curled. "Half a world of mages? Come on, Lisane, don't fantasize."

Detter said, "You should hear what she says about her family. Her father was a professional suicide, her mother was a prostitute mage, and Lisane herself is a cannibal."

Simon said wearily, "That's enough, Detter."

"It's true enough," I said. "Though you could describe all of us, my father, my mother, and me, as professional-suicide-prostitute-cannibal-mages." It sounded terribly funny in this language, not dignified or glorious at all. I snorted involuntarily, triggering myself into a fit of giggles.

Simon waited, his eyebrows raised, until I stopped being amused by myself. "Would you care to explain that, or is it too humorous for words?"

Since it was the words that made it so funny, I spluttered again, but said, "All right. I'll try." I collected myself, folded my arms, and said formally, "Kindly hear me now," as if they were a group of children being schooled.

Detter started to say something, but Simon waved him down. I waited until they were both still, then began, as far as I could in this language, to formally explain Mennenkalt government.

"We are a practical people," I said. "Like you, we understand that life, strength, and power are bought only with death, weakness, and submission. Unlike you, we prefer to pay afterward instead of in advance."

Simon started to object but I glared him down firmly.

"Our world is called Mennenkaltenei, meaning roughly 'male joined with female,' or 'union of gods,' though the most direct translation is 'this and that.' It is ruled by llerMennet, the Year-King or Father, and llerKalten, the Queen or Mother.

"The Mennet is chosen by his predecessor from the young men called Postulants, and rules for only a year. He has ultimate power of decision over the world, wields immense strength by reason of complete possession and mastery of magic, and lives life to the full, eating, drinking, dancing, loving, and siring countless children during his reign. He is gloriously alive and majestic, utterly wise and dangerous, fearfully transfigured and childlike. At the end of his year, he chooses a successor, and is then by him ritually slaughtered, going to his death insane, debased, and helpless, in payment for his reign. His body is cooked and consumed by his subjects as a celebration of life and an acknowledgment of death. My father was one such Mennet, and I have heard his reign was glorious."

Simon looked mildly revolted; Detter's eyes sparkled.

"The future Kalten is chosen as a young child by the reigning Kalten from among all Talented girl children of a certain generation. The child is raised to understand her duties, to learn the necessary skills, and to observe certain strictures. She is rigorously trained in what you call magic, learns the art of administration, and is taught the various erotic techniques. She remains virgin until her installation, has no real name, carries the voices of her predecessors in her head, and is never permitted to look in a mirror lest she forget her divinity. She is installed as Kalten at about the age of nineteen, when she first couples with the new Mennet and conceives his child. Where the Mennet has rights, she has responsibilities. She has ultimate power of administration, wields the strength of complete understanding of and coexistence with magic, and lives life to the full, loving, desiring, nurturing, producing. During her reign she is arbitrary, prophetic, whimsical and practical, comforting, punishing, erotic, and motherly. She continues to bear a child by each Mennet until she has borne twenty children. At the end of her twenty years, she abdicates her rule in favor of her successor, and becomes barren, wordless, and withered. Because she no longer has any interest in living, she usually starves to death in a short time. Her body is abandoned where it lies, ignored. My birth mother was Kalten, wise and good, wild and glorious.

"This is how my world is governed. The Mennet makes the laws, the Kalten carries them out, and they pay for their power with, as Detter has said, ritual murder and suicide, prostitution and cannibalism. The people they rule are peaceful, happy, and productive. There is always enough for all.

"Well, that's the way it was, anyway," I finished lamely. "The Enforcers walked in and blew everything to bits with no trouble at all, so it was obviously not as strong a system as I thought." I relaxed and sat back from the formal story-teacher's pose.

"So your father and mother were king and queen of your world," said Simon, frowning.

"Yes," I said. "For what it's worth, which isn't much anymore."

Detter said, "If it didn't sound so brutish, I'd swear you'd made it all up. It's wonderfully pat—if your mother and father were king and queen, what does that make you, Your Majesty?"

"High office wasn't hereditary." Detter assumed this was either a reluctant admission or an attempt to make my story more plausible.

He said to Simon, "And you thought I was the only savage on this trip. What do you think of someone who could say all that primitive stuff and still sound serious?"

Simon's lock of hair had fallen across his eyes. He looked very young in the firelight. He was thinking about something, and he didn't talk anymore until we were wrapped together in our blankets. I had one thigh over his hip and we were rubbing lazily against each other, hands and lips exploring luxuriously, when he stopped, raised his head, and said quietly to me, "Lisane."

"Hmmm?" I murmured, not interrupting what I was doing.

"You *were* chosen to succeed your mother, weren't you? Whether or not it was supposed to be hereditary? I could tell by your expression. And you've run away somehow."

I stilled my hands, and nodded silently in the dark.

"Do you ever feel that you should have stayed and done your job, even if it meant your death?"

This was unusually perceptive of Simon, but it felt like a blow. When I struck that soulless man down and stole the ship, I'd known I was leaving my duties behind, those pathetic people who tried so hard to be happy for my sake.

He said, "Never mind. I'm sorry. I'm feeling morbid," and lowered his lips to my neck again. For a moment, I toyed with the image of myself as a tragic, hollow exile, lost to honor by choosing to live. Then Simon said, "Ahh" in an almost inaudible tone, and began moving more purposefully. I put aside my cosmic considerations in favor of more immediate and urgent concerns, such as how to fuse my whole skin to his without losing the blanket. When it was all over, the blanket was crumpled somewhere beneath us and my skin was still identifiably my own, but I had a glowing sense of accomplishment nonetheless, not in the least bit lessened by Detter's strategic exercise in throat clearing at a crucial moment. Simon was a remarkably fast learner.

After a few days of being subtly and not-so-subtly scorned in

Telique, Simon began to wear a scarf wrapped around his neck to hide the ring. He dug a coin out of the bottom of his pack when we passed through a village on market day, and bought me a skirt and a headcloth. Simon explained apologetically that he didn't want to arouse any more attention than necessary. Detter seemed to take some satisfaction in my new costume. "What dishonor is there in dressing as other women do?" I asked Simon. "Why do you apologize?"

Simon was uneasily startled. "No dishonor, no dishonor, none at all," he said, waving his hands.

Detter said, "And when shall we see you dressed as a woman, master?"

Simon shot him a look, and Detter batted his eyelashes at him.

I thought about this odd event as I walked, kicking my skirts forward comfortably. It confirmed something I'd been noticing since Emsadorn. Women and men seemed very concerned with distinguishing themselves from each other. The costumes were the most obvious difference, but they also behaved very differently, women tending toward an odd delicacy and subservience, and men toward arrogance and physical display. Why would anybody want to make women and men seem any more different than they already were? I put it on my list of things to ponder when I didn't have anything better to do.

Whatever its implications, our slight disguise served to deflect any further unwelcome interest, and we made our way north through Telique without further incident. The days were getting shorter, though it was still heavily hot while the sun shone. We bypassed a city, though Simon said a fellow mage dwelt there, because we could not afford to lose any time getting to the mountains. It was early fall now, but Simon said winter would come on with no warning in the hills. We finally left the broad market road near its end at the northernmost tip of Telique, and struck inland on an unpaved track toward the ragged blue shadows we could see at the horizon. We had not seen the ocean yet, though we had been no more than fifty miles from it the whole length of the road. Were there seabirds and sand on this world? Was the sea salt? Did its waves have froth? I was reluctant to turn my footsteps toward the mountains again, and my Voices were suspicious and complaining, though they had no feet to collect blisters.

We passed by a few small villages and then some scattered single dwellings, but by the time we reached the foothills we hadn't seen any other humans for several days. I changed back into trousers, for while a skirt is handy for relieving yourself and making love, it does nothing but get in the way on rough terrain.

The nights were becoming crisp, and Simon drove us unmercifully toward the two peaks that grew to dominate the western sky. The range was much taller here than where we'd crossed before, and was crowned with snow even down to the join between mountains. The so-called pass we were aiming for looked as if it was as far above sea level as the tops of the mounts in the southern end of the range. This explained some of Simon's dismay when Kaihan told him to take this route.

We were all three in much better shape than when we first left the school. Detter in particular had acquired a long-legged effortless stride that made me look like a donkey scurrying behind a thoroughbred. But none of us was in any condition to take real hardship. I hoped we would have ller on our side—even if I had promised not to speak to ller—when we crossed that pass. My Voices were speaking to me sternly.

As we approached our goal, we kept walking doggedly, but the ground leaned further and further into us. The plants grew scrubby and gray, and there were places where their roots had failed to hold up the earth against gravity and half a pasture had fallen downhill. Soon we had to pick our way carefully to avoid falling ourselves, and when we reached a level spot we claimed it for the night, though it was early still. I listened to the foreboding conversation in my head, watched the sky-spirit swirl and cavort, and listened to the occasional rock or clump of dirt roll down the hillside near us. I suspected the people of Telique didn't visit Betzindahl very often, if this was the easiest path between the countries.

In the morning I unpacked my rope, and argued with Simon for another hour of climbing until he ungraciously agreed that we should tie ourselves loosely together. He made it a condition that he should go up first and I should go last, and that was what we did, though his reasoning was poor mountain-climbing practice. Detter was completely contemptuous of the rope, and it obviously chafed his pride to be attached to either of us in any way. I didn't care how either of them felt, just concentrated on keeping my feet steady and my handholds secure, just in case.

The footing was loose, and got looser. Bare outcroppings of mountain thrust up here and there through rivers of jumbled fallen rock. I tried to have at least one hand on solid rock, my heart pounding, while Detter and Simon scrambled along carelessly. It had been years since my one brief experience, an obligatory pilgrimage to the Solitary Temple.

Improbably, we reached the frozen height of the pass by afternoon, the two great peaks rearing awesomely away from us on either side, glowing rosily in the late cold sun. Simon started to plunge downward immediately, his breath huffing in impatient clouds, but I yelled, "Wait," and made him let me go down first. He and Detter kept trying to hurry me up, because they wanted to get to level ground before dark, but the footing was just as loose here and the incline a bit sharper.

Finally, Detter said, "Stop a minute." He was trying to untie the rope with his half-frozen hands. Holding on to a crevice in a sheer outcropping next to me, I yelled, "No, don't," as Simon half slid down near him.

Detter said to him, "She's holding us up. This is ridiculous. Help me get this undone."

Simon crab-walked across to him. I yelled desperately, "Don't untie him," and Simon put his foot down on a loose flat rock that wobbled, pitching him first backward, then forward, and he fell, arms splayed and headfirst, down the hill. I shoved my numb fingers into the crevice, and braced my feet against projections in the outcropping as Simon tumbled past me, jerking Detter off balance with the rope still tied to his waist. Detter's foot was wedged between two rocks as he fell in turn, and he screamed in pain. Then his bootless foot pulled free, and he slid downhill after Simon. The rope jerked taut around my waist, and I felt an agonizing wrench and snap in two of my fingers as the sudden weight knocked the breath out of me, but I held on and held on and held on.

Eventually the loose rocks stopped tumbling down the hill behind me, but the weight on the rope was still steadily dragging me away from my hold. Detter groaned, and I called thinly, with what breath I could gather, "Can you find anything to hold on to?" but he just groaned again.

I couldn't breathe; my fingers were slipping and screaming. I freed one foot and tentatively planted it into the rubble behind me. It didn't slip much, so I gradually brought some more weight to bear on it and then brought the other foot back until I was standing angled against the slope. Then I slowly let go with my fingers and sank to my knees, hoping my footing was firm enough to resist the rope pull.

Detter groaned once more as I got down on all fours and began shuffling down backward. He slipped further down as I crawled, but finally the rope slackened as he came to rest. I came up against a protruding shelf of rock that was solid, and turned around to look.

Detter was sprawled on his back, head downhill, between two large boulders. His leg was covered with blood and his left ankle was snapped sideways, displaying blood, bone, and shredded skin. His eyes were rolled up in his head but he was breathing.

Simon was farther down the incline, flung loosely like a rag doll, at the end of a trail of blood-blazed stones, blood that must have come from the dark stain on his head. He was breathing, but too heavily, his rib cage heaving.

I sat down on my shelf and thought for a moment, absentmindedly pressing a loose fingernail back into place with a wince. My Voices grunted and gibbered. I looked at my grimy, half-crushed hands, then down at Simon and Detter unconscious, and laughed, an odd sound in the whistling cold wilderness.

"Lle bevantegihn gehertelkallen," I said quietly. A wisp of ller trailed out of the wind and coiled around my hands in a figure eight, an opalescent silver glowing. "Ekestverten ller andanfellter, kavelnes ke," I suggested, and lle called more of ller into the loop, until I had a racing double loop the size of a skein of yarn flowing around the poles of my arms. I raised my hands with their speeding halo into the air, and shook ller gently toward the recumbent figures below me on the slope. My hands were partially healed now, the snapped bones straight and whole, the fingernails reattached, but the flesh was bruised and scraped. The silver glow rolled and roiled over and through Detter, then tumbled excitedly down to Simon. Detter groaned again, but now his ankle was merely purple and swollen, no longer shattered, just badly sprained. His eyes flickered open as the mass of ller flowed like a fountain over Simon. I tensed, then remembered Detter couldn't see magic. He probably wouldn't guess what I'd done. Simon's back arched as lle left him, and lle spun back into strands of wind as his eyes opened in turn. Even from where I crouched, I could see something was still very wrong with Simon. His pupils were dilated and he didn't seem really conscious. My spell had been designed only to mostly heal. If Simon was mostly healed now, he must have been nearly dead before. I didn't dare go to him yet until Detter was secured, though.

Detter said, "I think my ankle's broken," to the air. His voice was shaky.

"Hold on, I'm coming down," and I picked my way carefully to him. He pulled himself up to a sitting position and stared blankly at his swelling ankle.

"I could have sworn I felt it snap," he said calmly, his voice firm again. I looked at it, felt it, and said, "No, I think it's just twisted. Don't move it."

I scooted cautiously down to Simon, and confirmed my fears. He was badly hurt, though his skull didn't seem crushed. Detter didn't look so hot himself when I glanced back and caught him unaware. Could I get away with another spell? Detter seemed too alert. Things were very complicated already, and another spell might screw things up even more. It would have to wait.

I said, "Detter, can you slide real slowly down to us on your bottom? Without jiggling your foot?" He contemptuously did so without response, though his foot was obviously causing him incredible pain. His stoicism, if nothing else, was admirable. I inched us forward as a group in the gathering dusk, until we reached a broader rib of rock. I undid the rope and Simon's pack and began to wrap him in his blankets, then sighed exasperatedly, unwrapped him, and made Detter, now shaking and blank-eyed, lie down beside him. I covered them both with the rest of the blankets and the rain capes.

My teeth were chattering in reaction and cold, but I was going to sit and watch over them for a while and maybe sneak in another healing spell. Detter said shakily, "Come lie down, you stupid sow, I'm still cold," and I surrendered, sliding in next to Simon's warm, limp, breathing body. The next thing I knew, it was morning.

Simon was still unconscious, and Detter seemed still asleep. Detter's face was puffy and pale, and he looked sad and ill. I slid from beneath the blankets and hastily called another half-healing spell on both of them, working as swiftly and quietly as I dared. Detter's eyes did not open, but Simon's eyelids flickered and he arched his back gently, stretching his legs. His hair was still matted with blood, but I was pretty sure he would be all right, and I had given Detter's health an overall boost without fixing his ankle. I figured he wouldn't be grateful that I'd saved his worthless life. If he had the slightest suspicion I'd cheated and used magic, he'd use it on me somehow.

I stood up carefully on the ridge of rock and peered down the incline in the cold morning mist. How far was it to the beginning of vegetation and more secure footing? Assuming I could get my companions that far, I could rig some kind of shelter and get some food into them.

Detter cleared his throat elaborately and I jumped. He was sitting up watching me. "Done admiring the view?" he said gaily, his blue eyes shining. "Shall we all take a stroll before breakfast or do you need to meditate further on your sins?" A chill of revulsion ran down my back. I probably should have left him sick, I thought. Less trouble that way. Oh, well.

Simon was lying awake now, squinting and holding his hands to his head. He made a retching sound, but luckily there was nothing in his stomach. I wrapped him securely in blankets and cloaks, and began to drag him slowly downhill. That didn't work, because each bump and slide made him cringe in pain, so I left him and came back up. Some of the rope served to tie Detter's leg to a rolled blanket as a makeshift brace, and I got him started hitching himself downhill. He chattered cheerfully and inanely the whole time, and I didn't answer him. Then I collected the packs and hiked everything down, past Simon and Detter, to the first level patch of grass I found. When I labored back up, Detter had covered a good bit of ground, and Simon was sitting up. I slowly got him to his feet and helped him walk down. By the time I had him settled, Detter reached us, and we all sat on the cold patch of grass in the weak sunshine, drank the rest of our water, and ate the last of the food. Simon looked gray and frail, Detter looked hungover, and I felt like a bucket of mud, but we were alive.

7

In Which I Don't Get My Man

We were three grown adults shoehorned into a leaf-plastered lean-to night after night, and we smelled bad. At least Detter and Simon smelled bad, Detter like some small carnivorous cat and Simon like a dog with swamp-fever. I assume I had an odor of my own, but luckily I couldn't smell it myself.

The hut, a shaky bundle of branches and brush, was built into a crevice in the foothills of the mountain, well below the snow line, with trees all around us and a spring very near. A real little paradise, considering Simon couldn't walk any farther than that. Detter, though he defied pain, couldn't walk very well on his ankle. The winter rains had arrived, and travel was slimy, cold, and treacherous. I'd built a shelter for myself the year I was alone in the wilderness surrounding the school, which taught me that the smaller, the better. There was less air to heat that way. However, I hadn't had to live with anybody during that time. I'd been better off then than I thought.

Simon wasn't so bad. He slept frequently but restlessly since the accident, and I sometimes got angry at him just because he was sick and weak and recovering so slowly. Detter, though, had me completely on edge. He watched me all the time. Sometimes even in the dark I'd wake up and realize he was leaning on his elbow, breathing regularly, looking at me, though the darkness was total. In the daytime he would hobble around gathering wood or patiently waiting by a snare for some unwary animal, but when he wasn't working he was standing, staring at me blankly. It got so there was a weight on my back even when he wasn't near.

Oddly, he was helpful, restrained, and polite. He spoke only when spoken to, and his insults and sarcasm were mild and rare. That was almost as unsettling. He must be planning something, and I would only know what it was when he had sprung his trap.

I tended patiently to Simon, lost to me as a lover. He was pale, fretful, and childish. He no longer looked like a healthy woodsman but like some lost hopeless natural wandering around the edges of civilization. During the third week, though, a ghost of a smile began to quirk around his mouth when the pain in his head wasn't too bad, and I began to remember what was pleasing about him. It was a pity the rain was so heavy and the shelter so small. I was damned if I would invite Detter in on any activities, and given the size of the shelter there was no way to exclude him.

After we had been there about a month, Detter and I began to build another, larger shelter out of tree branches, sod, and compost, the first one having begun to deteriorate and leak badly. Detter's ankle was almost healed, though he might limp for a long time. I had no opportunity to cast any more healing spells, since Simon slept so lightly and Detter could as easily be awake as asleep. Detter was helping me lift and lash a cross-branch onto the framework, when he said to me, "Lise, what do you think of yourself?"

That had no meaning. It appeared to be a perfectly sincere question, though sincerity was a meaningless concept when applied to Detter. I just made a face at him and kept winding vine around a joint.

"I mean it. Do you ever think about yourself, who you are, where you belong, what you're supposed to be doing? Or do you just react?" His face was dripping with rain, and his hair was plastered to his neck.

That night with Simon on the other side of the mountain, I had wondered for a moment if I shouldn't be dead back on Mennenkaltenei or crammed in a dim hole on the ship. Other than that, I tried not to think about my purpose in life. My only purpose in life until I was fourteen was eventually to be llerKalten, nameless, fecund, and wise. After the Enforcers came I had no purpose except to survive and keep from upsetting my people, and I had not done very well at that. I ignored Detter, secured the end of the vine under the windings, and moved to the other end of the branch. He stood braced in the middle, his cold hands white and red gripping the crosspiece. He was still looking at me. He was always looking at me. My peripheral vision was filled with round wide blue eyes, as if everywhere I looked there would be Detter staring. I went back to get another branch from the pile we'd cut, and Detter followed me quietly, taking half the load as I lifted.

"Lise, how do you decide what to do? When you're handed a decision to make, how do you make it? What do you think about?"

"Don't talk, work," I said, my voice stupidly strained. He obediently lifted the new brace into position and waited. I knew this was a "don't answer." My tutor Jenneservet, teaching me the art of government, had told me there were two kinds of questions the llerKalten would have to deal with. The first kind should be answered immediately and with certainty, whether I was right or not, and the second kind should be ignored or passed on to the llerMennet.

Jenneservet asked me questions all the time, and slapped me if I answered too slowly, or if I tried to answer the wrong questions. "Make a choice," Jenneservet would say. "Answer or don't answer, wrong or right, black or white, but choose now and hold to your choice." For a long while I hated her, but as a capable and resilient five-year-old I began to figure the game out fairly fast. By the time I was seven, I rarely got slapped anymore. I missed Jenneservet. I wondered if she was still aboard the Enforcer transport, playing her double game.

So I chose not to answer Detter's question. I couldn't have answered him anyway. I tried to make as few rational decisions as possible. The last real decision I'd made had been to throw away my father's finger bone. I still missed it sometimes.

Detter was a wretched sight, no longer the rarefied angel I'd first met. His nose ran constantly, his hair was long and colorless with grease and dirt, and he had the strained gray look of long-term exposure to cold and rain. His eyes were as blue as ever, though, and his voice as dry and cool. He still moved beautifully, despite the limp.

We didn't finish the new shelter that day, and when Simon emerged exhausted from the woods with two limp, dead lizards and a handful of roots for dinner, it was too wet to even dream of kindling a fire. I hate raw meat, no matter how hungry I am. That night, still damp to the skin, I struggled out of my clinging old clothes in the wet darkness of the old lean-to and into a blanket that was dry only by comparison.

In the fetid, stinking dark while Detter adjusted the so-called door, I said almost inaudibly to Simon, "I suppose you've sworn some kind of oath not to use magic to help yourself or us, or you would have done something by now."

He laughed huskily next to my ear, and a cold hand found its way to my arm. He murmured almost silently, "Head injuries are hard on Talent, Lisane. Give me a little while yet. Don't say anything. Detter would find a way to make capital of it." His breath smelled like mushrooms, but the cold hand and the thready buzz of his voice in my ear unexpectedly stirred me. Detter crawled along and lay down on the other side of him. I felt my way along Simon's arm through the blankets to his moist chest, but his breathing had already settled into quiet regularity. He was asleep.

I lay awake and listened to the steady spit of the rain and the drip of the leaks in the roof. I'd dug channels and hung hollow stalks under the worst of the leaks to drain the water out, and pegged my rain cape under the center of the ceiling, so the water didn't hit us directly, but I was swimming anyway.

Simon breathed shallowly, and beyond him Detter began to gasp quietly and irregularly. Sometimes he did that at night, an ambiguous sound. It could have been pleasure or pain, sorrow or laughter. The sounds and the smells and the dampness kept on, and kept on, and I was awake still, queasily alert to the awkward and ugly mundane events of another ordinary, drowned, abandoned, crippled night in the company of my two involuntary fellow sufferers. My eyes began to burn and fill and my throat to close in the weary self-pity I had not allowed myself to feel since I was a small child worn out from too much teaching.

I struggled to hold my breath calm, but could feel my face drawing up in a rictus of grief. I was ashamed. It was not the end of my life, the time when I had always known I would be allowed to mourn. I had no license to weep, no permission to despair, for my reign had not ended. It would never begin. Yet I was lost and useless and hopeless and foolish. Detter's questions had set off all the bleak things I preferred not to think about. I had trained all my childhood to perform an office that no longer existed, and I did not know how to be a human being.

I drew a deep and shaky breath and oddly heard its echo from Detter on the other side of Simon's silent form. It was bleakly absurd. If I couldn't believe that I was weeping, I could even less believe it of the ice prince. The two of us, whimpering silently on either side of the unconscious body of our damaged leader, eventually must have fallen asleep, though I don't know when.

The next day was dry, though gray, and we got the larger shelter finished in time for the next bout of winter rain. Detter started dragging flat stones from farther up the mountain. We slowly built a clumsy fireplace, piecing the rocks together painstakingly against the wall of the shelter. Once we got the fireplace finished, we knocked part of the wall away in front of it so the fire could warm the hut. It seemed insane luxury to have warm, dry nights, though in the dim light of the banked coals I could now confirm that Detter did watch me when he thought I was asleep.

Simon mended faster once he dried out some. He began to seem more capable, and one night he called Detter over and firmly grasped his ankle. Over Detter's involuntary gasp of pain, he spoke two of the Healing Verses and a pallid glow flashed briefly between his fingers. When he opened his hands, Detter's ankle was firm and true, no longer puffy and flaccid, and gay wisps of ller flitted out through the crevices of the roof. Detter's face was stony while all this went on, but later I saw from the corner of my eye that he had his chin in his palm and his grave gaze resting on me.

I faced him, feeling defiant, but his expression did not change. "Lise, how do you decide what you should do?" he asked again quietly.

"I don't know, all right, Detter? I just decide. If I stop to think, I'm dead. How do you decide what you should do? Do you think about it, do you flip a coin, what do you do?"

"I work from a plan. I have goals, and I think about everything in terms of those goals. I'm very systematic. You have to have some kind of system if you want to survive and get ahead." He had dark smudges under his eyes and his lips were chapped. The last light had faded outside. Simon sat with his long arms wrapped around his legs, staring vaguely at the fire.

"What if your goals change? Does that make all your decisions wrong? How can you know you'll always want the same thing?" With each question, Detter's eyebrows lowered farther.

He burst out, "You never tell me anything I can understand. You just tell your fairy tales or ask your eternal questions. You question everything and you give me nothing in exchange. Is there anything inside you or are you just a question?" He was literally hissing at me, and I was bewildered and annoyed. I had managed to anger Detter, and I didn't even know how I'd managed it. Simon's face was buried in his knees, and his shoulders were quivering gently.

"What do you want from me?" I demanded angrily, and Detter just as angrily pounded his fist on the ground next to him.

"I don't understand you," he said. "I can't figure out why you haven't destroyed me or Simon or both of us, or put us both under your control. You have the Power and the Talent to make us do anything you want, you've shown you're not afraid of wizards or of kings, you don't care anything for conventions, and yet you do nothing. You didn't even choose to heal us all the way, and you could have done that at least. Why don't you use your Power? What good is it if you never wield it?"

Simon was suddenly attentive, the humor leaving his lifted face as he heard what Detter had said about healing. He looked at me speculatively. I didn't care what Simon suspected. But I felt a falling sensation as I realized Detter had known exactly what I'd done on the mountainside, and he hadn't chosen until now to say anything about it. I didn't know what he wanted from me, and I understood him not at all.

He took my puzzled silence for obstinacy and visibly began to collect his defenses again, the lighthearted mask sliding back over his face. No more sniping. I preferred Detter angry to Detter polite and nasty.

I asked, "Detter, what is it you think I should do? Why would I want to control you? Why would I try to destroy you? What would it profit me?" Simon snorted.

Detter said with a hint of his normal glitter, "If you ask me one more question, I'll break all of your fingers one by one."

I breathed in and said madly, "Why would you want to do that?" He lunged at me, Simon grabbed him, and they struggled for a minute. Unexpectedly, it turned into an amiable wrestling match that Simon eventually won. Some of the ceiling fell down, but luckily it wasn't raining.

Simon banged Detter's head on the ground, making his limp hair even dirtier, and said, "It's bedtime. Go to sleep and stop yammering. We start traveling again tomorrow." My face must have gone through some odd changes, for Detter caught my eye and gave me a wry smile. I'm not sure what my expression was in return, but Detter chuckled threadily as Simon let him up. We banked the fire, and the tiny hut darkened as we settled in for the night.

Unexpectedly, as if he had not been a fragile passionless wraith for nearly two months, Simon firmly overlapped our threadbare, greasy blankets and rolled me up in a tight cocoon with him. Though I protested for a minute, the feel of his suddenly insistent hands and thighs, the renewed urgency of his rhythms, made me suddenly frantic with postponed lust. He finally pinned me with my back to the ground, holding me down with his hands and his belly, because he wanted to take his time and I couldn't let him. In the dim red darkness of the hut, I could see past Simon's arm the faint liquid gleam of Detter's eyes as he lay calmly watching us. I turned my head to the other side. Why it should bother me I didn't know. I had once been prepared to mate with a god before a hundred thousand strangers, but sharing more mundane pleasures before one well-known enemy made me squeamish.

Later, still sweatily interwoven with Simon's limbs, I finally fell asleep, but I dreamed, a true dream. I was facing Detter and someone was standing behind me. Detter was naked, as smooth and pink as if he had never set out on this journey. His skin looked as if it had frozen translucently over his bones like a mountain stream in winter, eddying here, rippling there, glassy as the surface of a whirlpool. His eyes were shut, his hands loose at his sides, his chin slightly lifted. The person behind me reached hands forward in front of my face, grasped my lips, and began curling them up and back until my teeth and gums were bared. Then the hands inserted fingers at the back of my jaw as if I were a horse and parted my teeth, wider and wider, aiming me at Detter's face as if my mouth were a pair of scissors. I was forced forward, my head slowly twisted sideways, and I resisted and struggled as hard as I could, retching against the intrusive fingers. My neck was too weak, but I fought anyway, inches away from Detter's nose. I was nearly strangling, and I was afraid my neck would break. The hands couldn't force me any closer. Suddenly the fingers were gone from my mouth, the presence was gone from behind me, and Detter's eyes opened, enormous so close to me.

"Why not?" he asked, puzzled, his milk-white teeth perfect.

"You can't force me to," I answered, as weak and afraid as if I'd been running for my life.

"Oh, all right, if that's the way you want it," he said, disappointed. He started to turn away from me, but I grabbed his arms, leaned forward, and bit his lower lip as hard as I could, tasting blood. He grunted, startled and aroused, and as I dug my fingernails viciously into the skin of his arms, he melted against and into me. It stopped being a true dream after that, but it was a lot of fun in a nasty perverted way, as some dreams can be.

The next morning, after I woke up, and while we got ready to leave, I wondered. I'd never fought a true dream before, never deliberately changed what happened. Maybe my dreams weren't true anymore on a different planet, or maybe my discipline was falling apart. On Mennenkaltenei I would have had to do something about this dream right away, but here I didn't know what to do. There was no one to turn to, no one to tell, no dream teachers, no diviners. I shouldered my pack and set off down the hill behind the men. Simon had already started off, as if he hadn't been my nurseling for so long and I were merely a hitchhiker.

Over the next few days, I realized that Betzindahl was a very different country from Telique or Emsadorn. The country seemed older, tamer, though it was hillier. The rolling, glowing, buff hills were topped by dark trees shooting up like fountains, but the sides of the hills were grassy and rounded. Also, the first building we saw, though Simon steered us wide of it, looked from a distance much bigger and more elaborately constructed than the rustic houses the other side of the continent. It had two stories, a carved roofline, was half-timbered, shingled with slate, and had glass in its many arched windows. It wouldn't have looked out of place in the middle of Deistel Dom. Betzindahl was a more developed country, or at least had been settled longer.

"Why are we passing by?" demanded Detter, dawdling behind and staring back at the house now half-hidden by trees. "Couldn't we just see if they'd put us up for the night? A bed would feel wonderful right now."

Simon half smiled at him. Getting banged on the head seemed to have loosened him up a little; before, Detter's remark would have earned him a peevish reproof. "Nearly twenty years ago the King of Betzindahl swore an oath to deport or kill any mage who set foot in his country. He has kept his promise so far, though a few Talented children have been removed by stealth. I don't want anybody getting a close look at my neck, or my face for that matter, so we are staying away from people as much as possible."

Detter was scornful. "What are you afraid of? If you don't want people seeing you're a mage, why don't you just cloak yourself in illusion?"

"The neckring can't be hidden with magic, Detter. Illusion doesn't work on it; I'd have to be completely invisible to hide it. What good would the ring be if it could be hidden so easily?"

I said, "I understand why you don't want them to see your neck. But why don't you want them to see your face?"

Simon laughed ruefully. "That is just foolishness. I was born in this country, but I was taken so young I am sure no one would recognize me now."

So he was a native of Betzindahl. Who did he think might know him? He buttoned up his shirt but did not ask me to put the skirt back on.

We came across more houses scattered in the hills, most of them looking solid and well-built but empty. The track we were following became gradually a well-tamped cart road, unpaved, and apparently not much traveled in the winter. The rains kept on, but game was plentiful and we ate well. Both my companions had imperceptibly become much more endurable since we'd left the school, but my loneliness and sadness grew the longer we walked. I didn't know who or what I was. In spite of Simon's affections, the combination of Detter's questions and my strange true dream were making me realize more and more that I didn't know how anything worked anymore, or even how I thought.

We came to a place where the road joined another road, this one paved with gravel, and after a bit we passed through the first village. It looked as if it had once been prosperous, with four small shops and a blacksmith, but two of the shops were empty. The buildings, though solid, all needed minor repairs, and the inn at the edge of town was missing half its sign. The gray rain hissed down on the roofs, and only one or two faces peered out cautiously to mark our passing. When we were half an hour past the village, Simon called a halt and we rested uncomfortably under the trunk of a half-fallen tree.

He said, "Something's wrong here. The houses in the hills shouldn't all have been empty, and that town shouldn't have looked like that. There may have been a plague. We'll have to be careful." We shared some of last night's dinner and walked on, looking for a place to camp. We found a shallow cave in the bank above a stream, and Detter killed a fat bird with a stone for supper. Simon and I rolled ourselves up together, and Detter sat at the mouth of the cave a while longer staring out at the night, until he too lay down with a sigh.

The next morning, I awoke to strange, unfriendly voices. I kept still a moment in fear, feeling Simon stiffen against me as well. I listened until I knew the voices came from outside our cave. Then Detter's voice answered, casual and cheerful, and I realized he was outside with the owners of the voices. I wormed my way out of my blanket and crept to the edge of the cave, Simon following.

Detter was seated facing us with his hands awkwardly behind his head, and a man with his hair tied up, his back to us, was holding a ragged-edged spear to his throat. In typical fashion, Detter looked happy and relaxed, though a thin trickle of blood was running down his neck.

Surrounding the two of them were several other men, propping themselves on spears and staves and watching the entertainment.

The man had just demanded something of Detter, and Detter answered him, "Of course I am alone. Who would have me, diseased and vicious as I am?" He laughed, and the man holding the spear to his throat leaned on it a little harder.

One of the men, bigger than the others, said, "Melcom would have you, wouldn't you, Melcom?"

Another of the men, apparently the Melcom referred to, said, "I told you, Rambulf, if you don't slam your hole shut I'll shut it for you." His bravado sounded weak and his companions shifted away from him slightly. Not a favorite with the crowd.

Detter looked at him appraisingly out of the side of his eyes and said, "Well, I think you're adorable. Want to try me out?" The other men laughed, the man holding the spear against him shoved harder still, and Detter's head went back slightly.

Melcom said, "Oh, kill the snot-nosed apple-banger, Slevec, or I'll kill him for you." He moved forward and made as if to grab the spear, and the man holding it pulled back from Detter slightly to give Melcom a shove. Detter puckered his lips suggestively to Melcom, who pushed Slevec aside and swung his fist at Detter's face. Slevec, meanwhile, resented the push and grabbed Melcom's shoulder, while Detter jerked his head back out of the way, smiling and waving his pink tongue at his assailant. The other men were laughing even harder, even when Melcom and Slevec began to wrestle awkwardly with each other, grappling and punching. As they watched the entertainment, Detter backed cautiously out of the way of the two fighters. Beside me I heard Simon quietly chanting. It sounded like an invisibility spell, though since I couldn't use them I hadn't learned them. Lle was flowing lazily along the ground around Detter until lle was coating him evenly in what to my eyes was a glowing shell of royal blue glitter. A similar shell slid between the cave and the men, and if it was also an invisibility spell they wouldn't be able to see any of us if they looked.

Indeed, when there was a brief pause in the fight, they all realized their captive was "gone." Detter lay frozen on the forest floor, watching them carefully through the haze of blue, and luckily none of them stepped on him as they ran looking for their victim. Soon their voices were out of range, but they had left some packs behind and might return, so we gathered our equipment swiftly and left as quickly and quietly as we could, leaving the cloud of ller to disperse on ller own. I saluted ller surreptitiously as we walked away, and lle shuddered gently in reply.

It wasn't until noon that Simon felt it was safe to stop. He said grimly, "There is definitely something wrong here. Betzindahl is the safest and most civilized country in the world, in spite of its politics. Those men were definitely bandits, they didn't fear plague, and they didn't look hungry. They must be doing well for themselves, and nobody is stopping them." He was angry. He seemed to take it personally.

"Who would stop them normally?" I said. "Is there a government here, police or something?"

"The local lord should be policing his domain," said Simon, wiping cold rain off his face for the hundredth time. Detter was standing next to me, leaning weary and pale against a tree. The rain had washed his neck clean of blood over and over, until he finally stopped bleeding. He wasn't talking. I poked his leg, and when he looked down I offered him some cold cooked bird. He shook his head, spraying me with water. I swung my arm around, hit him as hard as I could in the leg, and said, "Eat." He looked startled, but reached down for the morsel I was offering.

Simon approved, or at least he didn't say anything, and Detter seemed to feel better, for a little later he hunkered down and said softly to me, "Dearest one, if you ever hit me again like that, I think we will have to get much closer, and I'm afraid you're not ready for that." He chuckled when I made a disgusted face.

The next village we passed through looked worse, and a small boy threw stones at us as we passed, his pasty mother frantically pulling him inside and slamming the door shut as if to protect him, not us. Simon began to walk faster and look angrier. The gravel road joined a paved road, and there was occasional dispirited traffic, a tinker or two and some solitary horsemen. The paving was crumbling at the edge of the road, and in the dips in the road there were immense potholes full of water. Simon's stride got longer, and he looked as if he were going to war. I finally said breathlessly to him, "Slow down. Wherever we're going, we won't get there today."

He stopped, looked around, and said, "Sorry." We slept secretly in somebody's abandoned stable that night. It was good to be warm and dry, though there were small animals rustling all night in the stale hay.

We entered more populated country, villages coming closer together with less countryside between them. The villages began to enlarge and melt together until they were large market and workshop towns with smaller villages between them. Still, the signs of decay and neglect were there. Doors were barred, some buildings were empty, and we were viewed with suspicion and distrust. It didn't help that we looked like homeless beggars, shabby, lost, and odd, and that Simon would speak to nobody, delegating that job to Detter or me.

Finally, Detter said to him, "You're supposed to be our guide and we're supposed to be students, not servants. Or have you forgotten?"

Simon said, "It is your job to do as I ask, whatever you call yourself. I do not exist here. I am invisible. I will give you no explanation." It didn't sound like pedantic Simon.

He saw me staring at him as if he'd turned into a fish, and I said, "You're going to have to do better than that."

He bit back something, frowned, shrugged his shoulders, and finally answered, "When the mages took me, I was declared a nonperson, to be shunned. Should any native Betzindahli acknowledge me, he would be punished. He is not permitted to see me. I would come to no harm, though, since I don't officially exist. It should be all right for you to speak to me, since you are not natives, but I don't want to get anybody else in trouble."

Detter said, "Ever since you got hit on the head, you've been as peculiar as Lisane," but he went along with the charade of invisibility after that, as if humoring an elderly relative.

I, however, was beginning to put a puzzle together in my head, and berating myself for being an idiot. Kaihan had said to me that he was Simon's ancestor. If he wasn't lying—I knew of no reason he should lie—and if he had not started Simon's line illegitimately—I could not see why the Master of Sassevin Council would want to admit to such a transgression—then Simon was the descendant of a king. I assumed that a king would trace his seed principally through the line of succession, especially through so many generations. How else would he know Simon for his descendant?

From what Simon had said, his father had denied him as son and denied welcome to mages perhaps eighteen years ago. Likewise, at that time the king of Betzindahl had forbidden the country to mages. Simon had been born in Betzindahl. Simon was a nonperson. It was my guess that Simon, like me, had been torn from his inheritance. Unlike me, his country and his father still lived, and he was beginning to think he was needed.

I said to Detter later on, "You don't happen to be related to anybody important, do you?"

"O most gracious majesty, empress of the night skies, I am the sixth son of a farmer and a weaver, neither of them particularly important, and I know they're dead, because I killed them both myself," he said. "Other than that, I am the first worthy person to be born of a long line of nobodies from nowhere, and I see no reason to claim otherwise."

"That's a relief," I said. He looked enigmatic, and I knew that meant he didn't know what I was talking about. I thought I might begin to understand Detter sometime. His lips were a darker rose pink than when I first met him, and he was growing a golden fuzz of mustache. As pretty as a wheat-snake in the sunlight.

Simon, his bones moving smoothly under his ragged brown traveling clothes, his scarf concealing his ring again, had a savage grace I'd never seen in him before, and I didn't think it was my imagination. It was as though he were breathing better air in Betzindahl, as though his pedantry and solemnity had been transmuted to arrogance and confidence. Though he was half-starved and determined to act invisible, his step was lighter and groups of people parted before him automatically. We entered unchallenged through the gates of the harbor city Linz only because Simon led us, his brows knit fiercely and his gray eyes clear and far-seeing. It was almost comic. If I had been in the place of the surly gate guard who waved us through, I would have stopped and arrested all three of us. We looked worse and less trustworthy than any of the bands of brigands we'd hid from on the road. But Simon glowed with purpose like a religious zealot, and besides we probably looked too hungry and poor to be successful highwaymen.

The city was great and grand, bustling and intense, nothing like healthy little Deistel Dom. The buildings were beautifully made, even the frequent inns, some of carved striated stone assembled without mortar, some joined together of smooth-finished woods. The streets wound through the city, down toward the sea and the inner city of tall towers within high walls that was the ruler's castle and the country's center. We could see the towers sparkling in the faint late winter sun, but it was going to be a long walk. I couldn't tell how long Simon planned to keep going. My legs were heavy, my pack dragged, my shoulders hurt, and keeping up with Simon was agony.

There were armed men strolling everywhere in the city, we had no money left, and the closer we got to the castle the less we belonged. The people in their exotic, structured clothing were scurrying nervously toward their homes as the day faded. Simon found his way assuredly through city squares, along side streets, and down long flights of steps carved into the hill, some kind of back way or shortcut, but it was nearly dark and we hadn't eaten all day.

We were cutting through a nearly empty plaza toward an alleyway when a gaudy figure hailed us. Up close, I could see he was a middle-aged man in a gorgeous burnt orange and brown uniform, a sword in a scabbard at his hip. He bore a scar across his nose, but his expression was not unkind, just indifferent. He spoke to Simon, as our obvious leader, "Son, the pickings are poor for beggars in this part of town. May I direct you to shelter before the night guard misunderstands your presence here?"

Simon stood as if at attention, staring past the man with a face like carved marble. This looked awkward. I said, stepping forward, "Excuse me, were you addressing me, sir?"

The man looked annoyed and said, "No, I was not, you young trollop. I was addressing your shabby friend." Simon was silent.

Detter said brightly from beyond him, "Oh, heavens, I must not have been paying attention. You were speaking to me?" The man's face chilled at Detter's tone, and his hand went to the pommel of his sword. This situation had the potential to become completely ridiculous.

I said with all the dignity I could muster, "It would have to be one of us two, sir, because as you can see there are only two here," and I laid my hand gently on Simon's arm. Simon did not move. I hoped he was right to behave like such a donkey. His black hair was dirty and matted, his broad cheekbones were toughened and gray with exposure, the clothes on his long frame were abjectly worn, but he had never looked nobler or wilder.

The man took a step back in sudden doubt, his eyes on Simon's face. "I am a foreigner here, good sir, new to the city today," I said, "and so is my friend. We are heading for the castle, but we are utterly lost without native guidance." I hoped I was doing the right thing. If my suspicions were correct, and if this man knew what had happened, and if he were sympathetic . . . if, if, if. My Voices were muttering gibberish in the back of my head, and I was on my own.

"If you are so strange to the city, how is it you have found your way to this point? You are nearly at the citizen's door. Who gave you directions?" he said, and I hoped it was working, for he was still staring at Simon.

"No one, sir. No one gave us directions," I murmured. Detter was looking enigmatic again, but Simon tightened the crook of his arm over my hand, and I felt a bit reassured.

There was a silence. Then the man breathed, "Thunder buzzards, I think you're too late, child." I pretended not to hear. Detter shifted from foot to foot, wearily, readjusting his pack and tucking his hair behind his ears. Simon seemed more relaxed, but he continued to stare into space, and the man continued to stare at Simon.

Then, briskly, the man turned to me and said, "The King is meeting with his advisers tonight, but I am sure he would always want to welcome foreigners. Why don't you and your friend follow me?" He spoke as if reciting lines. He turned his back on us deliberately, fiddling with his belt and waiting.

I said to Simon under my breath, "He knows you?" and Simon said in a normal voice, "My mother's brother, Quillas. We couldn't have met up with better. A fair, strong man and faithful to the King."

Quillas straightened his shoulders as if challenged and stepped off toward the alleyway that had been our original destination, not looking back to see if we were following. Everything had to be done according to form, apparently.

Detter said to Simon pettishly, "I'm hungry. Is he going to take us somewhere to change and eat?"

Simon said dryly, "He has his reasons for wanting me in particular to show up ragged and hungry. I may or may not go along with his plans, but it won't harm me to be prepared." We were scurrying to keep up with Quillas, who seemed to be a man of much importance in the city. Guards parted respectfully before him, however doubtful they looked when they saw whom he was escorting, and doors opened to him. We passed through several thick walls on our winding path, past stronger and stronger gates, until at one great iron gate a bearded troll of a man dressed almost as beautifully as Quillas gave him a spirited argument about letting us in. Quillas cited chapter and verse of some dusty law regarding the welcome of strangers, the troll spat in disgust and argued some more, but finally we were admitted. It was night, the sky had cleared, and the stars were out as we crossed a wide courtyard to a great open door ablaze with torchlight.

We entered an arched anteroom widening into a great chamber half full of people where some kind of dispute was taking place. We were half-blinded with the light, but I could see that the crowd looked bored and overdressed, showing scant respect for the frail figure in the high throne who faced them all, arguing with a small knot of people before him. I assumed the man in the throne was the King, but I found it hard to make him out. He was obscured by a malevolent haze of embodied ller, spirit-fire old and maimed and confined by some cruel force.

I said to Simon, shocked and angry, "That man up there is spelled to the gills, and has been for years. It's disgusting." Quillas was looking at me doubtfully.

"I can feel it," Simon said quietly. "Who is responsible? Can you see a source? Find out for me." No one besides the door guards had noticed our entrance so far, and the guards merely inclined their heads to Quillas as he led us in. He moved us to a spot beside the door. I guessed that the layers of gates and guards made these people careless of their safety, though far too many of them were armed for my taste. Quillas stood, arms folded, now looking a little worried. I hoped he didn't regret his decision all of a sudden.

An enraged graybeard was standing before the throne, berating the seated King in an infuriated but tremulous voice, only the graybeard wasn't the mystery mage. There was no sign of spells to accompany his gestures. The King, who through the haze of magic seemed barely conscious, looked bored, weak, and irritated, and responded in monosyllables.

I surveyed the room carefully, and came across a redheaded, black-bearded, lantern-jawed figure watching impassively from the side of the room. He seemed unconcerned with the argument going on, but his hands were rolling and rolling over each other, and between the palms was a spirit-glow, a blob of ller. His collar was open, but I saw no ring around his neck.

I murmured to Simon, "The redhead in the blue waistcoat."

Simon searched the room and found him. "A renegade," he said sadly, meaning the lack of a neckring. Pompous twit, I thought affectionately. I could count on Simon to be annoyed at simple rule-breaking when a major sin was being perpetrated here.

He said quietly, "I am about to betray your trust and my role as your guide. You had both better leave the room, for I have to do something about this, and it will mean I cannot leave ever again. Quillas will help you escape, and you must make your own way to Sassevin. It has been done before."

"Now you've gone completely insane," said Detter, pale with anger.

I interrupted. "Simon, if you really want to stop this, you're going to have to let me do it."

He glared at me imperiously. "You will do nothing. You are a student under oath. I will take care of it." A cadaverous character in purple seated near us turned and shushed us, then peered at us more closely. I was going to have to hurry if I wanted Simon to get off his high horse.

I said in a lower tone, "That's your father, right? The King?" He paused, then nodded, startled by my guess, the sweet idiot. "He's enspelled by a renegade and the kingdom is falling to bits, so you're going to stay and do your duty by him as Kaihan wanted, instead of going for your Sorcerer's ring, right?"

The man in purple was urgently talking to his immediate neighbor, a corpulent man with a nervous tic. Simon nodded again, and suddenly began to smile at me. His face was so much handsomer when he smiled.

I said, "Simon, you don't have the Power to beat this man. The spell is old and ugly, and the renegade is strong. This needs to be done, I can do it, and you can't. Trust me."

Detter said through his teeth, "You motherless offspring of pigs, I'm not going to let you do this to me!" The man in purple was standing up and motioning to a half-dozing guard by the door, and other heads turned toward us.

Simon said to Detter, "You don't have any choice. Since I may not speak until my banishment is lifted, will you be my voice, or must I speak with your mouth through spells? It is most uncomfortable, as I'm sure you know." Detter looked mulish, but as Simon put his hands to his neck, ripping his shirt open to reveal his neckring, Detter nodded reluctantly.

I said quickly to Simon, "Hide me. I need to be invisible." He spoke rapidly in an undertone, and a coating of royal blue entwined itself around me until I knew by his eyes he couldn't see me anymore. It wasn't a moment too soon, for the man in purple was calling out, "Who are you? What are you doing here?" to Simon. The graybeard at the front of the hall was too absorbed in his infuriated oration to hear, but the red-haired man's eyes shifted toward the disturbance. I walked rapidly away from Simon and toward the King.

Detter came in front of Simon. Simon muttered, prompting him, and Detter said loudly and elegantly, "Oh, gracious people of Betzindahl. I am new to the country, but even I can see that your King is under the spell of a renegade mage. Do you prefer your royalty thus enslaved, or do you perhaps not know what has happened? Could somebody enlighten me?"

There was noisy tumult. Half the people in the room went for their swords and the other half dived to the floor or out the door. They were definitely prepared for violence here. I turned to the saffron glowing spell enveloping the slumped figure of the King.

"Lle mehnes pertegressteren ihn beserglemt, san?" I said chattily to the spell, and the few people still near me recoiled in horror. Apparently I was invisible but not inaudible. Detter was shouting something else inflammatory and elegant from the back of the room. The mustard-colored spell stirred lethargically, and slowly unwound its long tail from the King's body. Lle was half-solid, almost material, and must have been congealed like that for years, poor thing.

I repeated, urging ller on, "Lle pertegressteren?" and lle shook like a jelly and flowed away from the King toward ller creator. The redheaded man's attention was entirely on the commotion at the back of the room. He was turning, coming away from the wall, craning his neck to see what was going on. I risked a glance backward and saw that Simon and Detter were half-surrounded by a slow-moving, cautious group made up of the more courageous gentlemen in the room, the rest having left entirely or cautiously concealed themselves behind benches. Simon was not without defenses, as I could see by the flickers of plum-colored ller that kept his attackers at bay. The redhead reached his hands out into the air and called globules of ectoplasm to him from the air. He molded them into ominous shapes and prepared to cast the product across the room at the disturbance. I admired his work. He was extremely good, the best I'd seen so far.

I turned and said encouragingly, "Yegger ve andersgerteren," to the immense spell humping across the room from the King back to his enemy. The renegade obviously sensed and manipulated magic by touch, not sight or emotion, so he probably wouldn't realize what was happening until the spell was on him. He released his crowd-control spell into the air, but I immediately told the new spell there was no need for ller to hang around. The renegade swung abruptly around at the sound of my voice and grabbed for some more magic, but as he grabbed, the spell he had cast on the King reached him finally and flowed back over him in rippling waves, shuddering with release. He was drowned in ller like a fly in amber, gasping and convulsing as lle tensed around him. He must have looked a sight if you had no spirit-eyes to see what was happening to him. He screamed, choked, screamed again.

With the new disturbance, the crowd was bewildered, fragmented, not sure what was going on. The King, bewildered and half-awake, stirred on his throne and said, "What is happening? Where am I?" No one heard him, and sick as he was, he grasped the arms of his throne, hauled himself to a standing position, and rasped harshly, "What is the meaning of this?"

In the sudden silence that followed, everyone heard the renegade choking and gasping in the corner, including the King. He turned and looked at his enemy, and after a measured moment said, "Whoever started killing off that vile little man, please finish the job."

I told the sulfurous gelatinous mass of ller to enjoy itself, and the redheaded man began to dissolve from the boots up, shrieking in pain and outrage. When he finished dissolving, I told the evil old binding spell its time was come, and lle faded gladly into undifferentiated sludgy streaks until lle had vanished. I turned to look at ller's erstwhile captive.

The King was almost as tall as Simon, and he must have topped him in his youth. The cheekbones were Simon's and the nose, but the face was more barbaric and closed than I thought Simon's could ever be. I made a mental note to ask Simon if all the men in his family lost their hair by late middle age, for the King's scalp shone smooth as Kaihan's in the torchlight. He was flabby and emaciated, wavering, like a man who had been seriously ill for a long time, but he kept himself upright by sheer will.

With a gesture and a word, Simon cleared the blue haze that surrounded me, and people recoiled as I "appeared" from thin air. I walked back to Simon, my head down like an elegant servant's, and he put his hand on my shoulder when I reached him. His other hand was on Detter's shoulder.

The King looked at us, a pathetic and inglorious group now the battle was over, and said to Simon, "Explain yourself. Why are mages here in defiance of law? Surely you must know of my edict. I am not swayed by the service you have done me." There were murmurs of agreement. What a bunch of legalistic loonies, I thought. What were they going to do, march us out and behead us for saving his life?

Simon did not reply. I started, "Majesty . . ." and Simon tightened his hand warningly on my shoulder, so I stopped. The King ignored me, waiting for an answer. Simon was not going to give it to him. There was a long silence. The King's arms were trembling with the effort to keep himself upright.

Finally, Quillas, leaning against a column not too far from us, said casually, "My lord, I should mention that you are once again without an heir now that Baron Laitallen has so tragically been taken from us." Somebody laughed sharply, and I guessed Laitallen had been the redheaded renegade.

"Now is hardly the time to discuss that. You overstep yourself," said the King angrily to Quillas. "Answer me, or suffer the consequences," he shouted at Simon. Simon stood stock-still.

"On the contrary, my lord," said Quillas. "It is time to settle the succession once and for all, since you have *no natural son*," stressing the last words. There was an appalled gasp from several of the people near us, and the man nearest to Quillas actually backed away as if afraid of contamination. The King peered at Simon more closely and then sat down suddenly. "Oh. Well then. Bring me syrup," he said hoarsely, but no one moved. "Quillas. Bring syrup," he commanded. Quillas sheathed his sword and strode clattering out a side door.

Simon said quietly to me, "It seems I have made a choice between my responsibility to my students and my duty to my father and country. I am very sorry."

"Responsibility and duty," said Detter mockingly. "It couldn't possibly be power and pleasure you desire. It must be responsibility and duty. Being Prince and heir to the most powerful kingdom of the Lesser Shore is simply your miserable duty."

Simon said gently, "There will be precious little pleasure and less power for me from now on. You will be far better off than I, Detter." He must have felt very dramatic and tragic, and all the apprehensive people around us appreciated the little show. Nobody knew better than I how important it was to truly be the character you play when you rule.

Quillas returned, bearing a pottery bowl full of a tea-colored viscous liquid. He said to me politely and pointedly, "Have you eaten today?"

I understood vaguely that the question was not meant for me, and said, "No, sir. We have been traveling empty since last night." I no longer felt very hungry, and wondered why.

"I will endeavor to see that you are fed later," he said, and bore the bowl gravely up to the King, laying it in his lap.

The King surveyed the room solemnly, as if it were not a frozen picture of chaos and battle, with people gradually coming out of their hiding places or falling back from fighting postures. He seemed not at all discomfited by being released from a spell, being presented with a long-lost son, or watching a man die from the feet up before his eyes. He began to speak solemnly in words that sounded ceremonial and dignified. I remembered how nice it was to have something suitable to say for every occasion, one time long ago when I was the straw goat of another world.

"My beloved queen bore one and only one child, a son, but he is dead to me," he said. "It is my right and my duty to declare an heir to follow me as ruler of the kingdom. I did indeed once choose an heir, but against my will and under duress, and the false heir has died in payment for his crime. Let all those present witness that I now choose my final heir, for good and of my own will. Are there any challenges to my choice?" He had blue shadows under his eyes and he was trembling, but I wouldn't have crossed this frightening old man for any reason, and apparently, though his audience shifted and muttered, neither now would anyone else in the room. "Will the candidate come forward?" said the King after the long pause.

Simon kissed my cheek, and unexpectedly Detter's too, though Detter pulled away from him. "This is how I was acknowledged legitimate as an infant," he murmured to us, and left us to walk to the front of the room. He stood before his father, upright and poised. Two sets of gray eyes stared at each other for an instant, and then the King dipped his index finger into the bowl of syrup. He extended the finger, and Simon leaned forward and took it into his mouth, sucking the syrup off as if he were a nursing baby. The sight disturbed me, an annexation of motherhood's nurture to the father, doubtless why the fostered child had to go hungry before the ceremony.

"This is now my son. I declare his name Saimin Leonais tzin Terhal mian Ankheleral, and from today until the end of time he will take the place of the son who was lost to me," said the King, and he was holding Simon's dark and dirty head in his lap. Simon's arms were around his knees. I'd lost a lover to ritual, though not in the way I'd always expected. I couldn't believe I was wishing Simon had been killed instead.

Detter said loudly, "How adorable they look. Just made for each other, don't you think?" and I nodded absently, tears running down my face. I really never would be llerKalten, I realized, and thought I could feel the presence of the goddess leave me absolutely.

Detter stared at me and said, "Am I really the only sane person in the world?" and I nodded again. He probably was.

8

In Which I Don't Take the Job

The suite where Detter and I were housed was comfortable enough, but lonely. No one but a pair of silent, disdainful servitors had visited us since Quillas led us out of the audience hall. He had said quietly, "We'd better get you out of here before somebody remembers you," and hustled us down a long corridor lit by oil lamps to the small, warm apartment. He shut us in the sitting room, said, "Somebody will come to see to your needs," and started to leave. He paused in the doorway and said, "Please stay here. I can't guarantee what might happen to you if you leave these rooms."

It was my guess that our main offense was not the practice of magic, but that we didn't fit the rules. I knew now where Simon got his legalistic bent and his lack of humor. This court was a web of unspoken laws, and if you made one wrong step you were spider food.

Three days had passed. I'd finally had as many hot baths as I wanted. The highly spiced food, though good, was hard on my stomach. The rooms were elegant and sophisticated, and smelled of perfumed smoke, but there weren't any books to read. The servitors brought clothes for Detter and me, but I made them take the woman's clothing back and bring me a man's costume.

Detter said, "Why do you need to dress like a man? Don't you think you make a better woman?" He himself was decked out in a pin-tucked costume of gleaming forest green, all shirred seams and elaborate beading, and he lay on his belly on the rug like a basking lizard, eating dried fruit. He was happy in this plush confinement. It was odd how much he loved his luxuries, considering he was equally comfortable with pain and deprivation.

"You'll never know how much better," I said, cheerfully. The real reason I wouldn't wear the gown was that it weighed about forty pounds and was as comfortable to wear as a butter churn. It was beyond me how the Betzindahli could be so comfort loving as to build indoor plumbing, yet design clothing expressly to limit motion and cause pain. Even the Emsadorn gowns had permitted some movement.

The servants, mutely conveying disapproval, brought me what I'd asked. I stripped off my worn traveling clothes and began changing. I'd gotten out of the habit of worrying what Detter might see.

Detter watched me pulling the knickers on and said, as if discussing the food or the weather, "Am I expected to be your consort now that Simon's out of the picture?"

I looked at him with such outrage that even he couldn't hold a straight face. I finished knotting my belt, my lips pursed, while Detter buried his giggles ostentatiously in the rug. I got up and kicked his ribs to get his attention. "The only way I would ever lie down in the same bed with you, Deteras Anhand, is if you were bound, gagged, and drugged. And even then I'd worry."

He rolled on his back, smiling relaxedly up at me, and said, "Don't you still have some of that rope in your pack? I'm sure the drugs and the gag could be arranged."

I considered kicking him again, just for the pleasure of it, but it wasn't worth the argument. Besides, that was probably what he wanted of me. I finished dressing, and roamed discontentedly through the apartment while Detter popped nuts in his mouth and hummed irritatingly.

The time went slowly, and no one visited us, not even Simon. That was all right with me. If I never saw him again, it would be easier for me. I could think of him as dead, then, rather than having the uneasy feeling that it was I who should be dead. I had no windows to look out of, nothing to do but eat, daydream, listen to my peevish Voices, sleep, and try not to talk to Detter. I felt as if we were a pair of embarrassing ghosts, fading gradually from reality.

Finally one evening, late, there came a quiet scratching. Detter, sprawling on the hearth, rolled swiftly to his feet and darted to open the door. Simon stood framed in the doorway, grave, dignified, and perfectly groomed. Even his forelock was trimmed and combed into place. He was still somberly dressed in brown, but the rich drape and perfect cut of the fabric made Detter's gaudy costume look shallow and cheap.

"I was unable to come before," he said quietly.

Detter said sarcastically, "I suppose you were held at sword point?"

"No. I couldn't seek you out without drawing attention to you, and there are people here who would leap at a chance to hold you hostage against me. My very existence threatens the plans of much of the court. I have arranged to get you both out of Linz and onto a ship to the Greater Shore tomorrow. There's a captain who's an experienced winter sailor, and he's agreed to take you. He doesn't know you're mages, though, so you must be cautious." It all sounded very dramatic, but his presence was annoying and I wished he would leave.

Detter answered sulkily, "I realize we are an embarrassment to you, but you needn't be in such a hurry to get rid of us."

Simon just made an exasperated sound, and continued, "When you reach Sassevin, you will go straight to the Beast, of course, but when you leave, find Kaihan. Tell him what happened, and tell him I said he is responsible for you."

Detter said, "Whereupon he will have us both locked in ward-chains, and he'll send the Finders to bring you to judgment. I find the prospect of your trial vastly entertaining."

Simon looked back and forth at the two of us, and his forelock escaped from its unguent and flopped forward. Then he sighed, came in, shut the door behind him, and sat down. "Detter, Kaihan has been trying to make me return to Betzindahl since I survived my Quest. I have done as he wished. He will take care of you, and I will not be punished. I thought Lisane had some idea of this. Hasn't she said anything?" He looked at me, puzzled, but when I didn't answer he turned back to Detter.

I was sitting in the armchair, my arms resting in my lap, feeling even more of a ghost than before. Simon sat there talking to Detter like some merchant saying he was out of fruit but the weather was fine. The Voices in the back of my head, my predecessors and prophecy guides, were chanting childhood rhymes in ragged unison. I could get on a ship tomorrow and leave this remote man without regrets, but I was leaving pieces of myself behind wherever I went, and nothing was coming in to replace them. I didn't know how to become anything but llerKalten, and none of what was going on fit in with my training. I was beginning to understand why the llerKalten always died at the end of her reign. She didn't know how to do anything else. I had lost my planet, my position, my pride, my prophetic powers shred by shred like a fish-nibbled corpse in the ocean.

Detter and Simon kept sparring, but I no longer listened to them. I wished Simon would go away. Now they were silent; Simon came closer to me, and I could feel the living warmth of him standing over me. Detter stood behind him, his arms folded, and I realized he didn't want to leave Simon either, though for different reasons. I stared through Simon's midriff, willing him to leave me alone, until he knelt before me and I was forced to look into his narrowed gray eyes. He already looked more like his father, purposeful and arrogant.

"So how is the King?" I asked coldly.

Simon winced, paused, and then answered. "He's already feeling much better, unfortunately. He's an opinionated, dictatorial bully at best. Even though he was enchanted by that rogue conjuror for nearly five years, he's recovered swiftly. I suppose it's good, because he needs all his wits to resist the political maneuvering that's going on, but he's a terror to deal with. He's unbelievably demanding, I'd forgotten how much."

"Didn't anybody here know what was going on?" I was willing to talk about anything but Simon and me.

"Not everybody has your Talent," he said quietly. "No one at court knew there was any magic involved. He just became more and more arbitrary and outrageous, and declaring an outsider his heir seemed only one more infuriating act. There was much dissension in the court, and the country itself nearly came to war. That's why the bandits could run around unchecked, because the lords were all conserving their soldiery for battle. Kaihan knew, somehow. He's been trying to convince me for a long time not to essay the test for Sorcerer, even though my father never requested my return."

He became aware he was rattling on, and stopped, embarrassed. At least he hadn't become completely pompous, though the potential was there. I didn't say anything more, but I put Kaihan on a list for painful revenge. It gave me something to live for, the prospect of flaying him alive. He'd planned all this with exquisite care, granted permission to Simon to seduce me so I'd support him, gave me just enough of a clue so I'd guess what was going on at the right time, and ordered Simon to pass through the country of his birth. He'd known I would be abandoned to make my own way with treacherous Detter as my only companion, and he'd cold-bloodedly condemned honest, well-meaning Simon to a political balancing act for the rest of his life. I closed my eyes. Simon put his hands on my knees, and in a sudden inexplicable burst of rage I swept them aside.

As I did so, the door flung open with a crash, and the King strode in. "I told you to come to me after dinner," he said coldly to Simon. "Instead I find you creeping back to your slut and your catamite. Are they merely your secret advisers, or are you their puppet? If you can't keep away from the kind of slime who stole you from me, I might as well throw you back to them." Simon, eyes slitted, sat back on his heels and waited out the tirade. Still furious, I had no such patience, and struck out at him with my harshest command voice, dredged from my oldest training.

"What rat-faced sludge of turtle spawn has beslimed this chamber uninvited?" I snarled. I was lifting, translated, from one of Jenneservet's better speeches. The King paused, his cape still swirling around him, and regarded me with alert attention.

I continued, "Were you not hairless, brainless, ancient, and badly addled, I would stir myself to be annoyed with you. Since your mother was obviously a kitchen drain and your father a festering rag, I must assume you do not know you have been rude. You may beg my pardon or remove your presence and its unbearable odor from the room." It was pleasant to feel anything, even rage, though both the King and Simon were watching me like snakes. Detter had edged halfway out of the room and was observing with prurient fascination.

Simon said, low and amused, "Father, she technically outranks you. You'd better do as she says."

I wasn't sure how he meant that, or if it were true, but the old man, astonishingly, took my instructions literally, a calculating glint in his eye. He inclined his head to me, said, "I do beg your pardon, madam," and I said, "Granted. I see I may have been deceived as to your character." I indicated the couch and he crossed over and took a seat, adjusting the skirts of his robe.

He said to Simon, who still sat on his heels before me, "You didn't tell me this adolescent would-be witch was actually a hundred-year-old queen with years of rule behind her. How did she make her voice do that, or is her appearance deceiving?"

Simon said cautiously, "You'd better ask her." The King waved his hand negligently, with no apologies. Simon rose, bowed to me, bowed to him, and left the room shooing Detter ahead of him. The King followed his progress with cat eyes but did not move. I'd never used command voice in a real situation before, and I was not sure whether it had worked or not, though it had certainly gotten his attention. For an exiled, dethroned ghost, I still had my resources.

The King turned to me with a rustle of fabric and said, "I thought you merely a witless, perverted, female apprentice conjuror. I must apologize. May I know your name and your station?" The old buzzard wasn't under any illusions, just looking for a different way to do what he wanted. My only recourse was truth, which might be counted on to disconcert if nothing else.

So I said frankly, "As for my station, I am indeed a student mage, which I assume is what you meant. However, I am in a manner of speaking the exiled, uncrowned queen and deposed deity of an invaded, defeated land. I have no name to give you, but you may call me Lisane. Your name, gracious sir?"

He said, "I am Terhal Leonais tzin Segevan mian Ephemener, and I am the previously bewitched and incapable King of a long-standing but heated permanent argument." We sat in silence for a moment. The fire popped and sent out a shower of sparks. I reached for the fire-tongs, and Terhal said, "I assume you are fairly close to my son?"

I looked up and in the flickering firelight realized I saw a man who was in some ways very like me. He'd been raised all his life to be a ruler, a human collection of strategies and policies who occasionally allowed a stunted emotion to rise to the surface. Though the question he'd just asked had all kinds of motives, he'd not been able to keep from showing a protective, fearful affection for his lost child. So I told him what I knew of Simon. Some of it he didn't like, but he was relieved to know for sure that Simon had been my lover.

"At least he's capable, then. I feared he was as twisted as most of the mages. He must be married soon, and I thought I'd have to find him some girl to marry who wouldn't mind spreading her legs to a man whose interest lay elsewhere."

He sounded like a cattle breeder with a reluctant bull, and I laughed, thinking of Jens and Annesil, and how complicated the practical romances of royalty must be here. It would have been so much easier for me. My consorts would have lasted only a year.

"He's a romantic, and naively honorable, so you'll have to choose well. He'll need a woman with spirit and brains, I'm afraid, or his eye will wander, whether to women or men I couldn't tell you." Terhal cocked an eye at me and I realized how cynical I sounded. I gazed at him levelly. His eyes dropped first, but I suspected from the creases around his eyes I'd lost the skirmish somehow.

We talked for another hour, and finally the old man lifted himself out of the sofa and kissed my hand. "You had better get out of the country fast," he said, "or I will find myself fighting my own son over the right to court you." The crafty old demon managed to make me blush, though I knew how much calculation went into the statement. He looked at me for a moment as if he were sorry for me, then left.

I went to bed. I added to Kaihan's list of offenses. I'd thought I had no illusions about the Master's reasons for mating Simon with me, but now I saw I had mainly served as evidence of the heir's potency. In the small hours of the morning my door swung silently open, and Simon climbed into my box of a bed, cold and shivering in his nightclothes. When he left at dawn I felt less solid than ever.

Quillas came after breakfast and escorted us down to a carriage, which took us the short distance to the harbor. He transferred us to a two-masted ship, manned by a silent, efficient crew, and loaded two chests of clothing and food for us as well.

Detter vanished in search of our quarters, and I said to Quillas, "Take care of your swell-headed nephew."

He leaned on the rail comfortably. "Saimin will be fine. He's already fitting in. He was a well-behaved child, and the courtier he killed all those years ago was a scheming pervert who deserved to die, so those of us who remember him support him." Seabirds were mewing shrilly, and wind-blown ropes slapped against the masts and dock in a pattering clamor. It was bitter cold, and I would have to go below soon.

Quillas reached into a pouch at his waist, and handed me two small boxes. "One is from Saimin and one is from the King," he said, and then dug out another box for Detter from Simon. Sentimental tokens of esteem, I thought sardonically, and considered tossing them in the water but refrained from politeness. Quillas grasped my shoulders and kissed me firmly on the forehead, then loped down the gangplank as the crew began to cast off. It was so cold I couldn't smell the sea, and I'd lost feeling in my fingers, so I sought out Detter and our cabin.

Detter's gift was a pair of earrings, small gold hoops. I watched fascinated as he matter-of-factly pierced his ears with them, leaving beads of blood on the wires. He left in search of a mirror, and I opened my presents. Simon's box contained a signet ring, sized for a man, with an elaborate dragon incised in intaglio. I was uncomfortably certain it was some kind of state seal. Also in the box was a tiny rosette of interwoven human hair, two kinds, both black but one coarser than the other. I wondered when he'd stolen my hair and found the time and the skill to fashion a love knot. I stared at it angrily for a while. He was an idiot and a romantic, and he did not deserve to be anybody's sovereign.

In Terhal's box was a locket, filigreed on the outside. Inside was an exquisite miniature, a mosaic in almost invisible chips of semiprecious stone, a portrait of a very young boy. He was solemn and innocent, perhaps five years old. The luminous eyes were silver gray and the forelock curling on his forehead was onyx black. I looked at that for a longer time, my eyes dry. Detter came in and went to his bunk, humming to himself.

We were the only passengers, no one else being so imbecile as to travel by ship in the pit of winter. Detter and I shared a mushroom box of a cabin with two shallow slots for bunks. As we inched out of harbor, the raised sails shuddered in the wind, and we began endless days and nights of pitching and rolling. Detter's stomach failed him for nearly two days, and my balance was unsure for a while, so it was some time before we ventured out.

The crew was a quiet lot, endlessly occupied with ship's chores or their handiwork, and they seemed to view us both with suspicion. There were no women among them, which startled me. I was used to women sailors, mostly. This whole planet seemed to have peculiar notions about gender.

The captain, a youngish man with a cruel mouth and remote eyes, avoided us altogether. After I had essayed polite conversation and been ignored, a young sailor told me gruffly, "The captain doesn't mix with passengers. Best leave him alone." I thanked him for his advice and he turned from me with a grunt.

So I didn't try to approach the captain anymore, just watched him covertly when I had the chance. There was a constant coalescence and dissipation of ller going on in his vicinity, never very intense. Every once in a while he would make a vague gesture and the spirit-fire would dissolve away into smears and blobs. He ate with his arm wrapped about his plate, as if someone might steal his food. He had no neckring, but he was obviously a product of the mage school, unless there was a similar prison for mages elsewhere on the planet.

The ship groaned and creaked, shuddered and plunged, day in and day out. The water was salt. Sometimes the wind sprayed ocean water on the deck like rain, tasting of salt, death, and life. Sometimes the rain poured down on us from the sky instead—bland, cold, and sweet. Either way it was deathly cold. We stayed in our cabin much of the time, driven out for meals and air. Detter was itchy, bored, and vicious, but I couldn't stir myself to fight with him.

In the daytime, the Voices in my head spoke in counterpoint to the wails of the wind. They had been making less and less sense, and now they spoke in fragments, irrelevancies, malapropisms. Sometimes I sat and listened to them for hours, as if waiting by a deathbed, pressing Simon's ring into the skin of my arms to make raised welts in the shape of a dragon. At night I dreamed in my confined bunk, but they were dreams that began in solemn ceremony and ended in intimacy with people I hated, or dreams of giant walking corpses bigger than the world itself.

One day in our cabin, Detter stood up suddenly and shouted, "What are you trying to do to me, drive me insane? Well, it won't work," and left the room. I was puzzled. I hadn't said a word to him for days. People kept acting as if I were a human being with motives and desires instead of a waking shell full of tools and training, voices and dreams. I still had obligations to Detter, I supposed, and a promise to keep to Simon, so I wouldn't lie down just yet. I wasn't sure I could even manage to die properly, if I had never reigned and never passed on my reign to another. I kept apologizing to Jenneservet in my head.

It was almost spring of the year I would have succeeded my mother. I kept forgetting to eat.

Detter took to sitting with the off-watch crew, though they ignored him completely. His mustache was growing out nicely, a delicate gleam on his upper lip, refined, slick, and absurd as a baby with a cigar. One day I saw the captain speak to him briefly and move away, Detter's eyes following him like a dog's. It happened again a few days later, and in spite of the bewildered deadness in my head, I vaguely thought I should do something, I didn't know what. The third time it happened, when the captain spoke and turned away, Detter stood and followed him to his cabin. The sailors playing cards did not change their expressions, though I could feel astonishment in the air. Detter did not come back to bed until late at night. I lay in my bunk listening to my Voices when he crept into the dark swaying room and clambered into his berth.

The captain ignored Detter again for some time. I could guess why, for the captain had fresh scratch marks on his neck and he walked as if something hurt. The flickers of luminous spirit were stronger about him and stayed coherent longer. Detter looked cold and self-satisfied. He thought he had gotten away with something.

I couldn't seem to rouse myself from lethargy, but one day when I had left my cabin with the half-formed and soon forgotten idea of getting something to eat, I saw the captain speaking to Detter again. I made my way across the deck to them, my Voices chorusing contradictory instructions to me, and was in front of them before Detter could finish standing up. The captain eyed me with a cold gleam, his harsh mouth compressed.

I said, ostensibly to Detter, "How often does a guide lose a student on the Quest? How often does a student lose his guide? What happens to mages who slip through the cracks?"

Detter, his eyebrows raised, thought I was threatening him, but the captain reacted as I thought he might. Small explosions of ller like fireworks were appearing around him. He was backing away from me imperceptibly, as well he might. I had no patience anymore with people who ran from their duty. No patience at all anymore.

I hissed, "What does happen to lost mages? Where do they go? Are they afraid of being caught? How can they possibly hide and whom do they have to hurt?"

Detter said, "Lisane?" bewildered.

The captain was backed up against the bulkhead. A crew member looked up from his knitting and began to rise. I don't know what he saw when I looked at him, but he sat down again, slowly.

I wondered what I was doing there. I said to Detter, "Just keep it in mind," and went back to my cabin. I shut the door and sat cross-legged in my cold bunk, with the beams creaking and the wind moaning overhead. My Voices inside had silenced for a moment. I felt weak, odd, and temporarily sane. What had I been trying to do? Keep Detter from running away? Where could he go? Was I trying to tell the captain I knew what he was? What purpose would that serve? I didn't think I was going to survive this voyage, and just as well.

Detter didn't come in and I didn't go out. In a while, my Voices came back in a clamorous rush. I moved legless and armless through true dreams, arguing with an old woman, chasing an animal through the dark, but I was wide awake for days and days, I think.

Finally, someone was apparently feeding me soup, and doing a clumsy job of it. I was very hungry, biting at the spoon, but he wouldn't hurry up. I tried to grab the spoon, but my arms were bound up in a rough blanket. The food went away. Someone wiped my face roughly.

I opened my eyes and Detter's absurd face hovered over me, looking irritated. "Are you awake, bitch?" he asked. I blinked and nodded at him yes. He said, "Good. Because I'm going to feed you until you get well, you'll stay alive till Sassevin, and when we leave the Beast I'm going to kill you."

I smiled up at him, absurdly happy to see his face. He screwed up his mouth and brought the spoon back, shoving more soup in my mouth. "What were you trying to do, kill yourself?" I nodded, my mouth full, and he continued, "I didn't think you cared that much for Simon." I swallowed, and shook my head no. Affection for Simon hadn't had much to do with it. My Voices weren't talking. Maybe I'd managed to kill them off. Detter shoved another spoonful in my mouth, and I didn't quite throw up.

Detter tended me carefully, though he disappeared for long stretches at night. He looked happy, and I kept seeing new bruises and broken skin here and there. I guessed he and his new friend were still hitting it off, as it were. I asked him, "What happened to the captain?"

Detter said, "You scared the stuffing out of him. Did you know your eyes were glowing and you were spitting sparks out of your mouth when you spoke to him?"

No, I hadn't realized that. No wonder that sailor had looked frightened. "That's not what I meant. He was obviously a student some time. How did he end up a merchant captain?"

"He and his guide took the route south to Perchel, but then his guide slit his own throat at the seaport. It happens. When he was on his own, he realized he didn't want to face the Beast, and he didn't really want to be a mage anyway. So he signed up as a sailor on the first ship out. A lot of students disappear that way on Quest, and there are so few Finders left, nobody came after him."

"Do *you* want to be a mage?" I said seriously.

He looked at me as if I'd lost my mind again. "Of course, darling. It's the only thing I'm good at, and I'll make a marvelous practitioner." I should have known. He was the perfect product of the school. "I'll apprentice myself to a Wizard in Sassevin for a few years, then become Sorcerer myself. I'll have students and apprentices of my own when you're still barking in the wilderness." He chucked me under the chin, and left the room. The ideal nurse, someone who liked making people do things they didn't want to do.

I made my way out of my cabin eventually, and found that spring had arrived. I must have been out for a while. The captain saw me pass by, but he didn't react. I felt helpless and inarticulate, but my Voices were still silent. Detter helped me up the ladder, and I surfaced on deck to a scudding wind and a deep blue sky. There was a darker blue streak on the horizon, land. We were almost there.

Without comment, the captain brought the ship close to land, and then, instead of mooring in the harbor, steered the ship up the wide river that fed the sea. We were heading into the heart of the Greater Shore, going straight to Sassevin. It took several more days.

We disembarked at Sassevin. I was almost a human being again, though my edges felt raw. Neither Detter nor I knew where to go, but we set off at random, leaving our boxes with the harbormaster. Could we just go up to someone on the street and say, "Could you please direct me to the Beast?" No one in sight seemed to be a mage. We wandered around like tourists as the sun rose pale and warm in the brisk spring air. It was a bewildering city, all dead ends, side streets, buildings on buildings, and crowds. I have never seen so many different types of clothing in one place. We were impolitely ignored by all and sundry.

Suddenly, as we paused near a thriving livery stable, I sighted a steady purposeful stream of spirit-fire condensing from thin air and pouring off down a lane out of sight. I grabbed Detter's arm and we followed the current. It wound from street to street, and was joined by other flows of ller, all different colors. Detter, resigned to trusting my peculiarities of vision, allowed me to lead him.

Eventually, the glowing torrents converged on a shabby stone building with an unfinished wooden door, standing alone on a hill overlooking the river. No one seemed to be going in or coming out. Detter said, "That can't be what we're looking for." He argued with me but finally consented to have a look.

We opened the door, Detter stepping in ahead of me, and entered a large cool chamber. A man, wearing a purple-striped single-strand neckring, sat at a desk. He looked up from his writing briefly and said to Detter, "You go ahead," gesturing to a set of ebony doors, then, holding up a palm to me, "You wait." Were we expected, or was this how all were greeted? As Detter walked forward, the doors swung open. A similar set of tarnished brass doors was revealed just beyond, before the black doors closed behind him. I sat down to wait, feeling like a customer at an expensive fortune-teller.

A moment later, a terrible harsh scream reverberated through the room, and a thunderous boom sounded. I jumped to my feet. The mage continued to write, ignoring the commotion. The screaming and pounding continued for a long time, and then there was a hideous silence, followed by the slamming of doors. I was shaking with shock and fear, but the mage just said, "All right. Go ahead." He didn't look up. So I stood and passed through the black doors. They closed behind me.

The tarnished brass inner doors parted slowly to the darkness like the inside of my eyelids when closed. A deep thrumming sounded, the dying echo of a gong, and a smell of raw meat and salt embraced me in thick folds as I passed through the opening. Once inside, I found to my surprise that my eyes were indeed closed, and when I opened them stickily and sleepily, I was standing naked, pale, and alone in a great warm crimson chamber the shape of an egg and the size of the entire Enforcer transport. Its walls were soft and moist, succulent, covered with a fragile membrane and pale veins as far as I could see. This room was far bigger than the outside of the building, and somehow more real. In true dreams but not in waking life, I'd felt this awful certainty of underlying reality, but even in true dreams I'd never noticed the small confirming details, like the dimples my feet made in the soft, wet, red floor, or the prickly rising of gooseflesh on my exposed skin.

A shudder ran over me, and I chafed my arms with my hands to make the startled hairs lie down. I stood for a minute, arms wrapped around myself, waiting for something to happen. It occurred to me to look for the door again, but when I turned around, the walls stretched just as far in the opposite direction, smooth and glistening and breathing gently. So this was the dreaded Room. Where was the famous Beast? I walked around, aimlessly, then stopped. There wasn't much point in moving around if the whole place was all the same. Whatever was going to happen to me, I was sure it would come looking for me, so I might as well relax. I felt somehow queasy about slapping my bare bottom down on the fleshy floor, as though that organic substance might some-how grow up into my insides. I stifled the nightmare thought, but com-promised by sitting on my heels, my hands resting lightly on my thighs. Nothing much happened, very slowly and for a long time.

There was a sense of presence all around me, remote and uncaring. Something or someone was thinking big rolling thoughts, thinking about things much more significant than me. I didn't like it. This, after all, was supposed to be my moment of truth. What if whatever it was never got around to noticing me? The room pulsed and glowed steadily around me, somnolent and inattentive, and eventually my left foot went to sleep. I was beginning to feel decidedly miffed and unwanted.

What if this setup didn't work for women? I was the first female mage these Wizards had acknowledged, after all. Maybe the Beast only came out to chew on lame-brained violent punks like Detter. Was he dead? There was no sign of him here. I hoped he had survived somehow, the nasty worm. He was my only family.

My back was starting to hurt, and the warm moist surface of the floor, though it rolled gently like the deck of a becalmed ship, showed no signs of intent to molest me, so I stretched forward on my front and laid my head on my arms, my breasts flattened beneath me. The floor quivered and gave gently around me.

Where was the big confrontation, the grand battle, the chance to prove my magical strength and wisdom and my natural fitness to rule something somewhere? Barring that, where was the door? Though being a ring-bound mage wasn't even my last choice on the list of desirable jobs, I had at least thought I'd have the choice of attempting to prove myself. I might not be able to die properly, but my training shouldn't go completely to waste. I think I had completely recovered from my funk at sea, for my natural arrogance was returning. In fact, it seemed amplified in this improbable room.

These dunderheaded mages, with their pettiness and caution and their perverted cravings, wasting their command of the spirit on mundane magical contrivances, these self-important misogynistic soul-shriveling snakes, had no idea who it was their Beast was ignoring. My destiny was greatness or death, but the Universe seemed determined to thwart me. Having managed to place the blame for my sidetracked life squarely on someone else besides me, I proceeded to work myself into a state of rage at each and every man with Power in the world, especially Kaihan. I spent a stimulating half hour figuring out a spell to give them all permanently sealed assholes and a case of galloping diarrhea.

The Room continued to swell and shrink imperceptibly like a giant heart, while I, the very important would-be llerKalten and Wizard, grimaced and twitched like a beached fish at the bottom of it, extracting the last teaspoon of satisfaction out of my imaginary revenge. But after that wore thin, I lay still, thinking of nothing at all. I had run out of paranoid fantasies and grandiose dreams. There was nothing I could do to occupy myself except worry, and I couldn't see much purpose in worrying, so I just lay and watched the Room pulsate, feeling useless.

An hour or a day or a week later, with a gasp and a sigh, an enveloping wind poured over me from the other end of the chamber, and I jumped to my feet. I now saw a dark misshapen figure ambling toward me from a distance. As it approached, I could not make sense of it, until with an adjustment of my sight I realized it was an immense centaur, with the squat upper trunk of a giant man and the massive black barrel and legs of a dray horse.

I stood waiting, shy and flushed as if just awakened, and the creature plodded steadily toward me, swollen-muscled arms swinging with each ponderous shift of his legs, until he paused a body's length away from me. His size and overwhelming masculinity overshadowed me, and I had to bend my head back to look into his face.

It was a blind, wild, ecstatic face, with great brown eyes all pupil like a stallion's, a hard strained mouth, and a blunt, flat, flared nose. I knew that face, though I'd only seen it before in diluted form, glaring through the mortal flesh of the Year-Kings who coupled with my mother. I felt a fierce pride in my knowledge, so fierce a pride that I didn't think to wonder why the avatar would show up in a glorified final examination room on the wrong planet.

"King and Lord, are you in this world as well?" I said. "I saw no signs you were awake among these people."

"I am in all human worlds," he said in a harsh voice like the scream of a horse. It was so loud and formless I could barely understand him. "Why should I not be here, whether people know me or not?"

"Where is your Kalten, Mennet? How can you be alone?"

He laughed, a cold booming sound starting from his horse's belly, and reared his forelegs in the air. His splayed hooves came down on the red membranous floor with a wet thwack and he danced sideways, looking down at me with his transfigured face.

"The Wizards called only me to this form, woman. They don't know of the Mother. How could they? They don't know their own mothers, they take no wives, they beget no daughters. They don't know the Mother, though she surrounds them entirely." He sidled back closer to me.

His skin was so white it was almost translucent between the black curls of his body hair, and blue veins rode over the threshing muscles of his belly and chest. At the base of his human half, coarse curly pubic hair blended gradually down into glossy horsehide. He was offensively, blatantly masculine and ugly, and my skin goosefleshed painfully at the sight of him. He switched his long coarse tail so it cascaded back over his haunches. The crimson walls of the curved chamber quivered imperceptibly all about us, with a repetitive thud like a distant heartbeat.

He began to move away from me again. He was going to leave me. I helplessly raised my hands as if to call him back. The centaur grinned fiercely, cantered back to stand before me, then knelt slowly so that his wild and hairy head was bent over me. Up close, his face was even more terrifying, savage, and remote, and his acrid sweaty smell made my eyes narrow and my nostrils flare. He spread his arms around me, and drew me half-willing to his curl-thatched chest. My brains were coagulated with lust and love and with the pride of the destiny I'd thought I'd lost forever, and I wanted to merge with him as with no mortal male, but a small cold voice was speaking dimly in the back of my mind, and it was not one of prophecy. It was a very mundane, stupid voice.

He slapped himself against me, front to front, like some humping animal in heat, and seized and sucked at my lips with his mouth, tasting me and groaning. My legs were straddled over his kneeling forelegs, and my whole body arched and peeled itself insistently against his, with a feeling like hot fluid pouring from my groin, up my spine, to my skull, where the small voice said, clearly and simply, "No." Against my whole desire, and with no clear understanding of my change of heart, I struggled, suddenly completely ashamed and fearful, against his grasping arms and groping lips, until, disgusted, he thrust me away from him at arm's length, dangling me in the air. "Don't you want to do what you were born to do? Why, then, are you here at all?" he demanded.

His unknowing animal eyes were wild and hot, his clutch was excruciatingly painful, and my throat swelled in regret and lust for him, but I knew I could not do it. The red walls beat steadily about us, looming somehow closer.

"I don't think this is my job anymore," I said inanely.

"Job?" he said, and laughed, jeering, in my face, his spittle spraying me. "You think you know what your job is, little bag of blood? If you want to be Mother, your job is to be my vessel, as mine is to pour myself into you." He flung me to the ground without effort and stood looming over me. I shrank back, afraid of his hooves, but he did not follow, just stood with his hairy knuckled fists on his hips and his tail arched high.

"I'm sorry, Lord," I said, knowing that I was blowing my last chance at eternity, "but you're talking about the real Mother, not me." His hard wide mouth opened, showing his teeth, and he was panting like a dog, but I lurched on: "You'd burn me into cinders from the inside out if I tried to join with you. I'm not enough for you, I'll never be enough for you. I'm just an ordinary woman with delusions of grandeur."

There went my childhood dreams of glory, and his great bared teeth shone, grisly and coarse in the crimson light of the encircling chamber. He hunched down and lifted me above him with his stone-muscled arms. His jaws gaped wider and impossibly wider as if he were going to gulp me down whole, and I felt I was about to die, my womb now forever empty, but my mind was saying inanely over and over, "No, I can't do it, no, I can't." I dangled limp and helpless in his grip above him as he rose, lurching and swaying, to all four feet. The egg-shaped chamber had closed completely about us, now so small it barely cleared my head, and it glowed with a hot ruby light, pulsing and flowing.

With a gasp, the membranous wall rushed in completely and wrapped us both in moist warmth and darkness. I was dropping down slowly, his hot arms still cradling me, and his dark wild voice, in unison with another, thicker, softer voice, whispered into my ear, "So you are only human, little one? Did you think we didn't know that? And now you know as well. Be well, beloved. Remember we are bound here when the time comes."

My feet were suddenly on a hard, bare floor, my eyes were closed, in a cold, silent space. I opened my eyes to lamplight appearing between two slowly opening doors. I stepped forward, staggering a little, and as I passed through the doorway I felt a sudden smooth cold weight settle around my neck.

I was in an ordinary hallway, with worn wooden floors. Down the center of the hall ran a thick congealing trail of blood, smeared with naked bloody footprints. A freckled red-haired Magician in a tunic and a single jade neckring, lazily mopping up the blood, gaped at me in silent consternation. His expression made me look down self-consciously, but it seemed I had my clothes on again, after all. I reached my hand up blindly to find out what had happened to my neck, and found a thick triple-ring collar bound seamlessly about it. Apparently, even if I was not a failed goddess, only a human woman and a cowardly one at that, the Beast had given me the badge of a Wizard.

Behind me the doors finally closed with a prosaic thud, and before the red-haired Magician could pull himself together, I strode past him down the hall, passed through the door at the end, and found myself back outside the shabby stone building. I didn't look back, just kept moving as fast as I could without running.

In Which I Don't
Poison Myself

"**R**ounderbean. Now, that's easy enough to remember. 'Round' for 'comes around,' for a woman's cycle. Takes the bloat away, that comes before your monthly flow. Chew till all the taste is gone, but don't swallow, and never take more than one a month." Charonne slipped the hard round bean back in its bag, then fumbled again with her wrinkled, spotted hands in her wicker medicine box.

I said, "Is that because it could be poisonous?"

She drew her mouth in, annoyed. "Lisane, is your head just on holiday or are you planning to think like a rock the rest of your life? I've told you and told you, everything in this box is poisonous if you take enough of it. You have to assume your customers will take too much of their medicine and take it too often. Though they're just as likely not to take it at all, but that doesn't poison them, just doesn't cure them." She found what she was looking for in the box, a creased packet of paper, and began painfully to unfold the end.

I was learning a trade. Since I'd chosen against being either a goddess queen or a practicing mage, I had to acquire some different skills if I wanted to keep on eating. Charonne was peevish and impatient, but in a way that was familiar to me. She reminded me of Jenneservet. She had agreed to teach me and lend me her vendor's squat on the pavement by the horse-dealer, if I would conduct her business for her so she could retire. She was getting too old to stand the cold, didn't want an enclosed shop, and, she said, was planning to die toward the end of next winter, so she wanted to take some time off before that. She'd spent half a lifetime selling medicine on Tinker's Hand Street in the Frog Belly quarter of Sassevin, and it seemed as good a trade as any to me. Though she was very careful to distinguish between her trade and that of the country herb-wife, she didn't explain the difference. I supposed it mattered to her, but I was content with the job, whatever it was called.

Now she spilled a little pale powder from the packet into her puffy hand, touched a moistened finger to it, and held her fingertip up for me to lick. The taste was bitter and lingered. She was stern-faced, which I was learning meant she was going to lay another trick on me. I worked my mouth and wrinkled my nose. She waited, impassive, for perhaps a minute, then darted her hand out, firmly twisting a pinch of skin on my arm. I laughed, amazed but completely relaxed. Though the pinch was viciously painful, the pain felt as if it belonged to someone else.

"What is that? It works fast," I said.

"Works fast, wears off fast. Called foster-pine. Good for short, hard pains—tooth pulling, bone setting, suchlike. Take a whole spoonful, it'll give you half an hour without pain, but you pay with shivers and spasms." She tipped the palmful of powder back into the packet. "I don't label it, so remember what the packet looks like. People like to steal it—an overdose is a good clean way to kill your enemy, or yourself for that matter."

It was afternoon, a merciless blinding summer day. Even dry old Charonne was sweating, and I kept blinking the salt out of my eyes. My three black neckrings chafed my skin red and raw in the heat, and I would have taken them off if I could. Charonne disapproved of them. Though I'd seen other nonmages in Sassevin wearing costume jewelry styled after the mage's mark, Charonne thought it poor judgment and bad taste for anyone to wear Wizard's sign. I hadn't tried to convince her I had earned it; I suspected she would think no better of me. She did not care for mages, nor did she see much use in magic, saying it was like harnessing sun's fire to power a candle flame. That was part of why I trusted her, in spite of her skin-scorching tongue. The innkeeper, Bielo Massim, had put me on to her after I'd been cleaning his stable for a couple of weeks. He said he was sorry to lose me, but I knew I really didn't do that good a job, and besides I distracted his customers from the working girls, who paid him tithe.

Charonne's pitch on Tinker's Hand Street was smack in the middle of one of the sweeping torrents of ller that met in the Beast's shabby shelter, but there was a little peaceful eddy around Charonne's pavement mat, where magic, it seemed, did not dare trespass. Lle had no such respect for any others, coursing through the crowds as if they were light-shadows, in frantic haste to supply the Beast. I wondered how the spell that bound the Beast had ever been set, and what would happen if it were broken. It didn't seem to me that any mage I'd met so far was capable of such an act.

I was here because when the Beast had finished with me, I decided I was finished with magic. I kept walking until my legs wouldn't work properly, which happened just outside the Cat and Apple, Bielo Massim's inn. I sat down, right there against the stinking wall. I was still wearing men's clothing, my hair was tangled and matted, I was only half-recovered from my confused attempt to die properly, and my neck was stacked three high with black mage-rings, but one of Bielo's drunken patrons still thought I was worth an effort. Bielo himself came out to see what the noise was, and after a series of misunderstandings, he ended up giving me a bowl of soup, a corner of the stable to sleep in, and the cleaning job. It all seemed so amusing to him I never felt the need to thank him.

"Lisane! Stop mooning about. You look like a chicken in the feed bin. Lesson's not done." Charonne was holding up another fingertip-full of smutty black dust. She had a terrifying gleam in her eye, though she was attempting to look sterner than ever. I began to stick my tongue out to lick the powder off, then backed up, uneasy.

I said, "That stuff looks evil. I'm not tasting that until you tell me what it is."

She cackled and waved the finger at me. "Spelldamp flour. Illegal as murder. I don't sell it, I don't have it, you haven't seen it. It wouldn't do a normal person any harm, but you give it to one of those insufferable mages and he's not a mage anymore. Can't do magic, can't cast spells, no matter how many chants he's memorized. Go on, taste it, it won't hurt you." I shook my head at her silently. "Aaah, I should have known. Do you think you were somehow born a mage but got overlooked somehow? Are you waiting for a Wizard to walk by and say, 'There she is—that one'? Even if you did have Power, girl, you'd be better off without it. Taste it."

"How long does it last? What's the dosage?" I said. The smudged finger was too near me, and I tried not to flinch. Though I had decided not to practice magic as a living, I found now that I didn't care to lose my abilities either.

She pulled it back, wiped her finger thoroughly in the dirt, and closed up the small black envelope. "At least you're beginning to learn what questions to ask. With this stuff, I don't know. When I was young, I was more than half a witch myself, so I've never dared taste it," and she cackled. I felt better. "The woman who gave it to me said enough to cover a fingernail would cripple a mage long enough for an enemy to knife him. Keep it in mind if any of those boil-faced mudthumpers causes you serious trouble. Not that you're the right sex for that."

Pelleter Tailor walked by, snapping her fingers briskly. Charonne unhurriedly stowed the envelope away and closed her medicine case. The finger-snapping was a signal that meant mages were coming. At all the stands, carts, and shops on Tinker's Hand Street, similar calm concealment occurred.

"Isn't it useless to keep secrets from the mages? One of them could walk through here invisible, for all you know, or cast a truth-telling spell on all of us," I remarked.

Charonne said impatiently, "The idea is to avoid rousing any attention in the first place. We're not important to them, and they're blinded by arrogance. They won't waste their energies on us if we don't do anything out of the ordinary. That's why your stupid neckrings are such a bad idea—they draw attention."

I obediently wrapped my headscarf around my throat, though I was instantly sweating twice as hard. Two mages strolled into sight, absorbed in their conversation and paying no heed to the colorful cacophony around them or to the relentless flow of ller that coursed over and through them. It was not usual for mages to stray from their luxurious quarters in Seven Snakes, but they did wander through occasionally. One was a dark-haired young single-ring Magician, and the other was a double-ring Sorcerer with curly white eyebrows and too much finger-jewelry.

As they passed us, the Sorcerer glanced aside and said vaguely, "Ah, Charonne. How goes it?" Charonne bobbed her head and smiled, showing too much brown tooth but not moving the rest of her face. The Sorcerer had already forgotten her, and the Magician had never looked at her. They kept walking and talking, and when they were out of sight Charonne calmly opened her case back up and I unwound the sweat-soaked scarf with relief. "You seem to have drawn the attention of at least one mage yourself," I said.

Charonne scowled at me, embarrassed. "If I haven't always followed my own advice, that doesn't mean it's bad advice. I'd be better off if no mages knew me." She started digging through her disorderly box again.

I lifted my rings up to let some air circulate on the abraded skin. According to the pocket mirror I'd bought with my first spare money, the rings were black as ebony, dull, smooth, and almost alive, the same color and texture as Kaihan's, though I would have preferred emerald green. With my long braided black hair, the rings formed a lustrous frame for the vivid face that still appeared to be mine. I spent a lot of time gluttonously, guiltily staring in the mirror, memorizing that face.

The afternoon wore on, hotter and slower, and finally Charonne latched her box shut, rolling it away with her back bent over. I stood, arching my back and stretching, feeling the flow of the indifferent spirit as I stepped into the stream. It was time for dinner. The air was thick with smoky food smells, sideways shafts of sunlight needling through the haze. I couldn't decide whether I should get sausage from Nicot's aunt or meat pastry from Sibby Gomm.

I set off down the street, winding my way between the buyers and sellers, the strollers and lookers. I knew about one in ten by sight, one in twenty to speak to, which wasn't bad, considering how new I was in the city. Working Charonne's pitch on Tinker's Hand and knowing Bielo Massim counted for a lot in Sassevin. I had been very fortunate in my flight from the Beast.

A little later, licking sausage grease off my fingers, I stopped and looked into the Cat and Apple. It was as busy as ever, but dark stocky Bielo stopped to talk for a moment. He always found everything vastly entertaining, as if all humanity were performing for his benefit.

"Mages are all stirred up. Something up north is eating them, one by one," he said gleefully.

"Eating them? You mean chewing them up and swallowing them? There's nothing big enough to do that." Bielo scurried across the room to serve a customer. "Who's been spreading tall tales?" I demanded of the room at large. I knew most of the customers there.

Dour Argevin looked up from his table. "It's true enough they're disappearing, but whether or not they're being eaten, I couldn't tell you." Argevin was Sorcerer Tilloke's manservant, an ill-natured, drunken gossip, but his information was generally reliable. It was Argevin who'd told me that Wizard Gelmas, a Council member notorious for his fits of cruelty, had a new apprentice, a blond-haired, blue-eyed novice Magician who'd already outlasted the three previous apprentices and earned a nasty reputation of his own. Detter's long-term plans were still working out, it seemed.

I came further into the room and sat on a stool by the wall, but Argevin went back to his greasy gray stew. He knew I was waiting to hear more, and he might tell me more in a bit if he felt like it. I leaned back and closed my eyes. It was as hot in the tavern as it was outside, or hotter, but the darkness inside made the heat feel friendlier somehow.

Argevin swallowed a mouthful, wiped his chin with a piece of bread, and finally said, "Any mages take the Dicedipper Road all the way up through Belmire to Asterman's Wood north of Falconhill, they don't come back. It's been happening for a long time now, but Council just decided to notice. Council's been fussing and gibbering all week." He stuck his spoon back in the bowl and put his hands on the table. "They won't do anything about it, though. Too busy scoring off each other to get any real work done, Kaihan or no Kaihan." He pushed his chair away from the table.

Before he could finish getting up, I said too eagerly, "Kaihan? What's Kaihan doing?"

He stood and shoved the chair back in without replying, then went out the door, a sullen, sour, gray-haired mutt of a man. I didn't know how his master could stand him. I certainly couldn't. I sat on the stool watching Bielo scurry about merrily among his customers playing inn-keeper until the inn was too crowded, then left. I didn't drink and I didn't hook, so I had no real business in the Cat once I'd already eaten.

The day was cooling slightly now that the sun was low, and if I walked slow and loose my clothes didn't stick to me. I turned down Tinker's Hand and decided not to go home yet, but to sit in Charonne's spot and watch the pretty men go by. Since Simon I had become even more wary, I was chaste again for the time being, but that didn't mean my thoughts were pure. I sat on the pavement and relaxed. My Voices had come back soon after I started with Charonne, unfortunately, but they seemed to like man-watching too, and I caught them sometimes making rude rhymes. They were becoming a giddy bunch now that I was no longer anybody important.

In the smoky dusk I didn't see Charonne and her unlikely companion approaching until they were almost on me. I rolled sideways and scram-bled behind Aggi's clothing stand, which annoyed Aggi. I peeked around the corner of her stand, my heart pounding, my mouth dry. Charonne strolled past, complacently arm in arm with a graceful Wizard all in black, the eternally unexpected Kaihan, who smiled down at her as if she were a lovely young girl. The expression on his face made me short of breath, and I could feel my face reddening. She smiled back, stumping along next to him like an animated bag of pudding. Aggi crabbily poked me with her toe, and I desperately ignored her until I was sure they were well past and that they hadn't seen me.

"What is wrong with you, girl?" demanded Aggi as I got back to my feet.

"Was I seeing things or was that Charonne and a mage?" I said weakly. "I heard no warning."

"Oh. I keep forgetting how new you are in town. That's Kaihan. He doesn't count—we don't warn for him." A customer claimed her attention, and she promptly forgot me.

I walked out into the street and stared after them. The Master of Sassevin Council and an elderly, poverty-stricken, mage-hating, acid-tongued street herbalist were ambling like a courting couple through one of the roughest sections of town, and nobody turned a hair. Something was skewed. This was the man for whom the King of Emsadorn held a reception and everybody came, all thrilled to share in his glory, but on Tinker's Hand he didn't count as a mage. I could see no logic to it.

Flat-footed in the middle of the road, I watched Kaihan and Charonne disappear into the crowd and thought how intriguing it was that men can perform the complicated act of walking without swiveling their hips at all, as if their legs were swinging loose from an axle. Somebody had been thinking well when they put that man together. Or maybe he put himself together. I wouldn't put it past him.

I sat back down at Charonne's spot, feeling stupid and depressed. I'd made the mistake of thinking I understood Sassevin just because I'd found myself a place and made a few friends. I wondered now if my concealment in plain sight had worked as well as I'd thought. Maybe Kaihan had known where I was all the time, and Charonne was his agent. He'd been able to make me do exactly what he wanted before, while all the while I'd thought I was on my own.

I was still sitting there in the half dark when Charonne herself sat down next to me, with a groan as her arthritic knees bent down. "I wish I had your body and my experience," she said querulously. The image of Charonne as anybody's agent dissolved in my mind. Then she saw my face. "Hey, spitfire, who died? What's the matter?"

"I just found I don't know as much as I thought I did," I answered shamefacedly.

She cackled. "Is that all? I've been telling you that all along." She reached out a puffy old hand, the skin swinging loose on her arm, and thumped me on the back reassuringly. "I just found out I don't know that much either, but ignorance is a much lighter sin on an old back like mine. What took you by surprise, then?"

I sat mum for a minute, but she prodded me impatiently with a forefinger. "Come on, out with it."

"I saw you walking with Master Kaihan. I thought you hated mages. It looked like you were old friends."

"We are. I've known Kaihan all my life. He's an old-style mage. He follows the old laws and even some he made up himself, but he never let a bad law get in the way of what's right. I respect him for that, though it's a waste of good meat for that man to play the celibate."

Celibate? The dark Master looked about as chaste as an old tomcat. "You've known him all your life? How can that be? He's only been here a year." It was almost dark. The vendors were packing up and moving off all around us.

Charonne grumbled, half-visible in the dusk, "Kaihan was Master in Sassevin before he ever played schoolmaster, and not just the once, either. He was Master before even I was born. You know him, don't you? And you're the young woman he's worried about, aren't you, hellion? No wonder you turned so white when I brought out the spelldamp." She reached out a finger and flicked my neckrings. "Those are real."

I nodded, watching her. She gathered herself up to stand. I stood myself and helped her up. "Well, it's time for us semi-respectable types to turn in before the fun starts," she said. "Do I have your illustrious Wizardship's permission to tell Kaihan you're all right? If I promise not to tell him where you are?" I nodded again, feeling weary and probably looking sulky.

"See you in the morning, you bat-brained young twerp," she said, and hobbled off in the direction of her room above the draper's.

I went home myself, out of sorts. Home was a lean-to on the side wall of the horse-dealer's yard. I liked having my own place. It kept the vermin down when you didn't share a bed or a room with anybody else. I had a hard time getting to sleep that night, shifting and turning on my lumpy straw-filled bed. I wished I could sleep on the ground as I had on my travels, but there were rats in the stable yard and I didn't care to be a rodent racetrack.

I did sleep, finally, and dreamed my first true dream in months.

A rabbit-cheeked boy was sitting at a table with a mixing bowl before him. He took a jar, unscrewed it, and poured colored sand into the bowl. He put the empty jar and its bulbous lid to one side, and the jar grew arms and tried to screw its lid back on. Meanwhile, the boy was pouring more sand in from a different jar. I moved closer and saw that the jars were men and the lids their heads, with blinking eyes and moving lips. He poured out another jar, and another, until the table was full of feebly grasping jars and the bowl was a swirl of colors. The boy smiled openly at me, grasped the last jar, unscrewed it, and upended the contents. When he put the jar down, the domed lid gleamed smooth in the dim light. The jar reached out nimble hands and grabbed its lid, leaping aside on agile legs. The head looked up at me with glittering empty eyes, and it was Kaihan. I struck the boy heavily behind his ear, and he fell, stunned.

I grabbed the bowl, but Kaihan's powder was inextricably mingled with the others. I poured it all out on the table, and the empty men leaped on it, scrabbling desperately among the grains.

It was hopeless. I stood holding the huge bowl in my arms, watching the antics on the table. At my feet the boy stirred and groaned. I looked down, knelt, and methodically began folding him legs first into the bowl. I might as well get some food for the Beast out of this mess, I thought. I folded and folded him until only his head stared up from the bowl, smiling at me. As I bore the bowl out of the room, I looked back. The manikin Kaihan stood at the edge of the table, watching me leave.

I woke with a foul taste in my mouth, and pried my body painfully out of bed. I'd hoped I was done with true dreams. I pasted myself together and walked to work, trying to forget the dream and wondering what Charonne was going to do with me now that she knew I was a mage.

She saw me coming and wheezed cheerfully, "Look what got swept off the outhouse floor. How much did you pour down your gullet last night?"

"You know I don't drink," I said defensively.

"So why do you look like the pig's dinner?"

"Bad dreams," I said, and sat down like a gross of potatoes.

Charonne hauled her wicker case next to her thigh, and dug through until she found a vial full of crimson liquid. "Stick out your tongue," she said, and put a single drop on it when I obeyed. The liquid tasted like cinnamon, so aromatic my eyes watered painfully. "For bad dreams," she said, and patted me clumsily. It seemed my open secret was still safe with her. A customer with palsy sat down before us, and the workday began.

The only other thing she said to me about it was a few days later. "A well-meaning innocent like you shouldn't have ended up with the mages, no matter how Powerful you were," she said. "Where was the herb-wife when you were born?"

"It's complicated," I said, and she let it go after a moment. I wondered what she meant, but I didn't want to raise the topic again.

That summer, I finished learning all the names of Charonne's medicines, and began to understand her system of diagnosis and dosage. Fall came, a blessed relief. The skin of my neck healed under my rings, and the streets smelled less like stale sewage. Charonne was letting me treat all the customers while she watched, and since fall was her busiest season, I had no time to think.

One afternoon after we had packed up early, I walked back along Tinker's Hand Street after dinner. The Hand was in full throat, all the vendors shouting out their wares and the customers discussing the merchandise in passing. I wound between the people, and almost collided with a man pulling a white shirt over his head at Aggi's cart. He had a small but appreciative audience cheering him on, and I was annoyed I couldn't find my way around them. The man's head emerged from the neck of the shirt, and I found myself face-to-face with Kaihan.

He was as startled as I was, his face for once unsure. His neckrings were entirely gone, though there was a ring of pink, smooth scar tissue where they had abraded the skin. He tugged the hem of the shirt down awkwardly over his surprisingly flat belly. "Lisane," he said quietly. The people who'd been watching him try on the shirt, three of them friends of mine, melted back into the moving crowd as if they had all just then remembered an urgent errand.

My stomach turned over, but rather than stand there gooping at him like a lackwit, I said, "What happened to your rings?" Kaihan turned, flipped a coin to Aggi, and offered me his arm with urbanity. I looked at the arm in astonishment, but he waited motionless until I caught on and clumsily slipped my arm through his. Off we went at a leisurely pace, people making way for us calmly. He wasn't much taller than I, which made me feel not that he was small but that I was a great galumphing galoot of a horse. My Voices were making indecent suggestions.

"I went for a fourth visit to the Beast," he said. Rings or no rings, his voice was still velvet. "I found out what outranks a Wizard."

"What possessed you to do that?" I demanded, and felt immediately even more awkward. We jerked to a stop to let the vegetable hawker trundle by us, then proceeded on, Kaihan deftly guiding me past a puddle.

He said ruefully, "I couldn't get Council to do what I wanted, though the fools should know by now I only put my foot down when the survival of the brotherhood is at stake. They called enough challenges on me that I could have fought twenty duels before breakfast. So I resigned as Master in a dramatic and satisfying way, with a rousing speech, and paid a call on the Beast." His tone was light, but I knew he'd intended suicide, not from self-pity but as a last political maneuver. I could understand that. Jenneservet had told me it was always a last resort, but an effective one if done properly.

"You must have felt very odd that the Beast didn't kill you. What are you going to do instead?" I asked.

He pressed his lips together and tucked his chin under, staring down at me over his nose like an owl, then spoiled the peculiar effect by snorting a stifled laugh out his nostrils. We had to stop while he searched for a handkerchief, and his eyes were watering with the attempt to keep from laughing. Finally he sat down on the curb and put one hand over his eyes, his shoulders shaking.

I was miffed. I hadn't meant to be humorous. Obviously I'd played the ignoramus again. I shifted from foot to foot, bored and irritated, while he recovered from his bout of laughter. Finally he dropped his hand, leaned his elbows on his knees, and said to me, "Yes, I felt very odd indeed, you horribly penetrating young harridan. Stop looking so mulish, I wasn't laughing at you. Sit down." Now I really felt foolish, but I uncomfortably lowered myself down to sit next to him. "As for what I'm going to do, I didn't lose my Power along with my rings," he said, "so I'll do what I wanted Council to do, and go north to stop whatever's taking mages. There are few enough of us as it is; we can't afford to lose any more, or the renegades will be the only abstract practitioners left and there'll be nothing but trouble."

If you go north, you'll be taken as well, you egotistical rooster, and what will that prove?" I said, still irritated with him.

"Don't be so certain," he said, not in the least stung. If Sassevin Council was anything like the madhouse Council I'd seen at school, he was fed a steady diet of insults far sharper than that. "I have had nine of your lifetimes to perfect my skills. I should have gone north alone to begin with."

"You will be taken as well. You should take somebody with you," I insisted. "What do you want me to do when you don't come back? Should I tell somebody?"

He started to say something, then stopped and looked down. I remembered again who I was talking to, and cursed myself for a dumb donkey. "No," he finally said. "Council doesn't believe you exist, because you never showed yourself to them after you left the Beast. They all think I conjured you up out of some perverse desire to humiliate them. And the herb-wives have no use for mages, or I'd send you to them. No, better off leaving well enough alone. My friend Charonne says you are learning a trade. I wish all mages would do so; they would then at least be useful for something besides conspiracy and mayhem."

He began to get to his feet. He'd assumed I was worried about losing his protection. He must think me very young and selfish indeed. I could take care of myself. "It's you I'm worried about, you pigheaded, arrogant, self-absorbed, power-hungry old tyrant," I shouted up at him from my seat on the pavement. "You think you're free to do as you wish, but that doesn't mean you have to behave like an idiot and get yourself killed for no reason other than lack of common sense." I couldn't see his face against the sun.

"If I were free to do as I wish, I would have become a horse-coper in Linz a long time ago," he said harshly. "We are not all permitted to make Charonne's choice. Power carries responsibility, and I do what I must. Nor are you so free yourself, but you'll find that out without my help." He hesitated, bowed lightly to me, then said, "But thank you for your concern. I have to go," and left, walking very fast as if running away, his new white shirt rippling in the breeze of his motion. I was so furious I could barely see, so furious my throat burned and the bridge of my nose felt hollow. Mother's milk and Father's blood, how I hated that man.

"Lisane, what's the matter? Why are you crying, dear?" said Sibby Gomm's mother, a woman I couldn't stand. I wiped my eyes casually, said, "Nothing, just smoke in my eyes," and went home to lie on my bed, argue with my Voices, and wonder what "Charonne's choice" meant. When I asked her the next day, she pursed her mouth up and said, "None of your impudent business, and Kaihan should keep his mouth shut."

I found out what it was at the end of the winter. Charonne died on a day she'd picked out, at the end of winter as she'd warned me, of heart failure. She'd wrapped up her affairs, given notice to her landlord, told her closer friends, and gone to bed to get it over with. She was mildly surprised I didn't object, but I said it made sense to me. I sat with her before she went to sleep, watching the flickers of spirit-fire that circled cautiously out of her reach, and said to her, "One thing before you go, Charonne."

She flapped a spotted hand at me impatiently. "I'm done. No more. Ask somebody else," and she pulled up her covers over her face. I put my feet up on the end of her bed, and waited until her curiosity got the better of her, and she peered out at me grumpily.

"Why does magic avoid you, make a wide circle around you? Wherever you are, there is a gap, an eddy, a hole."

"Oh. I thought you were going to ask how old I was, or why I'm going to die in half an hour, or the difference between powdered lungfish brain and puppy shit, or something important like that." She snickered and coughed, pleased with herself. I waited. "Magic doesn't avoid me. I avoid magic. I told you before; once I was more than half a witch, but I gave it up for real life a long time ago." She blinked her almost translucent eyes sleepily. "Anything else before I finally get some rest? I won't say I'll miss you, because I'll be dead and won't care."

"Kaihan told me he couldn't make 'Charonne's choice.' What choice is that?"

"What I just told you, silly girl. I gave up magic. I finished what I had to do, and chose to live, grow old, and die like a human being. Now let me get on with it." Her wrinkled mouth was turning downward, so I let her be. "You are such a silly girl, you'll never make a good herb-wife anyway," she mumbled, and closed her eyes for good. Half an hour later, rushes of spirit-fire tumbled through the walls and swept over her like yarn around a ball. Her body lay there glowing to my spirit eyes in the evening-darkened room.

"Zhe sselenter, devaghtel ains ye Charonne," I said to ller, but lle didn't even reply. I got up and left ller alone to mourn, telling the knacker on my way home that he could collect Charonne's body whenever he wanted.

A week later nobody mentioned her anymore, and her old spot on the street was "Lisane's pitch" in casual conversation. I heard no news of Kaihan. The winter rains poured down on the tarp over my space, I cured those of my customers who bothered to take their medicine, and the uninterrupted stream of ller poured over and through me down

Tinker's Hand to the Beast, now that Charonne's protective shield was gone. My Voices sang harmonies with the melodies that formed in the river of magic, and sometimes I thought I heard answering voices in the rushing swirl of Iler. But though I lived my days in an ocean of magic, I had never felt more real. I thought maybe this was real life, the thing that normal people lived. I hoped I was doing it right.

10

In Which I Don't Mind My Own Business

I lasted until spring. Once the novelty wore off, I tired fast of squatting on my haunches on Tinker's Hand, dispensing muddy-looking powders and murky liquids to people whose ailments could have been prevented by drinking less or taking one bed partner at a time. I tried hard, but one morning between customers I thought, what use am I? I can't do this for the rest of my life, I haven't the patience. Perhaps I had reached the limits of my maturity. I had turned twenty and therefore should have been grown-up, but I couldn't bring myself to settle down. Kaihan was right: I couldn't make Charonne's choice just yet.

I kept thinking about Kaihan striding away from me, his new white shirt flapping loose. He'd been afraid of something other than death, and he'd looked as foolish as I'd ever seen the man. He must have bought the shirt to celebrate losing his rings, for if he'd been a mage as long as Charonne said, he'd worn only black for centuries. He hadn't come back, for Asterman's Wood had swallowed him whole like the others, pretty new shirt and all.

I supposed it was really none of my business, as he had so clearly told me, but I had the uneasy feeling I should do something about it; I didn't know what and I didn't know why. My dreams at night mixed truth and wishes, and Kaihan walked in and out of them enigmatically.

Sometimes I struggled to distinguish what they were telling me, and sometimes I simply refused to care.

This cold spring morning, with the wind high and damp, I felt restless and worried, and the torrent of magic that poured past me day and night was fragile and itchy llerself. I stared up at the sky and realized I'd always depended on passing disasters to make up my mind for me. It was time I stopped waiting for things to happen to me and started making things happen. As another customer, uncomfortable and stone-faced, stopped before me, I made an appointment with myself to discuss my plans that night.

The evening was even colder, with hovering moisture crawling under my clothes, when I entered the Cat and Apple and found my stool. Sometimes between rushes of patrons Bielo came and sat on another stool next to me, silently studying me when he thought I wasn't looking. I realized I might have to find another place to eat dinner soon, for something I'd done the week before had made him take an interest in me, and I didn't think he was looking for another working girl. There had been an argument about the star patterns in the spring sky, and I'd let it slip that I thought they were just faraway suns. Everybody laughed at that, except Bielo for once.

Bielo wasn't the only one who was behaving oddly. All the patrons of the tavern seemed to be in a scummy mood tonight, though I marked most of that to the change in the weather. Twice arguments broke out in the other end of the room, and from the conversation I could hear, most people were doing nothing but complaining. After dark, Wizard Tilloke's servant Argevin came in with another mage-servant, a clean but sullen young woman I'd seen with him before. She had a bruise on her face tonight, and Argevin looked more than usually truculent. I hadn't been able to get any gossip out of him for months; he just stared through me. I was heartily tired of him and half the people in Frog Belly by now.

Argevin shoved my stool deliberately as he came around to his table. Taken by surprise, I nearly fell off, and grabbed at his jacket for support. He wrenched away from me, so I ended up slipping the rest of the way to the floor. He bent and lifted an arm to slap me, and I cringed. Bielo said curtly from two tables over, "Hold, Argevin." Argevin lifted a sour eyebrow at him but straightened and turned away from me.

He addressed Bielo instead. "I'm sick of the scum that hangs around this tavern. Especially this trull. Why do you defend her? She's a fool for mages, Bielo. Look at her, wearing those sham rings. She should be ashamed to show herself, wearing those things in this town of all towns, but I've never seen her without them." His companion frowned in agreement, looking at me sideways.

Bielo said, "She does no harm, man."

"She's always pestering me for stories about the mages, like they were bedtime tales. If I have to work all day for miserable backstabbing spell-weavers who give me half my pay in bruises, I don't want to think about them at night. My nerves are so shot I'm thinking of going to the Gutter Pony from now on, Bielo." Funny, he sounded really anguished. I hadn't realized I'd annoyed him as much as that.

Bielo said nothing, just looked at me in amused and embarrassed apology. Apparently, the accusations were fair. I said, "I'm sorry, Argevin. I didn't realize I was bothering you. I'll stop," but Argevin glared at Bielo, grabbed his companion by the arm, and left when he realized Bielo wasn't going to throw me out. "I'm sorry, Bielo," I said. So much for my quiet evening spent considering my future.

"Lisane, I know you don't care for conjurors any more than Argevin. Why do you have to wear those stupid rings?" said Bielo reasonably. "They'll only get you into more trouble. Come on, I'll get a cutter and do it for you if you like." Bielo's eyes glinted with his usual humor and more than his usual sharpness. I looked toward the door and realized that there were too many people between me and it. I wouldn't be able to escape if I ran, and I didn't like to think what would happen if someone tried to remove my chokers without the blessings of the Beast.

"You can try to take them off if you like," I said reasonably to Bielo. "I'd be happy to lose them." That was truthful enough, and might buy me some time.

As he turned to get his tools from behind the bar, I turned to run, but Onion Susa the water-broker, someone I'd thought a friend, grabbed my arms. I tried to pull her hands off me, my cheeks burning, but the tavern crowd had closed around us to watch the argument. Some there were friendly, but mostly they were just well-oiled idiots looking for amusement. It looked like I didn't have any alternatives. The rings weren't going to come off and I didn't want to be in the middle of this spring-struck mob with a sharp object near my throat when they discovered their mistake and my true nature.

So, as Bielo pushed his way back through the grinning audience with a rasp and a small latch-bladed jeweler's bow-saw, I said in a whisper, "Keff est perenteren, keff ge lesieg." They all roared, and Susa gasped with laughter, "She thinks she can even cast spells." Bielo by his expression was not so amused, and meanwhile a slender rope of faint green ller shot in through the roof, looping and twining like the lash of a whip around the body and arms of each person in the room, even the spectators still sitting, though none of them knew it yet. Then Bielo tried to come at me with his tools, and found he couldn't move, and the rest of the room erupted into shouting and fruitless struggle. I mouthed "sorry" at Bielo through the noise and snaked my way between the wriggling bodies to the door, nearly losing my dress and some of my skin in the process for they were standing too close together. I looked back. Bielo's face was completely alien, stiff and strained, and he was shouting nonsense at me. I left at a run to get my things before they could come after me. I had not asked the spell to last very long.

I didn't have much to take. I upended Charonne's box into my battered pack, put Simon's ring, my mirror, and the miniature into my waist-pouch, and threw my cape over me. When I emerged onto Tinker's Hand Street, I said farewell to the fountain of ller, and was shocked to hear ller sing me glad farewell and good journey in turn, very clearly as if in words. Lle had never spoken directly to me before in ller natural state.

I looked to the right, to the left, and found that my Voices already knew where I was going. Seven Snakes, the mage quarter, was all the way on the other side of the city to the northeast. It wasn't walled or guarded by anything but its foul reputation. All right, I'd go there first and look around, though I doubted I'd find much help there. I hadn't found yet what use the mages were in this world anyway. Magic to them was only subject for research or useful as weapon in war against each other. But I thought I might stir up some trouble and see what happened—in other words, look up Detter.

If I lived through that, I'd head up the Dicedipper Road. Why not? It was spring, another passing disaster had ripped me from my temporary respectability, and no matter what Kaihan had said, I was free to do what I wanted. And what I wanted to do was find him and curse him out for treating me the way he had. Even if I had to rescue him first to do it.

I walked briskly north in the dark through Frog Belly, more slowly through the workshops of Sunken Trunk, and cut east across the merchant's quarter. I didn't fit in here at all, either, and more than one window slammed shut as I passed by wishing I was anywhere else. It was too cold, my stomach hurt, and my knees were developing some kind of weary ache. Who did I think I was anyway? Maybe I could just hide in the country, and this wasn't such a good idea after all.

Before I knew it and before I could convince myself to give up, I was on the street that led into Seven Snakes from the south. I didn't feel any different crossing the invisible line. I just continued to be quite sure I wanted to be somewhere else doing something else. There was nobody on the street, nobody at all. The houses got bigger and bigger as I penetrated into the quarter. I was floating in cold blue shadow, all alone in the still, tidy, mage-lit streets. There were pale yellow lights in occasional windows, but though I was near the heart of the quarter, still I had encountered no one. It was late, but not that late. Did they all lie down and die when night came? Where were the mages?

Some of the buildings toward the center of the quarter reminded me of the school, all gussied up with useless ornaments, but occasionally I came across a treasure glowing dimly by the mage-light. One such was tiled from top to bottom, each tile a masterpiece, and each tile fitting perfectly into the whole. Another building seemed to soar eagerly like light into the dark sky, all arches and flying buttresses in cream-colored limestone. Each of these edifices followed a different taste, and I supposed belonged to the elder Wizards, members of Council.

I finally came into a gem of a square, a jeweled blooming garden full of lush trees and flowers, lit by a single flaming torch. Four buildings surrounded the square, four small castles. My Voices shared a joke about the spiritual significance of four, but I ignored them. One building was white, one was black, one was red, and one was every color I knew and some new ones. The multicolored edifice rose from a bulbous base to a point that glittered and sparkled in the fading sunlight, an impudent spire of no apparent function, too narrow to contain stairs. The base of that building was fenced in with curlicues and vines of wrought iron. The whole thing was in appalling taste, and exuded grotesque exuberance and good humor. Facing it across the square was the red structure, a massive lowering hulk like a giant's chiseled brick. That building was preposterously threatening and grim, a court or a prison.

I was standing next to the black palace, which reminded me of the Master's chair in Council. Made of a dull and porous stone, it grew from its base like a black flower, all its lines like those of living things. In the shuddering light of the torch, I could see that projecting windows swelled above my head like nodes on a stem, delicate and succulent, but there were no lights inside. The high-arched front doors hung open, abandoned. I put my hand on the wall, and it was warm and smooth and curved. I could almost feel its life. Nothing so obviously strong should feel so fragile. I leaned against it for a moment, then took a look across the square at the white building.

I didn't like it. It was restrained and clean, form following function, very explicit, very reasonable. It had doors and windows, and I felt that every door was where it was supposed to be and every window placed to let in precisely the right amount of light. It exuded clarity, purity, spiritual peace, and enlightenment. It was the smuggest building I'd ever seen. I crossed the tiny square and stood facing the peaceful white palace. The front door, set beneath a front arch, was white as well, a sedate marble panel with a white porcelain handle, and light gleamed invitingly through its windows. I turned the handle out of curiosity, the door opened, and so I walked in, though I hadn't planned to.

There wasn't anybody here, either, it seemed. It was annoying, though I had no right to quibble. My nerves, my heart, and my mind were geared up for confrontation, but apparently it was an off day for my visit. The entry hall was high-ceilinged and dignified, almost dowdy. Two stairs went up either side, bent back, and joined in the middle with self-important precision. I started toward the stairs, and heard a far-off clatter of metal. There was a kitchen somewhere here, and somebody in it working. How mundane. I took off my shoes, and padded up the stairs. I reached the top, and was looking down a long hall that led from the top when behind me the front door crashed open. My chest collapsed suddenly in panic. I dropped down on the waxed wooden floor and peered down from the landing.

A long-nosed, scholarly-looking, white-ringed gentleman Wizard with a cold glint in his eye was striding in, his white robes whirling around his body, and behind him Detter loped imperturbably, his face as sweet as ever. Detter's new neckring was a divine speckled blue like a bird's egg. He was carrying a satchel full of books over his shoulder that looked like it outweighed him, and he managed adroitly to avoid being hit by the backswing of the door. The two of them headed at the same furious pace for the stairs, and I scrambled in a panic down the hall in my stocking feet, devoutly invoking the Mother's intercession. I turned a corner, almost slipped and fell, and jerked open the first door I found. Behind me I could hear footsteps. I slid into the dim room, shut the door behind me, and looked around for a hiding place. It was a storage room or library of some sort with freestanding shelves full of books, objects, and stacks of paper. A pallid light came from the solitary window, half-blocked by a shelf. I stood with my back to the door, listening in complete paralysis to the approaching footsteps. They turned the same corner I had, came closer, but then continued past my door.

I took a breath and realized it was my first in at least a minute. My breathing sounded harsh in my ears, and the door behind me creaked as I shifted my weight. I froze again, but a door slammed indifferently farther down the hall. I cautiously took a step into the room. Mage-lights flared into life in sconces on the far wall, and I dove behind a shelf, barking my shin painfully. I felt like a fool when I realized the lights were lit by a captive spell reacting to my movement.

I got my breathing back under control and settled my back against the wall. I could hear muffled voices through it, one acrimonious and acid, one deferential and sweet. A door slammed open again, and the irritated voice shouted, "Then go get the right one!" I heard footsteps again.

The door to the library opened, and Detter came in, cradling a crystal globe. Behind him, the older man swept up and stood impatiently in the doorway. Detter was as sure of foot as ever, and visually musical in his movements. He passed down a range of shelves silently, carefully placed the lucid ball on a velvet stand, and more casually plucked a smaller one from the shelf below. Out of my field of sight, it slipped somehow through his fingers and smashed into the unforgiving floor, spraying glittering curved fragments out like a fountain. One must have passed his face, for a bleeding line appeared on his cheek.

"Clumsy, useless troll," came a tense and despairing voice from the doorway. The long-nosed one was half bent over, holding on to the jamb. If this was Gelmas, I was sorry for him. Detter had obviously been having his way with him. "How can such an oaf be so conceited and so inept at one and the same time?" Detter smiled at him beatifically, standing in the midst of the strewn shards. The Wizard straightened in fury and took an involuntary step toward him, then halted, his head back as if resisting a physical drag.

Detter said gently and impersonally, "I'm sorry I broke it, master. I'll try to be more careful next time." The older man surrendered to his fury and lunged at him, his hand raised to strike, and in the same instant Detter's face, indeed his whole body, seemed to rise triumphantly toward the falling hand. The Wizard checked himself with an effort and a disgusted noise; Detter's face fell and his eyes opened. Then the man hit him after all, as hard as he could, across his scored cheek.

"Clean it up, you calculating third-rate lump of gutter filth," the man said with contemptuous intensity. Except for the blotch where he was struck and the smear of blood, Detter's face was white, but he gracefully bent down and began to gather the shards together with his bare hands, ignoring the frost-thin curbed edges that made beads of blood appear on his palms. Light tinkling sounds were the only noise in the room aside from my back creaking in the effort not to move. His master stood over him, now looking cold, bored, and disdainful. I wondered whether Detter would get the reaction he wanted, or whether his master could stand to watch him systematically mangle his hands forever.

Detter straightened, holding a scintillating mound of broken glass firmly in his cupped hands. A thin line of blood promptly ran down his wrist into his sleeve. He looked the Wizard straight in the face, his blue eyes reflecting yellow in the lamplight, and held out his hands as if presenting a precious gift. For a moment they stayed like that, both of them pale, the young mage solemn, the older mage's lips drawn helplessly back, and then the Wizard swung around and swept out as if summoned. The front door crashed again below us. Detter let his hands open slowly, and most of the glass fell out to the floor; two pieces lightly embedded in the skin of one hand still jutted out, trembling with the intensity of his pulse. He let his head fall back luxuriously, smiling.

"I see you've finally found your proper home," I said dryly from behind the shelf. Detter whirled toward me, banging his elbow on the first crystal globe, knocking it off its stand and catching it in midair in one motion. As I suspected, he hadn't let the other one drop by accident. I stood up and stepped out into the light.

"Lisane, what are you doing here?" he said in a low voice. He was flushed now, perhaps embarrassed, but he looked me up and down with an attempt at elegant distaste. "I thought you were dead. I thought the Beast killed you off. What do you want?" He put the globe back and dusted the glass from his hands.

I shook out my rusty black skirt and sat on a towering pile of papers. "Was that charade all part of your long-term plan, Detter? For the apprentice to drive the master mad? You've got him well tenderized, I see. You should have him frothing, gibbering, and cutting your throat any day now."

His face was red. "This is my home, and you are not welcome here," he said. "You're dirty besides, and you've chosen to plant your stinking rump on some very important papers. Tell me what you want or get out of here, before I lose my temper." I laughed at him, for he was as disconcerted as I'd ever seen him. For Detter to resort to simple insult and open threat!

"I stopped by to say hello, Detter. I'm going off north on an expedition to rescue Kaihan from the mage-eater, with no plan, no backing, no equipment, and no companions. I thought I'd admire your face once more before I left, since I'm so fond of you. The Beast didn't kill me off, but I sure saw a lot of blood left behind from your visit. Was it yours or his?"

"I'm going to call Gelmas," he said, and turned to the door.

"Oh, good," I said. "I'm dying to meet him." He stopped.

"I never thought you would actually do that," he said. "All right. I'll do as you wish. What in the name of the septic weasel that spat you out do you want?" He sat down on a stack of books. Now I was off balance.

"You never thought I would do what?" I said blankly.

"Oh, don't play coy. You know, and I know, that you could take Gelmas, me, and any twelve other mages in spell-battle and plait your hair at the same time. Get on with it." He looked complacent and satisfied now.

"What are you talking about, Detter? I stopped by to say hello, and to tell you I was going north to find Kaihan. I'm not threatening you."

We sat and stared at each other. Detter said, "You're not threatening me." I shook my head. "You're going north to find Kaihan, and you stopped by to say hello." I nodded. "You don't want *anything* from me. What is *wrong* with you?"

"Well, actually, I did want one thing," I said cautiously.

"You may name your firstborn spawn after me, but I refuse to be the father, lizard lady," he said, flapping his hand at me contemptuously.

"I wanted to find out if you knew anything about what's been taking the mages in Asterman's Forest. I'm not up on Council affairs, since my source dried up."

Detter absently sucked on his mustache. I was afraid he was getting an idea, for his face changed, lighting from within with joy. "Take me with you," he said suddenly. "I'll tell you whatever you want, but you have to take me with you. I'll lend you a horse if you want. I don't believe it, what a wonderful idea, I'll run away with a street woman. It will infuriate Gelmas, absolutely demolish him. He thinks I adore him and want to be just like him, could you tell? He thinks he's corrupting me, the old toad."

"Detter, what happened to your master plan? I thought you were going to be the perfect apprentice."

"As far as Gelmas is concerned, I *am* the perfect apprentice," he said gently, as if I were short an upper story. "And he's the perfect master for me, a man who plays the hardest, highest game, and the next Master of Council if Kaihan's really gone. This will just teach him not to take me for granted."

"He's not dead," I said, and realized I knew that much. The Master was still alive somewhere, or I would have dreamed him dead. "You can come with me if you really want to, Detter, but I won't play your games."

"I don't think you can, sweetness. You're not equipped for it," he said lazily, rubbing his hands up and down his thighs suggestively like the golden boy I'd first seen in the school. Detter was all cheered up now. I couldn't imagine why I'd thought seeing him was such a good idea.

In the small hours of the morning, as our horses plodded jingling through the empty streets of Seven Snakes, I said to Detter, "Doesn't anybody ever go outside here?" There was no one to see us leave, as there had been no one to watch me arrive, and Detter had conducted our departure as if we were leaving on a Council-sanctioned errand in the middle of the day. He must have been very confident Gelmas wouldn't be back that night.

Detter looked at me through his lashes. It wouldn't be long before he stopped bothering to answer me at all, no matter what he had promised. "Hardly anybody actually lives in Seven Snakes, frogling, and the servants go home at night. You really haven't been in touch, have you? There's only Council members here, their apprentices, and a few working Magicians. Everyone else is teaching, traveling, holding down outstations, and finding wild Talents." I stared around me at the strange buildings. Most of them vacant, then, like the mostly empty school. Once this world must have seethed with mages. We left the mage quarter unchallenged.

Detter rode easily, long legs embracing the horse's flanks, his hands relaxed on the reins. He had adapted quickly to Sassevin luxury. I, on the other hand, rode like a getterhopp clutching a half-hatched shusslizard egg, slipping, sliding, hanging on for grim life, my skirt straining over the saddle neck and my calves sticking out. Back home when I traveled by palanquin, it had looked so much easier than it was to ride a horse. A horse is entirely too far off the ground. I would rather be closer to the point of impact if I fell.

The weather had changed. It was a good time for riding, the stars out sharp, hard, and high in the heart-stopping spring night at the northern edge of the city. No wind blew now, and sounds echoed close and still in the streets, in a foretelling of the intimacy of the summer.

Something caught my eye. "When your master knows you are gone, what will he do?" I asked.

The faintly lit figure beside me answered, "He won't do much for days, because he won't believe my message. Then he'll explode. I hope the pompous old gas-bag has a heart attack."

He apparently believed it. But a dimly not-glowing ward-spell gathering over his oblivious head had not been there a moment ago. His master knew he had left already, and was not stopping him, just keeping track of him. The sight made me sad for that baffling, furious disgusted man in the library. Unlike slim velvet Kaihan, Gelmas looked like my idea of a proper Wizard. He wore white robes, collected magical manuscripts, used crystal balls. His deep-set hood-lidded eyes and contemptuous mouth belonged with the sonorous chants they used for magic here. If he were senior Council, he must be controlled and canny. Along had come baby-blond Deteras Anhand in his precious speckled blue ring, and the powerful mage took his measure. He knew, but Detter didn't, that their war was being fought between equals.

We rode out of the city in the dark and kept on going until the horses were weary and we ourselves beyond weariness, riding into the light and the cold dew. As I expected, we didn't talk much, and Detter knew less than I'd hoped about the mage-eater, little more than I already knew myself, just the names of those who were lost and how long they had been gone. He wouldn't tell me what had happened between him and the Beast, just showed his teeth and smacked his lips unpleasantly. There was news of Simon, from three months ago; he was handfasted to a highborn woman, tall and homely, independently wealthy, notorious for her strong-mindedness, and three years older than he. Detter told me this gleefully, assuming that I would immediately go into a jealous decline, but I was pleased to hear it. Simon seemed very far away and long ago.

The horses were gentle saints, brown-eyed and soft-mouthed. They needed little guidance or urging, and by the third day I began to think I might like riding, though I still found them unpredictable. My mount's name was Amlik, and when I was grooming him at the end of the third day he unexpectedly knocked the length of his immense head flat against my side, landing me splat on my hip in the grass. Detter, done with his horse and sprawled on a moss bank, laughed at me, but after a couple of days' travel, Detter no longer looked so refined or elegant himself—or so driven, for that matter. The ward-spell still hovered over him, though, a reminder that Gelmas had not surrendered him.

At the end of two weeks' leisurely travel, we inquired and found we were within a day's ride of the forest, and that the local people went in and out of the wood with impunity. Whatever lurked in there, it took only mages. I still had no idea of any strategy, and Detter didn't care, for he said he was turning back as soon as we sighted the forest.

His masquerade ended even before that, for as we tethered the horses that evening, I heard hoofbeats on the road. Over a rise came a blue-eyed, sweating white horse, and on it was Gelmas, looking like a close relative of the plague. He reined up when he saw us. The horse's sides heaved in and out, and its eyes showed too much white.

Detter, absolutely glowing with suppressed satisfaction, looked up at him calmly. Gelmas addressed him, ignoring me completely. "I look for you to fulfill your bond, and find instead you have pranced off without permission in the company of what is either Kaihan's infamous nightmare or a diseased trollop with horrible taste in jewelry. Is this mere rebelliousness, major delusion, or just another instance of your ineffable ineptitude?" Detter looked innocently aside at me through his lashes as if to savor the description, but stayed silent, turning back to his horse.

Gelmas waited for Detter to answer his rhetorical challenge. He was quite a sight in the sunset, proud and cruel with long strong bones and paper-thin skin, all dressed in white on the half-dead white beast. I said, "You'd better see to your horse, it's nearly foundered," and pulled off Amlik's sweaty blanket.

Gelmas continued to pretend I wasn't there, watching Detter move off, then slid off his heaving horse, his back contemptuously to me, and began unsaddling it. It was like having two Detters to deal with at once, the group of us grooming our mounts as if each was alone in the wilderness.

I got my comb and my mirror out of my pack and rebraided my hair while the two of them ignored each other. I really was an awful sight, my black dress gray with dust. I had slit the skirt up the middle so I could ride better, and the edges were unraveling. I took off my battered shoes, wiggled my toes, and set about building a fire as dusk settled. Gelmas sat himself down regally, still not looking at me, still silent. I began to understand that I should be afraid, for Gelmas was jockeying his forces for battle.

We ate in silence, equidistant around the flames. I noticed that Gelmas' long fingers flickered in the shape of a summoning as they lay in his lap; I spoke languidly to the glimmer of spirit-fire that started to form, it dissolved, and I realized Gelmas thought I had Detter under spell. He didn't understand Detter any better than Detter understood him, then. Gelmas looked at me under his brows, moved his lips in the beginning of a chant; I requested the approaching hesitant tendrils of plasm to leave. He straightened his back and glared, beginning to speak; I hastily interrupted, convincing a shell of ller to form a space all around us free from other spells. Gelmas closed his mouth as he realized how strong the spell was. Neither of us had yet spoken above a mutter, but Detter was beginning to look sulky. I finished off my melted cheese and licked my fingers.

Gelmas sat staring into the flames. Detter unrolled his blankets and prepared for sleep. Soon his breathing was regular, his sweet lips relaxed, one broad hand pillowed beneath his face. I didn't believe him.

I began cleaning my toenails with my knife, with great concentration, hoping to irritate Gelmas into some action. Gelmas did not move, but stared silently at the campfire. It was as relaxed in appearance as a catfight in the making. Any moment the squalling, spitting, and scratching might start, or then again it might not.

I put the knife away and hugged my knees. I didn't have anything left to pretend to do, but I knew if I were the first one to speak, he would have me on the defensive. The fire hissed, and glowing honeycomb coals shone hotly beneath the burning branches, while all around us, like a soap bubble about to pop, evanescent spirals chased each other in the spell I'd set, humming inaudibly as they swirled. Magic is so happy, I thought, gentle, willing to oblige if asked, pleased to be of service, even to harsh, irascible old mages like Gelmas and grubby, half-baked bawds like myself.

Gelmas got to his feet finally, but I didn't. The fire was dying. I resisted the urge to feed it just for something to do. He stood there, waiting or thinking or preparing a spell, I didn't know what, but then he spoke aloud to me. His voice made me leap inside, so bemused had I become with the fire and the silence. "Why steal this particular apprentice, witch? If it was only to call me out in battle, you could have done it much more easily. I admit I am puzzled. I could name you ten other young Magicians you might find more suitable."

I said to the fire, grinning inside, "You have made an incorrect assumption. I did not steal your apprentice." He'd made the first move. Apparently he was reasonable enough to want to negotiate, in spite of his bad temper. There was a long silence. The fire really was getting too low now, so I got up and put some more wood on it. The blaze leapt up again soon. Gelmas folded himself down on the ground again, staring at me over the flames. That was better. I relented enough to look him in the face, and regretted it immediately, for it gave him license to look me over in a way that made my skin crawl, but now I could not look away. Round two to him.

He tired of his game when I did not waver, and with a flicker of his deep eyelids dismissed me, looking away. Detter was truly asleep now, his face slack, his closed eyes fluttering. We were both watching him dream, and Gelmas said, "You must be a powerful mage indeed, to make this wretched mongrel obey you." His voice was amused and almost tender, but I did not let it deceive me. He thought to flatter and distract me.

"I haven't spelled him," I said. "And he wouldn't bother to obey me unspelled if I had a knife to his groin and a rope round his neck. He came away with me only because it amused him to. I didn't try to prevent him." Gelmas did not look convinced. I was getting a cramp in my calf, and massaged it wearily. My face was drying up in the heat of the fire. "We have traveled like this before, when we made our Quest, in company together but not as friends. You of all people must know how impossible he is."

Gelmas looked sharply over his nose at me. "You claim to have earned your rings honestly from the Beast, then."

"I make no claims, and would prefer I didn't have to wear the rattling things," I said impatiently. "I have no desire to play Wizard."

But he did not believe my disavowal. He couldn't, now that I confessed to Power, the Talent to use it, and the blessing of the Beast. He couldn't imagine someone having those gifts and not finding them valuable. "Kaihan has made the claims for you. Are you true life, or did he conjure you for some purpose of his own? If so, now that he has gone, there can be no value in your existence. Why do you linger on, plaguing the world like an unsatisfied ghost?"

"Kaihan didn't make me. And he's not gone. He may be a twisted schemer, but he's the only mage out of all of you who doesn't see me as a threat." I was horrified, for my throat was swelling in a wave of sentimental self-pity at the thought of Kaihan dead. I must be more tired than I thought. I found I was either going to have to wipe my eyes or sit there with tear tracks on my grimy face.

Luckily, Gelmas looked not in the least swayed by my histrionics, or I would have broken down completely. He said grimly, "Then this is yet another of these hasty, ill-thought rescue trips? A woman and a lackwit against strength that has vanquished ten of our most powerful mages. I begin to believe that you are human, woman, for you are a fool. You should have simply killed Detter and yourself in Sassevin and saved yourselves and me this useless trip."

I wiped my nose on my ragged sleeve and smiled blearily at him, saying, "Detter wasn't planning to help. He was just coming along for the ride. It's too bad you're not human enough yourself to stay and help me, because I'm going to get Kaihan out one way or another." I knew how insane it sounded, but it was the truth.

His head went back as if I suddenly smelled bad. "I am here only to reclaim my assistant; he may be deranged and deficient but at least he's trained. If you have any brains, you will let us leave."

"Leave, then, old man. You can have Detter if he wants to come with you, but I have nothing to say about that. He probably will go back with you. You're made for each other. Suspicious, vicious, and warped. Go ahead and leave." I stood up and shook out my blankets. "Now, if you want. I'm tired, I'm going to sleep. If you want to argue with me, can we do it in the morning?" He didn't move. I turned away for a minute, and when I looked back he was futilely trying to form another spell.

"Keff ge lesieg!" I said sharply, and the shell of ller collapsed around him like a net. Encircled with veins of crawling not-light, he sat glaring at me, immobilized. I sat down again facing him, and rubbed my puffy eyes with the heels of both hands. "Please," I said. "I'm tired. I want to go to sleep. Can we fight in the morning?" By his expression, he refused to surrender, so I asked ller to make him sleep, and soon was drifting to sleep myself. Detter slumbered, mouth open, between us, the picture of peace and contentment. It must have been relaxing to have no conscience.

11

In Which I Don't Perform Any Magic

I couldn't move, and I couldn't open my eyes. Not my favorite way to wake up, no matter how fine the morning. "Thank you for the restful night," came Gelmas' voice bitingly from above me. Detter must have awakened early and released his master from his enchanted sleep, the petty, perverted little wretch. What for? It ran against his grain to curry favor. He probably just awoke, saw an opportunity to cause trouble, and couldn't resist.

Gelmas' foot nudged my side ungently. "I know you're awake, you needn't sham. If you tell me the truth now, I'll cause you no pain. Why did you steal my apprentice? What did you need him for?" I heard an annoyed intake of breath from farther away.

"She didn't steal me, you old fool, I left of my own will. You think too well of yourself. Didn't it occur to you I might not want to stay with you?"

"Be silent when you've nothing to say, boy. You'd never have gone off with this simpleton witch on your own. She's not devious enough to please you; you'd be weeping of boredom if you were in your right mind. She's just got raw Power. I have to find out what's going on. Go tend to the horses." Detter wheeled and strode off, far too agreeably, I thought.

I worked my mouth and found Gelmas had not sealed it, but as I opened my lips, he said, "If you start to conjure, I will break your teeth. What were you going to use Detter for, bait?" I started to laugh, and a hand came out of nowhere and belted me in the face. "I warn you, child, I'm going to enjoy this," he said austerely, and then I heard a sudden jingle of tack and the sound of hoofbeats going away.

The Wizard inhaled sharply, started to rise, then roughly lifted my head and gagged me with some kind of sweaty cloth, knotting it tightly behind my head. He ran from me and I heard another horse, but soon all the sounds faded into the distance. I was left behind snug in my blankets with my eyes closed, the picture of lazy serenity, and feeling like an utter idiot. I didn't know if something had scared them away, but as nothing came to eat me I realized Detter must have decided to demonstrate his independence by running away.

As the sun rose further, I began to feel even more uncomfortable. I was too hot, my bladder was full, and I had lost sensation where I lay on one arm. I was too distracted and upset to think clearly, but I could hear a background hum, peaceful and soporific, like bees in summer. Finally, when I stopped berating myself long enough to listen, I realized it was lle singing gently as lle held me immobile. Fascinated, I listened harder and began to make out a tune, and lyrics that weren't exactly in words. I forgot my discomfort.

It was a song about comfort, and pleasure and obedience; it celebrated closeness, and was thankful for direction. It pleaded for intercession, forlornly questioned fate, asked for forgiveness. I was enthralled. It sounded like lle was singing a hymn.

Lle noticed I was paying attention, and lle was grateful. I couldn't move my mouth to speak to ller, but while I framed a tentative wish in my mind, lle loosed ller bonds and whirled away. I sat up awkwardly, opening my eyes, and watched ller dance about me and slowly dissipate. I gazed up at the fading vestiges of the spirit-fire that had held me, and wondered at the way lle seemed to know and speak to me, more and more as lle had on Mennenkaltenei. Was all of ller connected, from world to world, as some said? My arm began to wake up, all flaming prickles, so I put theology out of mind, eased the gag out of my mouth, and tended to my mistreated body.

Amlik grazed nearby, still tethered from the night before, and possessions lay strewn about the cinders of the campfire. Detter had acted like an ass, but it was all the better for me. Gelmas really did seem to value him, though I couldn't see why. I was better off with both of them out of my hair.

Ten minutes later, I was up on Amlik and back on my way to the forest. The sun was warm, the road was smooth, and the sprouting baby leaves were throwing a green haze over the countryside. It was earlier in the day than I'd thought, not yet noon. I must not have lain bound as long as I'd thought.

The road came to a ford, and almost by chance I noticed a mess of splattered drying muddy hoofprints on the far side of the stream as Amlik lumbered out of the water. With a queasy sense of foreboding I realized Detter's escape had led toward the mage-eating forest. I kicked Amlik to a trot, but soon admitted neither he nor I would last long at that rate. I let him slow to a walk. There was no sane way I could overtake Detter or his master before they got to the forest. Maybe they would stop, maybe Gelmas would catch Detter, maybe they would veer off. I don't know why I didn't think they could take care of themselves, or why I should care, but I was even more worried than I'd been before Simon and Detter fell down the mountain, and this time I didn't have any rope.

Abruptly I reined the horse in. I was going at it all wrong, I thought. This was a problem in magic, and I was trying to outrun it mechanically. Why not take advantage of my Power for my own purposes, for once? I settled my thoughts, opened my mind and my mouth, and a cataract of elemental power poured eagerly over me before I could speak. Lle came with a rush and a glad roar, understanding what I wanted before I could get the words out. I found myself and my frantic horse surging into the air like froth on a breaking wave. As we soared giddily forward, high above the ground like a misshapen, improbable bird, I lunged forward to get my hands over Amlik's eyes; it helped, but not enough. The horse was shuddering, whinnying, and flailing his legs. I felt like doing the same.

It was awe-inspiring, what we were doing. We were a good thirty feet off the ground and racing along like a tidal wave or a grass fire. The only thing suspending us in the air was the massive curling crest of a wave of elemental fire, invisibly flaming in crimson and orange. The ground raced past so fast we must have covered a good twenty miles in the time it took me to remember to breathe. Then, slowly, we drifted down, skimming the surface of the turf and gradually slowing, until Amlik's dangling hoofs touched delicately down. We came to a halt, and Amlik, head down, sweated and breathed as if he'd run the whole way. Lle circled with me as ller center, rising and roaring like a tornado, and dissipated back into the sky with a whoosh. I was exhilarated and terrified, feeling the same way I had as a child being blanket-tossed.

I looked around, and found myself perhaps a hundred feet from the first trees of a dark, thick forest starting above me on the hill. Detter and Gelmas, still mounted, were almost beneath the branches of one immense dark tree, arguing. Improbable as it seemed, they hadn't noticed my apocalyptic arrival; I supposed it hadn't been visible or audible to them. I approached cautiously, for I could see that a miasma of ller filled the forest like water in a bowl of pebbles, reaching out all along the border between grassland and tree to the very tips of the tender leaves. Lle seethed and simmered, dark, sad, confined, and malevolent, and Detter was within arm's reach of it. As I came into hearing range, Detter was shaking his head sadly, his face set and cold, while Gelmas said, "You are defeated. Admit it. If you come back with me now, you will at least have understood your limitations. That's part of growing up. Only children think in terms of pure victory, and you are no longer a child."

Detter said, "You're so blind, old man. You're so sure the woman took me against my will, you can't see the truth. *I will not* go with you." His lips were parted, and he was enjoying himself, but his restless horse sidled sideways one step, backward one step, even closer to the forest.

Gelmas said irritably, reaching out one hand for Detter's reins, "You should know by now that inner certainty is just as easily inspired by bewitchment. Come on, grub, I'll take you back and straighten you out. There is no use in running from me."

Detter wrenched his horse's head vindictively away, and it pranced back another step. He was almost within the circumference of the straining spell, totally unaware of its nearness. "Stop trying to control me," he said, and then he saw me.

"Oh, dead gods, Lise, go away and leave me alone!" he shouted, and his restless horse backed him full into the arms of the enchantment. He stopped in midsentence, chirruped to his horse, and rode gaily, utterly enspelled, into the woods. Before Gelmas could follow, I kicked Amlik forward and around him, forcing him back as he struggled to control his offended horse.

Before he could collect himself enough to get nasty, I hissed, "Lle got Detter, whatever lle is, and lle's one step away from taking you too." He stared at me wildly, not comprehending, and I said, "The spell, idiot, the spell. The mage-eater. Get away from the forest—can't you see, fool?" But he couldn't, of course.

"If Kaihan isn't already dead, I'll kill him myself for bringing you into the world, you miserable abortion," he said, and tried to wrest his horse away from me.

I lurched forward, grabbed a handful of his robe, and said with utter sincerity, "There is one evil grandfather of a spell extending all along the edge of this forest. I don't care what you do, turn blue, just as long as you don't throw yourself in there too. I've got enough to do as it is."

He was red in the face. "You've done what you wanted with him, haven't you? Let me go, rot you," and he tried to beat me off. I fell unexpectedly off my horse, dragging him with me, and he hit the ground heavily beneath me. I found myself intimately entangled with an enraged but breathless bag of bones.

Before he could get his breath back, I gabbled a hasty incantation to hold him for a minute. I extricated myself from his legs, and turned back to look at the forest. Detter, oblivious, had gone out of sight by now. The forest trap obviously took any mage lle could get. Lle was bigger and meaner than any spell I'd seen since the Beast's. I spoke to ller, and lle didn't even quiver. Lle was massive, indifferent, answering to something far stronger than me. It was far beyond any one mage's Power to dispel. I'd been afraid of this. It was going to take something other than magic to break this spell.

I didn't have time to play any games with the Wizard, and I didn't want to think about what I was going to do, so I turned away from him and rummaged in my pack. I found the small black envelope. What had Charonne said—enough to cover a fingernail would take away a mage's abilities long enough to knife him? How long did it take to knife a mage? If the mage-eater's source were at the center of the forest, I'd have a good long way to go. I'd better take a larger dose, just in case. I tipped the spelldamp, black and feathery as mold, into my palm. There was a healthy spoonful.

Gelmas, his eyes wide and wild on me, writhed away from me on the ground. He obviously knew what I had there.

"It's not for you," I said disgustedly. "It's for me. This disgusting forest captures mages," and licked the foul stuff off my hand. It was hard to swallow, clinging to the inside of my mouth, and it tasted bitter, oily, and decayed. In fact, it tasted like long-dead animals smelled. I looked up, waited for the medicine to take effect. Gelmas was gray in the face. I said, irritably, "Don't gape," and realized I had to release him from my spell or leave him bound until I recovered. I let him go.

"What are you doing," he gasped, "killing yourself?"

"What I'm doing should be obvious to one of your discernment and intelligence," I said sarcastically. "The forest only eats mages. I have to get Detter out now, as well as Kaihan. If I'm not a mage, I can go in. So I'm taking spelldamp."

And then the dose hit. I said, "Uh," and "Uh," again, as if I'd been hit in the belly. It was like being struck blind, deaf, dumb, and sterile all at once.

I dropped the black envelope and groaned. I felt like I'd been spun in a circle and left staggering. All around me, things were just things, just lumps with no life. Colors were flat and were only colors, sounds were crisp but tuneless, the sky was empty blue space. There was no spell in the forest, and Gelmas was a skinny old man with the stupidest look of chagrin on his face.

"Oh, Mother and Father, I just killed the world," I said in dismay. It was too awful. I wanted to dig a hole and bury myself, but the stupid old man was suddenly holding me by the arm and slapping me. I tried to stop him, and instead he started shaking me until I was forced to look at him.

"Pull yourself together. It's done now. Don't waste it," he said. Everything looked like it was made out of wax, including his pop-eyed, intense face. I almost laughed at him. He shook me again. "I was wrong. You're even more naive than I thought. You actually didn't plan to use Detter, did you?" I remembered why I'd done this incredibly foolish thing. It was worse than I'd imagined anything could be. "Oh, girl, you're worse than even Kaihan," he said. I nodded vaguely at him, and he thrust me from him roughly. "Get that fool Detter back first," he said. How nice, I thought. I'll go get Detter for him to beat up and at least somebody will be happy.

I clambered back up on Amlik, and Gelmas in his rumpled robe watched me with something like fear in his face. I turned and rode back under the trees. Nothing changed. The trees were just trees, dark damp boles and high branches, leaf mold and rotten logs. My head was empty. It was impossible to believe that a few minutes before I had been riding in the sky on a wave of joy.

I caught up with Detter in a few minutes, for he was riding slowly, blank-eyed and content. I grabbed the reins and turned his horse, but he slipped off its back and strolled in his original direction, ignoring me. So I dismounted myself, found a smooth rock, and hit him behind the ear with it. He fell to his knees, holding his head, and I hit him again. I hauled him up, staggering under his weight, and managed to lay him across his horse without rupturing myself, though it was a near thing. When I emerged from the woods, Gelmas rushed to him and got him down, cradling his head in his lap and doing something that made the blood on his scalp disappear. Astonishing, I thought. Magic really looks like magic when you can't see ller. No wonder mages take themselves so seriously.

"I guess I'll go look for Kaihan now," I said, "before this stuff wears off."

The Wizard, startled, remembered my existence. He took a deep breath, paused, and took another. "I don't know if it wears off or not. I've seen it used, twice. It's Council's ultimate punishment, and both mages killed themselves after taking it, so . . . I don't know."

"Oh. Well, then I've got all the time in the world, don't I?" It didn't seem to matter to me. I felt drained. Everything was meaningless. How did normal people navigate in the world, with all the intention taken out? I aimed my horse back at the boring trees anyway.

Behind me, Gelmas said stiffly, "Before you go." I twisted around and saw him staring up at me with his arms around his unconscious apprentice. "What are you, girl? Are you human after all?"

"Last time I looked," I said. He was silent. It took far too much work to win an argument with that man. I wished Detter joy of him.

I rode off into the idiot forest on my mindless horse on an empty day in spring. I rode alone in dark silence, though it was a sunny day filled with birdcalls, the hiss of breezes, and the steady crunch of Amlik's footfalls. I'd never known how much my perceptions were colored by the spirit that sang and flew in and through all there was, all that lived and died around me. Now I was moving in a cardboard world, shallow and sketchy, the scenery for a play. It was as if I were a character in a story-singer's tale, a shadowy puppet of the mind aping the action behind the words.

So I was a puppet in a story-song, going through the motions. Who's singing the story, I thought tiredly. Let's get to the last verse so we can all go back to real life. At least in the songs people knew where they were going and why. Maybe this was supposed to be a funny song, and I was the goat.

Not feeling particularly amusing, I meandered generally toward the north until I came to a well-cleared trail, then followed that. After a bit, it joined a road, and by early afternoon, Amlik and I were standing looking up at a translucent castle, delicate and airy in the sun, impossibly perched like a bird in the arms of the trees, with the road passing beneath it and the sun shining through it to the ground below.

I wondered whether for the first time I was seeing an illusion as others might see it. I rode closer, unsaddled Amlik and tethered him, then walked up to take a look. It still looked real enough. I found a tree with low branches and climbed up to rap the base of the building with my knuckles. No, it was solid stone, and rough enough to scrape my skin. I couldn't see any way to get in. There were doors enough and windows, but they opened out far above the ground.

I walked underneath it, between the trunks of the supporting trees, staring up through interlaced branches at the watery image of the sun and faint body shadows moving far above me. The castle was inhabited, apparently. I came to the center of the base, and nearly walked past a crystal spiral staircase wafting delicately up to a square opening in the foundation like a trapdoor. The stair was the only part of the building that actually touched the ground. The rest was all impossibly borne on the inadequate shoulders of the trees. I put a tentative foot on the bottom step, and the entire structure rang out, singing, like a bell. I backed up in haste and hid behind a tree, but no one came to investigate. After half an hour I made up my mind to try again, and this time put my foot on the second step. This time, there was no sound. I tiptoed up the treads cautiously, holding on to the insubstantial railing, and poked my head up into the building to investigate.

Once I was inside the castle, its walls were perfectly opaque. I guessed the light of the sun was somehow routed through the castle to emerge unaffected beneath. It seemed a lot of trouble for an aesthetic effect. The entrance hall was shadowed but solid, lit by glow-lights of an eerie steady blue. I came the rest of the way up, and cautiously opened the far door. In the next room, there were more glow-lights, but they were green. Somebody had an odd taste in decoration; the color made everything look putrescent. I had seen no lights from beneath the building, either. I wondered what those moving shadows had been—birds, perhaps.

Growing bolder, I crept through the hallways, checking side doors and looking for stairs. All the rooms were furnished fancifully, like pictures from a child's book, and each was different. When I opened one door, it gave me a horrid turn to be looking into a torture room, complete with tools and equipment. The next chamber I looked into was a sprightly sitting room, its absurdly affected furniture upholstered in maroon silk, with fussy pictures of landscapes on the polka-dot papered walls. It went on like that, an endless variation of unexpected contrasts.

Finally, one narrow door I tried opened into a cramped back stair. I trudged up, peered out at the next landing, and decided to go as far up as I could. Three more floors and the stairs ended, opening out into a light and airy gallery full of plants and sculpture. Feathery arching branches nearly swept the high ceiling, vines trailed from hollows in the walls, and stone creatures peered out here and there from between the greenery. I walked along, trailing my fingers through the leaves and caressing the smooth stone sides of the carved and polished animals. Hot sunbeams slanted through the moist and dusty air, and dead leaves curled in the corners. The soporific atmosphere made me feel languid and careless, and I made more noise than I should have. I nearly walked past a lattice archway opening off the gallery, then I glanced aside and realized I saw human forms moving there in a darker room.

There was no way to hide; I was standing in the middle of the doorway, backlit by the sun. I stood frozen in indecision for an instant that felt like an hour, but as I stood, I realized that no one was paying attention to me. Were they also illusion? I couldn't make out faces, my eyes were dazzled still, but the shadowy figures were moving casually, sitting, standing, shifting about, gesturing. Something was very wrong with the picture, something besides the fact that they were ignoring me.

I stepped farther into the room and stood beside the door, waiting for my eyes to adjust. It was cooler than the gallery, a square room with a fountain in the center, stone platforms ranged around the fountain, and a darker arch-framed passageway running around the outside wall like the roofed porch in a courtyard. Low tables were scattered around with food on them, and the people occasionally selected something to eat.

Still no one acknowledged me. I realized that they didn't acknowledge each other either. Though no one collided, they walked as if they were blind or seeing something other than what lay before them. As my own eyes finally began to work, I saw that their eyes were all closed.

I had found the captives, still alive, still healthy, and still thoroughly enspelled. There were more of them than I'd expected, perhaps twenty. Half bore no rings and three of the ringless ones were women; the spell saw no distinction between recognized mages and those who had never sought the Beast. Their restless movement dizzied me, and it took me a while to pick out the man I was looking for. Kaihan was seated, relaxed and still, on a stone platform, his chin on his hand and his eyes closed. He was still wearing the white shirt I'd seen him in last, though now it was worn and stained. I wove through the pacing figures toward him.

I passed a hand casually in front of his face, if only to confirm what I already knew. He didn't move, he didn't see. I shook his shoulders gently, and his head rolled forward and back. When I was done, he was still entranced. I sat down next to him and poked him in the side. It was like poking dough. I tried to wrestle him up, and managed to get him standing, but as soon as I let go, he sat down again. Maybe I could hit him with a rock as I had hit Detter, but then I'd have to get him through the halls and down the stairs, hoping he would stay unconscious. Even if I managed to get him down to the ground, I'd still have to get him out of the forest, and still all these other mages would be captive.

This was no good at all. Everything was wrong. I hadn't thought through the consequences of giving up my Power. Here I was at the center of the enchantment, exactly where I planned to be, and I was useless as the eyes on a mole. I sat next to Kaihan, kicking my heels. At least I could rest a little while before I decided what to do. I snagged some bread and cheese from a nearby table and had a meal. Kaihan continued to meditate, oblivious of me. It was a small comfort, but comfort nevertheless, that he was still alive.

A shadow came across the blazing archway I'd entered by; someone stood there as I had. I tried to duck behind Kaihan's body, but Kaihan, like everybody else in the room, was standing and turning to face the newcomer. I slid behind the platform, sure I'd be discovered, but the man strode into the room as if everything were normal. He stood by the fountain in the center of the room and waved to the spellbound mages to be seated. They obeyed. This man must be the maker of the spell, then, though he was not marked as a mage.

He gestured, and the fountain vanished; in its place stood a jewel-encrusted throne, and sunlight haloed it from above. Fresh flower petals appeared beneath his feet, still glistening with moisture. He took his seat, and surveyed his thralls, still not seeing me. The room began to change shape weirdly, as if sleeping life was waking beneath the surface of the walls and floors. I realized that if I were still a mage myself, I would not be able to see past the magic that must be surging and boiling in this room. Somehow he was using and channeling the power of his twenty slaves.

The man's face was eager and glad as windows appeared in the walls and the mages slid from their seats to kneel before him. He didn't look evil. In fact, he looked more like a boy than a man, someone who hadn't reached his full growth. He looked familiar to me, and I remembered my dream of the jars with heads. This man's smooth childish cheeks and innocent eyes were those of the boy in the dream. He looked passionate, visionary, and prophetic, as the ceiling rose higher above us. He was doing something he believed in, whatever it was. I began looking for something I could use as a club.

There was a heavy pottery jug on one of the tables. It was awkward, but maybe it would do. I hefted it in my hand, and walked boldly up to the man on the throne. He still didn't know I was there. I felt free to circle around him looking for the right angle, and finally poised myself behind his left ear, jug upraised, like a vengeful brewer's god. I swung as hard as I could, praying that it would work.

He fell on his face, landing full on his nose and scrabbling in panic on the floor. I stooped and hit him again, not caring if I broke his skull. The blow took effect; he collapsed limply. All around us in a vague supplicant circle the mages knelt, in hushed unison.

I grabbed hold of Kaihan's slack arms, trying to wrestle him out of the room. He came with me to begin with, but the closer we got to the door the slower he moved, until I could force him no farther. I tugged and tugged until I had to stop and catch my breath. Then, serene and sightless, he swiveled and paced back to catch his place in the circle surrounding the felled spell-master, who was starting to move again. It was worse than chasing a room full of half-swatted bugs. I grabbed up the jug and swung it again at the head of the boy. The jug shattered. Finally he lay still, and stayed there, but everything else began to come apart.

The captive mages groaned in unison, a sorrowful chorus. Two fell to their sides, backs arched, twitching. Several others simply clutched their heads, and a small hardy group, Kaihan among them, stood up and began purposefully walking away. As they walked and as I watched, they looked as if they were striding into swampland, sinking lower somehow. I looked closer and realized they were up to their shins on the floor, which was gelatinously softening and yielding to their feet. My own legs were half sunk through the surface, like standing in the surf at the beach while the sand wears away beneath. The walls were sagging, the ceiling drooping down to us in the center, everything was turning gray, and I was afraid I was going to drown or be smothered in the disintegrating building.

Now I was up to my hips, and I felt a falling sensation. I held on to the nearest body, which turned out to be that of the renegade conjuror

I'd hit. He and I both continued to sink, and the stupefied men around us were half-covered with the cloudy translucent slime everything had turned into. The ceiling drooled over the top of my head and trickled into my hair just before my nose disappeared under the surface of the floor. In the dark miasma, still clutching the unconscious mage, I sank holding my breath forlornly, faster and faster, until my feet hit something solid with a wrenching thud and I fell to my knees. I thought for a moment I'd broken both my legs, not that broken legs would matter if I suffocated to death. I lost my grip on the boy as he fell farther to the bottom, and just as I was about to surrender and gasp gray sludge into my aching lungs, my head broke the surface and I could breathe.

All around me, the building continued to dissolve and disappear, a shallow gray pool broken by the trunks of the trees and rapidly settling into the ground like water in a desert. A scattering of large lumps revealed themselves as human beings, crouching and lying on the ground, moving feebly. In a short while the dregs of the castle were gone, and there in an unsullied, sunny clearing in the forest were twenty mindless mages, an unconscious puppet-master, and myself, battered, breathless, shabby, and sweating. My horse, still tethered, placidly tore with his teeth at the undergrowth not fifty feet away.

I wavered on my feet. My head swam, my ears roared, and I nearly fainted. I sat down and closed my eyes, wondering why I wasn't dead and not sure I wouldn't prefer to be. I put my head between my bruised knees, waiting for the feeling to go away.

Finally, I felt I could raise my head again without passing out, and to my horror saw only myself and the renegade still in the clearing. There were three men still staggering out through the trees, all three in different directions, as fast as they could force their half-useless legs. I jumped to my feet and again nearly passed out. I stood swaying in the sun, ready to throw up. I wanted to do something but I didn't know what; I didn't know which direction Kaihan had gone, and I knew I would lose him if I went the wrong way.

At my feet, there was a scratchy wheeze. The renegade turned over with an effort, then lay flaccid again, squinting his eyes painfully up at me. "What happened?" he asked weakly. "The kingdom is gone. Am I dead? Is this the afterlife?" Then he threw up on himself. He really was no more than a boy, a young man barely showing a beard. I turned him on his side with my foot so he wouldn't throw up on himself again. He began to cry like a bullied child, hopelessly and quietly. I walked over to the horse so I wouldn't have to listen to him, but as I untethered Amlik I could still hear the occasional painful gulp.

I wanted to kill him to shut him up. I sat on my horse staring into the forest, wondering where Kaihan had gone and knowing I had lost him again. At least he was alive, but if he'd been himself he would have known me and stayed, not run off into the forest like the rest of them. And I was a mage no longer. I couldn't send a search spell after him or call him back to me. It would start to get dark soon, too.

I turned back to the renegade, walking the horse back to loom over him. His chest was still shaking, and he stared out in complete despair. He didn't seem to be afraid of me, just completely hopeless and incapable. I must have given him a bad injury with that last blow; like Simon on the mountain, he had no magic for the moment. I considered trying to kill him now before he recovered, but I didn't have the stomach for it. Besides, in my true dream I hadn't killed him, though there was no sense in the dream for me.

I got down, and kicked and shoved him until he hauled himself up onto the horse. I got up before him, kicked Amlik's sides, and set off back down the road. I'd let Detter and Gelmas figure out what to do with him. Maybe they would kill him for me. Maybe they could find Kaihan for me, too. I couldn't do much for myself or anyone else at this point, and my dress was an absolute mess as well. The monster-boy-mage clung to Amlik's mane, shaking, looking as if he'd never ridden a horse before.

It was a long ride back to the edge of the forest. I took the path, turning right when I emerged from the woods, to skirt the trees and find Detter and Gelmas again. It occurred to me to wonder if they had waited for me. The light was low, the grass and trees glowed in the dusk, and I could see a few stars shining through the mother-of-pearl sky when I finally came on a low campfire, two men relaxed beside it, two horses placidly grazing. It was so hard to see through the dusk. I realized that if I no longer could see ller, nights would be even darker. No wonder normal people preferred to travel in the day.

"Well, if it isn't what the dog wouldn't eat," said Detter, healthier than ever. "What's this grimy piece of fluff?" he said as the boy slid off the horse and fell weakly to his knees.

"This is what set the mage-eater spell," I said. The boy stared up at me glassily. He hadn't said anything since the clearing, though his shoulders shook occasionally in stifled sobs. I didn't know if it was the head injury or if his mind just wasn't too well assembled in the first place, but he was not my idea of a malevolent necromancer.

Gelmas still sat by the fire. I lifted the boy to his feet, walked him over to where he could get some warmth, and sat him down. Gelmas looked him over without interest, while I wrapped him in a blanket. The boy sat huddled, shivering. "I don't understand you," said Gelmas. "Why haven't you killed him? Where are the lost mages? Are they all dead?"

"You're never happy, are you?" I said to the long-nosed old bastard, and flopped myself down on the grass. Detter came over and sat beside his master, not quite touching shoulders.

"Oh no, Master Gelmas is always very happy, aren't you, Master?" said Detter with his eyes very wide and innocent. An even sourer expression settled over Gelmas' face, but he didn't move away. Detter sat tucked up into himself, self-contained, smug. Although I'd explained it all to them in my head on the way back, I realized now that they probably weren't going to believe my reasons, my dreams, or my Voices.

"The spell is dissolved. The lost mages are alive but mindless, walking in every possible direction at great speed in the forest, and I don't know whether they're going to recover. The only one who stayed behind when I broke the enchantment was this one. I hit him pretty hard in the head. He's harmless for the moment." I paused. Gelmas was barely visible in the firelight, but what I could see of him was unreceptive. "What do the Finders usually do with renegades?" I asked.

"Take them to the Beast and throw them in unprepared," said Gelmas. "Sometimes they live."

"Oh." I was very tired, my head hurt, and I had little hope, but I went on anyway. "Can I ask two favors of you?" He didn't respond, but I went ahead anyway. "Could you take this creature back to the Beast for me, that's one. The other is, would you cast me a search spell so I can find Kaihan? I'm worried he'll hurt himself."

Gelmas said coldly, "Ask me no favors." Beside him, Detter lifted his eyes to me luxuriously. "It is not my place to give ear to your petitions, woman. You should not be asking favors of anybody. That is a serious error of judgment." Detter turned to him, puzzled. "I have been listening to my apprentice attempt to slander you for hours, and from that I have gleaned a few things. In everything you have faced, whether disabled or no, you have managed to tear success out of a situation where any mage of sense and ability would lie down and die, and you try to cut your own head off between times. You disgust me. You have obviously been very badly trained, and I am glad I had nothing to do with your upbringing, or you would have been killed a long time ago." Now I was puzzled too. He took a breath, and continued, "If you *com-

mand me, I will take this pathetic slug back to the Beast, I will provide you with a search spell, and I am afraid I must also insist on providing you with some different clothing. You are about to fall out of that disintegrating rag, and while I am immune to your dubious charms, I am sure you wouldn't want to frighten any unwitting passersby with the appalling sight of your flesh."

Detter said disgustedly, "You're raving, man," and Gelmas said, "Shut up, hotheaded thug."

I wiped my nose on the sleeve of the maligned dress. The halfwit renegade mage was weeping again, silently, inattentive. I said, "I am really very hungry. Is there anything to eat?" Gelmas chanted a change spell, and my clothes shimmered and changed on my body. I was now wearing something suitable for my purposes: trousers, high boots, and a warm tunic. Detter got up and walked away. Gelmas tossed me a hunk of meat, and I promptly got grease on my new clothes. Gelmas looked away, pursing his lips, and Detter smiled in the background.

That night I lay looking up; the sky arched empty of life above me. I had always liked to watch the little wisps of spirit plasma chasing each other in the heavens, appearing and disappearing, swirling and changing faint colors, but lle wasn't there for me that night. Maybe the night sky dance would never be there again. I wasn't sure I could sleep. The pathetic, horrible renegade mage lay rolled in a blanket on his side, with a sleep spell on him, both hands nestled under his battered head. Detter and Gelmas, to my foolish surprise, were lying indistinctly intertwined, in intent mutual motion, over at the edge of the circle of light from the fire. Well, at least somebody was getting something out of the situation. I turned over on my face, listened to the solitary dry sounds of wind and leaf, and eventually went to sleep.

12

In Which I Don't Please the Master

When I caught up with him, I'd been eagerly examining every wayfarer I passed for three solid days, shading my eyes to peer at figures barely visible in the distance, even turning around to look behind in case I'd missed Kaihan somehow. The road west of the forest was a well-traveled one, and Amlik was getting nervous at my constant twisting and turning. Maybe Gelmas' spell had been intended only to take me far away, not to find Kaihan.

Then I came upon my quarry.

I was even with Kaihan before I recognized him. He smiled with all his teeth at me. There was no recognition behind those flat black eyes, only limitless greed. He darted suddenly at Amlik's head, grabbing for the reins, and as I pulled the startled horse away, he ran after, planning I don't know what. Once I was out of reach, though, he stood blinking at me, and I circled around him while he followed me with his eyes like a trapped and dangerous bear. He had a feral grin on his face. He looked healthy but somehow goblinlike, shrunken.

"Kaihan," I said cautiously, but he sprinted toward me suddenly, and I wheeled the horse and cantered away. He chased me for a moment, then stood in the middle of the road, his chest heaving, his face somehow flattened and animallike.

I reined up and said, "Master Kaihan," entreatingly; he took another step toward me; I backed the horse away and he stopped; when I halted, he moved again. We repeated the dance for a while, until I felt like a beast trainer with a large untamed tiger, or like the taunting Lady Fair in the Knife Dance. It was pathetic and frightening, and he never answered me.

Finally, he gave up, lost interest, and sat down in the middle of the road, looking like a broken machine. I drank from my waterskin, then threw it to him. He was thirsty, but it took too long for him to unplug it; his hands were as nimble as ever but he wasn't quite sure of the concept. When he had done drinking, he let the skin fall to the ground, and the rest of the contents dribbled out, making a small circle of mud on the road. He sat and stared at me, his black eyes bright and empty, and I stared back, feeling just as empty.

Though when in full possession of his powers he'd infuriated and disturbed me, now, staring at this husk, I found I'd suffered a loss much bigger than I could have imagined. What had I hoped to find? Someone who would make it all better, someone like Simon's long-lost father who'd tell me what to do? This was as bad as when I found the Adepts had taken my name from me, and just as puzzling. I couldn't put words to what I felt, but it was painful.

Eventually, he rose and kept walking, leaving the waterskin lying shriveled in the dirt. I followed the slim, shabby figure, hoping to wear him out or wait until he fell asleep. Other people on the road, seeing him approach, seemed to understand something was wrong with him and kept carefully away. He was staying alive by no obvious means, for he didn't seem to have the sense to eat. His time in Asterman's Wood had taken his mind away, perhaps for good. Gelmas had said that persuading Council to organize a rescue expedition for the lost mages would take a while, so I was Kaihan's guardian for the time being, and must figure out what to do.

Toward the end of the day, he sat abruptly down by the side of the road, rubbed his face, lay down, and curled up into a ball. I sat and watched him for a time until I was sure he was going to sleep, then retreated farther down the road to make my own camp. I turned it over in my mind, and decided to try sneaking up on him in his sleep. That way, I might bind him and take him back to Sassevin, where presumably the Council might consent to care for him. I didn't feel afraid at the prospect, more mournful, like I did at butchering time back home when last year's lambs were this year's mutton and the King was due to die. It wasn't as if we were going to kill Kaihan, I told myself firmly, just keep him from hurting himself.

When it was dark and the birds were finally quiet, I cautiously rose to my feet and started back down the road with my rope slung around my shoulders. The stars were blocked out by cloud, and there were no dwellings nearby, so I could barely see in the ller-bereft murk of the night. Once I nearly turned my ankle, and twice I strayed noisily off the road into thick underbrush, flailing and staggering. If my quarry were in command of his normal mind, he would have been long gone by the time I reached him. Instead, by the sound of his quiet snoring when I came near, he slept peacefully.

Taking a long breath, I readied the rope in my shaking hands, crept forward silently. Then I stepped full on one of his legs, tripped extravagantly, and fell on top of him. There was a roar of rage, wordless and furious, from Kaihan's throat, and a strangled grunt from me. I frantically untangled myself from the rope and from the man and tried to roll away, but a hand caught me, and I found myself in the middle of a random maelstrom of limbs and blows. Strong hands gripped and shook me, and I screamed, "Please, no, Kaihan." They relaxed slightly at the unexpected sound of my voice and I ripped myself free, feeling the fingernails tear my skin as I pulled. I crawled away as fast as I could. It almost wasn't fast enough, for something nearly caught my foot before I got free. My plan obviously had defects.

I heard scuffling noises off to my left, Kaihan casting about for his attacker, and I turned myself around, trying to find the road by sound. It was motherless dark and I had lost my rope. Then the scuffling ceased, and a deep voice, slightly slurred, sent a muddy wave of shock through my viscera. "Who it is?" Kaihan said, "Who it is? Who?" I took a step forward involuntarily, feeling my throat close. It was horrible to know he could speak after all. The scuffling sounded again, nearer, and suddenly a hand brushed my ankle and grabbed at me. I leaped with a yelp, and ran in the other direction, finding the road by accident with my face when I tripped in the ditch.

In the distance, the deep voice said again, "Who is?" I limped back up the road over the rise to my camp, while I heard the occasional question fade into the distance. It sounded like Kaihan was staying put, sending his garbled queries randomly into the darkness.

I finally found my blankets by the dim coals of my banked campfire. I sat shivering, and swallowing to keep from crying, for a long time. Kaihan was mixed in my head with the image of the Father-God, aggressive, angry, foolish, out of control, terribly sad, and utterly foreign to me. That we'd needed to resort to the hostile dance on the road, the hard struggle in the dark, made me want to throw up. I didn't like the mindless animal he'd become; I was angry that the self-aware, amused, restrained man had been swallowed up as if he had never existed. I didn't think I would have made a very good Kalten after all, if I was so easily disconcerted, but I knew that by now. I didn't make a very good anything, I thought, laid myself down to sleep, and passed imperceptibly into a true dream, in forced and garish colors.

Kaihan, Detter, Gelmas, and I were sitting on the ground with our backs to each other, triply guarding the rabbit-cheeked boy, who stood in our midst. My arms were pulled almost straight back in their sockets, my hands in the boy's hands, and so also were Detter's and Kaihan's. I noticed now other mages, their arms extended behind them, backed up to our seated knot and took their places between us, the renegade mage taking each offered hand and adding it to his grasp, which kept getting harsher and stronger and tighter on my own fingers. He grew taller, and the ring of seated mages surrounding him expanded and began to circle around him like a human maypole with human ribbons, until we were all flying in a circle around him, our arms stretched almost past bearing, and getting longer and longer.

We began to enter the clear blue sky as if it were a sea, swinging through blueness and dipping up, surfacing only to breathe. The blue became thicker and harder, and our spinning bodies battered through it. It glowed, glared blue, and I realized it was no longer the innocent sky, but the blue spirit-fire of the Enforcers, filled with knives and needles, ripping, tearing, burning. One by one, more mages joined the ring, falling in and dissolving into the wheel, and then more came, merchants and sailors and elderly ladies, until there were thousands, hundreds of thousands.

Suddenly Kaihan, still beside me, began to slip away from the wheel. I screamed, the first sound of the dream, and as his arms lost their grip, I somehow hooked my legs around him, holding him safe but dangling, twisting, spinning in the air. While he clung to my waist with desperate hands, his extended body tore a gaping hole through the blue fire, sliced it into fluttering shreds. He looked up at me with his black eyes, calm as ever and smiling, and I said to him as if we were not reeling and spinning madly through space, "I will not let you go this time." My legs began to slip, and the boy's hands tightened on mine brutally until I passed out of the dream with the pain. It was a harsh, fragmented dream, like someone shouting up the stairs.

When I got up in the morning, I felt like the gold-grain finder on harvest day, excited and anxious. I never knew how a true dream would affect me, and I couldn't interpret this one, but it made me feel good. I broke my fast, and went to find Kaihan. He was sitting still where we'd struggled the night before, with his arms around his knees, warily waiting for his assailant to return. There was an ugly scrape on his face, and his shirt was torn, but something else seemed different about him.

As I cautiously approached him, he spoke first. "I have nothing left worth stealing. You are wasting your time." He could speak clearly now. One layer of his mind had healed, though his memory had not returned. Perhaps the fight of the night before had hastened his recovery.

"I'm not a thief," I said. "You've been ill. I'm trying to take you home."

He was bitterly amused. "Do you often attack sick people in the dark? I assure you, if I had not been completely healthy, I could not have resisted you so well last night. Whatever it is you want of me, I do not have it. I beg you to leave me alone."

I grinned at him. "No. I'm not letting you out of my sight." He stood, offended and impatient, and started walking west again. I nudged Amlik after him, feeling like a disobedient younger sister trailing after her big brother. Kaihan even walked in a different way than the day before. Then, he had been an aggressive animal; today, he was without question a man, though not the man I knew. I didn't like this particular man much better than the animal he'd been, though I was less sorry for him now.

The next day, Kaihan, growing more articulate and more irritated by the hour, tried everything he could think of to lose me. He threw stones, ran off the road, shouted at me, tried to enlist the aid of passersby, attempted to frighten the horse, and made speeches. I listened to the speeches, avoided the stones, and ignored the rest. At night I offered him some food and a blanket, which he first refused and then took ungraciously when I left them in the road. I withdrew a good way and set up my own camp, but half an hour later, as I sat hugging my knees and missing my Voices, he stepped into the firelight with the blanket rolled under his arm.

"Since I cannot lose you, I will use you," he said, and slept near the warmth of the fire that night.

The next morning I woke early, before he did. Kaihan was neatly wrapped in his borrowed blanket, his hands tucked up under his chin, an exquisitely drawn picture. The sideways morning light caught one sculptured ear and then spilled over his cheekbone, but the rest of his face was shadowed, the sparse feathers of his lashes, the hard flared nose, the wide firm mouth no more relaxed and no less aware in sleep than it was when he was awake. As I lay there, my head propped on my elbow, allowed for the first time to stare at him unhindered, I realized guiltily that I thought him beautiful, that I had thought him beautiful when I was dragged in to see him in his study at school, and every time I'd encountered him after.

I didn't know precisely why I felt guilty about it. After all, in this world I was free to admire whatever man I wanted. Why couldn't I look at the Master if it gave me pleasure? But it was an embarrassed pleasure, nonetheless.

Of course, to the Lisane, the child who'd been raised to be a public oracle, queen, and breeder, even his apparent age was ancient to me, let alone the centuries he claimed. If I had been installed the year before, my partners for the next twenty years would all have been young men, boys in their early twenties, the only age idealistic enough to sacrifice itself for one year's glory. So the forty or fifty years Kaihan appeared to own seemed terribly old, and the two hundred or more he claimed was unimaginable.

Yet it was undeniable that I had been overwhelmed by his presence every time we met. I was fascinated by him, he passed through my thoughts constantly, and yet I denied him. Well, here I was lying on the hard ground, having followed him into the wilderness on a wild chance and the whim of my Voices to find him, and there he was, asleep and mindless as an infant instead of the old, hard, powerful lord he was. Now that I knew how I felt, I wanted to get up and leave him now before I could make myself a bigger fool than I already was, but I dared not leave him until he had recovered.

I stole one more self-indulgent look at him, running my eyes up the long line of his legs under the blanket, the elegant curve of his rib cage, over the raised shoulder, and ran smack into the cold gaze of his now open eyes. He had woken up while I was mooning over him.

"I see I cannot escape your attentions, Lisane," he said flatly, and I froze at the change in his voice and face. "I take it you came after me, after I told you not to?" He had changed again in the night. He was no longer the irritated, amnesiac, middle-aged man being harried for no reason by a juvenile vigilante. Now he was the Master again, and the frigid blaze in his eyes reduced my musings of the moment before to a stupid fantasy.

"You didn't come back," I said. It already sounded lame enough to me; the powerful leader of mages hadn't returned to let me know he was all right, so I'd taken it on myself to chase after him into the countryside.

"What vagrant brainstorm made you decide to herd me back like a stolen sheep?" Kaihan continued. "Didn't you have anything more valuable to do with your time than to waste it playing catch-up after one useless old man among many? You would have better used your energy attending to your own business, not in an uninvited, dragged-out, inept rescue of one solitary captive. What did you hope to prove? I expected better of you."

"Oh, you're welcome, I'm sure, you rat-faced, bug-headed, sister-splitting tree frog," I said venomously, shoving my hair out of my face, kicking my blankets aside, and standing up. I stamped past him, resisted kicking him in the side, and grabbed Amlik's bridle.

"If you felt you had to tag along after me, you could at least have cast a spell to keep me from wandering, or have you forsworn the use of magic even when it would be ordinary common sense?"

"You sound just like Gelmas," I said, throwing Amlik's saddle over him. "Is that part of the requirement for being a Wizard?" I was so angry my head hurt, and my mind was incoherent. I didn't feel like explaining anything to such a wrongheaded lout. I wanted to leave. He was obviously back to his old pigheaded self. He didn't need me. I could leave now if I wanted to. I bent over, cinched Amlik's belly-strap, and started to loose his tether.

From behind, Kaihan grabbed me, turned me around, and said, "Don't you run from me. Are you a complete idiot? What possessed you to do such a stupid thing?" His face was inches from mine, and I hated every arrogant scrap of it.

I kicked his shins as hard as I could. He exclaimed in anger, but he didn't let me go, so I screamed at him, "Yes. I'm a complete idiot. I should have left you there. Let go of me, you worthless old bag of wind." At that, he did let go of me, his eyes burning. I turned and vaulted up on Amlik, then realized I hadn't finished untethering him. Kaihan contemptuously loosed the line, tossed the end back up to me, stood back, and let me go. I rode away, back in the direction of Sassevin, without my pack or my blanket, knowing I'd been a fool all along. When I got out of range, I put my head on Amlik's stolid neck and began weeping in great gulping sobs, angry, shamed, and devastated. I didn't want to live on the same planet as that horrible man. I began, for the first time since I'd landed on this world, to wonder if I might make myself another ship to leave it. Then I remembered I had no more magic. I kept riding.

In the late afternoon, grim and growing tired, thirsty, hungry, having long since regretted my flight, I was still riding. Amlin tossed his massive head from time to time, annoyed and sweaty, poor mutt. It wasn't his fault. I leaned forward and rubbed his coarse and glossy forelock and rested my head a moment on his neck. His sweat-stained hide smelled like sea air and shoe leather. As soon as he felt my weight on his neck, he stopped walking and dropped his head to search for grass, almost tipping me over. Just as I had pulled myself together and decided to keep going, someone cleared his throat not two paces away, and I jerked up my head to see Kaihan standing there. I looked wildly around but found no sign of another horse; he must have enchanted his feet to come so far, so fast.

"I am sorry," he said. "May I apologize for my behavior this morning?" He looked as if he found me, and the entire situation, funny. I was stern and still by an effort of will, though my belly was hollow and I knew my eyes must be purple.

"No harm done. I lost my temper, too," I said, meaning it to sound gracious and forgiving. It sounded sad and silly instead.

"You certainly did," he said, and laughed unexpectedly, his face creasing up in startled warmth. I couldn't bear it, and must have looked as dismayed as I felt, for he took a step backward and put his hands behind him. "May I accompany you?" he asked politely. "I think our paths lie together."

I wretchedly nodded my head, and shook Amlik's reins to stir him forward again, but Kaihan stopped me. "Perhaps you should rest awhile," he said. "You have ridden far. Let me help you down." I let the reins slip from my fingers, and Kaihan helped me from my horse, help I didn't want but needed, and then settled me under a tree while he went to catch dinner. He behaved impeccably, like a well-trained servant, which made me feel even more the fool.

I leaned my back against the tree and looked up. The sky was barely visible through the unfolded leaves; early summer had welled up and flowed over the country while I was charging around saving people who shouted at me and thought me funny. The air was almost warm, and smelled of the white flowers that come just at the break of summer, all dusty pollen and heart of honey. I took out my comb from the pack Kaihan had graciously restored to me, tugged my tangled hair straight, and rebraided my hair tightly. If nothing else, at least my hair would be under my control. I rummaged for my mirror, and regarded my face intently. It was even grubbier than usual, thinner, and very sulky, but the eyes were liquid green, the skin was clear, and the hair was neat, black, and shiny. Somewhat reassured, I started to put it back and was startled to find Kaihan watching me.

He said only, "Would you care to eat?" and offered me his arm. I didn't want to take it, but I did. I was never going to be able to stand being near the man. His voice sliced through air like a knife through a grape, his figure cut a fluid, subtle silhouette, and even in a stained peasant shirt with a scrape on his face he looked as commanding as he had when he sat on the black throne.

As we sat down to eat, I looked through the corner of my eyes at him, at the corded neck, at the wafer-thin gap between his shirt's open neck and the firm skin of his chest, and thought, if you were anyone else in the world, I'd know exactly what to do with you, but you are Master Kaihan, and I'm lost.

After the sun set, I sat staring in the fire, trying not to think. Kaihan had said nothing more to me. A wind in the distance sighed, and I turned my head to one side to look into the night. As my eyes adjusted to the dark, I realized with surprise that the world had begun to be alive in my eyes again. In and of each leaf, each trunk, each weed, and the air itself, lle was glowing, swirling, and living dimly. "I can see," I said softly. "I can see again."

"You were blind?" said Kaihan, looking up under his brows at me. He had been staring at his hands for half an hour.

I opened my mouth and found there was nothing I could say. I didn't want him to know what I'd done for him. He would only get angrier. "It's nothing," I mumbled. He looked back at his hands again.

"I was very rude to you this morning, and I had no right," he said painfully, as if the admission embarrassed him. Mother and Father, what a lovely voice.

"You apologized already. I said to forget it."

"I'm afraid I must ask you. How was I freed? You did free me, did you not, or was someone else responsible?"

"I did it," I said, grudgingly.

"How did you do it?" he asked. "Were the others there freed as well, or was I the only one?"

"The others are all free, but they're scattered across the hills. If you're worried about the renegade, I sent him back to Sassevin with Gelmas and Detter."

"It was Gelmas who aided you?" he said quickly, looking relieved but puzzled. "He is the last I should have expected. What did you do to make him help you?"

"He didn't do anything at all until afterward," I said hotly, still burning with the injustice of it. "That idiot Detter insisted on running away with me to annoy Gelmas, and Gelmas chased after us to bring him back. Neither one of them was any help, and Detter even managed to get himself caught in the spell as well." I stopped, reminding myself suddenly that I was not going to explain myself.

"Then how *did* you do it, lady mage?" he asked insistently. "I am counted the most Powerful Wizard in the world, and my strongest shield spell wilted against that enchantment in an instant. I was taken as if I had no defenses at all."

"Then maybe you're not the most Powerful in the world after all," I said snidely, and regretted it in an instant. "No, I'm sorry, I didn't mean that. It had nothing to do with Power at all—in fact, just the opposite." Then I shut my jaw. I'd gone too far, I could see. The black eyes glittered at me angrily, a dawning realization arriving.

"What did you do, woman? What did you do to yourself?" The veneer of politeness had vanished. He was about to start lecturing me again, I could tell.

"You have no right to speak that way to me," I said. "I did what I had to do, and it's done. Take it as it is."

He drew breath to speak, and then paused, looked instead at his hands, and bitterly said, "I have gone to absurd lengths to ensure you a place in the fellowship of mages, at great risk to my own reputation, I might add, and you have rewarded my efforts by systematically sabotaging yourself. You have maimed yourself in some way, haven't you?"

"Whatever you have done for me, or done to me, I am not your property," I hissed at him. "I'd be better off if I had stayed in the forest starving—at least I wouldn't be jerked from disaster to calamity by your endless plots and plans. I didn't maim myself, if you must know. I just took spelldamp." My admission seemed to leave him unmoved. He sat like a statue, still staring down at his hands.

"It seems to be wearing off now," I finished lamely. He didn't answer. I turned back to the night and watched what blurry traces of spirit I could make out, fuming.

It was so reassuring to see ller again, even if my not-sight was still blurry and faint, that it took me a while to realize that what I saw of ller was agitated, frenzied. I was beginning to hear something, too. What I thought the wind was the foggy howling of many spirit voices. I strained my mind's ears, tried to make out the distant statements, and when lle realized I was trying to reach ller, I was suddenly drowned in ller.

It was like the day Gelmas had bound me, but this time the song was aimed directly at me. Lle knew exactly where I was, and was trying to sing, or more precisely shout, in my ear. I could almost make out words, thoughts, ideas. There was something about return, recapitulation; something about danger—I tried and tried to make it out, but it wasn't working. Kaihan was standing, saying, "Do you need help?" and I held my hand up sharply for silence. Lle wailed about me, swirling and swinging in loops. I was supposed to do something, supposed to finish something, I didn't know what.

"Ye essertver, lle benk, ye essertver," I pleaded, and abruptly found myself awake in the midst of a true dream. I was a hundred miles tall, and I stood straddle-legged above Sassevin looking down through the world to the other side. High above the mountains at the center of the Lesser Shore, there was a hole, a blackness, an absence, circling the world toward me and descending. It was a cancer on the world. It would consume everything, kill everything. All life was dying already. Fear was rising like hot air all about me, dancing and shaking, saying Death, Death, Pain, and I said all right, all right, let me go, let me go, I understand. The dream dissolved in a spiral around me and I found myself staring into Kaihan's concerned face.

"Whose spell was that?" he asked, and I answered, "Nobody's. Free the horse, we'll have to leave him behind. We're going back to Sassevin now. The Enforcers are landing on this world, and their ship is killing the magic." I started kicking dirt over the campfire as Kaihan ran to untether Amlik. When he returned, I grabbed his hand. Without any warning, a force that felt like all the ectoplasm in the world formed a canted whirlpool with us at the center, sucking us up into the cringing sky so fast my skin sagged. We shot southeast toward Sassevin as if flung from a sling.

13

In Which I Don't Know
What I'm Doing

Kaihan looked exhilarated, his body arching like a diver's, his mouth half-open and his glittering inlaid eyes staring into infinity. I couldn't stand looking at him, so I mostly watched the convulsing stripes of luminiferous ether that were acting in concert to shove us home, and listened to the chaotic roar of the wind, thinking worriedly about something odd.

I had just had a true dream. Of that there was no doubt. But I'd been shoved into it by a frightened thunderstorm of spirit-fire trying to tell me something. I'd always thought my dreams were direct extensions of myself to the future, aided by that part of the Goddess that lived in me, and filtered through my limited human mind. But this was more like a crude message from another part of the present, and lle had been as terrified as if lle were a person being tortured, instead of the bland, serene, sacrificial servitor of the gods. What was going on?

What if my dreams were instructions instead of visions, planted in my mind by the spirit-fire? I had understood that the Beast was revealed in his Room by magic, but what if he were made of magic too? Who was making whom do what here? Where were the Mother and Father in all this, or were they somewhere else entirely, paying no attention at all?

Finally I decided that whatever the spirit-fire was doing, I had never been treated badly by ller, and I would do anything I could to protect this world from the Enforcers. Maybe later on I could sort things out.

We landed in Sassevin just before dawn, outside the building that housed the Beast's Room, and I remembered he had told me, "Remember we are bound here when the time comes." I guessed the time had come. The instant my foot touched the ground I headed for the nondescript door at a run. Kaihan staggered and fell, but as I put my hand on the door, he grabbed me and said, "What are you planning?"

"Magic is alive, and afraid, and must be free to fight," I said. "I'd undo every bound spell you mages have set since the beginning of the world if I had time, but I'll settle for the biggest one." He didn't move.

I said urgently, "This is the end of your world either way. Do you choose to sacrifice and start over, or be destroyed still clinging to your old life?" I didn't want to have to force him.

Kaihan said, "If you are sure those are the only options, then loose the Beast, for he is no longer really needed." I opened the door, and raced past the drowsing door-mage, who lifted his head wearily. Behind me, Kaihan spoke a word and the outside door fell off its hinges. The door-mage started to his feet, shouting at Kaihan.

As I reached the ebony doors, they flung open of themselves, ripping free of the jamb, and behind them the brass doors followed. It was as if magic needed only my intention to work of llerself, as if I were only along to serve as hands and will to ller desire and energy. With both sets of doors open at once, the Room was as bright as the heart of the sun, a seething, molten, essential Mind. I didn't dare stop, but plunged through to open the far doors as well. The essence of the captive Beast flayed, scalded, scraped me, turned me inside out so that the raw surfaces were lifted to the scorching heat, but when my rush carried me to the door, and it opened, I burst forth into the exit hall unmarked but without my neckrings.

The same jade-ringed Magician was there as when I came through before, asleep on a bench but awakening and rolling up to stare half-awake at me. The door shattered soundlessly into fragments, and the unbearable glare flowed out, liquid crystal, quivering flame.

I kicked the Magician off his impromptu pallet, screaming, "Run! Get out of here, fool!" He backed away, slipping and stumbling, calling "Help! Help!" as I ran past him. Outside, Kaihan was standing there watching the disintegration, the melting of his fellowship's heart and center, as if warming himself by a fire. The substance of the Beast was swelling out of the building, bowing and bending the walls.

Kaihan said, "Where now?"

Two dreams had told me to look to the puppet-master, so I said, "The renegade who captured you in the forest. I hope he's still with Gelmas." Kaihan turned and ran, and I followed. Behind us, I heard a screeching tearing sound and a loud crack, and I knew the low building that had housed the Beast was broken. Debris clattered down all over us, and streams, gouts, cataracts of ller shot past and through us, ravening, craving, clutching, but not touching us.

We pounded into Seven Snakes, past the provisioners' wagons and the mage-servants on their way into work. It was still barely dawn. I was gasping for my breath, my legs felt leaden, and sweat was burning my eyes, but Kaihan raced ahead, his legs pumping smoothly like pistons. We entered the tiny garden square at the center of the mages' enclosed quarter, and Kaihan flung himself through Gelmas' white front door, the door slamming back against the wall like thunder. I came in behind him, and stood half bent over, my chest on fire, wheezing and gasping, as he shouted in a voice like a gong, "Gelmas! I have won the wager! Gelmas!"

I wheezed, "What?" and half stood up, panting still.

Gelmas was coming down the stairs, settling his robe about his scarecrow frame. His white hair stood half on end. Waspishly he said, "Never mind that, Kaihan, some wretch has loosed the Beast," as if Kaihan's crack-of-doom reappearance among the living were entirely to be expected.

I gasped breath in, and wheezed at him, "Gelmas, where's that renegade? Do you still have him?" He spared me a glance, then jerked his head toward the top of the staircase. Detter was coming down, followed by my quarry, who paused and paled when he saw me again. He was still wan and foolish-looking, with a multicolored bangle of a mage-ring about his neck. What was I going to do with him? How could I persuade him to help? The house was filling up with a seething flood of ller, swirling and lapping about my thighs and crawling up the stairs.

Kaihan said, "The Beast is gone, Gelmas, but I have won the wager. There *is* life behind the skies and it is coming to kill us *now.*" He sounded almost happy. Detter noticed his charge was dawdling, grasped him by the ear, and dragged him briskly forward.

Gelmas stopped, fastened the neck-catch of his robe, and said peevishly, "Where's your evidence, man?"

I said to Kaihan, "We've got to figure out a way to make that pasty outlaw geek up there link mages together without all of us going insane."

Kaihan said, "What?" in surprise and Detter said, "What?" in outrage. Gelmas just scowled, and said, "Who, Salki here? He's as close to useless as the tail on a pig. What are you talking about?"

"He can link mages together and somehow combine their Power and their minds. If we can get him to understand what we need and keep him from straying, we can join together—"

Detter, leaning at me and snarling, "Lise, you're such a fool!" must have inadvertently twisted Salki's ear further, for the new-minted Magician squealed in pain. Kaihan loped up the stairs past Gelmas and grasped the puppet-master by the shoulders, shaking him free of Detter.

The seething slurry of ller grew up over them like vines as Kaihan said gently to Salki, "Remember the forest and the palace?"

The young man nodded, smiling in relieved recognition, saying confidingly, "You were with me there." I could barely see them through the tangle of magic.

Gelmas said, "Will someone tell me what is happening?"

The walls were shifting and changing, slithering with spirit-fire jittering up and down around us. My Voices were yammering over the pounding of my heart. Kaihan said to Salki, "I can be with you again, and others as well—"

Detter said, "No!"

Salki nodded, placidly, trusting Kaihan, who said, "We need a larger space." They calmly proceeded down the stairs together, oblivious of the riot of power thrusting at them impotently, and walked out the front door.

"We don't have any time," I said to their backs, but they kept walking. The air, the ground, the buildings around us surged with elemental plasm, bright, hot, purposeful. We were the focus of a lens of magic. All the power in the world was forcing llerself into this tiny wedge of land.

I dithered, half-blinded, behind the two, saying, "Hurry, hurry, holy Mother, hurry," but they didn't move any faster, just walked to the square red granite building and up the wide ceremonial steps. The high rectangular door opened into a wide hall full of stone benches with a raised podium at one end. The room was bloated with magic, but Kaihan sat Salki gently down, took the young mage's head between his hands, and spoke to him in a low voice, Salki nodding earnestly all the time. I was dancing with impatience and fear, though I was deathly afraid of being swallowed up by Salki's spell. We all might end up like those ghostly people in the dark room, permanently lost in the pathetic mage's cage of a waking dream, but I remembered the tearing blue death of the Enforcers and how my mother had died. Kaihan linked one hand with

Salki's, and jerked his head at me to join them. Gelmas, dragging Detter, joined the chain, to my surprise.

"Look to her for guidance," said Kaihan to Salki. "She will know. Remember to look to her." The rabbit-cheeked boy nodded one more time, looking at me doubtfully. He wasn't going to do any such thing.

It wasn't until everything was well under way that I realized something changed at that moment. At the time, it seemed perfectly reasonable to think of myself as five small animals running around in one human-shaped skin. Salki was the head, Kaihan was a hand, Gelmas was another hand, Detter was a foot, and I was the other foot. I said, "Wait a minute, wait a minute," and squirted up the leg, while Salki ran in circles in the skull trying to find the way out. We tangled, squeaking and gasping, and Salki rolled and tumbled down the neck, while I stood on my hind legs and peered out through the eyes.

I looked down at our body. The skin, whatever reality it stood for, billowed and rippled like an unfilled hot-air balloon in a high wind, with squirming lumps pushing out where my partners were. We obviously needed more. This body was too empty otherwise. I said so to Salki, and he said, "We're coming." Now I saw we were indeed. A clot of twenty or so half-dressed mages were running to the central square, to alert the senior Wizards that calamity had befallen the Beast. As they entered, they came within the reach of the spectral grasp of the body, and were gathered in, cursing and protesting for only a moment. Suddenly I wasn't sure who the Lisane was or where the Lisane ended.

We'd felt clumsy and hungry before. Now we began to feel a wash of well-being as we filled out our form. It felt so good to be whole that we almost forgot what we were doing in the general glow. Somewhere in the mix of our mind, a ghost of Gelmas' sardonic, acid thoughts sent out irritating sparks of discontent, and we turned back to our task.

I turned our eyes outward, and scanned the city. There were still more mages sleeping in the sparsely settled quarter. It was, after all, still well before the time that normal people pried a gummy eyelid open. Our hands reached out. Kaihan and Gelmas teased the sleepers imperceptibly in, and the feeling of well-being flowed through us, a drugged bliss. No wonder Kaihan had been mindless when he left this meld. It must have been like leaving the womb.

The feeling of joy as we all joined together was indescribable, better than sex or a good meal, better even than thinking a new thought. We could spend years this way, exploring. . . . I shook our head ponderously, to wake ourselves up. Every time we added more mages to our body, the euphoria nearly overwhelmed us. Some of the squirming souls that made up the whole tried to drift further into intoxication, but the rest of us struggled and screeched, shoving them into place, I thought, like a fat woman adjusting her breasts. That particular mental image was unfortunate, for it struck most of us as funny and we sniggered distractedly for a few minutes.

This wasn't working well. I shook the head again, feeling like a mouse at the reins of a rubbish cart full of rats, and plunged farther out into the world to gather more stuffing for the body. The more mages that melted into us, the more difficult it became to stay focused. It shouldn't have surprised me so; I already knew that the mages preferred argument, speculation, and dissension to action of any sort. I called out anxiously. I wasn't sure anymore where Kaihan and Gelmas were. The metaphorical hands of the imaginary body continued to harvest new minds. Suddenly I found Kaihan and Gelmas again, and acid Detter joined us snarling at Salki.

We were locked together in the center now, and the Lisane's eyes opened for a moment to see that the original five people still sat relaxed in the chamber, while others walked casually in and sat down, or paced back and forth, looking abstracted. She shut her eyes again, reassured to see they hadn't actually all dissolved together.

We, I, our body, our self, stood up gradually until we straddled Sassevin completely like the giant of my dreams. We were staggering, lurching, arms and legs elongating and shrinking, wobbling and sobbing. There were too many bright ideas winking into existence every moment to remember what we were supposed to be doing. I understood why Salki's fantasy palace had so many rooms, all so different. I purely hated mages, and shook impotent fists at them all, while our imaginary arms still stretched out toward the horizon to touch and seduce more minds. It was going to fail.

Then, outside the limits of the city, an annoyed woman was dragged into the bond. "Mages!" she said, exasperated. "Always fiddling with things they should leave alone!" Then she realized what was going on, and in an instant our luck changed. She set down her pestle and mortar, wiped her hands on her smock, and concentrated. Suddenly, we began to grow exponentially. Every village and hamlet outside of Sassevin had its herb-wife, and every herb-wife stilled her hands and joined in with us, generally with something acid to say about mages. I finally realized what herb-wives were. The mages protesting and resisting, our body shimmered and jelled into something firmer, and a terrible practicality washed over the lurching giant.

We finally remembered to look up at the sky, and saw an absurd globe spiraling half the world away, a swollen ball of leaden ugliness, shoving itself with grudging labor and sharp blue knives through the clouds. The coarse orange skin of the ship was broken at senseless intervals by hatches, portholes, access bays, and patches where the skin had worn away and been replaced by other material. All around the ship, dead waves of blue fire chopped the ller-filled air into rotting fragments that drifted and swirled like paper ash after a fire. The ship of the Enforcers was moving toward us, carrying my people and wielding death.

We could hear ller crying, sobbing, as lle died. Lle was dying in enormous clots, murdered by the movement of the ship. Hastily, with a lurch and a desperate grab, we flung our arms over the whole world, reaching for every Talent revealed and hidden on the planet, and found our body-skin stuffed like a sausage to bursting. There was only one ringed mage for every ten Talents we found. Somewhere in the part of me that still existed, I laughed in delight. No wonder there were so few mages. Council's Finders found only the incorrigible children they were meant to find; the herb-wives took the others and raised them right, teaching them to leave magic well alone. They were smiths and weavers, mothers and fathers, laboring farmers and greasy tinkers. I had fallen in with the dwindling criminal set—and Kaihan said acerbically, "Where you belonged"—when Simon took me to the school.

Still swaying slightly, we stood over Sassevin, dwarfing the mountains to the north, feeling clumsy, satiated, and bewildered. The Enforcer ship had almost reached us, was just above the air. From a warm corner somewhere, we found the strength and structure to straighten up, and there, just outside the atmosphere, the ungainly, wretched ship spun weightily, beginning to make an arc downward. The Enforcers were coming right at us, and I hadn't the least idea of how to stop them.

The end that aimed toward us, I saw, held the drive, the thing that cut with knives. It was like an axle, keeping still while all else around it revolved, but it dragged the rest of the ship with it. In the center of that axle, a dark translucent bulge stuck out like a dead cow's eye with a cracked pimple on it. That was the place where the people had marched out when they landed. I wondered if the brutish crew was staring out of that eye, bored as ever, and if twelve thousand Mennenkalts still milled mournfully in the swollen cells of the ship or if they'd been exchanged for some other set of victims. All around the ship, deadly razors of blue essence crackled, like fissures in the skin of the universe. We reached out one hand tentatively to touch the ship, but with a shrieking blast of pain, twenty of us died in the touching. The ship didn't even swerve. How could anything with a soul use such a terrible force merely to move from star to star?

Windmilling our arms, we managed to maintain our balance, and, once steadied, looked around us for answers. We saw that in addition to the magic that made up the fabric of our body, there were worms, trailers, clouds of magic coiled over and around us like snakes, and more swimming to us from everywhere, even from the guts of the planet and from the airless void above us.

We shouted, most of us wondering what we were saying, "Bel genteren, lle sesselfer, lle palkertes, lle sesselsechern," and the magic wound llerself into strands, into ropes, into a cable with a tiny loop at the end, just the right size for a human body.

The Lisane stood up suddenly, took a step forward, and started to rise up into the air. Kaihan opened his eyes, and leaping up, grabbed her feet before she got out of reach, yanking her down harshly. She tumbled with a thud to the floor, mewing and gasping in pain. Kaihan turned casually and flung himself into the air like a bird, passing up and out of the building.

One of us physically put himself into the loop, which tightened gently around his waist. The Enforcer ship revolved slowly down toward us, like a ball thrown from a long way away, spiraling in excruciating slow motion. We grabbed the multicolored, coruscating cable of ller that coiled in the air around us, pulled one immense arm back, and put all our strength into a whip-stroke that flicked the cable, with the man in the loop, straight at the starred crack in the eye at the center of the ship. Just as lle reached the ship, lle braked just enough for the man it held to fling himself unharmed at the crack, the iris hatch that led to the drive. The end of the cable itself flamed, shattered, and died under the blades of blue that, dead and mindless, flailed about the ship.

The man, who knew what all of us could know about the ship, efficiently worked the outside control of the hatch and slipped inside. We couldn't see him anymore, because we couldn't see past the skin of the ship. We stared up at the abomination. We were waiting, an imaginary giant with hands upraised, an invisible skin with thousands of souls pulsing inside it, poised for final action or for death. The Enforcer transport still continued on its implacable arc, spinning closer and closer. It seemed the ship would splash through us like a rock through still water. We could track its trajectory, a hard clean line coming straight at us.

Then the blue went away. The ship began to fall freely, governed only by momentum and gravity, the still center suddenly revolving with the rest of it in an ungainly wobble that slewed the ship like a slowing top. Small struggling figures of men hurtled out of the central hatch, losing height and tumbling end over end. One of them was one of us.

Half of the captives aboard the ship suddenly became part of our union. They were indeed Mennenkalts, some sputtering about heresy and some just glad to be doing something, Jenneservet commenting sharply while lending a hand. We reached out one long, strong hand and grasped the powerless ship, guiding it gently in a powered fall to hilly land north of Sassevin.

Almost all our attention was on the ship, except for one shrieking, dancing, gibbering Lisane that caused us, as an afterthought, to reach out the other hand and catch the falling man in our cushioned palm. Most of us cared not at all for the individual minds that had come together to form our corporate self. Even the herb-wives were swept along into the grandeur of it all, and the rest had long since sunk beneath the surface. But the Lisane, screaming solitary in the center of the brain, wakened another mind, and Gelmas' voice, harsh and weary as a crow's, was added to the tiny dissonance.

The fallen man was still held in one immense cloud-hand. He looked around him for a moment, then ran to the edge and leaped off. Instead of falling, now he glided gently, down to the squat building far below him. We forgot his existence, forgot to bring him back in with us, engaged as we were in a desperate argument with ourself. Most of us wanted to continue our mass identity, intoxicated with the surge and flow of intention and agreement that animated us, but a very few were struggling against the tide, an angry herb-wife or two, a knife-sharpener, Detter drawling sarcastically.

Kaihan limped in the door of the hall and looked around. Every mage within walking distance had come into the chamber and was milling about among the benches. Salki, smiling, serene, stood in the midst of his enthralled subjects. The Lisane, Detter, and Gelmas were each surrounded by silent guards of mages, who moved only enough to keep them separate from Salki. Kaihan stepped into the room and began worming his way through the crowd. As he did, the Lisane opened her eyes with a tangible effort. Moving as if seeing double, extending her hands in front of her, she wriggled between two guards, then fell to all fours to scuttle away from them as they pursued her. Kaihan and the Lisane got to Salki together, the Lisane grabbing the boy by the legs and Kaihan grasping his shoulders, shouting into his ecstatic face. The other mages were plucking and pulling at them, their eyes still closed, like crabs at a carcass. Then Salki threw back his head in anguish and opened his eyes, flinging out his arms as if throwing something away.

I was on my aching knees as if praying, holding Salki's knees and staring up at Kaihan, when everything shrank back to normal. There was an appalled silence all around us. Several mages, finding themselves in the chamber with only the most tenuous and improbable memories of how they had gotten there, dashed for the door in panic. The others straightened and looked around, bewildered.

Kaihan, after imprisonment, insanity, pursuit, magical flight, destruction of the Beast, sabotage of the ship, and free fall from a crippled spaceship, was finally showing his age. His skin was flaccid, pale. He stood with eyes closed, breathing heavily, trembling, his shoulders slumped and sweat soaking darkly through his clothing. I didn't care. I wasn't sorry for him.

I said, "So you decided to play the hero again, did you?" His eyes jerked open, but he was too exhausted to move. "You decided it was all right for you to toss your life away doing something you didn't know how to do, just because you saw me doing it first? Blast your wrinkled hide, do you think you're expendable, fool? If you want to kill yourself again, kindly do it when nobody is depending on you."

Detter giggled crazily. "She'll kill you if you try to kill yourself again, Kaihan. You're warned." Gelmas casually smacked him across the face. The blond angel struck back at him like a snake, and the old man knocked him to the floor.

Kaihan was still staring at me, panting, exhausted, when the rest of the befuddled mages discovered a woman's presence in what was, apparently, Council Hall. The group had found something to focus their outrage on, and I was grabbed and flung down the steps outside, adding some juicy bruises to what was already going to be a major grape harvest. I dragged myself upright, limped to the little garden in the center of the square, and sat down on a bench. Inside the red hall voices began to rise. I figured the mages would be busy arguing for hours before they even got around to finding out what had happened, much less start think-

ing about what they were going to do with twelve thousand foreigners
and a handful of dreary Enforcers. Not that it mattered, for they weren't
nearly as important as they thought they were. Between the herb-wives,
the Mennenkalts, and wayward ller, everything would probably be settled
long before the mages finished shouting.

I heard footsteps. Gelmas swept up beside me and paused for a
moment, his hand on the back of the bench. I was surprised he wasn't
in there arguing. "Very impressive display," he said in his harsh, crowlike
voice. "I hope Kaihan is properly humbled." My face reddened, and I
looked down. "Who are the people held captive on that sky-ship? They
seemed very strange."

"They're my people," I said. "I was on that ship myself once."

"If they're all like you, we will have serious trouble."

I shook my head. "They're not like me. I don't even know what
they're really like." I sighed and shivered.

"I am going to get properly dressed and have breakfast," he said.
"When you are finished moping, come tell me what we will do about
these people of yours." He stalked back into the white house, his robe
flapping about him. His white hair still stood on end, I noticed. Tell him
what to do about my people? Moping? Senile bastard. To gehenna with
them all. My feet hurt. I took off my shoes and wriggled my toes in the
turf.

Somebody else's feet intruded into my field of vision. I looked up
involuntarily, and Kaihan was standing there with his hands on his hips,
looking at me. I squinted back at him, for the sun was shining in my
eyes. "What am I to do about you?" he asked sadly.

"Why don't you just leave me alone?" I said wearily.

"If that is your wish," he said. His voice was too quiet.

I stared up at him. "It matters to you."

He walked away from me. I got hastily up and jogged after him,
shouting, "Wait!" He kept walking, and started up the low smooth steps
of the black building before I could grab his arm. He shook it off impatiently and strode through the open doors, as I said wretchedly, "Kaihan, please," and Detter laughed behind me. I whirled, saw the
impeccable creature leaning against the side of the bench we'd just left,
his face shining with pleasure.

"The ingratitude of it," he said softly. "Poor little Lisane. But you're
going after the wrong man, you know. I've heard he had his troublesome
parts removed a long time ago. You'd find it very frustrating."

It was finally enough. Detter had finally won. I stood white-faced, speechless with rage. His eyes widened when he realized his victory, and as I bore down on him with my fists clenched he straightened up and laughed again, amazed. I swung wildly at his belly and he grabbed my arm. I hit him in the neck with my other hand and he grabbed that arm too, and held me easily away from him, smiling merrily and holding his sleek head cocked back from my struggles. I twisted and kicked against him frantically, but he was stronger than I and held me still. I finally stopped, my face twisted in a grimace and flooded with angry tears.

"Your nose is running," he said calmly. "You're not very good at this, Lisane." Then he looked past me in surprise as a pair of stronger hands grasped and pulled me away from him. I struggled to pull free from my new assailant, who said imperiously in a voice I could feel in my bones, "If you ever touch her again, I will flay you myself."

I learned something new right then—Detter was actually afraid of at least one person in the world, for he said hastily, "She struck me first, my lord," and took one step backward.

"Is this true?" said Kaihan sternly to me like a schoolmaster.

"Yes, and if you take your hands off me I'll do it again, you flatulent old goat," I said breathlessly, but Kaihan didn't let me go.

Instead, he said to me, "Have you no pride at all, to scuffle in the gutter with every little pig who wanders by?"

I screamed at the top of my voice, wrenched free with a strength that surprised me, and stood between the two of them, panting, my fists balled, looking back and forth at them both. Then I stormed at Kaihan, who stood with his hands on his hips again, and I shoved him in the chest with the heels of my hands. He rocked, and looked disgusted, but didn't do anything, so I shoved him again. He stumbled back slightly, not resisting, looking down his nose at me like an owl. I shoved him again, started to laugh like a madwoman, and buried my face in his neck with my arms flung around him.

He snorted, his abdomen shook convulsively against me, and he started to laugh himself. Fiercely he wrapped his arms around me and rocked me back and forth, saying helplessly, "I am too old for this."

I mumbled into the neck of his shirt. He stopped moving.

"What did you say?"

I gripped him tighter and turned my head to one side to speak more clearly. "I said I hate you. I hate you, I hate you, I hate you." He freed one hand, and gently turned my head up toward his. The fathomless black eyes, with the humorous creases fanning from the corners, were only inches away from my tearstained face. I felt surrounded, enclosed,

consumed by his embrace, and an exuberant and vulgar Voice chortled
that Detter had been quite wrong.

"Lisane, what would you have me do?" he whispered.

I told him. Kaihan bent a little, sighing, and those lips found mine.

Detter said from somewhere, "Do you still need an audience for
this performance, or can I go now?" I don't know whether he left then
or later.

OF SWORDS AND SPELLS

1
The Salute
(**Malka,** Indicating Intent)

The big dark room echoed with the silvery sound of moving feet and blunted weapons striking against each other. Light came in the high windows and got lost in the moving shadows below. All around the circle containing my teacher and me, the students moved back and forth in pairs, dancing with no music, trying to hurt each other. In the center, we stood still, facing one another, teacher and student, surly gorilla man looming over cantankerous monkey girl.

The sword-fighting lessons always began and ended the same way, with a salute. The Sefir Zul, his thick stiff hair standing on end, raised his glittering blade and touched his forehead with the flat, then swept it to one side with a hiss of divided air. I raised my practice sword to my brow in turn and swept it as grandly as if I were bigger than Zul, instead of half his size. I had been studying with the Sefir Zul for three years. *Let me do well,* I said inside my head, as gently as I could.

He did not speak himself, but only began to circle around me. The Sefir Zul never talked much anyway. Following his motion, I stepped sideways, facing him, inside the bouting ring painted on the dark wood floor.

He moved too close and dropped his hand a fraction of an inch too low, as if he were underestimating me, but I wasn't fooled. It was only a standard opening, the Ibrah Kohim, suitable for use against overaggressive opponents. I jerked my hand as if I were about to attack into it, the first variation to the Ibrah Kohim. In response, he pretended to cut at my arm, which would have been naked if I had really attacked. I feigned a flinch, and his real cut came on the other side. I had my weapon back where it was supposed to be, so his sharp edge bounced harmlessly off my bell-guard.

With his height he could have just reached over and whacked me on the head. Or maybe he couldn't; maybe I was good enough to stop him. Or he was lulling me into false security. Or maybe he wasn't.

That was one of the two things I liked best about sword-fighting: the carefully built layers of deception, the strenuous exercise of the mind at high speed, the lightning-fast decisions you had to make. The other thing I liked about sword-fighting was getting to hit people. I rarely got to hit Zul.

He drew back, circling me again. Zul's sword shone in the light. He kept it cleaner than he kept himself. The blade splashed light around the room like honey. Words, cut into the lustrous surface, flowed from the curved guard to the tip. I didn't know what they said. My own sword was a dull gray stick with an imaginary edge painted in white.

I watched everything and nothing, seeing him move smoothly for all his bulk, watching the small shifts in his hand position, feeling the changing angle of his weapon as if it were resting in my own hand, seeing the library of actions scroll past me unrealized.

I lifted my toe a little, as if I were about to make an attack. Zul began to take a half step back, as if he believed me: the first moves of a suite, one I dimly recognized. When my foot came down, he had changed the back step to a forward step and his hand was flying forward, but knowing he would do it, I spun my blade under and around, struck his blade to one side, and thrust my point toward his chest. He danced backward smoothly, pretending to be surprised, but I didn't bother to follow because from the rhythm of his steps I knew it was the fourth Aanandani variation and all the branches that followed from that ended in my defeat. We circled one another again.

He came forward again, light on his feet for such a big man, cutting to my head, but he intended a cut to the side instead. I was there, binding his blade with mine and levering past it to drive point first at his shoulder. He disengaged his blade sharply—

—and we were fighting at twice lesson speed.

We wheeled about each other, stepping in and out, in and out. I could feel my hand flying without thought to take the proper positions in each of the phrases: The Hand-Mihalek, the Meekum, Anthony's Stab, the Sideways Schnell. There was a name for every movement, for every pair of movements, for every combination and rhythm, and he had taught me every one himself. I could hear our blades striking against each other as if we were alone in the room. The Sefir Zul's stiff hair was jerking from side to side. He was red in the face, but then he always was. His hands and feet, as always, moved like those of a man admiring himself in the mirror, but for a change he wasn't watching the other students out of the corner of his eye. He was watching me. He was going to do something horrible again.

Well, I had nothing to lose. With Zul, I was never right, so there were endless possibilities for ways I could be wrong. I decided to try something. I increased the speed again. He followed the tempo change. All of a sudden, I was directing the lesson. He was following my moves. That had never happened before. Well, if I was in charge, I knew what I would do.

Cut, parry, feint, thrust, deceive the blade, step in, pretend to thrust again, and step out. It was a well-worn pattern he had taught me long ago, the Aegyptus. He would believe that I couldn't do anything complicated and go fast at the same time. He thought I was his student, his creation. He wouldn't be the first human to make that mistake.

Cut, parry, feint, thrust, deceive the blade, step in, pretend to thrust, and step out; his face looked bored, and I did it again. The third time, when I moved as if to make the predictable change-cut that was the first variation in the pattern, his blade was exactly where it had to be if he believed my lie, but I wasn't doing the Aegyptus anymore.

He was sure I would be. I had fooled him. So he missed me, because I wasn't there. Instead, I was striking him with a loud whack on the join between his shoulder and his neck. The whack was too loud. I realized the room was silent. His face red with anger—or was it astonishment?—Zul lifted his thick finger to acknowledge the blow, stepping back.

The skin where I had hit him was red, right between the grimy edge of his collar and the roots of his beard. A welt was already rising. He was going to have a dark blue bruise there, a big one. If I'd had a real sword with a real edge, I would have been looking down at him on the floor. There would have been blood. It was exactly what I had always wanted to do to him.

I was still holding my weapon out, ready for defense, but now I dropped it so that the tip touched the floor. "Sorry, sir," I said.

Then the whole side of my head felt as if it had blown up. He had slapped me with the flat of his blade. He didn't look angry anymore. Now he looked triumphant. "Is your opponent dead, troll girl?" he said with confirmed contempt. "Never drop your weapon until your opponent is dead."

I closed my eyes. Somebody in the back of the room snorted.

Zul went to the tall mahogany cabinet in the back of the room and reached inside. He came out with a neat pile of leather in his huge hands, and a long glittering thing lying on top of the pile. "Go away, Malka," he said, handing it to me. "I can do nothing more with you. You are done."

I took the pile in my arms, staring up at him in rage. He raised his blade and touched his forehead, brought the sword forward, then swept it to one side with a hiss. I put my practice sword in my other hand, lifted the glittering thing from the top of the pile, and swept it grandly back at him, looping it in a final flourish. Somebody else gave a tired laugh. Zul glared around him, the clatter and slide of practice started up again, and a student stepped into the lesson ring and faced the Sefir. As I turned and walked away, I heard him blow his breath out.

He was making me graduate, even though I wasn't done. There was more I wanted to learn.

There wasn't any ceremony besides the clothing. When Zul gave you your armor, whatever grade it was, you were finished. You put it on and went away and couldn't come anymore.

I walked stiffly back to the locker room, stuffed the cotton student armor in the laundry bin, and laid out my new gear to see what grade I had attained. I picked all the pieces up, one by one. I put them all back down, one by one.

This armor was soft, thin, and flexible. It was almost dusty-looking, not so rough it would catch a blade, supple but strong enough to turn a point. The helmet was no more than a cap. The plastron, carapace, and arm-guards were sewn together into a padded jacket with a collar. The leg armor was just trousers. It was armor that said its owner didn't need armor. It was armor just like Zul's, and I knew I deserved it, but there was something fishy. Zul would never grant Sefir rank to anyone if he could help it.

Since I had it in front of me, I tried it on anyway, pulling everything on over my black shirt and skins. The jacket's waist and shoulders fit me exactly. There wasn't anybody else as small as I in the school, so they must be mine. I felt wonderful in it, and I didn't want to take it off.

The sword was long, thin, sharp, and almost weightless. It caught the light with a watery gleam and sent small reflections skittering over the room. The gleaming guard swept over my knuckles when I grasped it, and the grip fit my fingers exactly. When I cut the air, it hissed. I put it in the back-scabbard and drew it a few times, listening to the sliding noise. The mighty Sefir Malka.

I put the cap on, tucked my curly black hair into it, and cocked it slightly. In the middle of the locker room, I stood in the on-guard position, my knees slightly bent, my back straight, my shoulders relaxed, and I drew the blade a few more times, cutting grimly at phantoms. Malka the monkey, fighting back! I could smell the leather. I closed my eyes and shuffled over to the full-length mirror at the end of the locker room, banging into the benches on my way and feeling along the fronts of the lockers. I wanted to surprise myself.

I opened my eyes. There I was. It was a surprise, all right. The surprise was, I was still Malka, still a small maiden with big wide eyes. From the neck down the image in the mirror was a mighty sword-fighter, the way a scale model looks like the real thing. Every detail was perfect, but I looked like a doll in a costume, or a dressed-up cat. At least I didn't have big furry ears and dainty whiskers.

I made a snarling face at myself in the mirror, and laughed. No matter how fiercely I squinted, my eyes were round and clear. Even when I glowered, my brow just crinkled. I felt as if I were scowling, but the scowl looked like a sulk on my rosebud mouth. A Malka doll in a sword-fighting costume. Grr. Ha.

Zul's joke was a nasty one, but if he had given the stuff to me it was mine. I would go wave my sword at him like the performing monkey he obviously thought I was, and then I would march out of the school, I would keep the armor, and Zul could boil his head. I screwed my face up, stuck my tongue out at my image, drew the sword, and strode back into the hall.

And stopped. There, in a perfectly staged scene, was my next-to-worst nightmare.

A man in the orange uniform of a Web Witchfinder, an Enforcer, was standing there talking to Zul.

2

The On-Guard Position
(**Igor's Crouch,** Facing an
Unfamiliar Opponent)

I *am not here,* I said.

Zul towered over the man like a small mountain. His hair was standing on end again.

"It doesn't do you any good to deny it," said the Forcer, taking a step back with a puzzled expression. Zul's bath habits had that effect on people. The Forcer was another Caliban, of course, a short bland echo of Zul, with quill-like black hair and broad cheekbones. Most Enforcers, Web-wide, were Calibans. The personality was suitable.

"I have no need to protect against witches," said Zul with fine contempt. "You people protect me. Correct?" Only Zul, I thought, would dare talk to an Enforcer that way, but even Zul needed to watch his step.

The Forcer's face didn't move for a moment after Zul's breath hit him. "Correct. Yes. My point exactly," he said finally. "In fact, a witch could hide in the shadow your machine is creating. This is why they are forbidden. So please turn it off and hand it in." He talked in a clumsy, formal way, as if he were reciting. He looked afraid of Zul.

Zul's face didn't change. He didn't repeat himself for his students, and he wasn't going to repeat himself for a government flunky who was interrupting his work.

"You don't understand, sir," continued the Forcer when he realized he had to do all the talking. "There's a huge hole in the flow of magic around your school, a blank spot like a whirlpool. Our detectors are accurate. We know you have a strong magic suppressor."

"You know nothing," said the student who had been taking the lesson after mine, and I didn't even see Zul's hand move, but there was a thin red line on the student's cheek and he was flinching, too late.

"Go look," said Zul to the Forcer, gesturing widely. "No magic suppressor." He turned his back and saluted his student, who sullenly saluted him in turn, the thin red line getting thicker, a red droplet forming at his chin.

Zul was right. There wasn't any machine sucking the magic out of his school. There was a blank spot, though, and it was me. I had better take myself and my blank spot away, and my new sword and armor while I was at it. Time to leave another world. If Enforcement had tracked me down, my long-lost master would be close behind, humming a little tune and carrying a small sharp knife. *I am not here. You cannot see me,* I said carefully inside my head, feeling the thin wash of my words like the last slide of a wave across sand. *Not here.*

The Forcer was still just standing there, as if waiting for a cue. Everybody was still just standing there. I went to the heavy entrance door, and turned the knob. The door opened silently and smoothly. I stepped forward through the widening gap, and I did not run. Very important not to run.

The cobbled street outside was thick with people, as always, and all of them were armed and dangerous, or else just plain dangerous. Zul's was one of ten weapon schools on the block, in a martial arts district, in a city of trained fighters, in a world that provided security guards, soldiers, and Enforcement employees for the whole inhabited Web, all of the Thousand Worlds. I slid into the flow of people walking. Between the shoulders I could see a woman in orange standing beside a gray van. There was a single orange stripe running along its side, and a round logo that said ERC in the center and "Enforcement, Regulation, Control" in neat orange letters around the circumference. It was more serious than I'd thought. The Forcer had brought backup.

The woman moved her head on her neck, peering between the pedestrians. *I'm not here,* I repeated silently, gently—at least gently enough. She obligingly didn't see me. I walked past her, not hugging the building, not moving too close to her, not looking at her, not looking away, not running, fitting in with the crowd.

Behind me, Zul's door thudded open, and there were footsteps above the crowd noise. The Forcer jogged by, swinging his head from side to side to stare at the people he passed. Three gray vans striped with orange bumped past in the road.

"What does she look like?" called the driver of the third van, loudly, leaning out his window. The first Forcer said, just as loudly, "Tiny. Tiny little thing. Short dark hair. Wearing black."

The crowd of people had slowed. They were staring at the vans, and listening to the conversation. All I could see in front of me was shoulder blades. I turned and worked through the mob the other way, trying not to bump into anyone. On Caliban 5, you didn't jostle people. You could get yourself killed. That was one of the reasons I liked it so much here. I always felt safer when I didn't have to pretend to trust anybody. I was going to miss it. I was going to miss the Sefir Zul, smell and all. I was going to miss the hostile, mocking students. I was going to miss my silent days in the school, and my solitary, simple nights.

I stood and breathed at a less busy intersection. Three more gray vans turned the corner and rolled past me, heading back the way I had come. *Don't see me,* I begged, trying to look taller, but their drivers didn't even notice me . . . *The skin where I hit him is red, right between the grimy edge of his collar and the roots of his beard . . .* I had dropped my weapon and apologized for hitting my sword-master. What had happened to me? I had never regretted hurting anyone, ever. No time to think about it.

I walked another block to the subway, and stopped, muttering, *I'm somewhere else* inside my head because in the subway entrance a man was standing at the top of the steps, watching the crowd, holding an instrument in his hand. The patch on his orange jumpsuit read ERC. People went past him down the stairs, not looking at him until they were past. Even on Caliban, it paid to be afraid of Enforcement. Though the Sefir Zul was an exception; I didn't know why.

The Enforcer didn't see me, but I didn't dare go past him. I would have had to bespeak him too *loudly* if I wanted to squeeze past him down the stairs. People noticed if I got too *loud.* I walked past, threading my way among the people. I realized I was walking toward the nearest Web terminal, as if I were a rabbit running down the center of the road in front of traffic. Not a good idea. It would be better to do what I had planned, to go across the continent to the terminal in the next state. They wouldn't be looking for me there. I could slip into the Web and disappear again.

But back behind me I saw another gray van rolling into the intersection. I couldn't go back that way. I shuffled from foot to foot on the corner, then plunged on toward the antiques district. Tobiah might help me. Even if he couldn't, I needed to warn him. All these Forcers couldn't be here just for one little blurry spot in the current of magic. There must have been another conspiracy in the Web, another wiped planet somewhere, and it was tough-on-witches week in the Enforcement head offices again.

The street where Tobiah sold his clocks was full of trees, hedges, and small stuffy stores, their woodwork picked out in dark colors and gold leaf, their windows each displaying one perfect object, usually an antique weapon. Tobiah's shop was an exception; in his window was a great round clock with its face inlaid in Lorimer gweneal-wood, so that you saw the deep patterns in the natural grain before you realized the separate pieces of the inlay formed a mosaic themselves, a bearded face in an armored helmet, with staring eyes and with wrinkles fanning out across the cheeks. I trotted up his stairs and swung the door open.

As usual, Tobiah sat behind the high wooden desk, surrounded in the dimness by softly clicking clocks. His round pale face was calm, his straight wood-colored hair was neatly combed, and his soft nimble hands were folded on each other in front of him. Next to him on the desktop was his familiar spirit. Tobiah's familiar was a clock, of course, a gleaming brass-bound ebony box with brass claw feet and an ivory moon-face. Every witch I'd ever met had a familiar, but every familiar was different, unfamiliar. "Tobiah," I said.

Tobiah didn't stir. He looked through me, or rather he looked at nothing. His smooth face didn't stir. His paper-thin eyelids didn't quiver.

"Hey," I said. Silence. His milky blue eyes regarded some nonexistent spot in the middle distance. Tobiah was always so calm, as if he had all the time in the world. He might have the time, but I didn't.

I cracked the door open behind me. Down in the street, several people were hustling along, looking behind them, and following them came a line of Forcers, turning their heads back and forth, back and forth.

I backed away and let the door close gently. "Tobiah," I said. "Tobiah. Enforcement is on its way. We have to go." Nothing. "Tobiah, *move,*" I said, raising my voice and putting force into it.

He blinked.

Tobiah.

His upper lip got sweaty, tiny beads revealing themselves like the mosaic in the gweneal-wood clock.

I waited, but he didn't budge. Paralysis, magic, force field, I didn't know what, but he was frozen. *Tobiah, Tobiah, move,* I said, pulling at his hands. His mouth opened but made no sound, and he fell off his stool. I didn't know if it was my imagination that he looked annoyed for a moment, but when he rolled onto his back, his eyes were still looking into the middle distance, pale blue smudges. A trap, a trap. Tobiah was bait in a trap.

I ran to the back of the store. My sword got stuck in the doorway. I'd forgotten I had it. I had to back up and go through again. I wormed my way through the piles of boxes and old clock cases in the back room, my sword banging into things on either side of me, and found the back door. I wriggled out and slammed the door behind me. *Hidden, hidden.* Behind me a door opened, and there were footsteps, but the alley behind the shops was clear—no, there was a van idling at one end. I scuttled the other way. Three streets over I found myself walking in the direction of the local Web terminal again.

As I walked, my new sword banging against my back and sweat running down my skin under my new armor, three vans came up the hill in a smooth rush, one after another, the orange stripes on their sides flowing past me, the eyes of the drivers fixed ahead of them. I kept walking.

The Web terminal was at the top of a rise, the tops of the main building and the tops of the parked ships peeping above the low sandstone wall that circled the crest of the hill. The entry road to the gate was the only break in the close-cropped lawn surrounding the wall and rolling down to the wide swampy ditch at the bottom of the hill. The agents could see everyone approaching the terminal. There was a glint of light from the slit window nearest to me above the wall.

No one important is coming up the road.

The glint of light flashed out.

I walked through the sandstone gate into the main terminal building. Inside the doors, the station waiting room was crowded, and all the benches were filled with armed people, their luggage piled around their feet. Trained Calibans could get work anywhere on the Web as mercenaries, guards, and martial arts instructors. But there were figures in orange standing at every door. I turned around and a man in orange was moving into place beside the one I had just entered, though he didn't seem to have noticed me. I walked to the other side of the terminal as slowly as I could.

The entrance into the shipyard was a pair of doors with a high stone arch above them, guarded by a Forcer. He stood a few feet before it with his arms folded, looking bored. He was too close to the door, but there was only one of him. *Oh, please move over. Oh, please don't see me.* He unfolded his arms and put them behind his back, rocking back and forth. *Just a little to one side.* He began pacing in front of the doors, still with his hands behind his back, and then while I held my breath he walked over to one side of the doors and leaned against the wall, closing his eyes. *That's it,* I breathed to myself. My whole head felt waterlogged with all the bespeaking. Rivulets of magic surged from side to side behind my eyes. It wasn't good to stir the currents like this. I would have to find a safe place and be still for a week to settle the tides afterward.

I walked up to the doors, past the Forcer. The doors were heavy, but I opened them slowly, and slid through the crack. I eased them shut but let go of them too soon. They thudded gently against each other. I darted to the right, flattened myself against the wall, and froze. *Bump on the wall. Part of the wall.* "Hey!" the Forcer shouted, and he shoved the doors open again, glaring from side to side suspiciously.

"What?" said a woman's voice from the other end of the building.

"Nothing. Could be the midget, could be the wind."

"This is so stupid," she said. "I didn't sign up to play his games. It's all a game to him. Boxes inside boxes inside boxes."

The first Forcer didn't answer, just went inside again. Whose games?

I peeled myself off the wall. I jogged between the lines of parked ships, my scabbard banging on my back and reminding me how sweaty I was. Funky little Malka. I never used to sweat, back when I was smaller. I was changing too much.

Every other ship I passed was Enforcement, with the orange logo painted on the side. I couldn't use those. They had the chilly new killer engines, the black-matter ones you didn't need to be a witch to drive. A black-matter engine would slice me up or blow me away if I walked into it. Even this far outside them, the Enforcement ships made me feel cold when I walked by.

Here was a civilian ship, a white cube with a blue-and-yellow logo. It gave off a warm smell of natural magic. I walked all the way around it, but it was locked, the cargo hatch was closed, and it didn't even have any scratches in the paint. I knocked on the main entrance but nobody came.

I jogged on. Another ship farther down looked less carefully maintained and I had my hopes, but it was locked up, too.

Something quiet drove by in the access lane behind the ships and I saw a flash of gray and orange and the shadow of a head in the driver's seat. *Don't see me.* I had to hurry. This was the most dangerous time, when I was actually at a terminal. This was where the Forcers could catch me, this was where my sharp-smiling master could find me. People kept records at terminals. I jogged on.

After a row of Enforcement jitneys, there was another ship, all angles and shadows. I moved toward it, slowing down as I approached, staring up at it in recognition. When I was little, the houseboat was a fashionable model, and this one looked exactly like the ship my thin-fingered master and I hid on when we left Forest. This one was made of white-painted wood, and it had a porch and shutters, and a paneled front door. The front door had a brass knocker, there was a mailbox next to it, and it looked like someone's weekend cottage.

I walked up to the front door. It was closed, but I put my hand to the knob anyway.

The door swung open in my face. The man inside was just as surprised as I was. He looked down into my face. Then he smiled with delight, a sweet smile. "Come in," he said. He was good-looking in a sad dark way, and very lifelike. His eyes, fringed with astonished black lashes, were the color of river water flowing over white sand. I recognized the model. He had been an expensive android, once upon a time.

He stepped back, holding the door open for me, but I didn't move forward. "Pleased to meet you. I'm Roder Massim," he said. Even his first name was old-fashioned, the name of a cinestar in the first part of the century. People all over the Web named their boys Roder then, but it was a joke name now, a grandfather's name.

I still didn't move. I didn't bespeak him. I was too close, and he would notice.

He held his hand out as if to touch me on the arm, then paused before his fingers reached me. He pulled his hand back and put his arms behind him. Very perceptive. I hated having people touch me. "And you are a witch," he said.

I shook my head. Out of the corner of my eye I could see orange people moving into the open. They were small in the distance, but they were coming.

"Yes, you are," he said. "You are a wandering patch of fog on my instruments. You are a blurry spot in the porch scanner. They are complaining about you on the Enforcement communications channels. I like that. Come in before Enforcement decides to help me with you. I hate it when they're helpful. What's your name?"

He stood waiting, looking polite and sad and clear-eyed. So I did not answer him, but I came in and let him shut the door behind me. Anyway, he wasn't killing me just yet, he didn't smell as bad as the Sefir Zul, and he wasn't my little dead-eyed master.

The Extension of Blade (**Blessed Shanahan,** To Convey Potential Threat)

Inside, it wasn't what I expected. It was dark, shabby, and cool, and it smelled of wood and dry leaves, and of the things that live in old upholstery. The ship I stowed away on so long ago had been bright and very clean, and it smelled of nothing at all.

The floor creaked under my feet. My eyes didn't adjust to the dark right away, because the only light came from the door Roder was already opening for me farther down the hall.

I walked toward him, trailing one hand along the wall of the corridor, which felt smooth and damp. Both walls were plaster-white and lined with wood-framed doors, all closed. Each door had a tarnished brass number on it. Beneath each number was a brass frame, holding a card with a hand-lettered label. The card on the fourth door to the right said ENGINE ROOM, NO ENTRY in faded blue, and I couldn't see any lock on it, but the deep warm smell behind it told me there was a fine big drive there.

The other cards had people's first names on them. It looked like a dilapidated guest-cottage inside as well as outside.

He sucked his chest in so I could get past him into the room. He had on a loose shirt and trousers in a weathered woven fabric, and the top of my head came to the middle of his rib cage. That made him medium height for a man.

"You can stay here. The woman who had it has left," he said, pulling bleached cotton curtains aside and lifting the heavy sash of the window at the head of the bed to let in sunshine and a pale breeze. The bed, the wardrobe, and the chest of drawers were of honey-colored wood. Across the room was a desk of the same wood. The room smelled like starch and soap and pine trees. The window looked out through the black arms of an enormous pine tree and down a long sloped pasture to a wooded stream. I could see the water flowing, and a crow called from the sky. There was no stream at this Web terminal, no woods, no pasture. I'd never seen a crow on Caliban, or a pine tree.

Roder's ship was bigger on the inside than it was on the outside.

You could do that with magic. I did it myself. Magic was indifferent to the concept of space. To magic, everything was in the same place. But it would take a bigger engine than this houseboat should have to maintain this scenery.

He stood with his hands behind his back still, watching me. I supposed he was waiting for me to say something, but I'd said what I had to say, which was nothing at all. He raised his eyebrows. Somebody banged at the front door. He ignored it, but the banging came again. "Excuse me," he said, and walked out, closing the chamber door.

I went to it immediately, but it was locked. I was stuck here.

Footsteps went past in the hall. I knelt on the pillow at the head of the bed and leaned over the windowsill. The branches of the pine tree brushed against the house's walls on either side of me. There was a sky above me, and the ground, a bone-pale carpet of dry needles, was right about where you would expect the ground to be below a first-story window. The wall felt warm in the sunlight and cool in the shadows of the tree branches. Flakes of paint fell to the ground when I brushed them off the wall. This ship looked as if it should be condemned, but an internal space-fold pocket this big would draw enough power from the engine to light a small city.

Enormous power, but no money for repairs to the walls and floors in the corridor, no money for paint.

I leaned farther, looking out. The door clicked open behind me. I pulled back and banged the back of my head and the hilt of my sword on the window sash on the way in.

Roder said from the doorway, "I'm sorry. I startled you. I meant to tell you, don't lean too far out the window. It's too high to reach from outside if you fall. My new employees are always getting stuck outside, and you're shorter than most."

I was his new employee, was I?

A woman squeezed past him in the hall. She didn't glance into the room. Roder left the door open and followed her. Four more people came past, carrying someone whose arms dangled down and whose head dangled back. His head flopped to one side as they passed my room. His eyes were open in his round pale face. He didn't see me. It was Tobiah. He looked dead, and I guessed I would be next, no matter what the android said.

There was only one thing I could do now, what I had always done when I couldn't run instead. I was crouched on the bed with my hand on the hilt of my sword, so I climbed down off the bed and went to the open doorway, drawing the sword as quietly as I could.

"There," said Roder to someone, coming back down the hall. "That's it. Go ahead." Down the hall a door opened and closed, and I could hear his footsteps coming toward my room.

The moment he was within distance, not before, I whipped my new blade around and sliced through him.

Well, I would have sliced through him if he had been there.

Somehow, he didn't finish taking his last step, so I cut through the space in front of him instead, hearing the blade hiss through the air. He didn't look frightened. His face was calm.

When I realized the cut had missed, I took a pace forward, changed the angle of my hand, and swung again. I would have hit him this time if he had stayed where he was, but as I took my step, he drew away, as smoothly as the Sefir Zul. The tip of my sword skimmed the air in front of his shirt, not even rippling the weave.

When I saw the point passing him, and saw him move forward and raise his hand, I was already moving backward, cutting the point of my weapon at the back of his extended hand to make him stop. He didn't stop. Instead, he circled his hand at the last moment and grabbed the flat tip of my sword. His fingers were like a vise.

I struggled with him for an instant, then let go and ran backward down the hall, yanking the front door open. I was facing the backs of two Enforcers on the front doorstep. They started to turn, hands to their guns. I closed the door and put my own back up against it.

Roder hadn't moved. He just stood there with the tip of my sword between his fingers, still calm, still sad and vague. The guard of the weapon bounced up and down, up and down, catching the dim light in the hall.

Roder said, "Here, take it. I don't want it." He paused. "That boy you saw is still alive, by the way, and we weren't the ones who hurt him."

I took one step forward. He didn't move. I took another, and another. When I had my hand on the grip, he separated his fingers. He put his hands behind his back again.

My blade was unsheathed, and he was so close even he couldn't get away if I decided to thrust. Never drop your weapon until your opponent is dead, Malka. We stood facing each other in the dark hallway. I could see his chest rising and falling with his breathing. I didn't know androids had to breathe, though of course they would. They weren't really humans, but they were grown like humans. Besides, I wasn't human either, and I breathed.

Now he looked faintly interested.

I had studied sword-fighting for three years now. I was a professional killer.

Roder was waiting to see what I would do, his fringed sad eyes wider than before.

Please, I began, and then didn't know what to say. I closed my eyes and then opened them again. His expression shifted, as if something had happened, though I hadn't moved, and then he sighed and rubbed his face with both hands and turned away. He hadn't been so sure I wasn't going to kill him after all.

He didn't stick around to gloat. He walked away and went through the door at the end of the hall.

While he was going, I whacked my lovely new sword against the wall next to me, so that little pieces of plaster pattered down on the floor, and I stamped my foot as I did it, and then struck the wall again with my fist, making a wordless noise. What was happening that I couldn't kill an unarmed opponent? I unstrapped the helmet from my head and threw it on the ground. I jumped on it and kicked it. I was going to throw my sword down on the ground and jump on it too, but it was too pretty.

Then I picked up the helmet, dusted it off, and stuck it back on my head. I wiped the dust off my sword with my arm and sheathed it. I strode to the door and flung it open.

He was standing at a counter with his back to me, and he didn't turn around. The room was large and square with a yellow pine table in the center, thick sturdy chairs all around it. A row of china mugs sat on the windowsill, and a gray cat was beside them; it poured itself out the window when I came in. Outside the window was a walled garden, with a stone fishpond in the corner. The thick grass was wild and seedy, and there were pale green vines winding up the stone walls. More space-fold scenery. More threadbare display of power.

I yanked a chair out and sat, scowling.

Roder brought a large steaming bowl over to me, carrying it carefully. It held rice and beans and a thin fragrant red sauce. I stared at the pinhead-sized flowers that floated in the sauce. My head felt empty except for a faint image of my master hunched over a bowl just like this, watching me go hungry while he ate.

He said, "Those flowers are spices. They won't poison you. They're from a world where all the people look like you. Eat up. Then I'll introduce you to the others."

The spices were veronicas, and they didn't grow anywhere anymore, and nobody looked like me anymore, not since Enforcement wiped Forest. Most people didn't know what Foresters looked like. There weren't any of us around anymore and they don't teach the history of wiped worlds. All of us were small, though few as small as I. Foresters were all slight and dark with black eyes and quick hands, and with a taste for the sour veronica in their sweet bean dishes, and all the Foresters were dead, all of them, except for my master who left them all to die.

"Is the sword your familiar?" asked Roder.

Startled, I looked up at him, then at the hilt of my sword. "No. I'm not a witch."

That was enough conversation. I picked up the wide spoon and dipped it into the soup. He had gotten the taste just right, and the texture of the veronicas. I swallowed. He was old enough to have met some Foresters, if I had the year of his manufacture right. I met his eyes and took another spoonful. *Go away and leave me alone,* I urged him.

He smiled and left the room. He knew he had me where he wanted me. He knew exactly how nice the smile was, too, even with all his sadness. Or maybe it was boredom, not sorrow.

The gray cat jumped in and landed on the windowsill again, freezing with her legs bent and her wide eyes fixed on me. There was something about her eyes.

"Hello," I said to her.

The cat hissed back. In words. "Mine," she said. She angled her whiskers forward when she spoke, and moved her mouth in a way that was distinctly uncatlike. She sounded rusty. She was somebody's familiar, starting to fade. Her creator must have died.

"Mine," she insisted.

"Yours," I agreed. "Your ship. Keep it. I don't want it."

I didn't want any of it. I wanted to be able to kill my enemies. I wanted to be a mighty sword-fighter. I wanted to know what that android saw with those eyes. I wanted to know what was going on, and why Enforcement would decide to make me land on melancholy Roder Massim's doorstep. I took another mouthful in the meantime, saluting the room with my spoon. Malka the Mighty, Nemesis of Soup.

4

The Intentional Pause (**Ram Dass,** For Appraisal of Opponent)

"**G**ood heavens," said a voice from the kitchen doorway. "So small! How old are you?"

I wiped my chin. The owner of the voice was a woman with an expectant smile, holding a smooth, round pink-nosed animal the size of an orange in her nervous hands. I put my spoon down.

She came in and pulled a chair out, sitting sideways with her knees together, placing the animal on the table and keeping it from running with her hand. Her long dark hair was wound into a multiple knot at the back of her head, making her long oval face even longer. She rippled her fingers over the top of the animal in an odd motion. "Welcome. I'm Electra. What's your name? What's your Talent? What's your story?"

She had white lines tattooed on her neck, too. I kept looking at her until she shifted and leaned back, still moving her fingers restlessly over the smooth surface of the animal. The motion made me want to hit her, or to get up and go to the other side of the room. She was a witch, then, and the animal was her familiar. It blinked at me with eyes pinker than its nose. I blinked back *hello* and it shut them.

"Oh, I'm sorry, I suppose I'm being awfully forward. But welcome to the ship anyway. I'm sure you'll tell us all about yourself when you're ready. Has Roder shown you your room? You can change the decor any time you like, you know, you don't have to stay with it, the ship may be old but it was luxurious in its time. The room used to belong to a very nice girl, a very nice girl indeed," she said with emphasis, though I hadn't contradicted her. Interesting. "Her name was Akamai. She liked the country look, but everyone can't have the same taste, now, can they? You look like you would, let me see, you would like tile floors, and sandalwood furniture, and those lovely old-fashioned grass-mat screens. Am I right?"

My master's house. The feel of cold tile on my bare feet, the aroma of the fragrant wood pervading the house, and the hushed rooms with those soft woven walls and the yellow sand reaching out in every direction outside. I remembered my master's dog Bear, too, his nails clicking on the floor, his yelps when my master pinched him or cut his skin, but she didn't mention the dog. She didn't know. All it meant was Roder had told her I was from Forest. Push, push, she was pushing on me. I could feel it.

"Or perhaps not," she finished amiably. "But I'm chattering on, as usual. What would you like to know? How can I help you? You'll be wanting to know the name of the ship, and what Roder does, and who the rest of the crew is, and why he recruited you, of course—"

How could I stop her? Something that would make her uncomfortable. "Akamai?" I said. The girl who had my room before me, whose name she had said with such false affection.

Her dark eyes went darker, and so did the rest of her face, and her fingers stopped moving for a moment. In the space, I could take a breath. She'd been smothering me.

The cat, still perched on the windowsill, said, "Aaaaaa-kaaaa-maiiii," in a long low call.

"Oh, stop it!" said Electra to it, and it jumped out the window. The woman's mouth was tight, and her fingers still weren't moving.

"Electra, thank you. Let it be," said Roder from the doorway. He stepped in and laid his hand on her shoulder, and she briefly leaned her head against his arm. It made his sad face sadder.

"She asked me about Akamai," she said.

"Ah." He said to me, "Akamai decided to leave the ship without permission. You saw those two when you opened the door? We have an arrangement with Enforcement, but it ends on the outside of the ship. Unless we're on official business."

I waited, evaluating the implied threat, thinking about the way Electra was pursing her lips in disagreement as he spoke. She lowered her eyes. She laid her familiar back in front of her on the table, and fluttered her fingers again. He squeezed her shoulder and let go. "Electra is our interviewer," he said.

Other people began to come in.

The first was a slender boy with a black ponytail. He glanced at me sideways as he came in, not exactly flirting, just sizing me up, a wide-eyed stare like a cat's. An Alcibiadan party-favor just past employment age, he didn't look like any Polytechnic graduate I'd ever seen, but Roder, absently running his fingers over the ponytail, introduced him as "Octavian, our communications officer." Octavian, unperturbed by Roder's caress, ghosted to the table and sat cross-legged in one of the chairs. He continued to watch me as if he thought he must know me from somewhere.

A very tall man with a large head and wide-spaced eyes followed him in, ducking to clear the top of the door. He held a loop of amber beads in one huge fist, and bobbed his head at me kindly. He was definitely a Calypsan priest, one of the People of the Hands. But he was "Cully, our cryptographer," according to Roder, who stroked his shoulder as he passed. Whatever the arrangement Roder had with Enforcement, it let him hire non-Polytechnic witches to run his boat.

They came in the door and Roder, touching each one gently, introduced them and their jobs: Octavian the communications officer, Cully the cyptographer, redheaded Fergus the engineer, brown Pegeen the navigator, toothy Wladyslaw the archivist, gray Julia the cybernalist, and Electra the interviewer with her animal. They were as different from one another as if they'd been taken from their home worlds only the day before.

They all sat around the table, leaving spaces empty, and the room was awash with the warmth of bodies, the creaks of chairs, and the shifting of feet. They were looking at Roder, faces too open and trusting, waiting for something. Electra continued moving her fingers over the skin of her pet, which was bulging its eyes at me.

I felt as if I were struggling to breathe in the thin flood of magic that was drooling all over me. I stood up abruptly, pushed my chair in, and leaned back against the wall. Now they were looking at me instead of Roder, but I didn't care. I didn't want to be a part of that large warm fuzzy group. *Get on with it.*

"Folks, this is our new shipmate," said Roder. "Don't expect her to tell you anything. Electra didn't get anywhere." I heard a couple of inhalations.

"Doesn't look like the Forcers damaged her much," said Pegeen the navigator, whose hair was knotted in furry spirals that made her dark brown skin look like carved wood in comparison. She wore gold-framed eyeglasses. Except for the glasses, which you didn't see much except as jewelry, she looked like an Afrigael businesswoman.

Roder answered for me when he saw I wasn't going to say anything. "Enforcement promised and delivered the young man in the stasis tank, who may or may not be the chronologer we were looking for, and who is certainly damaged. No, this young lady apparently arrived on her own. I only knew she was here because they were talking about her on the channels, trying to track her down. She tells me she's not a witch."

They all laughed, a big warm sound, and I pressed my shoulder blades back against the wall. Nothing more dangerous than the confident innocent. Did he really think I had come here by accident? I'd been herded every inch of the way by Enforcement. Electra squeezed her animal more tightly, staring at me. The animal made a grimace and the pressure increased.

"Don't be frightened," said Roder. "You're safe here."

I bared my teeth at them all. Malka the Savage and Ungrateful Captive.

"Oh, she's not going to tell us anything, I don't know why I'm bothering," said Electra, and let go of the familiar, putting her hands down either side of it while it shook itself and started furiously licking one front paw.

I took a deep breath and sat back down. I was all right now. When witches went to work on me, they sucked the air right out of my lungs, the water right out of my sea.

"I don't know about you people, but I'm hungry," said Cully firmly into the confused silence, and the room slipped into chatter and motion. Roder went to the refectory niche and began handing out platters of food, and the toothy man called Wladyslaw distributed silverware, smiling at me shyly when he gave me mine.

The slim Octavian was still staring at me. He opened his mouth to say something, but Wladyslaw nudged his shoulder and handed him a spoon and the moment passed.

Cully, seated to my right, reached his long arms out to snare a plate, still holding his amber beads in one hand. He offered me a plate of things that looked like tiny rabbit ears, and I shook my head. I laced my fingers together under the table and watched them eat. My armor was hot and uncomfortable, even if it was soft for armor, but that would help keep me alert in this fuzzy cloud of kindness, good food, magic, and interplanetary coziness.

There was a Calypsan and an Alcibiadan, and Fergus, the engineer, was Matrish. I thought Electra was a Murikino. Wladyslaw the archivist had that pale Slavic face with large teeth that could have been Copernican or Szycielist, while Julia could only have come from one of the nontechno prudish worlds of the Gray People. Yet Julia held the highly skilled job of cybernalist, and she was definitely flirting with Octavian, who had forgotten me and watched her with half-opened eyes as if she were wearing a few scraps of glitter. His other arm was draped over the back of Pegeen's chair. He was stroking Pegeen's neck with the back of his forefinger.

It was so rare these days to see so many kinds of people in one room. The Polytechnic training made the government witches in ship's crews into shaven-headed lumps less distinct than a pack of beagle dogs, and most other people stayed home these days unless they had business. People who traveled regularly traveled in families, and carried their worlds with them. The big interplanet shipping consortiums, for instance, were mostly owned by members of the Guese tribes, and passenger lines were owned by the Chemdiah. Accountants and auditors came from Arre-Catte Waho and wore those stupid crests. And the Forcers were Calibans like the Sefir Zul, pale people with thick quill-like black hair and broad cheekbones, who moved their eyes but not their faces, who had no magic and didn't care to have any, and who liked to hit.

The conversation around the table sharpened from general chatter to a single argument, one that sounded old and well-worn. Pegeen was saying hotly, "Invisibility isn't invisibility unless the light waves aren't reaching your eye at all. I'm sorry if I'm being a purist. If you mean misdirection, say misdirection."

"If you're being a purist, do it right, m'love," said Octavian, his finger still caressing her neck. "The word 'invisibility' just means not perceptible. Not visible. If I can't see it, I can't see it, whether the light is there or not."

"Don't tell me this—" and she vanished from her place at the table and reappeared "—is exactly the same as this," and did nothing I could tell, except for putting her hand to her glasses and letting some tepid magic swirl around her.

"As far as I'm concerned, it is," answered Octavian, still unperturbed. "I can't see you either way, even though I can feel you."

I was puzzled.

"But in this one—" She vanished again but her voice still came from the center of the roiling spell-vortex in the spot she had occupied. "—I am changing the physical behavior of local space, while in this one—" and she reappeared and kept on talking "—I am merely influencing your mind, a much easier task."

"It's what the target sees that matters, not what happens at the source. Either way I can't see you," he said.

"But our visitor can," said Roder from where he sat at the side of the room, not eating. "Can't you, visitor?"

His eyes must have been on me the whole time.

"Can you really?" said Pegeen. "Then what am I doing right now, runt?" and she made a quick gesture at me, one I happened to know because I'd been insulted on Afrigael. I looked away.

"She's blushing," said Octavian with interest. "What did you do, Pegeen?"

"What!" When I looked up again, Pegeen was staring at me and so was everyone else.

"You're an immune?" cried Fergus from the other end of the table. "Martyred Mother's underthings, an immune!"

"You knew what that meant?" asked Pegeen at the same time. "Heavens. I'm sorry. I didn't realize—most people don't— Oh, dear, I apologize."

"But what did you do?" asked Octavian again. "I'd love to be able to make somebody blush like that."

Leave me alone.

Cully cocked his head to one side, looking at me, drawing his beads slowly through his fingers.

"All of you, leave her alone, and watch your mouth, Fergus," said Roder like a preoccupied uncle. Fergus grinned toothily.

A long bell-like tone sounded. Everybody stopped talking. Fergus tipped his chair back and slapped his palm socket to a jack on the counter. "Mennenkaltenei," he said. "Convicted of Class Two offense under the Control Act. Disciplinary action to commence in one hour. Physical wipe."

If they got copies of official communications routinely, their arrangement with Enforcement apparently extended past a little personal privacy inside the ship.

But Mennenkaltenei? With the physical wipe, you got a nice clean planet without any tiresome living things on it. Physical wipe was corrosives. That's what they did to Forest just before I left. Mennenkaltenei must have really annoyed Enforcement now.

Roder's crew didn't believe it, either, and apparently they took it personally. "Mennenkaltenei? The religious planet, the one with the exemption?" Pegeen said, and then she shot out of her chair. "Oh, Lords of Chaos, no!" Abruptly, everybody was cleaning the table. Wladyslaw gave it one last wipe. Fergus, the engineer, had already shouldered Roder aside to get at the engine controls, and the others were turning their chairs around to face the counter. The kitchen was full of people who were used to working with one another, and none of them was looking at me anymore.

I stood up, slid sideways over to the door, and slipped out of the room.

5

The Simple Retreat
(**Scuttling Bug,** For
Drawing Attack)

No one called after me. I stood in the dark shabby hall and breathed.
I hadn't been in a large group of witches like that since I was tiny.
Fingers and hands all over one another, ripples of power escaping and
fluttering into the room, surges of intention wearing away at my skin.

I went to the end of the hall, past the scratches I'd made in the wall,
and opened the front door. The Enforcement guards were gone, but there
was nothing at all out there, or rather Nothing with a capital N. We were
already in midtranslation, temporarily a dream in the mind of the engine.
I'd have to wait until we were somewhere in real space and time before
I could escape these lovely fuzzy people.

All the other doors in the hall were locked except for one, and it
was the last one I expected to be open. When I put my hand to the knob
of the engine room door and it opened, it startled me so much I let go
of the knob and the door banged into the wall, but nobody looked out
of the kitchen door to find out what the noise was.

Most engine chambers were locked. It wasn't to protect the engine.
Engines stayed where they were because they were told to stay. The
chambers were locked to protect the passengers. If the crew were the

only passengers, though, I guessed they knew enough to stay out of it. I walked into the engine chamber and looked around the room, breathing in. Fergus had called me an immune, but I wasn't immune to magic any more than a fish was immune to water.

The engine chamber was the same size as my bedroom, with a window in the same place, but otherwise completely bare. Why decorate what nobody ever saw, after all? The average engine was packed with magic, and the human eye was blinded by the blaze. If the particles of magic in here had been normal atoms, I would have been a black hole inside a neutron star, but magic has no mass and takes up little space.

A single light glared from the rough ceiling, the plaster walls were raw and unpainted, and the floor was splintery planks, gray with age. The window looked out into Nothing too. I stood in the center and turned around once, then sat down where I was and closed my eyes. They would never find me here, if they didn't notice the little blurry spot in the middle of their engine.

Any human being except the strongest witch would be melted by a drive. I wasn't a witch. I basked in the impersonal glow. People pushed, but engines were just there. I could taste them at my leisure.

No, I wasn't a witch, but there was a time once when I wanted to be a witch, when I was little. My little master put me on a leash and took me to see the Forest Cybernal, which everybody called the Old Green Brain. It was examination time for a school group of children who had tenth birthdays that week, and we got in line behind them to walk through the outer chamber.

The Forest Cybernal was a real antique of a magic computer from the old days, sealed in a great big globe of solid shielding as if it were radioactive. The children pushed and giggled into the outer chamber, which was narrow and dark with round portholes of foot-thick quartz looking into the vault. Apparently all the children saw a glow coming out of the portholes, judging by the gasps and whoops. I saw no glow. I smelled the dry, blinding heat, and saw magic moving through the big spherical room, which was painted institutional green with dead flies lying around on the bottom. The group of children filed ahead of us, with two shaven-headed Polytechnic cybernalists yelling at them to keep moving.

When everybody came out of the room again, the children chased one another around, some of them pretending the Old Green Brain had talked to them. They thought it would be exciting and dangerous to be a witch and go work for the government, even though they could see how boring the cybernalists were. The cybernalists, meanwhile, were talking in mutters to another staff member, heads down and hands making little irritated movements. "I've never seen the measurement go *down* before," said one of them. "All right, boys and girls, we're going to go through again," she called, and the children, all excited, took twice as long to get in line again. I wished I was with them, but my master yanked my leash and took me with him. When we got home and he measured me and I saw his triumphant expression, I was glad for him that I wasn't a witch. It took a lot to make my master look glad. He wasn't what you would call a warm person. Even when he was hurting me he didn't look happy, he just looked intent.

Something made me open my eyes now. The room looked different. Light was spreading diagonally across the floor. The window didn't look into Nothing now; it looked out over a flat stretch of farmland and a blue-green sky with a blazing yellow sun.

It was outside, it was real, and I could escape.

I was at the window and lifting the sash. It rumbled upward and stuck halfway, though it left enough room for me to squeeze through. I dropped down to the ground. We had landed right in the middle of a field, with plants in neat rows all the way to the horizon. There weren't any buildings in sight. I walked around the back of the ship. Nothing there, either. I rounded the corner to the other side—

—and was tripped, knocked down, picked up by one arm, and dangled in the air.

Cully stood holding me up, showing little strain in his shoulders, but mild surprise in his wide-spaced eyes. "Don't let her go," said Roder, and set off at a run toward the low fieldstone house a hundred yards away.

I hauled myself up by my arm and launched my fingernails at his face, but he grabbed the other hand too. I kicked him. He flipped me upside down and held me by the ankles an arm's length away, and followed Roder at a brisk walk.

Roder was speaking Mennenkalt, calling over and over, "Guardian! Guardian! Come to the door!" but nobody answered. He pounded on the door, yelling, "Come out! Come out! Rot you, Guardian, come to the door!"

"Lord Disorder's panties," sighed Fergus, coming up behind us, his freckled mug flushed and sweaty. Cully lowered me far enough that my head was resting on the ground, though I wasn't carrying much weight on it. When I grabbed his ankles, he kicked me away and held me up again.

Roder backed up, leaned, and rammed through the door with a splintering crash. We could hear him yelling through the house.

"Veremteren koppert," said a thin voice from behind us, and Cully turned around, shoving me behind him for protection. I peered around Cully's side. It was a tired man with a beard and a hat, wearing blue homespun and leaning on a worn wooden stick. He repeated that no one was home.

"Roder!" called Fergus, and began to babble in fractured Mennenkalt so badly pronounced I couldn't make it out. The bearded man shook his head, taking Fergus for an idiot. He made a wiping motion with one hand, then indicated the horizon and the sky. "Go away. No one is home. The Forcers are going to destroy the world in less than an hour. Go away," he said in Mennenkalt.

We were on Mennenkaltenei itself? How had Roder gotten permission to land on a world about to undergo a Class Two wipe?

Roder burst out onto the porch and ran toward the bearded man, who began to repeat what he'd said once again as he watched the android approach.

"You know about the Enforcement action?" said Roder.

The man shrugged. He nodded.

"We can't talk here. It's about to happen. Please come with us," said the android.

The Mennenkalt looked annoyed and shook his head.

Roder lifted his hand. Something sparkled in it. He hit the man's shoulder with it, and the native looked surprised, and then even more surprised, and then his eyes rolled up in his head. The sparkling thing had been a stunner. He slumped forward, and Roder ducked under him as he did and stood up with the man draped over his shoulders. "Fifteen minutes," he said, and everybody ran.

Cully dropped me once we were in the front door of the ship, and I rolled to my knees, rubbing my head. Fergus and Roder ran down the hall, while Cully made me get up and shooed me ahead of him. "How ever did you get out by yourself, spider? You need a baby-sitter. You could have had your chowder boiled for sure," he said. "That planet is about to get cleaned off, and everything living with it." He hustled me ahead of him into the kitchen and made me sit against the wall.

"Let's go, let's go," Roder was saying over and over, and Fergus, with his palm socket already on the plug, was shaking his head.

"Something's wrong with the engine. It's complaining about a draft. It says it's cold."

"If we don't get out in five minutes, we're dead," said Roder.

Fergus was rubbing his head. "It says there's a hole."

"Oh!" I said, and got up. Cully casually put his arm across the doorway to stop me from leaving. "I left the window open in the engine room," I said to him. He stared. I repeated, "I left the window—"

"Go, let her go, go!" shouted Roder, and I slipped under Cully's arm and ran down the hall and into the engine chamber. I hauled at the sash. It was still stuck halfway, and I couldn't jiggle it loose. I reached up to the top of the panel and hung my whole weight on it. *Please shut, please shut,* I muttered to myself, and I heard a grinding noise, but it stopped. *Shut, shut, shut,* I chanted to myself, and it stuttered down inch by inch until it slammed.

Cully was at the door. "Okay, go," I said, but he couldn't hear me. He couldn't see me, either. He was blinded by the light of the engine. I ran across the room, pushed him out of the doorway, shut the door, and said, "Okay. You can go."

He turned and called, "Go ahead," to the people in the kitchen. Then he grabbed my arm and began to shove me down the corridor. "You walked into the engine room, waltzed through the engine, and jumped out the flaming window, just like that, did you, squirrel girl?" he said, giving me a push.

I broke away, ran three steps, whirled, drew my blade, and met him with its point squarely in the center of his chest just in time for him to stop. "Don't push me," I said, stamping my foot. "Don't yank me, don't drag me, don't throw me, *don't touch me.* Don't ever touch me again." I pleaded silently for him not to notice I wasn't pushing the weapon in. What was happening to me?

"If you don't climb into the engine chamber again, I won't," he said, not moving. He had a small dark red spot where the point had gone through the fabric. I was glad he hadn't moved closer, and ashamed that I was glad. I yanked the sword away and smacked the wall with it. I glared at him, breathing hard, but he didn't look at me.

"Aaah!" I said, and kicked the wall, and stormed ahead of him into the kitchen.

Nobody paid any attention when I came in. Slender black-haired Octavian the communications officer was apparently having an epileptic attack, with Roder and everybody else watching him. Octavian's teeth were bared, his dark eyes were slits, his back was arched, and his whole body was vibrating so that the black pendant he wore bounced on his chest. The Mennenkalt was out cold on the floor, his hands folded over his staff and his hat to one side.

"Mmmm!" said Octavian with vulgar satisfaction, and opened his black-lined eyes wide. He was still vibrating.

"NeverMind?" inquired Roder.

"NeverNeverNeverMind," answered Octavian in a deep voice not his own. He was one remarkable communications officer if he could reach the Web Center Cybernal all by himself.

Roder began talking rapidly. "Monitor Roder Massim filing Petition of Appeal against the Office of Enforcement, Regulation, and Control, requesting stay of disciplinary action against Mennenkaltenei for Class Two offense against the Control Act, reason insufficient notice to Monitor of action, absence of due process, endangerment of public safety, violation of civil rights, hindrance of government officials— Pegeen, am I missing anything?"

"Wasting public funds," said Pegeen. "Looking ugly, kicking puppies, and spitting on the sidewalk. You really going to put civil rights in there?"

"—and wasting public funds," he finished. "NeverMind?"

Octavian rolled his eyes. "It's thinking," he said in his normal voice. "If you can call it thinking." Then he shuddered and said in the deep voice of the NeverMind, "Petition of Appeal filed, thirty-day stay awarded, all evidence must be presented by then. Web Center Cybernal has spoken. Ouch," he finished in his normal voice and rubbed his arms. "Completely insane."

"The larger the Mind, the loonier," said Cully tritely.

"No, the NeverMind's getting worse. Really." Octavian's voice was remote, and his eyes were watering. "And you are so noisy," he said to me. "Be quiet when I'm trying to listen."

I set my jaw, but nobody was listening to him now. "Thirty days, folks," said Roder. "Thirty days. Pegeen, I'm willing to bet the Mennenkalts didn't do anything serious. They're not like that. I can get Enforcement on the failure to file notice, but the most important part of the charge is violation of civil rights. I think we're finally going to get them with that one."

There was a dead silence. Cully nodded kindly, passing his beads through his fingers.

"Thirty days," repeated the android. "Cully, you have a stain on your shirt."

"The new girl poked me with her sticker thing," the Calypsan answered, and everybody turned around and looked at me as if it were easier than looking at Roder.

"Cranky little sprat," said Octavian.

"Malka," I said. Roder raised his eyebrows.

The bell-like tone sounded again, and Fergus went over to the palm socket.

"I'm not a sprat. I'm not a squirrel, or a spider, either. My name is Malka," I repeated, sticking my chin out, but Fergus was talking over me.

"Folks. People. Enforcement is starting the wipe," he said in a flat voice. "They started it anyway. They started it anyway. They're killing Mennenkaltenei."

Maintaining Distance between Opponents (**Bumper Gap,** With Mismatch)

Nobody said anything for nearly a minute. It was so quiet I could hear the click of Cully's beads. Something rustled outside the window in the weedy garden.

"They wiped Mennenkaltenei in spite of us?" said Electra. Gray Julia looked even grayer than before.

Pegeen said, "Well, shall we have a chorus of 'but they can't do that!' and get it over with?"

"But they really *can't* do that," said Roder. "The petition should have stopped them. The NeverMind will shut them down completely."

Pegeen looked at him over her glasses. "Will it? Can it?"

"Be realistic. They might not need witches to run their engines, but they still need the NeverMind."

"That we know of," said Pegeen.

"Communication. Information storage and processing. News. They can't just sidestep the Web. The galaxy's too big, there's too much going on."

"So say they've made their own black-matter Web. Say they can communicate with the new stuff."

Roder sighed. "Oh, Pegeen, don't be paranoid."

"That's it," she insisted. "That's got to be it. That's why they've put so much work into developing the black-matter drive. It isn't just to reduce the dependence on witches, it's so they won't have to depend on the NeverMind itself."

Fergus nodded slowly, but Roder wasn't going to listen, though she was right. "We'd better find out what happened on Mennenkaltenei to make them do this." He leaned over the kidnapped native and put something to his neck, then stood back, putting his hand on Octavian's arm. The communications officer's boyish face was tired and his skin had a damp shine to it, but when Roder touched him he seemed to settle in on himself and relax. Now I knew what Roder and his group reminded me of: a man I'd known on Fetuu who had seventeen dogs. When he took them for a walk, it was hard to tell who owned whom or who was in charge, except they expected a great deal more of him than he expected of them.

The Mennenkalt opened his eyes, clutched his staff, sat up, and twisted around to retrieve his hat as if he had known exactly where it was all along. He placed it firmly on his head, tugging the brim down all the way around. Then, using the staff, he stood up, with the crew of the ship taking a step back from him. He looked just as annoyed as he had before Roder knocked him out.

"Elder, your world has been destroyed by the Enforcers," said Roder. "I took the liberty of rescuing you."

"You were too hasty. I was permitted to stay behind because I had a vision and a mission," the Mennenkalt said. He peered up into Cully's face. He shook his head, and then walked over to Julia. She lowered her eyes. No, Julia wouldn't do either. I was afraid I knew what was coming. I went over to the window and looked out. The cat was washing one ragged ear out by the stone wall. It froze when it saw me.

"Mine," it said. It stared at me with blank gold eyes, and then gradually began to wash again. It had a patch of fur missing over one shoulder. If it were the familiar of a dead witch, it was going to lose more fur. It would turn into a rack of cat bones with a skin slung over it, and then into a small pile of something like fallen leaves. Then it would blow away. That was what happened most of the time.

Behind me everybody was talking at once, and then Roder's voice said, "Malka?"

He'd heard me say my name. I thought no one had noticed. I swung around. The native was pointing at me. Oh, well.

"Kurfurst lle zhatter," he said when he was sure he had my attention. "Ekestverte yer andanfellter, kavelnes lle helster." I scowled. Mennenkalts.

Fergus said, "He wants to cure her constipation?" He really didn't speak Mennenkalt very well.

"The pronoun 'lle' makes a difference, Fergus," said Roder.

"I don't think she understands the language," said Electra helpfully.

I understood him fine. He was saying, "O, shackled spirit, consent to aid us and we will release you at the foreseen time," just like the Mennenkalts were always saying to me.

"No," I said. In Standard.

The native repeated to me very slowly and clearly, as if like Electra he thought I merely didn't understand, "Kurfurst lle zhatter, ekestverte yer andanfellter, kavelnes lle helster."

No. Go away, I said inside my head.

He bowed his head to me. "Kavelnes lle," he repeated once again, with great respect. He swept them all with a look and made a gesture with his hand.

"Oh, no, he disappeared," said Pegeen and they all put their hands out to try to catch him. Confused for a moment, not understanding that the others couldn't see him anymore, I watched him duck under Cully's arms and slip sideways out the half-open door.

Roder said, making me jump, "Malka, what is he doing?"

I pointed.

The crew rushed to the door and right past the Mennenkalt, who was standing with his back to the wall. "Hey," I said, but they didn't listen, and he was following them now anyway. He pushed a door open behind them and went in. "Hey!" I said again, and went to the door. It was the engine chamber, and he was standing in the middle looking completely normal. "Wow," I said. I'd never seen a human do that. The others shoved up around me and looked too, but of course they couldn't see anything.

Inside the engine, the Mennenkalt held his staff, with his chin up. He had his hat at his chest as if he were in church. His eyes were bright. "Lle kepelst, lle begest, lle koppelteren ne hals bekmelter," he said to the empty air, and then he began to fade from sight. He saw me and bowed again, then disappeared. Nice trick. Use somebody else's engine to squirt you through the Web.

"What are you looking at?" asked Roder, peering through his fingers at the empty engine room.

"Nothing, now. He went away." I closed the door again.

"Oh, damn," said Pegeen. "He deep-fried himself? Are you sure?" They started going back down the hall, but Roder stayed, looking down at me.

"He went away? Where did he go?" the android asked me politely. Cully glanced over his shoulder and slowed.

"He asked the engine to take him to his people."

"Oh, sweetie," said Electra, "you don't have to make anything up. It's all right."

"He said, 'Thou spirit be adored, thou spirit be respected, thou spirit take me to my people,' and he disappeared," I said to her, narrowing my eyes.

"Oh, for heaven's sake," said Electra, turning away. "What a show, child."

I narrowed my eyes some more, but she wasn't looking.

Roder looked amused. " 'To my people,' hm?"

"Ha." Pegeen stopped. "His people would normally be on Mennenkalt—"

"—but there aren't any Mennenkalts left on Mennenkaltenei, not if Enforcement did the wipe," Cully interrupted.

"Exactly," Roder agreed.

"Mennenkalts don't travel. They won't use magic that way," said Pegeen.

Roder said slowly, "I would have said they wouldn't use magic in *any* way that would upset Enforcement."

"You're saying they ran away before the wipe? Where?"

"We can find out, if it's a world in the Web," said Roder, and grinned at Octavian.

Octavian groaned. "Oh, my head. Come on, Roder. Please. There's more than a thousand worlds in the Web."

"Then we'd better get to work," said Roder. Pegeen rolled her eyes and slipped her arm around Octavian's waist. They all moved back to the kitchen down the hall.

"I need to talk to you," said Roder. "Come on."

I followed him. A talk about what? There were so many things I didn't want to talk about.

The third door down in the hall opened to his touch, though it had been locked when I tried it before, and he showed me in. It was a cold shadowy room, all smooth metal, and there were tall human-sized tanks in slots along one wall. In the fourth slot over was Tobiah.

He was naked in a blue-tinted fluid, his eyes closed and his hair waving in a slow current. I stopped and looked at him. Roder drew me to a stool in the far corner and sat me down facing him.

"First, I want to take care of some routine business. May I?" he said, holding his palms up facing me. He was asking if he could touch me.

I didn't move.

He put the hands back down on his legs. "Just a physical exam."

I didn't see what I could do to stop him, and he wasn't asking me to take my armor off. I nodded slowly.

With a blank face, he quickly, lightly ran his hands down the tops of my arms and up the undersides, down the rib cage to my hips, then repeated the sweep with my legs, as if he were feeling my skin through the armor.

"Stand up and face away from me." I could feel the travel of his hands down my back, up the back of my neck. It was as impersonal as falling rain. He felt behind my ears and slid his fingers over my cap. Then he had me sit down again so he could trace the orbits of my eyes, press down either side of my nose, and look up my nostrils. Even when his hands were directly on my skin, he did it without the meaning that humans always gave to touch.

"Hm. Open your mouth."

I didn't. I shook my head.

After waiting a beat, he leaned back against the counter. "It's all right. I would just like to measure your temperature. That's why I asked."

"Everything in the universe has a temperature," I said, keeping my mouth narrow. I didn't let people take my temperature since that doctor on Halyard got so upset, and it hadn't gone down any since then.

The mournful river-colored eyes rested on me. He took a breath to say something and thought better of it.

"All right. Let's have our talk. What would you like to know about us?" he said.

It was the one thing I hadn't expected. What would I like to know? I tried to think of something to ask him that wouldn't give me away.

So I pointed at Tobiah.

"Him? I am mending him." He walked over and regarded Tobiah, who looked as if he had drowned while asleep, though now I could see the slow ripple of his ribs as he breathed something, not air, in and out. "Enforcement delivers my recruits in poor condition. They tell me he's a chronologer, but he's got some stuff inside him I can't identify, and he doesn't read as a witch on my scans."

I nodded. Silence.

"What else can I tell you?"

I thought. "What are you?"

"What am I or what do I do? You knew *what* I was when you saw my face."

That almost stopped me, but I said, "I mean what do you do."

"I'm a Monitor. I work for the government. I monitor Enforcement. I'm a glorified referee with a little shiny whistle. I blow it whenever Enforcement goes over the boundaries."

I didn't laugh. That made sense. I'd always thought the Monitors were nothing but a fairy tale, but apparently they actually existed. Once upon a time, the government had a dim clue it wasn't a good idea to create a police force that had unlimited power, so they created a mosquito, gave it perfect freedom, and sent it to buzz about Enforcement's ears . . . Tobiah had turned a quarter inch to the right while Roder was talking, not a voluntary movement but a combination of breathing and flow inside his container.

"So you already know about Monitors, too," said the android, startling me. He leaned against the tank.

"Are you going to put me in one of those now?" I pointed to the tank.

"No. You don't have any suspicious implants and you're not injured, so no, I won't put you in there. I don't use the stasis tanks for cages. This is an infirmary, not a jail."

I set my jaw. He could try that on somebody else.

"You're not the first recruit to try to kill me, Malka," he said. "Pegeen used a knife."

"I bet I—" I stopped.

"No. She wasn't nearly as good as you are. She didn't even come close. Mostly they try to use magic on me instead, but I'm completely encased in shielding. In case you were wondering."

I shifted around uncomfortably.

"I need a crew. I can't drive an engine or do a proper investigation without witches. But I can't use the Polytechnic graduates. They're conditioned too well. They'd have nervous breakdowns trying to even think about Enforcement the way my crew needs to. So under the law, Enforcement supplies me with unconditioned witches right out of their nets, whenever I ask. Some of my recruits try to kill me, like you. Some of them aren't in such good shape, like this gentleman. I'm used to it."

I didn't say anything. It sounded like a bad deal all around, for everybody concerned.

"We're in here now because I have some standard hiring procedures. I'm going to make sure you're healthy, give you an implant so I can ID you to Enforcement when you're off the ship, and socket you in to officially record your hiring."

I shook my head.

His face went blank. Inconvenient Malka. "Why not?"

"Doesn't work," I said, showing him the socket in my right palm.

A long pause, while he stared at it. "A forgery. It must have been hard to get that done, but why? It just gives ID?"

I nodded. That was all it did. It wasn't a line to my brain, it was a local echo that went no farther than my wrist.

"Do you want a real one you can use? I can give you one."

"Won't take," I said.

"Won't take? Your brain rejects it? So I guess I can't give you a locator implant either?"

I shrugged and repeated, "Won't take."

He sat back on the counter and swung his legs. I watched Tobiah breathe blue fluid.

"So. Tell me about yourself," he said.

I could feel my jaw muscles ache. *No.* Nothing to tell.

"No? Then I'll tell you about yourself." He held up his fingers and folded them down one by one as he talked. "You tell me you're not a witch. You don't have a familiar that I can find. But your shielding is better than mine—I couldn't detect any body functions just now. You can walk in and out of an active engine, see what's inside, and see people when they're invisible. You speak Mennenkalt, and probably Matrish— you understand Fergus when he swears. You're an expert Caliban sword-fighter, but you're not a Caliban. You figured out the homeworld of every one of my crew in less than a minute. I watched you do it."

It was just as impersonal as his hands, and just as steady. *No. Stop it.* It was louder than I'd intended.

Roder swung his legs again, looking vague, and then gathered himself with a visible effort.

"Corrections? No? I'll go on. The forged palm socket you have was made for a very short time thirty years ago, on Didrika. You looked at my face and knew I was an android. The company hasn't made a new Massim in over sixty years, and there weren't that many of us to begin with."

I began to see where he was going, and pushed my heels down as if braking a slide downhill.

"And you're Forest born and bred. I'd swear to it. But Forest was wiped forty years ago, and I was there to see it. So even though Electra seems sure you're about fifteen, you're—what?"

I scrambled off the stool and drew my sword, backing away from him, but he didn't stop swinging his legs. He didn't look pleased with himself, though.

"Fifty? Fifty-five? And you've managed to avoid Enforcement for half a century?"

I crouched, ready to defend myself.

He stilled his legs. We stared at each other. He was taking me seriously, just as he did when I attacked him before, but he wasn't backing down, either.

Once again, we passed some critical moment, and he relaxed. "I'm sorry I upset you. I'll ask you how you did it some other time. You can come back in when you're ready."

He left the room, closing the door, and left me crouched over, all my muscles tense.

I screamed at the top of my voice, and jumped up and down. I whirled in place, swinging the sword so it hissed. Then I did it again. Then I climbed back onto the stool and sat there with my eyes closed, breathing in and out, holding the sides of the stool. It was like somebody had taken my skin off whole and then handed it back to me so I could put it back on, and it was the handing back part that bothered me . . . The skin where I had hit Zul was red, right between the grimy edge of his collar and the roots of his beard, and I dropped my weapon and said I was sorry. I said I was sorry. And I had not killed Roder, or Cully.

I must be falling apart at the seams. It was inevitable. I wasn't meant to get this big.

There was a scratching noise at the door. I opened my eyes, and for a moment it looked as if Tobiah were staring at me in fury from his blue tank, but then something scratched at the door again. I got up and opened the door, looking out and then down. It was the gray cat, its tail wrapped around it. "Mine. Mine," it said, lifting its crumpled whiskers with each syllable.

"Yes. Yours," I said. "I'm just passing through. I'm leaving as soon as I can." It walked in anyway, waited until I sat down again, and then jumped up into my lap with its back against me, its shabby sides pumping in and out with a silent purr. The cat smelled ugly, not ugly like the Sefir Zul but ugly like old butter. With each breath it sent tufts of fur above it in the air, where they hung like smoke and disappeared. The cat was falling apart at the seams too, poor thing. I put my hand down on it, and it laid its chin on my hand and closed its eyes. I watched it for a while. Fifty-five years ago, my master's dog Bear liked me, better than he liked my master, but I couldn't remember now what Bear even looked like.

7

The Probing Attack
(**Arachne's Needle,** For Finding Out)

When I got uncomfortable, I tried to put the cat down on the floor carefully, but it started struggling and ended up jumping down with a thud and darting out the door. When I looked out, the hall seemed dimmer than ever, though there was a gap of light beneath the kitchen door. It was some kind of official night on the ship. In the kitchen, it was dark outside that window too, but the crew of the ship was busy and no one looked up when I came in.

Octavian, slim and supple, lay on the floor with his chin on his hands. His eyes were closed but you could see them flicker under his eyelids as he said, "No . . . No . . . No . . ." while Electra read him a list of planet names. Pegeen sat on a chair next to him, with her feet together and her dark hands over her bespectacled eyes, nodding when he spoke. Wladyslaw was staring at a screen scrolling data so fast it blurred, somebody's backup text records.

Roder, like the rest, was watching Octavian, but I was sure he saw me come in, though he didn't look right away. He shifted his eyes to look at me, just slowly enough that I could be looking away myself

THE WAYS OF MAGIC

before our eyes met. Not only did he see things, he knew when he shouldn't see things. He said, "We're trying to find the Mennenkalts."

I still didn't look at him. He continued, "There wasn't anybody left on the planet when it was wiped. The Mennenkalts all left before it happened."

He was still looking at me. I could feel it on the side of my face. I didn't know where they'd gone. Just because Mennenkalts recognized me when they saw me didn't mean I understood them.

He finally said, "Whatever they did or didn't do to deserve the wipe, they're in for it now. Flight to avoid discipline is a Class One offense."

"I guess that blows their religious exemption," said Fergus.

I'd never quite understood how the Mennenkalts pulled off the exemption as long as they had, though it might just have been a grandfather clause in the Control Act. They'd been around forever. They believed magic was god, they ate their kings, and they were stuffy and boring and obsessed with food, crops, and fertility. They took immigrants, though they turned down the ones who were interested in them for their sexual practices. I had tried to emigrate there once, but they told me I was a benighted slave and they attempted to free me from my spiritual bondage, right then and there in the immigration office.

"Gagarin . . . Annawon . . . Tatanka Iyota . . . Worthy Montgomery . . . ," said Electra in the silence.

"No . . . No . . . No . . . No . . . ," answered Octavian to each one.

Cully slid his beads through his fingers. "It doesn't make sense. They're so conservative. So rigid and moralistic. It would take something outrageous for them to defy Enforcement."

"Um," I said, and again nobody heard me but Roder.

"Yes?" he said.

"Enforcement disciplined Mennenkalt three years ago," I said. It was a planet-wide punishment, the one for a Class Three offense. Enforcement executed all the government officials above department head, deported random chunks of the population, dumped refugees on Mennenkaltenei, and poisoned the crops. It happened just after I tried to emigrate.

"I would have heard about it," he said, and I supposed that was that.

"Monahan . . . Polydionysus . . . Chapman . . . Laelah's Mask . . . ," read Electra.

"No . . . No . . . No . . . No . . ."

"Enforcement just didn't happen to get around to notifying you this time either, Roder," said Pegeen, with her hands still over her eyes.

"You're really being paranoid now, Pegeen," said Electra, interrupting herself.

Roder opened his mouth, and closed it again, then looked at me. I shrugged, but he kept waiting.

"It was a Class Three offense," I said. "Breeding for the gift."

"They're allowed to encourage the birth of witches, sweetheart," explained Electra. "It's part of their religion." I wished I hadn't said anything.

Roder said, "Where did they put the people they deported? They usually dump them on the next planet they punish."

I shrugged. *Leave me alone,* I thought.

Roder seemed lost in thought. Cully, who had been hunched over his station, swiveled around in his chair and watched us, fingering his beads.

Electra continued, "Gitalong 2 . . . Morbid . . . Eight Horses . . . Ong's Hat . . . Guilty as Charged . . ."

"No . . . No . . . No . . . No . . . No . . ."

"How do you do that?" Cully asked me suddenly, and Roder glanced at him under his brows.

"How does she do what?"

"She did it before. She mutters under her breath, and people do what she says."

"No, I don't."

"Roder asked you a question, you said, 'Leave me alone,' and all of a sudden he didn't care anymore."

"I did not. I didn't say anything."

Roder laughed. "So that's what— When we were talking a little while ago, in the infirmary, it felt like someone was hitting me with a hammer. Malka, you're a witch, all right. You're not only an immune, you're a spell speaker. No, you didn't say anything, but you're so strong you don't have to open your mouth."

I set my mouth grimly, and flinched when they all laughed.

"Speaker," said Wladyslaw, his eyes not leaving the screen. "Talks about as much as mud."

"Just *leave me alone*," I said, aloud this time.

Pegeen took her hands off her eyes momentarily. "I see what you mean, Cully. That made my head ache. So *can* we leave her alone now? We need to finish this."

Roder nodded.

"And so you get what you wish," said Cully. "No, no, don't say it," holding up his hands to stop me.

I went to the window. It was dark outside, and I couldn't make out the fishpond or the stone walls, just a darker blur below the horizon and a deep gray sky above, a different sky than the one outside my bedroom. This moth-eaten little houseboat must have a different space-fold outside every window. The cat jumped up to the windowsill next to me and leaned on me, hard, ramming the top of its head into my arm.

"Heaven . . . Carmichael . . ."

"No . . . No . . ."

Wladyslaw, still staring at the scrolling screen, froze it suddenly and said, "Here it is. Three and a half years ago. Class Three offense. Genetic manipulation contrary to Title Eight of the Control Act. Twelve thousand Mennenkalts were loaded on the *Hilma K. Lewis*, and they're still on board."

"Still on the ship?" said Fergus in horror. "Brother Conrad's tail-wrap. Sorry. But really."

Knowing the Mennenkalts, Enforcement was saving them to dump on some planet that really ticked them off.

"Where's the *Hilma K.* now?" asked Roder, ignoring Fergus.

Wladyslaw answered doubtfully, "At backup time, it was off the Web chasing a prisoner that got away."

The whole group laughed. "One of those Mennenkalt farmers saw a cow that needed milking outside, and there was no stopping him," said Fergus.

"Victoria . . ." said Electra firmly, bringing them back to task.

"No," answered Octavian, still chuckling.

"Caliban 5 . . ."

There was a long delay. At last, Octavian said, "No answer. Can't get through to their Cybernal. The Forcers have it locked for administrative review."

"But we were just there! Oh well, we'll come back to it. Hovering Flower . . ." Electra sounded annoyed.

"No . . ." They continued.

Administrative review. My sharp-nosed thin-lipped master was getting swifter. He'd already been in and out of Caliban looking for me, and they were all busy locking the stable doors now. I needed to get off this ship before he tracked it down. My little persistent master. I could feel the hairs on the backs of my arms standing up.

"Octavian's querying every planet Mind to find out if they've logged any Mennenkalt visitors," explained Cully next to my elbow, running a finger down the cat's back so that it arched happily. I turned my face away slightly. I didn't want to be friends with him, I wanted to be friends with the cat, and he was being condescending. I knew very well what Octavian was doing.

"Dobrovolski . . ."

"No . . ."

"Nitoh Mahkwi . . . Lazarus . . . ," read Electra.

"No . . . Yes," said Octavian, opening his eyes. "Yes, yes, yes. Lazarus. Mennenkalt agents bought all the old-style gray-matter ships in the Somnus Terminal yards, paid cash, supplied the crews, and left over the course of a week."

"Lazarus it is, then," said Roder. "Fergus?"

Fergus plugged in, and grimaced. "Woof, the engine's in a bad mood. Lazarus, Lazarus," and his face went still as he spoke to the magic furnace back in that empty room. "Ahh . . . okay," he finally said. "Prepare for translation."

They all went pale. Being in translation never bothered me. Humans said being neither-here-nor-there was some kind of a transcendent state. The idea was, when they were in translation they were inside the nonlocal universe of magic where all places were one place, all times one time, and all things were one thing. They could think thoughts, understand ideas, imagine things they never would let pass through their minds otherwise. From the way it looked, they weren't very agreeable thoughts.

Pegeen, for instance, looked as if she were repressing a belch, and gray Julia looked even grayer. Cully had his eyes closed and his head rolling back as if he were trying to unkink a stiff neck. "This is our fourth translation today," complained Octavian in a faint voice, shifting around, and nobody bothered to respond. They were all linked in their uneasy discomfort. Roder was watching me again, so maybe his expression had to do with another thing he'd noticed about me. I hoped not.

The cat was washing one paw complacently. She didn't feel it either.

It was a short translation. My stomach jumped as the ship tilted sideways, the crew looked relieved, and then the floor thumped and the ship gave a settling lurch. "Somnus," said Fergus on a descending note, looking truculent.

"Right. We'll talk about that landing later," said Roder. "Electra, you and I go to the terminal offices to interview the stationmaster. Julia, tap the data stream from the station to the Lazarus Cybernal and see if you can find flight plans for the Mennenkalts. Pegeen, conceal Wladyslaw so he can get into the transaction record backups; I don't have time to go through official channels to request them. Fergus, Octavian, check the gossip in the crew lounge and *please* don't make any unnecessary comments about the Polytechnic. Cully . . ." He raised his eyebrows at the tall Calypsan and nodded at me.

"Baby-sit," finished the priest, nodding. The room emptied except for Roder, Cully, and me. Cully stretched his long legs out and began sliding his beads along their cord very slowly with both hands, concentrating on the task. There was still a spot of blood on the front of his tunic. He hadn't bothered to change it.

Roder, still sitting, said to me, "I advise you not to leave the ship, but it's up to you."

I didn't move. Didn't say anything.

"Cully's not your guard. He's here to keep you company and keep anybody from getting into the ship while we're away. Cully, you aren't to try to restrain her in any way, understand?"

Cully said, with emphasis, "No problem."

"Malka?" said Roder.

I waited for him to leave.

"You remember Electra mentioned Akamai, the woman who died? She went outside on Rilievo when I asked her not to go, and without notifying the Rilievo Cybernal. As a member of my crew, she wasn't a wild witch anymore. She was a deserter, and therefore Enforcement treated her differently than they would a wild witch. They didn't try to catch her. They just killed her."

Enforcement wasn't the problem, if I could sneak aboard another ship fast enough. My nasty little master was the problem. He could make me do whatever he wanted.

Roder exchanged a look with Cully, and left. Cully slid another bead, and didn't look at me.

Out in the hall, doors were banging and there were footsteps and voices. I looked, and they were all wearing armbands that reflected the light as they trooped out. I glanced at Cully, and he still wasn't looking at me.

I waited about a minute, walked down the hall, opened the door, and looked out. It was day here, though it was night on the ship. We were in another terminal like Eliot, though it wasn't in the center of a city. Here the air smelled of clay, damp, and moss. There were fewer ships, and the sky had a yellow tinge to it like the inside of a melon.

The crew members were going down the alley between the lines of parked ships.

I stepped out. The surface was a deep gray ceramic, and beyond the rows of ships I couldn't see any fence, just a marshy expanse of grass and some low buildings at a distance. I couldn't remember anything about Lazarus, though I'd been here once. It was hot, and my armor felt like a turtle shell. I went to the edge. The grassy marsh sucked at me when I tried to put a foot down in it, so I went down the alley where the crew had gone.

When I had gone no more than ten feet, a bulbous orange shape winked into the sky, a small Enforcement patrol ship, and it dropped and squatted down in an empty parking spot between two ships just ahead of me. A front hatch slid up and two orange figures stood framed against the interior, their arms folded, looking in the direction the crew had gone. I stopped. *No.*

Then another orange ship came down across from them, and another. The third one was a full-size transport that lowered its hold door and began unloading orange-and-gray vans. The two Forcers in the first ship turned their heads. They jumped down and ran toward me. I drew my sword with a hiss.

Then two more Forcers appeared in the hatchway, and I turned and ran.

I ran back to Roder's ship, but the front door had closed and locked behind me. I hammered with my fist once, then again. *No.* I could hear their footsteps.

Cully swung the door in and walked away as I jumped back in.

I carefully closed the door and stood just inside, breathing in the air of the old ship. No noise came from outside. I ran my finger along the plaster wall, feeling the damp, the cracks, and the holes in it as I walked back to the kitchen. The floor creaked under me.

Cully moved a bead along the loose cord, then moved it back. "How many Enforcement ships?" he asked.

"Three."

He sighed, and met my eyes, then shifted them away.

"Do they . . . ," I began, then stopped.

"Do they follow us everywhere? Yes. Can they do that? Yes. As long as they don't interfere with our work. Can they kill us? Yes. If we leave without permission, or if they can make it look like a mistake."

A soggy night breeze blew across the garden outside the kitchen window, ruffling the ferns and rippling the surface of the fishpond.

"You might as well resign yourself to it. Settle down, settle in. This is your home now."

Home? I didn't think so. It was a mobile prison. It was a leghold trap, meant for some other kind of animal, but its jaws had closed on me instead. I was trapped here until my master came to punish me. I had better start getting ready.

8

The Footwork Pattern (**Astaire,** With Known Opponent)

When the door slammed open, I had been practicing for an hour, and still had an hour to go. Two hours of footwork a day, no matter what, the Sefir Zul said.

The foot is the most important part of sword-fighting, not the hand. Beginners don't know that. If you hand a beginner a blade, he plants his feet and waves the blade around, or thrusts with it, or chops. That's because he doesn't understand that the blow is only the finish of a sword-fight, not the beginning. In order to end the fight, you have to move. You need to be too far away for your opponent to hit you, and close enough for you to hit him, and you need to convince your opponent that he's close enough to hit you and too far away to get hit. That sounds like a joke, but it's not.

I watched the Sefir Zul demonstrate this to a novice, a few weeks after I got over the humiliation of having it done to me. Zul dropped his weapon, and the novice charged forward to attack, raising his blade high. Zul retreated smoothly, then halted his retreat an instant, like a hiccup, before continuing backward one more step, an elementary Radomil maneuver. Fooled by Zul's tiny pause, the beginner swung his blade too early, missed him, and nearly fell over with the force of his swing. Zul smacked him on the top of the head with his blade and sneered.

Bewildered, the man took up his on-guard position again, and this time he decided to wait for Zul's attack. Zul stepped forward, bringing his shining weapon up in a sharp motion before he was really within striking distance, the straight Taylor feint. The novice jerked his blade across to parry the false threat, missed Zul's weapon entirely, and stood in dismay as Zul stood with his blade bent in an arc, point buried in the student's cotton armor.

"You're just too fast for me," said the novice, trying to laugh.

"Not too fast, too far," said Zul and slapped him on the side of the head so the man glared with his jaw thrust out, obviously not understanding. I don't remember the beginner's name. He didn't come back for his second class.

I hated Zul too, and not just because he probably washed his face with his tongue and farmed mushrooms in his armpits. He made no secret of his contempt and impatience for me. "Troll girl," he called me. "Time for the troll's lesson. Come, troll," and I would march over and stand grimly on guard while the other students laughed. I never understood why he insisted on keeping me as a student.

He smelled bad, he was unkind to me, and he didn't care if I lived or died, but the lessons were a dance of understanding for me. From the first grudging salute to the last, they were a conversation conducted at sword's length, without words, and even if they always ended with Zul smacking me, I learned something new every time.

Even though he showed me no favor, the other students resented me. They didn't think anyone but a Caliban should study in a Caliban school. They made fun of my size and my temper. When we free-fought, they went for the painful spots, and they struck with too much force. For the first year I hurt all over. Then, when I finally learned to use my feet, they stopped being able to hit me.

So now I made each movement perfect. I concentrated on form, practiced each foot action separately, and then combined them into patterns. I tried not to think about where I was, though the smell of the air kept intruding. The ship was almost as old as I was, and so was Roder, but both of them were expensive when they were new. How long had he been buzzing around the ears of Enforcement without getting swatted? Longer than I had, though he could do it out in the open.

No, I wouldn't be distracted. I would practice my footwork. My skin was sweating, my feet were burning, my legs were aching. I wouldn't think of myself as a captive. I might be imprisoned for the moment, but I was a mighty sword-fighter and I would fight my way out of this. I was the Prisoner Malka, scraping away at her shackles with a pebble, keeping her skills strong, laboring in the dead of night while the Forces of Evil ran ceaselessly outside, barking.

That was when the front door crashed open. The Prisoner Malka squeaked in surprise and flattened against the wall, her heart pounding.

Roder charged past me carrying Pegeen in his arms. He was followed by Electra, her face swollen and dark stains down the front of her clothes. Roder disappeared into the infirmary. Octavian and Fergus tore through the door a moment later, and Fergus slammed it shut behind him. He stopped halfway down the corridor to lean on his thighs and gasp. Octavian grabbed him by the upper arm and pulled him along. "I have to breathe," Fergus protested.

"Later," Octavian said. "Breathe later." He sounded as if he'd been crying. He pulled Fergus into the kitchen.

I looked into the open door of the infirmary. Roder was leaning on his arms against the third stasis tank, where dark brown Pegeen floated in the middle of a cloud of darker liquid that was draining out of her.

In the fourth tank, Tobiah Gregg lifted his chin, shook his head slowly, and closed his eyes again.

While I was frozen staring at him, Roder stood up. I quickly got out of the doorway and Roder slid past me and into the kitchen. I heard Fergus say, in response to something Roder had said, "I'm working on it, I'm working on it!"

There was a thud. It came from the direction of the front door. Roder came out and pushed past me again. Another thud came, more like a boom this time. Roder put his hands to the door, moving them about as if he were blind. The next thud made his fingers vibrate, but he kept them pressed against the panel.

Boom. The inside of the door bulged this time, and he backed away. "Fergus!" he said.

"Keep your bottom on," yelled Fergus.

Octavian stuck his head out. "Engine trouble, boss."

"We can't afford engine trouble," Roder said calmly. "They're using a shock cannon." Boom. The door bulged again and subsided, though this time it wasn't quite flat when the force of the impact went away.

"Right. No engine trouble." Octavian popped back into the kitchen.

I looked down and saw my sword still in my hand, my knuckles white and the grip all wrong. I was holding it like a club. It didn't matter. My little pointy stick wouldn't stop whatever was hitting the door.

The next boom finished with a high screech. The peak of the bulge had a white crown of frayed door, as if something sharp had almost penetrated. The door snapped back again, but now there was a protruding dimple. Roder took another step back, stood with his legs apart, and put his arms behind his back as if he were standing at attention.

In the pause between that shock and the next, there was absolute silence. Then came another boom, and a tearing sound, and then a crunch so loud it made me lean with the impact. The door ruptured, sending sparkling splinters bouncing down the hall in a corona around the android. One came to rest by my foot, a translucent glass shard that looked like the door surface on only one side. Roder brushed his face off and I heard more splinters falling from him. Through the torn opening in the door there was bright daylight and movement, and then something dark swung forward, blotted out the light, and struck the door once again, distending the hole and rolling its edges back. When the dark bludgeon swung back, and let the light back in, Roder still didn't move.

A large head appeared in the aperture. Against the bright light, all I could see was thick stiff hair standing on end, and then it disappeared and a big orange-covered arm was reaching through the hole, groping for the doorknob. He couldn't reach.

"You are out of your jurisdiction," said Roder. "I am going to file an official protest."

That was it? That was how he planned to defend us? I took a step forward.

The man withdrew his arm.

"Fergus, *please,*" called Roder, almost quietly.

The battering ram slammed against the door again, and widened the hole. After it swung back, the man appeared again, groping blindly but with complete scorn for whoever might be watching. This time the hand almost reached the doorknob.

"This ship and its employees are the property of the Department of Monitoring and Compliance, and not to be tampered with," said Roder in a conversational tone. I was right behind him now.

The hand pulled out again. This time the tip of the conical ram nearly touched Roder's face when it swung through, tearing the hole to shoulder width. The android didn't flinch.

"You have to kill him," I said. "You have to fight back."

"I can't," he said calmly. "I wish I could. I have my limits. I can run, I can hide, I can argue, or I can file a protest, and if they kill me outright I have a transmitter implant that notifies the NeverMind. I can't use force against them."

"Can I?"

He thought about it.

The Enforcer's head thrust through again, and this time, because enough light surrounded it, I could see his face. I recognized it.

He peered down and checked the location of the doorknob. "You're fired," he said to Roder. I recognized his voice, too. He pulled his head out, stuck his arm in, seized the doorknob—

—and, raising my arm as if I were holding a butcher knife and not a precision instrument, I ducked under Roder's arm and nailed the Enforcer's hand to the door, striking the Sefir Zul for the second time that day and drawing blood this time.

There was a familiar yell of rage. I yanked the point of my sword out, and the arm whipped away. Zul's head appeared again, looking, and I poked at it like a woodpecker, but the head slipped aside. Roder slid out of my way and put his back to the wall, watching me.

"Troll," said Zul's voice contemptuously from the other side of the door. "You think you are my student. I taught you nothing. Nothing. Nothing."

I listened.

"You hack at me from behind a wall, like a frightened animal. Fight me as a fighter should, face-to-face. Come out and fight me."

I shifted my grip on the sword.

"You are afraid? You are afraid? The Sefir Malka with all her fancy armor is afraid of a mere Zul? You struck me twice today—can you not do it again?" he taunted, his voice thick.

I bent my knees, and breathed hard. He never talked this much. I knew what he was trying to do. I struggled to keep him from getting me to do it.

There were other voices outside, arguing. "Be silent," Zul snapped. Now there were muttered complaints. In a harsh whisper, deliberately loud enough for me to hear, Zul said, "I trained her. I know her. She has the bad temper of a squirrel monkey, and less brains."

He stuck his face back in the hole. I stabbed at it again, and missed again, and he laughed. "Come out and get me, Malka," he said. "Or kill the android for me, like you were supposed to. You weren't good enough, were you?"

I reached for the doorknob, and Roder's fingers were grasping my wrist, lightly. "Don't touch me," I hissed, white-hot, glaring at him. He separated his fingers gently. He was still leaning against the wall, watching me with that grave expression. We stared at each other.

An arm, holding a needle-gun, came through the hole next to my head and shot down the corridor, once, twice, three times. I could hear the spitting sound of the needles hitting the kitchen door.

I still couldn't move. *Help,* I said in my head. *Help.* Malka the Paralyzed in Battle. Roder flinched and closed his eyes.

I raised my blade, saw something, and stuck there, frozen in place. The arm was wearing orange, but it wasn't big enough to be Zul's. He'd sent a sacrifice in his place.

Go. Leave now, I said shakily. *LEAVE.*

There was a cheer from the kitchen.

I still held my blade high, but all by itself the arm fell to the floor, the hand falling open and the gun falling from its fingers. Through the hole in the door I could see Nothing. We were in translation, and the Forcer's arm was the only part of him that got to make the trip with us.

9

The Establishment of Tempo (**Marching Band, Taking Control**)

I stood with the sword in my hand. The tip was red. The Sefir Zul taught me never to put a sword back in the scabbard bloody. But then, the Sefir Zul was an Enforcer, and everything he told me was a lie. I leaned against the wall opposite Roder.

"Three years," I said. "I was with him for three years."

I could hear him breathing. "Are you all right?" he said finally.

Well, no, I was not all right. Now that I had reason to distrust the Sefir Zul, I didn't believe anything he did. He had given up too easily just now. It smelled, just like the scene with the Forcer in Zul's academy this morning would have smelled if I'd used my common sense. It was like the inlay in Tobiah's clock, one set of layers concealing another set.

I heard Roder's feet moving away, and then the kitchen door closed.

My scalp was burning. Absently, I rubbed it and said, "Ooh," staring at my wet hand. The Forcer shooting down the hall had been aiming for my head, not the kitchen door. The tip of the dart had missed, but it scraped my scalp on the way past.

Three years. The Sefir Zul took me on because he thought I had potential, not as a sword-fighter but as an ignorant assassin. A tool. A trained animal, a walking bomb, a rabid mole wrapped up as a present. I knew Enforcement had chased me directly to Roder, and now I knew why they had done it that way. They wanted him to believe they had nothing to do with my arrival, so he wouldn't mistrust me like poor Tobiah, wouldn't stick me in the stasis tank right away.

I hadn't killed Roder yet. I probably wouldn't kill him, either. But it still wasn't enough. The Sefir Zul always nested his real attacks within false attacks. I would have to be on guard. I would have to keep my eyes open. Something else would happen, I didn't know what or where or when.

The arm still lay on the floor, the needler next to it. I pitied the Enforcer who offered it up to me, now standing on Lazarus looking at his empty shoulder in shock while the Sefir Zul doubtless strode away, ignoring him.

I put the needler in my pocket, picked the arm up by the sleeve, and shoved it through the hole in the door, giving it a sharp push so it wouldn't just hang there. As the arm slid into Nothing, it ceased to exist. The information about the arm slipped the engine's mind completely. Conservation of energy and matter didn't exactly work in translation. After staring out the hole for a while, briefly homesick, I walked down the hall trailing my sword behind me with the tip on the floor. I didn't care for this game at all.

When I walked in, Fergus was glowering at the console and Electra was sitting at the table with an ice pack on her jaw. They all looked pale again. Nobody looked at me.

The room seemed to rise in the air and then fall, and I stumbled.

"*What* was that landing?" said Roder.

"I can't help it. I can't help it," said Fergus, yanking his palm off the socket. "The engine is ignoring me."

"Well, we're here, anyway. Octavian, put in a call to the Never-Mind." Octavian put his head in his hands and began jiggling and jittering again. He was sweating, and droplets flew off him as he shook. It seemed as if everybody in the room except Roder was vibrating with him, wavering in and out of view. I shook my head. *Concentrate,* I said.

"Ow!" said Octavian, sitting bolt upright and glaring at me.

"NeverMind!" Roder leaned forward.

"NeverNeverNever—" started Octavian in that rough voice, and began to cough.

"Code Monitor Roder Massim filing complaint against the Office of Enforcement, Regulation, and Control, alleging harassment and assault of employees of the Code Monitor, systematic hindrance of Code Monitor investigations in progress—"

"Enforcement ships landing," said Fergus.

Roder jerked around. "Already? How many ships?"

"Three, four . . . no, six now."

"Okay, take us out the moment Octavian's off-line. Try Cloud Farm. Nimbus City terminal, it's so big it'll take them half an hour to process us." He swung back to Octavian. "Where was I? Trespass on property of Code Monitor. That's it, I think. NeverMind?"

There was no answer. Octavian's mouth was open as if he were about to speak, but nothing came out. I noticed his makeup was smeared.

"NeverMind?" repeated Roder. "Don't lose the connection, Octavian. Stay in for the acknowledgment. Stay in."

"It's fading," said Octavian in a bewildered voice.

We were all leaning forward, as if we could shove him into closer contact with the NeverMind. *Focus, focus,* I realized I was saying inside my head.

"Ow!" he said again. "Complaint registered. NeverMind. Malka, don't do that."

"Okay, ready? Translation," snapped Fergus, and everybody looked even more ill than they had before, but relieved at the same time. The cat jumped up into the window and stretched luxuriously.

Still standing in the doorway, I looked around. The crew was all sitting with their hands dangling between their knees, looking shocked. No, not the whole crew. Where were gray Julia and the toothy, shy Wladyslaw?

"What happened out there?" said Cully. I braced myself.

Roder shook his head, but he didn't mention what had just happened in the hall. "Electra and I were talking to the stationmaster when Pegeen called for help. They had just started looking at the backup when Enforcement came in the building already shooting. Julia's signal stopped at the same time. Electra, Pegeen, and I were cut off from the yard, so we went outside, stole a taxi, and rammed the yard gates."

Electra said through the bag of ice. "I feel like I rammed them with my face. You could have told me we were going to do that."

"I'm sorry," Roder said, and he meant it, but she just closed her eyes.

Cully clutched his beads. "They just attacked? They didn't say anything?"

Roder shook his head. "Octavian, Fergus?"

"We hadn't even gotten to the driver's lounge," said Fergus. "There was a ruckus in the station so we turned around and ran. That's what we were doing when we met up with you."

"Pegeen was shot as we were coming up to the ship. They were still shooting as we were heading for our ship," said the android. He shook his head and kept shaking it.

"Is she all right?" Octavian burst out.

"What?" Roder looked up. "Pegeen? It's a shallow wound. She'll be fine."

"Still think she was being paranoid?" said Octavian.

"No. No. It's some kind of coup. I have to figure out some way that I can make myself think about this. I'm not designed for it." He looked down again, his face patient and tired. They all watched him expectantly, his pack of faithful, needy dogs.

Leave him alone, I said, and Cully said, "Protecting somebody else for a change, mouse?" Now they all looked at me.

I was not a mouse. I was Malka the Eternally Deluded, but I wasn't going to have people calling me a mouse.

"Hey. You're bloody," said Roder, leaning forward. "What happened to your head?" I put my hand up and felt it. The sharp pain had changed to a throbbing burn. "Did he shoot you?" He stopped running his hands over my scalp just before I was ready to hit him. "Come on. Infirmary for you."

Well, I like that," said Electra fiercely through her ice bag. I didn't know if Roder heard her, because he left without commenting.

In the infirmary, the fluid around Pegeen was clear now, though there was a long ugly ditch across her belly. Her face was hard and still, and she was still wearing her glasses. One earpiece dangled free, bobbing. Roder sat me down and reached into a cabinet while I watched Tobiah. He'd always seemed young, but right now he looked like an unborn baby. I could see the pulse in his neck. His bones stuck out like a wet bird's and he was corpse-color.

"Don't look so nervous," said Roder. "I said you weren't the first of my crew to attack me. You're not even the first one planted on me. I find their efforts intriguing."

"I didn't know I was a plant. Well, I knew that Enforcement chased me here on purpose, but I didn't know he was behind it. That man was my sword-master. I thought he let me into the academy because I might be good."

"Calibans don't share," he said. I knew that. I should have known that.

"Ouch!" Roder had done something to my head that made it burn again, worse.

"I have to clean it. You lost more than scalp," continued Roder, reaching in the cabinet again. Tobiah's pulse seemed quick, fluttering rapidly like a small animal's, and he opened his eyes, blinked them, and shut them again. Roder began doing something that hurt even more. I concentrated on my breathing. "Good," said the android, swinging me around on the stool to face him. "Now. That will repair itself, but if you let me put you in the stasis tank for a little while, it will work faster and hurt less."

I shook my head.

"If you're afraid of being trapped, it's easy enough to set the controls so you can let yourself out."

I shook my head even more forcefully, and he smiled. "You're a tough character."

Malka the Tough. Malka the Leathery. Malka the Extremely Chewy. "Can he let himself out?" I pointed to Tobiah.

His expression as he looked at my friend was sad. "No, he can't. And I can't let him out, not yet. They've stuffed him so full of gadgets I'm not sure he's human anymore, and there's something in the middle of him I can't read at all. I think he's a walking bomb."

"But you can't read me either," I said sharply.

"With my hands I can't, but with X rays I can," he said, and laughed at my expression. "That's how I checked you for implants. Good old-fashioned X rays. Like poking your patient all over with a long needle to find out what's inside."

He was relaxed and easy again, talking to me as if I were a normal person. People usually talked to me as if I were a child, or a small animal. *Let Tobiah out,* I wanted to say. *Please let him out.* But I couldn't ask him that.

"Roder!" said Cully from the door.

The android's head snapped around as if he'd been asleep. Maybe I'd been bespeaking him after all. "What?"

"Fergus can't get us *out* of translation now."

"Coming," said the android, giving one of the dials on Tobiah's tank a swift turn as he left.

The room felt smaller instead of bigger when he was gone. Left alone, I looked at Tobiah again. His pulse was still fast.

He was my only friend, if you could call him a friend. I first met Tobiah when the Sefir Zul sent me to his shop to pick up his antique bout-timer, which was being repaired. Tobiah hadn't finished fixing it, but he dug it out of a disorderly pile of other gadgets and said he'd have it ready in a couple of minutes.

I sat and waited while he worked. There was another customer in the shop, a young woman. She was lifting a clock to look at it when Tobiah said something under his breath and traced a loop in the air. The young woman stopped moving, though Tobiah was working briskly. The clocks stopped ticking. Everything stopped except Tobiah Gregg.

I didn't move. I'd learned not to draw attention to myself when things got strange. I didn't think it was a magic spell at first, because I didn't feel any pressure, but about ten minutes into the silent freeze one of his clocks ticked for the first time. It sounded like an elephant cracking its knuckles. That was when I figured Tobiah had slowed the progress of time, at least within the shop.

Slowing time was not a common skill. Like stretching space, it took the energy of a lot of magic, an accumulation of magic as big as an engine. Tobiah's familiar must be as enormous inside as my master's familiar was.

It took the customer nearly twenty minutes to finish turning the clock around to look at the price. It took Tobiah nearly an hour, an hour in which he didn't ever look at me, to finish repairing the timer. It must have been very convenient for him to be able to do that. When he was done, he made the gesture again, the customer started moving, and he presented me with the timer and a bill for the Sefir Zul. He crooked his finger, and I leaned in to listen. "Don't tell," he said without noise. I shook my head quickly, clutching the timer, and left. I hadn't moved. I hadn't breathed. I hadn't even blinked for that hour, except when he couldn't see me. How had he known? That was one of the reasons I avoided witches, because you could never tell what they would see.

I swore I wouldn't go back after that. I avoided the part of the city where Tobiah had his shop. When the square clock that hung above the main door in Zul's academy stopped working, I tried to stay out of Zul's sight, hoping he wouldn't send me, but he did. I was Zul's scholarship student, so I ran all his errands, or at least the ones that weren't important.

It wasn't as bad as I feared the second time. Tobiah smiled when I came in, looked at the clock, and said, "I can fix that while you wait. Sit here," and I sat on an old stool and watched his nimble fingers work. I passed the time by looking around for his familiar, and only when he rested his hand on it like a man caressing a pet did I realize that Tobiah's familiar was a clock, a well-worn thing of ebony, brass, and ivory. It was quiet and restful in the shop.

"Come back and visit," he said quietly as I left, so later on I did. I came and sat in his shop and watched him fix time so it ran smoothly and everything happened when it should. He never pushed on me the way other witches did. He never slowed time after that first visit. He never talked, and he never touched me, so I kept coming back, and now he was comatose in a blue tank, without his familiar. He was the only friend I'd ever had, besides my master's dog, and he didn't ever make me feel as bad as that dog did. Until now.

Now his eyes opened again, and this time it was no illusion. He was awake. "Out, out, get me out," he mouthed. *I'll get you out,* I mouthed back. *I'll get you out. I'll try.* Toby lifted his palms and pushed against the transparent cover of the tank, making his hair flow forward over his face. He made fists of the hands and pressed them on the glass so that the skin whitened in flat patches.

I ran my hands over the surface of the tank, looking for controls. There was a smooth pit the size and shape of a hand at the base, and I could fit my palm into it, but it didn't do anything that I could see. The dial Roder had turned had markings but no numbers, so I didn't know what it measured. I drew my sword and hammered the hilt on the tank, but the clear material didn't even scratch. Tobiah's face was impatient. He pressed his hands against the cover again. I put my palms up to his, and he yanked away.

He closed his eyes again, and his face went still. Though I stood with my palms on the cover for a while longer, he didn't move anymore except for the pulse.

Something soft and feathery brushed against my ankles. I looked down. The cat was there, working its front paws up and down. Its face looked less raggedy than before. I scooped it up, holding it in my arms. It purred into my face, and said, "Mine. You are mine."

"Oh." I'd thought before it was warning me off, and here it was claiming me as its own.

"Miiiine," it whispered, and butted into my chest. I stared at it in astonishment, forgetting the Sefir Zul, Rafael, and even Tobiah for a moment.

"Hey there," I said softly to it.

At the same moment I heard Fergus yell "Yes!" from the kitchen, and this time when we came out of translation, everything slid sideways and stayed on a slant, so I fell against the wall.

10

The Exchange of Parried Blows (**Flock of Crows,** Conversation of the Blades)

The cat struggled in my arms and jumped down, crouching. It stared at me, ready to run away. A tuft of its hair floated into the air, caught in the light from the opening door.

"It's all right. I'm sorry," I said to the cat, and followed it into the kitchen. They all looked up at me. "Does this animal have a name?" I asked.

"Akamai didn't call her anything," said Electra. Her mouth was turned down. She didn't approve.

"Then I'm calling you Bear," I said to the cat, which ignored me. "Bear" after my master's dog, the one he killed.

"Whoa," said Fergus, and rolled his eyes, hastily turning his face from Roder, who ignored him. The exchange wasn't about me or the name or even about the cat herself. The name of Akamai made everyone angry every time I said it.

"You can't adopt someone else's familiar," said Cully, trying to be kind. "It's like adopting somebody's leg, or their ears. The cat will be gone in a few more days, anyway. Familiars don't survive on their own."

He was wrong. *Leave me alone, leave me alone.* "I'm not adopting her. She adopted me."

"Leave her alone, leave her alone," said Octavian in a soft singsong, his cat's eyes wide on me. Electra squeezed her mouth even more tightly.

"We know," said Cully. "We know."

Roder, who had been sitting with his face like a sad patient mask, stirred and said, "We still have a few minutes on this planet. We need to decide what to do, where to go. We can't just keep running away." They were silent. A damp breeze blew in through the window behind him. The night sky had cleared, and the stars were out.

I cautiously touched the cat's back and it—she—Bear the Younger— shoved her back against my hand in return. I never had a pet except for the dog Bear. He cared about me, he even bit my little master for me once, when little master came after me to explain something with a stiletto. He might be the master's dog, but Bear loved me. My master wasn't easy to love.

"I can't believe Enforcement has this much power," complained Electra as if she thought Roder should do something about it. Octavian began tapping his fingers.

Cully shifted, glancing at him. "Do we know they killed Julia?"

Roder shut his eyes. "Her implant went dead. I felt it."

There was a long, resentful silence. Electra glowered at the table.

Fergus blew his breath out. "You didn't promise us we'd live forever, Roder, but I thought we'd be taking Enforcement on one infraction at a time, not all of it at once. And," looking at me, "why should we believe Malka came here on her own—"

No.

"Did you find out where the Mennenkalts went?" Cully interrupted suddenly, speaking to Electra. Then he winced and shook his head.

"They were just chasing the Enforcement transport that carried out the earlier sanction, the *Hilma K. Lewis*," said Electra, startled. "I guess they're rescuing their deportees. If they followed the *Hilma K.*, they ended up off the Web. We'll worry about them later, if there is a later."

"No," said Roder, straightening up. "Fergus, try the Mennenkalt flight plan. You know how methodical and cautious they are. It won't land us inside a sun or a black hole."

They were already interrupting him.

"Ah, Roder, come on," said Cully. "Whatever might have happened to the Mennenkalts, we need to take care of our own problems right now."

And Octavian said, "If we're off the Web, how are we going to get back? Enforcement will be there before us, besides."

"Saint Jabob's salty thong!" came the voice of Fergus through the exasperated racket. "Three—four—I have a whole fleet of Enforcement ships coming in." He continued talking carefully under his breath, a Matrish litany of terms for underwear.

They were all looking at the android again, but Roder shrugged. "Where, then? Where do you want to go next? Ephrayim? Nice Sky? Vernon Two? Big Dry Pile? We either stay in the Web and let them chase us around, getting nothing done, or we leave the Web with a chance of learning something useful."

"Twelve and shock cannons," said Fergus. "Give me a destination. The drive has been fighting me like crazy. I have to start *now* if we're going to go."

Their faces were pale. They didn't want to be here, any of them. Neither did I. I wanted to be absolutely elsewhere. *Let's go,* I thought, as if it would help.

"Roder, tell us what to do," said Electra.

The android said, "Follow the Mennenkalts."

Fergus hunched over the palm jack.

Something hit the house with a loud thump.

Let's go.

Fergus closed his eyes. "The engine's doing it again," he said in a hollow voice.

Go. Get away. Get away.

Then something really hit the house. I saw a train wreck once. It was that kind of noise. Malka the Doughty in Battle stood up, flapped her hands, and squealed, *"Get away get out get out get out NOW,"* and the noise simply wasn't there anymore.

"Lords of Disorder, we're in translation," said Cully. "Fergus, I love you."

"I know you love me, but I have no idea what I did," said Fergus. "We're not even where I aimed us. We're somewhere else."

They all ignored me pointedly, and I realized I was still flapping my hands. In the silence, Roder leaned his head back and let out a long breath.

"No Mennenkalts? No Forcers?"

"Not that I can read," agreed Fergus.

Roder turned those eyes on me. For a moment, I was too frightened to say anything. He knew what I'd done. I couldn't let anybody know what I could do. My master's orders, underlined with the gentlest touch of a razor in his small neat hand.

Roder glanced away. I breathed in.

Cully put his arms around the redheaded engineer from behind and hugged, and Fergus gave a comfortable grunt.

There was a crash outside in the hall. My ears popped, and the kitchen door thumped like a drum. Fergus said in the same moment, "We're out of translation already."

"And in vacuum, not atmosphere," said Roder. "That was the front door blowing the rest of the way out, along with all the air in the hall." He sounded as if that were nothing out of the ordinary.

Octavian got up. "Don't things explode in vacuum? What about the infirmary? What about Pegeen?"

Tobiah too, trapped awake in his tank, I suddenly remembered. Tobiah too.

Roder raised his eyebrows. "The door to the infirmary is as well sealed as this one. Pegeen's fine." I'd never been in real space before. I'd never had to be. Translation skipped that in-between stuff.

For the moment I was safe from Roder's insight. They all got to work. We were within a solar system and near a planet the engine didn't recognize, completely out of the Web. There was no organized communications traffic, Fergus said. He brought up a dark speckled screen from his console. The specks in the screen moved, and I realized he was looking outside the ship in real time at the stars. Something round swam into the middle of it, blue and white. My eyes didn't adjust right away. Then I knew what it was.

I had never seen a planet from space before, except pictures in school. The rest of them were all watching the screen too. That small thing was a whole world, suspended there in the middle of black nothing, and it made the Web seem immense, almost infinite. The Web I knew was close, border to border, a slithery pile of big balls crowded with people. This space was mostly empty and very lonely.

I felt something bump under my feet, a soundless reverberation, as if the ship had hit something. "What was that?" Electra said.

"Don't know. Automatic force field is up over the door opening and pressure's back, Electra, if you want to take a look," answered Roder.

Electra tried the door. It opened easily to her hand and she went out. "Gracious, the hall's a disaster," I heard her say and then the door shut behind her.

"Take us in closer. I want to take a look at it; it looks habitable," said Roder. "Do you know how to put a ship in orbit?"

"Orbit?" said Fergus, "Are you kidding me? Not since simulation training. Orbit. Free fall. Wow."

Cully, having taken a seat in the back of the room by himself, was talking to himself, though the others didn't stop what they were doing, nor did they seem to listen. He bowed his head, recited something in a quiet gabble, said, "Julia," clicked one of his beads, and bowed his head again. He worked through the routine again for Wladyslaw, Akamai, and some other people named LeRoy, Yannis, Cosima, Louise, Satterthwaite, Bo Dog, and Duchese Kanani Isabella. Nobody said anything to him, though Fergus bowed his head along with each name.

People did that. They mourned for the dead, like clouds regretting the loss of their rain. I would regret my own death plenty when it happened, but someone else's, no. Or maybe I would. Since earlier today—yesterday?—I hadn't been able to kill anybody. Not even Roder, who I realized was watching me again.

"That should do it," he said, shifting his eyes smoothly back to the screen. Fergus still sat staring at his tiny little screen. It was filled to the edges with blue and white now, and a black curved edge that was space. I guessed the white was clouds. I would have expected a world to be green and brown, somehow.

Roder leaned back and stretched his arms above his head. "Now, Malka," he said. "We need to talk some more."

No.

"Shouldn't we be working on a plan?" interrupted Cully.

"I am," said Roder. "I have to find out what we have to work with. I'm a Monitor. What powers do I have as a Monitor?"

Cully said, "The right to place administrative hold, the right to inspect evidence and interrogate witnesses, the right to investigate independently, the right to be informed of all Enforcement operations . . . Oh."

"That's it. Those are rights, not powers. Who grants those rights?"

Again Cully said, from some memorized text, "The government by means of the Charter." He was starting to look unsure of himself.

"No. Who tells Enforcement they have to do what I say?"

"The NeverMind."

There was a long wait while everybody got that straight in their heads. "Right. And they're ignoring the NeverMind. The only power I had depended on was the ability of the NeverMind to make Enforcement do what I wanted. Now all we have left is ourselves."

"Ourselves and Malka. Malka's a little messed up," said Cully, finished with his litany, leaning back and regarding me. All their eyes were on me again.

Stop staring at me.

With surprising suddenness they were all looking elsewhere. My head felt light.

"It's like an electric shock when she does that," said Fergus, who was back staring at his screen.

"Or a breaking wave," agreed Roder, looking down at his hands from beneath his eyelashes as if they were fascinating. "Malka, you cast spells with words so easily it's scary. You haven't known you were a speaker long, have you? You told me you weren't a witch, and you believed it."

I didn't answer. I wouldn't repeat myself.

"I bet you bespoke only when you really wanted something?" he persisted, glancing up at me. His eyes creased at the corners when he did it. "That's how most bespeakers get started."

All I ever really said to myself was *leave me alone*, and I said it now.

Roder shook his head as if to clear it. "Stop it. Please."

Cully wiped his forehead with his beads. "My mind went completely blank. What happened to Electra, anyway?"

Roder squeezed his eyes shut. "Concentrate, people."

"I'm going to see where she went," Cully said, got up, and left the room. Roder brought his hands together, leaned forward to say something more, and then Cully yelled, "Roder!" from the hall. He rose and looked out, and then went out. Cully yelled again, higher and louder. "Roder! He's trying to get into the drive chamber! Roder—"

As he stepped out, something crashed in the hall. I went to look.

Roder's back was toward me. His knees were bent and his arms were in front of him. He was carefully inching forward toward someone facing him, someone who was a black shadow against the glare of planet-light through the shattered front door. Electra lay on her face in front of the drive doorway, her back slowly falling and rising. Cully was on his knees nearer to me, trying to get up.

"Malka, move please," Octavian said as he slipped past me. Slight as he was, he grabbed Cully by the shoulders, dragging him back into the kitchen.

"Malka, get him. I'll get him from this side," said a familiar, calm voice from the other end of the hall, and the silhouette moved forward. "You can do it. Run him through."

It was Tobiah. He'd gotten himself out. Or maybe I had gotten him out.

11

Attack with Reprise (**Biter's Bark,** True Action Behind False Action)

Roder didn't look behind him. He took another step forward, moving very slowly. "You know this young man, Malka?" he said.

"Yes."

Tobiah was dripping blue fluid still, and his round face looked naked. "Come on, Malka, get him for me. Kill him." Tobiah never talked to me like that before. "He works for Enforcement, Malka. He's a Forcer."

Now that wasn't right. Even after such a short time, I knew Roder wasn't exactly a Forcer. I could understand why Tobiah would think it, though.

Roder said, still moving forward, "How long have you known him, Malka?"

"You've known me for years, Malka. Who do you believe, him or me? Who do you believe? We've got to get out of here. I know how to take over the drive."

If he was Tobiah, he could make time slow down and take care of Roder himself.

"Who do you believe, Malka?" he repeated, moving closer, his eyes fixed on Roder. As he neared me he looked like a drowned man or a dead man.

He could take care of Roder himself. He could.

I heard a piece of Octavian's voice in the kitchen, hushed, and Cully's voice saying, "Electra."

"Slow time," I suggested to Tobiah. He made an annoyed face, just as he had in the tank, just as he had when I tried to warn him in his shop. He crouched and he hurled himself straight at Roder. It was all wrong.

"Now!" he yelled as he jumped.

Slow time. Slow time. Slow time.

Fergus started, "Sweet Cecil's under—" and then the voice dipped to a lazy growl and fell below hearing. The air turned to honey or hot mud or thick dust, and I had to struggle to pull it into my lungs. It felt different from the time when Tobiah did it in his shop. That felt normal, just looked and sounded funny. This felt like a very bad dream or a drowning.

Tobiah hung stopped in midair, his mouth open and his teeth showing. Both his thumbs were inches from the android's eyes, and his thin muscles stretched his naked skin like tent ropes. It was a commando's leap, coordinated and athletic, but he had already failed. Roder's hands were sweeping Tobiah's arms apart, and balanced neatly forward on one foot he was already kicking one of Tobiah's legs aside with his other foot.

Tobiah and Roder were together in their agonizing dawdle. Tobiah was moving even more slowly than the android. I had made the time drag, not Tobiah.

Something leaned against my leg. I looked down. The cat, moving normally, stared up at me with her mouth open, panting. She was in slow time with me.

When I looked up again, I could see Tobiah's eyes getting even wider, his teeth showing more. He looked like an ogre or a machine. I waded through the air to look at Roder's face. It was calm and intent. When he was this focused, he didn't look sad. Tobiah's arms were separated now, missing Roder's eyes, and the android was turning him around, using the spin he had applied with his foot.

I still had time to do something, if I wanted to. Tobiah had been something like a friend to me. Or maybe he hadn't. Slow time really didn't feel anything like what I felt in his shop. I was wheezing. The muscles that pulled the air into my lungs were hurting.

Now Tobiah had his back to Roder, and was falling to the floor. In a gradual motion like a snake going into a burrow, the android hooked his arms under the clock maker's arms and locked his hands behind his neck, and at the same time he brought his knee into the center of Tobiah's back. They were falling together now, but Tobiah was stuck in Roder's hug. His face, approaching the ground, still had the same masklike grimace. Roder had him down, safe and alive, even though Tobiah would have killed Roder without a qualm. I coughed from the effort of drawing the air in.

There was another cough at my feet, light and thin. The cat was crouching with her head down and her gums showing, trying to breathe. I kneeled down and she stared at me but didn't see me. Then she rolled to one side with her ribs pumping in and out. No. I'd never had a pet before. She couldn't die on me now. *No, no, no, faster, please, no,* I said to her.

"—pants, we're at the end of nowhere!" it sounded like Fergus said.

The time had quickened again. There was a thud and a struggle and Roder was kneeling on top of Tobiah, holding his head back and up at an uncomfortable angle. Tobiah continued to fight. His legs were kicking all over the place. "Get Octavian," said Roder to me. "I need to get your friend back in the tank. I have to keep him from hurting himself."

Even with Octavian's help it wasn't easy. They wrestled Tobiah into the infirmary and I could hear grunts and splashes. Then they came back and got Electra, not looking at me.

I understood why. But Tobiah wasn't my friend. He wasn't even a witch. I'd been fooled twice. Was there a third level to Zul's deception?

The cat bounded ahead of me into the kitchen, tail high. Fergus, oblivious, was muttering to himself and staring into his screen. Cully was leaning on the table, holding his beads to his big chest. "Is it over yet?" he asked me.

"It's over," I said. I went to the window. The imaginary wallpaper sun had started to rise, bright as the real one, and a sweet heavy smell like lilac flowed in from some flowering bushes the other side of the garden wall. The cat jumped up to the sill next to me and leaned on me, hard, her warm fur going up my nose. I snorted in annoyance and she jumped down into the garden.

"How did he get out?" Octavian said, coming in.

"I don't know," said Roder. "It wasn't broken. He got the locking mechanism to disengage somehow."

"I think I must have let him out," I said, "But I don't think he's really who I thought he was." A hand on my shoulder, hard, turning me around. Cully stopped because the tip of my blade was beneath his jaw. He lifted his chin, swallowing, but I followed his movements.

"You forgot what I said about touching me," I explained to him.

"Cully," said Roder.

Cully took a deep breath. Roder watched us and did nothing to stop me. I let the weapon drop, and noticed it was still smeared with the Forcer's blood, mostly dry now. I scratched at it with a fingernail.

"Roder, you won't believe it," said Fergus, still staring into his screen. "I was trying to get a fix on our absolute location, and I can't map us. We're so far outside the Web there aren't any standard beacons—" Still talking, he had turned excitedly to Roder and stopped. Everybody in the room excepting himself and Octavian looked as if they had just survived a tornado.

"Where did Electra get to?" he said. "What happened?"

"She's in the infirmary tank," said Roder. "The boy in the tank got loose and gave her a concussion. I had to wrestle him down. I sedated him, but I think you're right, Malka, and whoever he is, he's not a witch either. While he was conscious the instruments didn't even jiggle, until you did what you did."

Roder was rummaging in a cupboard above the refectory console. He pulled out a white cloth and tossed it at me. I caught it by reflex and realized he was giving me something to clean my sword. Bribing the bad dog, I thought to myself, but I sat down and started to use it. Tall Cully still stood there gloomily staring at Roder just out of my blade's length. He looked like his feelings hurt all over.

"Leave her alone, Cully. She told you not to touch her, didn't she? And she didn't stop me from taking the boy down when she could have. She had plenty of time. Come on, Cully, come on, I'll take care of that arm." Cully's shoulders didn't relax, but he turned slowly toward the android.

He had seen me in that long instant when I slowed the time. Roder had seen me.

"I'm sorry," I said.

He gave me such a sweet smile it made my teeth hurt.

"Stop that," I said, and his smile widened. I was going to get off this ship. He was dangerous.

"You resist my charm? Deep woman," he said, and took Cully out to the infirmary.

It wasn't hard to get the dried blood off the shiny surface of the blade. I worked in silence, as I had most of my life. Roder had asked me if I talked to myself when I really wanted something. Most of my life I didn't want things much. Mostly I wanted people to leave me alone, and Roder wasn't leaving me alone.

Of course when I was little I did want something badly. I wanted to leave my little master, wanted to run away, wanted to escape his slim-fingered clutch. That was all I really cared about. And when I wanted something badly, I did something about it. I ran away from my master and stowed away on a ship that looked like this one. I went to Caliban and found the Sefir Zul. No magic spells required. As simple as that.

Well, Caliban was not exactly simple. It had seemed simple to begin with. I did some research, and I chose Caliban on its reputation. It was as grouchy as they said, but it had the best martial arts center in the Galaxy, so that's where I went. I didn't realize that like most worlds these days, they trained only their own people. When I arrived, it took me weeks of going around to every dojo and salle I could find before I gave up. The sword-teachers were grim and silent and none of them would take on a newcomer.

So I found myself a job as an errand runner, and settled down to wait until I wasn't a newcomer anymore. I wanted to be a fighter badly, very badly indeed, but I didn't talk to myself, didn't cast any spells. I just waited. It was before I came fully awake, so waiting for weeks or months or even years wasn't a problem.

While I was waiting, the Sefir Zul found me. He was one of my regular drops. I delivered uniforms like the one I was wearing now. If he was my last job for the day, I would stay by the doorway watching his students. If anyone caught me looking, I could slip out fast. I loved the noise of the people crossing swords. I loved the movements of the fighters. Zul taught his students to dance the game, and they didn't know it.

One day, Zul caught me looking, but I couldn't slip out because he was standing in my way, towering over me. He looked down at me from under his caterpillar eyebrows and then he watched his students instead, but he still didn't move from the doorway. He stood there a long time. I could smell him all the while. When he moved into the room as if he had forgotten me, I slithered out, my heart pounding. The next three times I made my deliveries and escaped. The next time, feeling safer, I stopped to watch again, but Zul caught me again, and he forced me to stay again. He did it again and again, until one day when I stopped to watch, it was a Wednesday and a new class was starting. When Zul was handing out uniforms, he threw one to me. I stayed and learned. I felt like an alien, but things worked out—I thought. I hoped Zul didn't know what I really was. I hoped he thought I was a little witch with a hair-trigger temper, just the way Roder did.

My little master still controlled me, no matter how far away I ran. He ordered me never to let anyone know what I really was, so I never did. And I never would. He didn't really need to use pain on me to make sure of that, but he liked doing it.

The blade was clean now. I didn't really need to keep polishing it the way I was. I slid it into the scabbard with a hiss. The cloth was smeared red-brown. I folded it up into a small wad, but I didn't know where to put it so I set it neatly on the table in front of me.

I could not believe I was so naive, after all this time running and hiding. Tobiah was not my friend. I should have known. The Sefir Zul was not my hero. The Sefir Zul was an Enforcer, one who could order another Forcer to sacrifice his arm. No wonder that poor Forcer in the school had looked so frightened, reciting his nonsense about magic suppressors. No wonder Zul had chastened his student when he mocked the Forcer. And Tobiah was not a witch. And he was not my friend. Was he part of Zul's plan? Had I been sent to Tobiah so I might think him a witch, and free him when Roder captured us both? Were all the Sefir's students Forcers too? No, that was too complicated a web for one small grim Malka with a bad taste in her mouth. Malka the Sleepless, Malka the Rumpled, Malka the Flapper of Hands.

12

The False Parry
(**Dick Johnson,** Defend-
ing What Is Not Attacked)

Some time later, something smelled like grilling sausages. Octavian was sitting opposite me at the table eating a thick sandwich with both hands. The others were leaning against the wall near the door, talking in muted voices. I heard Cully say, "You know, like when you're trying to pick up a mouse and it sinks its little teeth into you. It's such a shock, even if it doesn't draw any blood."

Fergus laughed up at him, but Roder said, "Not a mouse. Think of a sparrow hawk, maybe, if that makes it easier." Cully loomed over the other two like a pigeon in a group of sparrows himself, but there was no doubt who was leader there: the slim sad android leaned back against the wall and they arranged themselves on either side of him. All his people acted as if they were in love with him.

I got up and walked over to the food console. The men fell silent when I approached. As I feared, the only control was a palm jack.

"Could I have some food too?" I said to them. There was a time I didn't need food.

"Sure," said Roder. Cully, expressionless, moved forward and I moved back to give him room to work. He gripped his beads in his off hand to ward against me while he did it. Humans and their talismans, setting magic to catch magic. That was why I was in such a mess.

I took my food back to the other end of the table to eat. I was giving them space, since they didn't want to talk near me, but their conversation had ended and they all got something to eat as well. Roder stayed leaning against the wall, his worn blue shirt creasing between his folded arms.

"Octavian, you're sure the planet has no mind of its own?" he said quietly.

Octavian finished his mouthful. "It has concentrations of magic here and there mumbling to themselves, but nothing I recognize as a Cybernal. Nothing large enough or clear enough." He tore off another mouthful.

"Magic doesn't organize itself. That tells me there's human presence on the planet and they have talent."

Octavian stopped chewing. "A renegade world?"

The others looked away as if he had said something embarrassing. It was the witch's daydream, the inspiration for all kinds of stupid insurrections, the Eden where the talented could play witch without persecution. My master and his associates—not his friends, he would have no friends—had talked of it as if it were a certainty. To me, it sounded like a nightmare, a world all full of witches, all poking and prying and pushing on me.

"Possibly," said Roder. "They do exist, you know. Usually not for long if there's a trail to follow, but the Web is a bigger place than most people imagine. I don't know how the Mennenkalts got these coordinates in the first place unless they set the world up themselves. I would have sworn they never went off-planet."

"But these aren't the coordinates the Mennenkalts gave in their flight plan," said Fergus. "I thought I told you. We're somewhere else completely."

Silence.

"We're lost?" said Octavian.

Roder finally lifted his head. "Well, no wonder they weren't here when we arrived. Malka, where are we?"

"You're asking *her*—" began Fergus.

I shook my head.

A thump, a crash, and then another crash came from the hall. Octavian stood up suddenly, saying, "The drive is screaming." The android ran to the door and went out. "Malka!" he shouted.

He was standing at the broken door of the drive, covering his face with his hands and peering through the fingers. I came and stood at his shoulder. I saw what Roder couldn't see, and I said, "I didn't let him out this time."

"My fault," he said grimly. "I should have checked. He reset it for self-release when he got out. Can you see him? Is he still alive?"

"Sort of."

The room was as empty and silent as ever, except that Tobiah sat cross-legged in the center. Tobiah, or something from which Tobiah's face and body hung like an ill-fitting suit. He was obviously as blinded by the drive as Roder was, and his skin was crawling. I'd seen that happen before; the compressed magic was changing the stuff he was made of. He didn't seem to mind. His face was as still and empty as it had been when he was in the tank. "Tobiah," I said. He lifted his head and turned it this way and that, searching for the source of the noise. Then he opened his mouth wide, and shoved two fingers of one hand down his throat and leaned forward, making a coughing, strangling sound. A small sphere was the only thing that came out, a shiny cold sphere the size of a walnut. It bounced on the floor in front of him and lay still. He looked at it.

He held it between his nimble clock maker's fingers, cracked it open, and stared at what was inside.

Then his skin melted away like a pile of sand in a high wind, starting with his hands and face, peeling away and leaving behind an opalescent stick figure with Tobiah's blue eyes. The opalescent figure began to get to its feet.

A chilly breeze blew past me from the chamber. It wasn't a breeze, it was the cold I felt when I went near one of the new Enforcement ships. The stuff drifting out of the sphere was black-matter. It killed live magic.

No, no, no. The escaping waves of magic from the terrified engine broke over me, roaring. If you wait for just the right moment, if you go loose and stay open, you can ride on top of a breaking wave. It feels like being in an earthquake or a high-speed accident, and it is as hot as an explosion.

A quiet voice came from the kitchen: Fergus, shaking. "Roder, we're losing the drive. It was screaming, and now it's fading away somehow, like water going down a drain." Around and around and around, down the drain.

"Well, then, take us down. Fergus, take us down," said Roder in a voice so calm, it felt like the end of the world, or the beginning. He disappeared through the shattered door of the infirmary; I heard shattering. Blue fluid flowed out the door on the floor, and he splashed out supporting Electra and Pegeen. Both of them were half-asleep. Pegeen's abdomen was nearly healed already, though a pink stripe went from one hipbone to the other. Fergus was already bent over his console. "Prepare to evacuate, people," Roder said, leading the way to the door.

"Evacuate?" said Cully.

"The moment we touch down. Run as fast as you can, as far as you can. Everything in the ship is held together by the drive."

The floor shook and we bounced. "We're down. Petrus!" said Fergus. I thought it was another swearword, but he ran past us to dive into his bedroom, resurfacing a moment later with an enraged-looking parrot clinging grimly to his shoulder. They crowded past me heading for the front door, Cully clutching his beads, Octavian holding his pendant, as if their familiars were all the baggage they needed.

Where was the cat? Unsteady on my feet, I went to the window. She was sitting washing herself on the garden wall. "Hey," I said. She swiveled her ears at me and kept washing.

I climbed over the sill and dropped down. The grass was high and damp, and my slippers were wet the moment I landed. The cat jumped and whirled to face me. "Bear, we have to go," I said, wading toward her, reaching my hands out. She crouched, her hindquarters up, her eyes staring. "Don't run, puss," I said, slowing down and reaching out to her.

"Malka!" Roder's voice from the window startled the cat, and she jumped down on the other side of the wall. I climbed over after her. She had her back to me and her tail twitching.

"We have to go now!" Roder said. She crouched again but didn't move. I bent my knees as I approached her, reaching out and calling her name.

"Malka, come now, please," Roder said just as softly and just as gently as I was talking to Bear.

She twitched her tail one more time, and then I had her. I was clutching her around her middle and holding her to me while she tried to climb off me with every claw. I rolled over the wall and ran to the window.

It was too high to reach, but Roder was still leaning out of it, stretching his arms down. I didn't want to let go of the cat. I held her to me with one arm and reached up until he caught my fingers. It hurt worse than when Cully had caught me. Halfway up, the whole world went boom and I could hear rocks falling off the top of the garden wall behind me. I scrambled over the sill with Roder's help into the empty kitchen. Everyone was gone. Something soft smacked me in the back of the head, a clod of dirt. Dirt and grass sprayed past us from the window.

"Come on," he said, and we ran down the hall and out the door, burst into an open plaza between tall buildings, and kept running. A hundred yards ahead, I saw the crew standing and watching us, Octavian supporting Pegeen, Electra with her arms hanging over the shoulders of Fergus and Cully. "Run! Go!" shouted Roder, flinging his hands out as if releasing birds, and the crew obeyed him. They kept going until they disappeared over the neatly paved crest of a hill. From the square openings of a big red building, people were coming and looking out.

A crack and a roar like thunder sounded behind us and echoed off the buildings. Roder slowed to a walk and turned around. The cat seized the opportunity to jump away from me and land. Her tail was lashing.

There was another crack, and more thunder, and the house shook, and another crack, and then the windows blew out. Seven crows burst cawing out with them, leaving feathers swirling behind, and rocketed toward the horizon. With a crash, the frame of the front door fell forward, and an opalescent stick figure leapt out and ran past us, blue eyes staring and mouth open, the hand that had been inside Tobiah-puppet.

Behind him a solid fountain of earth and rocks poured out of the apertures, which held for a moment and then began to crumble outward. The sides of the house were buried in dirt, rising higher and higher. Then an entire side of the house bulged out and a black clump of tree roots thrust into the air, followed by the rest of the tree, the pine tree outside my bedroom. The other side of the house simply tore off, and more trees fell out. Then the roof, making a groaning sound, began to rise, wobbling, into the air, propelled by a crumbling mound of clay and topsoil. The house disappeared, covered by the geyser of soil, except for the roof, which like a hat was perched atop the growing hill. Finally, the roar began to subside, and streams of mud bubbled from the sides of the earthen mount, joining at the base into a clay-colored stream that spread out over the square and rippled over the hill going away from us. Fish flopped and jumped in the shallow stream.

"I always wondered what would happen to the scenery if the drive went," said Roder.

13

The Engagement of Blades (**Birdy's Clasp,** Suspicious Embrace)

A clod of dirt landed a few feet away and rolled toward us, stopping a few inches away with roots sticking out of its underside.

"I guess we're marooned for the moment," said Roder calmly, prodding with his toe at it.

Some of the people coming out of the red building were arguing with one another, shaking their arms at one another so the bright sleeves trembled. Two, gaudy robes swirling, were walking toward us. The nearest of the crowd, a broad-faced bearded man swathed in magenta, shouted something at us, something that pushed against me. I wriggled my shoulders in irritation, said *I am not here*, and began to walk in the opposite direction. The cat too leapt into motion and bounded ahead of me, but then skittered off to one side and disappeared. A moment later she sauntered out again and sat down, letting me pass her by, and then cantered past again. "Malka!" I heard Roder call. I looked back. His expression was wary, he was leaning as if he wanted to walk, but he wasn't moving and the first of the colorful gentlemen was almost upon him. They were witches, then.

I watched for a moment. It wasn't my problem.

Roder isn't here either, I said anyway.

The natives came level with Roder and went past, making harsh comments, huddling around an empty spot on the pavement, and grasping at air with their hands. He backed away from the group as they began to snarl at one another.

I saw in my head the red blotch on the neck of the Sefir Zul, and Zul's face, the expression on the android's face in the corridor when I faced him with the blade he had handed back to me. Cully's face, too. I was coming apart at the seams, sparing people, saving people like this. It was bound to happen. *Not yet, please, not yet.*

I looked around me. The street was narrow, winding, bumpy, and deserted. The houses on either side gaped empty. If you could call them houses. The street was like an amusement park, or a museum, because each one was odder and more beautiful than the next: encrusted glass mosaic next to limestone arches next to carved marble inlaid with wood, all of them different heights and widths.

I was going the opposite direction from the one Roder's crew had taken. He would follow them and I would be free from them all, and from the troublesome way they made me feel.

The air smelled of dusty resin and a tarry, dark tang I recognized after a while as wood smoke. The houses stayed absurd, but they got smaller. Then I crossed an invisible dividing line: the road straightened, and the houses became nearly identical bungalows, sane, smug, and boring. The smoky smell intensified, and then a nagging whisper of sewage. That was another odor you rarely found on Web worlds, though humans always smelled far stronger than they knew.

The cat passed me again, tail up, her soft feet pacing lightly, went diagonally across the road in front of me, and disappeared down an alley. Two houses later, she trotted out and cut across my path, looking intent. At least one companion had stayed with me.

I turned left at a fork and continued downhill, slowing to a walk. The staid villas gave way to rows of less substantial houses, some of them with peeling paint and injured dignity. There were people here, sitting on the steps, talking in groups, not staring at me because I *wasn't there*, after all. I saw no cars, and the people's palms were smooth, no sockets. It really was a world outside the Web. Enforcement wouldn't know where I was. My empty-eyed master wouldn't know where I was, then. I was safe here. I could live here.

If I was staying, I needed more people than this. I needed a busy tavern, or a roof-raising, or a party, some place where people talked and talked and I could sit and soak up the words. Farther down the hill, perhaps.

Behind me, someone made a chirping noise. I ignored it, but the cat, ahead of me, cocked her ears back and sat down in the road. As I passed her, the chirping came again. I glanced back, and saw Roder a few paces behind, scooping the cat up into his arms and scratching with one finger behind her ears.

I am not here, I insisted.

"The rest of my crew has implants. I can find them when I want them," he said vaguely to a spot just past my right shoulder, catching up and walking even with me. "They'll find me."

Malka is not a member of your crew.

He strolled along holding the cat for a few steps, then shook his head. "It's remarkable that you can do that to me. I told you I'm shielded against magic, didn't I? You bespeak me so strongly that it takes a few moments for my shield to recover. It's as strong as what that whole pack of Talents were just doing before you rescued me up the hill."

Was there nothing I could do that he wouldn't notice?

He continued, "Did you know that you have grown about two inches taller some time in the last hour?"

No. I broke into a run, startling a young woman who was just opening her front door so that she jumped back and slammed it. I ran to the next cross street and swerved left, then cut back up the hill on the next turn. I could run like this for hours if I needed to. I passed a man trudging up the hill holding the hands of two small children, and they all turned to look.

"I *am* an android, I *can* keep up with you," said Roder from next to my elbow, and I yelled and drew my sword. He backed away just enough for me to miss him every time the flailing edge cut past. His footwork was really wonderful, some part of my mind commented. Meanwhile, the calm-eyed cat watched me from his shoulder, and the man I had passed picked both children up by the midsection and escaped, the children giving high thin complaints.

"You're not going to kill me. You're not the murdering type."

"I've killed millions," I hissed, and put some shoulder into my attack.

"Lately?" He leaned back out of the way, taking another step back.

I was found out. He knew. I dropped the blade and stood with it hanging from my fist, glaring at him.

He smiled that sweet smile, a genuinely happy one. "I like you," he said. "You interest me. One of the disadvantages of a long life. After a while, you don't run into really interesting people anymore. I'd hate to pass up the opportunity to get to know you better."

I closed my eyes. When I opened them again, he was still there. He did look interested. The river-colored eyes had a distant sparkle in them, and he wasn't sad at all.

"I am not a member of your crew."

"No."

"I am not a witch."

"If you say so."

"I can't help you."

He shrugged and fell into step beside me. Somehow, we were walking down the hill again. The man and his children peered at us from behind a house. I saluted them gravely with my sword and sheathed it. Malka's Surrender, as painted by a second-rate half-blind artist for a memorial picture commissioned by a fourth-rank office of the civil government, to be hung in an unused corridor. Everything had gone from bad to worse to calamity today, but there was no point in struggling. I could escape him later.

He put the cat down and it sat and washed while we passed it, but I knew it would catch up. Now that he mentioned it, my beautiful new armor was tight on my chest and shoulders. I had always been a growing girl, but the food had been rich today.

The odor of smoke and poor drainage intensified. We turned left, then right, and then we walked into the midst of a full-blown market. Ramshackle wooden buildings spilled out their contents on jury-rigged shelving. Leaning into the street were rough-built stands and half huts bulging with shoes, fly-ridden meat on ice, toys, spices, and frying dough. People were lined up shoulder to shoulder reaching for things or working their way through the crowds, and banging one another with their string bags and baskets. The stink was rich and complex: well-aged garbage, fish, urine, resin, sweat, sawdust, the metallic tang of meat and overripe apples, and a sweet reek of caramelized sugar.

In the middle of the road, a man squatted on a loose-woven blanket next to a carved wooden model of a skeleton and a pile of water-smoothed rocks. He saw us between the people, raised one weather-beaten hand, and called something to Roder. The android shook his head and kept going through the crowd.

I couldn't see the cat anywhere, and when I looked around for her I saw the squatting man beginning to rise. I started to walk faster, snaked between a woman as wide as a milk cow and a bent man counting out coins to her, and heard someone shouting behind me. I ducked and burrowed under somebody's arm. I found myself in Roder's shadow again.

People were speaking to him and nodding to him as he passed, saying the same thing the man on the blanket had: "Bielo, Bielo, Bielo?" Roder kept shaking his head, and I watched their faces get doubtful, one by one. Another shout came from behind us. Roder led me in between two fruit stands and out into the street. The cat skittered out after us.

Roder stopped and laughed. "Thought I felt a beacon." We were facing a house with a porch, shutters, and a paneled front door. The house had started out small. The base had been built upon sideways and upward, with wood, stone, slate, and straw. A roofed walkway of weathered wood led to something in the back, probably stables from the smell. Over the door hung a heavy wooden sign painted with many coats of enamel. There was a second story and an attic, and it was all painted a crumbling white, but the original house had looked exactly like Roder's ship. A Monitor's ship.

"I have a brother here," said Roder, and entered. I could hear footsteps behind us.

Inside the tavern—it was obviously a tavern, smelling of food and sour beer—a man behind the bar looked up. Here, yes, was Roder's brother.

"Hello, Bielo," said Roder.

"Roder. I knew it was too good to last," the man, or rather the Massim-model android, answered in Standard, putting a mug down. He was not Roder. He was thicker, with a small round belly pushing the waistband of his trousers down and a dish cloth flung over his shoulder. The lines at the corners of his mouth were sharp folds, and his eyes were the eyes of a man who did business. I obviously had to adjust some of my notions about androids if two identical models could be so different. "Were you the thunder earlier?" It was his name the people had been saying outside, then, the name of another cinestar from the twenties.

Roder lifted his eyebrows. "Thunder?" People were crowding into the room after us, curious and loud. The cat had disappeared again.

"There was a big noise and half my mugs fell off the wall."

"Oh. My drive blew and the scenery turned inside out," answered Roder.

Bielo got a mug down. "You're marooned here too, then? Have a

drink? And a drink for your little Forester? Where'd you get her, anyway?
I thought you hunted them all down a long time ago."

Hunted them down?

Roder flicked his eyes at me. "Ask her yourself."

"Oh. My apologies, madam. I'll give you a drink, Roder, but I can't
help you."

Roder leaned forward on his elbows. "Bielo, it's full-scale war now,
not just government politics. Enforcement is trying to take over the
Web." The room was full now, and noisy with conversation and laughter
in the language I didn't know. A man was talking to my back, tinny and
insistent.

Bielo raised his voice. "That may well be, but I still can't help you:
I don't have a drive. This is a witch world. When I found it, nearly
ninety years now, I set down right where I am now to have a look around.
In less than half an hour the local Talents happened by—"

The man's voice behind me got louder. I turned in irritation. It was
the skeleton man from the road, and he was asking me something about
Roder, jabbing his finger at him. Three other people stood behind him,
their faces eager with inquiry. I shook my head and turned back.

"—zoning violation of some kind. They sucked the drive hollow,
and did it without blowing my space-fold pockets. I don't know where
the scenery went. When I came back I had to pretend I was a local
squatter and I put my crew to work in the kitchen until they learned the
language. I've been here ever since. Actually, I'm the great-grandson,
as far as the locals know."

The skeleton man was repeating himself louder, as if that would
make me answer him.

"I understand," said Roder. "Can you at least house us for a day or
so?"

"I'm a businessman. I need my rooms. I'm always right on the edge
as it is."

The native poked me in the ribs from behind, and I jumped off the
stool to face him. He flinched back, and then laughed down at me,
showing a mouthful of stained but healthy teeth.

"Malka, don't," said Roder quietly. "Bielo, she's very cranky when
she's pushed. I need to get her out of this crowd. And you're still government."

"The government's awful small and awful far away; I bet Enforcement's taking care of everything just fine. And if you're stuck here like

OF SWORDS AND SPELLS

283

me, money's tight. I'd give you and your lady friend a room, but I'd have
to ask you to help me out."

The skeleton man stepped forward and poked his finger down at
me again, saying something different now. I put my hand to my hilt.

"Malka, don't, please. Bielo, I'm not staying long if I can fix this,
but I promise I'll help if I'm stuck here. I invoke your contract."

The skeleton man poked me in the middle of the chest, squatting
to do it, and laughed. Then he looked down in amazement at my blade,
which was touching the hollow of his scrawny throat. The room was
silent.

Bielo moved slowly, hands up. "I'll see what I can do. Make her
drop that, all right? The man's harmless, and a good chiropractor to
boot."

"And I need the language if you can give it to me. Not her. Implants
don't work on her. Malka?"

"He was poking me," I explained. Roder sat there with his arm on
the bar, looking at me with the tea-colored eyes as if we were old friends
and he'd heard it before. The other Massim, with his hands half extended,
was a stranger whose eyes were flat and anxious. Roder cocked his head,
I put my blade back, and the skeleton man bared his brown teeth at me
in a nervous grin. I bobbed politely at him, and he bobbed back at me.

The room Bielo gave us was tiny, with a stained bed in a rope-hung
frame that took up half the floor. It was obvious why Bielo begrudged
us the space from the noises either side of us: loud conversations, splash-
ing water, rhythmic thumps, and occasional moans. Bielo wasn't exactly
running a hotel. He got his money's worth out of those rooms, and we
were taking an entire room's income for the rest of the day. I felt the
bed with my hand, looked at it dubiously, and sat on the floor instead
with my back to the wall.

Roder laughed and slid down to sit against the door himself, stretching his legs out so his feet nearly touched mine. They weren't actually
touching, though. The man knew exactly what I could stand. It took him
only a few hours to know me when no one had ever known me before.
I closed my eyes to stop the feeling that the room was moving . . . Bielo
said Roder had hunted all the Foresters down?

I opened my eyes again. Roder was watching me. We stared at each
other in the dark room for a long time until I closed my eyes and closed
the contact. *I am very very boring,* I said, but didn't open my eyes again
to see if it worked. I didn't want to know.

14

Pretense of Trust (**Gorm,** The Feint of Innocence)

I woke with a start when someone knocked on the door, and found myself halfway to my feet with my hand reaching for my sword, and Roder's hand clamped around my forearm to stop me. There was a brief scuffle, which I realized I would have lost if I'd kept going. I rubbed my arm. He didn't apologize.

"I did a copy of my language center," said Bielo, when Roder let him in. The landlord's hair was even more rumpled. "I don't know how good it is. The equipment's pretty old. I won't apologize for the vocabulary. You're getting ninety years' worth of slang and curses."

Roder turned the small thing over, then lifted the hair behind his ear. There were three sockets just like the one in my hand, in a row. He plugged the implant in. He closed his eyes.

Bielo, ignoring his inattention, complained, "My customers are not pleased, Roder. This is the second time this week a woman has caused trouble in the bar, and that doesn't go over well. There's rules for women and men here, and she's breaking them just by going around looking like that, let alone hauling out her pigsticker and poking poor old Duber with it."

Roder opened his eyes again. "I think it's working, Bielo. Thank you. Yaschutt zhay, Bielo." It was a harsh language. I'd thought it was the people, but even Roder sounded ill-tempered when he wrapped his throat around the sounds.

"Not bad, not bad. You don't have to sleep on the floor. I'm spelled against vermin," he said, letting himself out.

Bielo's footsteps faded away. Roder sat down on the bed with his eyes half-open, staring at the opposite wall. "Lie down," he said. "Go back to sleep. Oh, you can have the bed if you want. It will take me a little while to absorb this."

I shook my head and leaned back against the wall. Something scrabbled in the window above my head, and the cat crawled in through the fist-sized opening between the sash and the sill. She was carrying something small and furry, which she took underneath the bed. I saw her eyes reflecting the light and listened to her crunch. "Good," she said finally, coming out to wash. She was sitting so close to me that every time she bobbed her head her whiskers brushed me. I ran my forefinger along her back. "Mine," she said. "You are mine."

"My name is Malka."

"Maallkkaa," she enunciated carefully. "I am Bear."

"Yes."

"Good," she said again. She settled with a thump against me and put her nose under her tail. I knew the android was contemplating me but I didn't look. Your opponent should never know where you are looking; you should watch nothing and everything.

He said, "I've never seen that happen. Familiars and talismans are always keyed to their makers. You keep surprising me."

I shrugged.

"You're unusual in a lot of ways. How did you come to leave Forest?" he said. "It wasn't the kind of world people left."

I considered the question, turned it around and looked underneath it, found another question hiding behind it. "You hunted Foresters down. Bielo said."

"Ah. Yes, I did, or I tried to."

I watched the cat breathe.

"I was looking for someone," he said. "Not you."

If I looked up, the clear eyes would be watching me.

"Enforcement was very upset with Forest," he said. "I came in because they were threatening to do a Class Two wipe. Some Forest witches had built themselves an unsanctioned Cybernal—it was more than just a computer, it was an engine of enormous size. The thing was incredible, powerful enough to move a world, small enough to fit in a hand, a pocket NeverMind. They were going to turn the planet into a ship, move the whole world, take it out of the Web, make it a renegade world."

Yes, they were. I had been around for that. It wasn't something I had been looking forward to.

"Something really frightened Enforcement. They started the wipe right after I arrived. Some of their own people were still on the surface when it happened. ERC barely let me lift off even though I was already in my ship." He shrugged. "They stayed frightened. I think one of them got away, the one who had the idea in the first place. Something keeps happening on different planets, an unexplained drain, just like the one that alerted us in the first place. I've been looking for him, and so has ERC, ever since," he said. "I even thought you might be him when I first saw you, but you're not." He closed his eyes and leaned back.

No, I wasn't him. I was mostly myself these days.

It was getting dark outside. The air drifting in the window smelled of charcoal, bread, cooking meat, and vinegar. The ugly language came in, with people laughing and shouting in it.

Why did I leave Forest? My master and I caught a ride in the engine of a small houseboat just like Roder's. Maybe it *was* Roder's, if he was there when they started the wipe. My master found out the wipe was coming. We ran away from home, from sandalwood, woven baskets, my master's dog, veronicas and sweet bean soup, because Enforcement was going to wipe my world. My master tied Bear up and muzzled him and made one neat thrust under the foreleg into the heart while he looked into the dog's eyes. "Not as interesting as I'd hoped, after all our years together," he said to the dying dog, wiped his knife on Bear's fur, and left him staring on the floor.

"Beautiful place, Forest," Roder said, and I jumped.

He continued with eyes shut, talking softly. "Those deep fragrant woods. With the russet trunks, and that apple-colored fog in the middle distance. And the moss, and ferns, and those round planked houses your people built in the branches. I could lie on my face down on the ground and stare into the moss, and it was just like looking down through the tops of the trees, I could see into a miniature forest with all those tiny green branches, and insects marching through the stems like bearer-beasts going through the woods. And that wind, that rushing wind bending the treetops, with that heavenly smell drifting down in the eddies. The whole world was forest, trees marching down to the edges of the beaches, trees rolling up the mountains with only the peaks showing, trees on every bump of an island, fat leafless trees covering the desert, thin short evergreens all across the tundra up to the edge of the ice caps. All those small dark people with the shy eyes." He fell silent again, with his eyes still closed.

How very odd, and what a pretty story. Why was he lying to me? I hadn't thought about my home much until today, when Roder gave me the food. I hadn't really been awake until a couple of years ago, and when I was on Forest I was too little to take much in. I tried to think about it now, but all I could remember was the same litany of pictures. My master's hands, holding a bowl of sweet bean soup and eating it, watching me hungry and tied to a chair. The dog Bear, limping. The fragrant bedstead, and my feet on the cool tile floor in some room somewhere. The Forest Cybernal. The breaking wave. The growing darkness outside wasn't as dark as the inside of my head.

Roder rubbed his temples. He lay down full length on the bed, kicking off the soft shoes he wore, and turned his face to the wall, resting his head on his arm. He was a long dark wave against the white wall, breathing steadily.

The breaking wave. My oldest memory was the breaking wave. I always thought it was a memory of my birth. I was in the water, and the wave was rising before me, approaching me. The top of it, above my head, whispered foam into the wind. The long green slope below it, veined with white, crawled up and up, curving until the whole wave sucked in its breath and became a long rolling tube, a green glass cave all around me with the sky barely visible through the roof of seawater. I was in the moment before the crash for what seemed like forever, and then all those tons of water fell into me all at once, and I swallowed them all. My master's long-fingered hands grabbed me and lifted me up while I coughed and screamed in fury, and he held me above the surface, my legs dangling. "Perfect," he said, and squeezed me so hard I thought my heart would burst. I remembered his small blue eyes watching me cough and gasp.

At least I remembered that much, though it had parts I must have filled in since then. When he held me up, for instance, I was bone dry and we were inside a big hollow room full of magic just like the Forest Cybernal, not outside at the seashore.

I got up and took my armor off in the dusk, folded it neatly, and used it for a pillow on the floor, though I laid the sword down beside me and held on to its hilt. I'd slept on plenty of floors over the years. I slept on a floor on the first night on the first world my master and

I came to after Forest. I slipped from the ship when it landed, and let my master out from the place I had concealed him, and together we slipped through the terminal and into a part of the town where there were abandoned buildings. The floor had splinters. My little master, his lips pursed, slept on a ruined couch, and I slept on the splintered floor. In the morning, he sent me out to get some food for us, but before he did, he took me by the ears and spoke to me.

"There are people out there who will hurt you worse than I ever can, Malka," he said, holding the ears tightly so I couldn't look away. "Don't trust anyone. Just get something to eat, that's all. Don't talk to anyone, they'll just hurt you. Stay away from anybody who can hurt you. Hear me?" and he lifted me by my ears and gave me a little shake. Then he gave me a bigger shake, watching me. He sighed. "You could be interesting. Pity. I need you." I remembered how torn he was when he realized Forest was going to be wiped, how much he wanted to stay and watch in spite of the danger. It would have been fascinating, he kept repeating in his dry voice as we escaped. I remembered his dog, its muzzle tied, eyes open. There were other creatures that died in our house from time to time, eyes always open.

I nodded solemnly once he put me down. I had to do everything he told me, of course, but he hadn't told me to come back this time, and he *had* told me to stay away from anyone who could hurt me, so I would take him at his word and stay away from *him*. I was awake enough for that. My ears still burning, I went back to the terminal, stole a little food, and stowed away in the engine of the next ship leaving.

I stayed away from everyone who could hurt me, stayed in the shadows, slipped from world to world invisible and asleep. After a while I realized my little master was still hunting me across the Web, always a few steps behind. I'd stayed out of his sharp grasp, until I decided to turn and fight, until I went to Caliban, until I met the Sefir Zul. It had seemed like such a good idea.

The Sefir Zul, stepping and turning, caressing me with his blows, admiring himself in the mirror and parrying my cuts. Stepping and turning, striking and blocking, dancing around and around, I swirled to the bottom and slid down the wave back into sleep—

The door burst open. Again I was standing blinking with my sword out, but Roder was in front of me. The light in the room was the color of old wood. It was dusk, and Bielo was talking urgently in a low voice.

"You didn't tell me the mages had already seen you. Two of them are downstairs asking me about my brother. Do you have the language yet? I need you to calm them down; they're mostly harmless, but they can be impossible if they think there's real danger."

"Yes. I'll go be your brother from out of town. Don't worry." Bielo ran down the stairs after Roder, who had brushed past him and was walking down the creaking stairs, smoothing his hair with both hands. I padded after them in my bare feet. It was only when I had gotten all the way downstairs that I realized I had left my sword behind. What was I thinking?

In the otherwise empty bar, Roder blinked sleepily at a gaudy pair of dandies. One of them, with ginger hair and muttonchop whiskers, was costumed in slashed pantaloons in acid green and mint. His stockings, tunic, and tubular necklace followed the color scheme with unmerciful faithfulness. The other, more muted, was a sour-looking scholar in deep crimson from his long gown to his gaiters. He likewise had a neat hoop—crimson, of course—circling his neck, and it was he who was addressing Roder in the brusque local language, made even more brusque by his manner. The other one glanced at me standing *not here* in the doorway and dismissed me without a thought.

Roder, his shoulders stooped forward and his hair standing on end, answered him in the same tongue. His voice sounded like Bielo's, but with a whine in the back of it. He was pretending to be a local. The crimson scholar answered him sharply. Roder continued to explain. Then the green-clad man said something and made a sharp gesture that *pushed*, and they both turned to leave. Roder's shoulders sagged and he shuffled after them, still playing the part. Bielo said something tentatively, and the green one answered with one word. The door swung shut behind them. Just like that I had what I wanted, an escape from Roder. Back into the shadows for Malka, safe again from people who could hurt her. I waited to feel good about it.

15

Displacing Target
(**Canard,** Duck-Squat)

Bielo's hand fell on my shoulder while I was waiting, and I wriggled away from it. "Stay, girl," he muttered under his breath. "He can take care of himself." I didn't know what he was talking about. I wasn't going to chase after Roder, no I wasn't. No. The innkeeper went to the door and peered into the dusk, his arms folded. He turned around and looked at me. "What am I going to do with you in the meantime? What's your Talent, girl?"

I shrugged. "Don't have one."

"You're not a witch? Don't tell me—Roder wouldn't—well, the boy must have some juice in him after all."

No, no. The image of Roder embracing me flitted through my head, incongruous and startling. I had never been anyone's bed-partner. I would have scalded anyone alive if anyone had ever noticed me long enough to try. *No.*

"Well—" Bielo stood staring at me even more doubtfully, then wriggled his shoulders as if shaking something off. A head peered around the doorjamb and inquired something in a husky voice. He snapped back at it, and it withdrew.

"Not a witch. Well, you're pretty enough, but I don't have enough customers who like that sort of thing—don't look so offended, girl, I'm trying to figure out how I can help you until Roder gets himself out."

Not now. Not ever.

His face smoothed out. "It can wait," he said vaguely. He was as well protected as Roder. Another head popped into the doorway, this one belonging to a stout gentleman with curly gray hair and broken veins in his cheeks, and this time Bielo let him come in, walking back behind the bar to take his request.

Yes, Roder would be all right. And it wasn't my job to worry about it. Here I was, where I wanted to go in the first place, a place where people talked, and I would take care of my business. I scuttled sideways along the wall and ducked under a counter on the side of the room, sitting cross-legged on the sticky floor. In my black shirt and skins I wouldn't stand out in the shadow. If I was going to survive here for more than a day or two, I needed to listen to people talking for a while.

Every time I landed on a new world, I got away from the terminal as quickly as possible and found a place where people got together to talk. Then I sat down and listened in the background until I knew the language. Every world had its own way of talking. Even if they spoke something they called good Standard, the natives of a place had their own speech, their slang, their cadences and singsongs, especially these days since people had stopped roving from planet to planet. When I arrived, it was always gabble to me, but by the time I'd been in a place for a while, I could untangle the tune and sing their song well enough for my one-word style. I'd always had the ability. My master had given it to me, so I could find my way and feed wherever I was.

I wasn't going to learn good diction from the people pouring into Bielo's inn tonight, that was for sure. The harsh language sounded even harsher in their crowing voices. It was a dissonant score played on pots and pans with rocks. It had a tune, though, as all ways of speaking did. The tune got louder and louder as the evening progressed, and it was a tired and worried tune.

The turnover was considerable. No one stayed long, though I noticed that some of them returned. The gentleman with the broken veins, for instance, left and came back several times, each time coming back in to confide something to Bielo. Most of the others followed a pattern of arriving in the door, asking something of the group at large, and moving to join the first person who answered. The talk was general, someone on one side of the room answering a question from the other side, with someone in the middle interrupting to disagree with the answer, but no

one took offense. They all loved Bielo, too, just as Roder's crew loved
Roder. Their faces lighted up when he spoke to them, and they gathered
around him as if he were a warm fire.

As the evening wore on, Bielo's several female employees went
upstairs with clients less and less often, and stayed to lean in on the
conversation themselves, their damp-looking tendrils of hair swinging
from their earnest foreheads and their beaded bracelets clinking. Somewhere in the first hour, Bielo stopped giving them quelling looks and
hand motions and surrendered to his lack of income for the evening.
Somewhere in the second hour, the cat picked its way through the room,
crouching here and there to bolt down scraps from the floor, and then
sat under the counter with me. Somewhere in the third hour, I began to
understand a few of the words.

Around midnight, something shifted in my head.

Broken-vein was back again, explaining something to a cadaverous
man with a long jaw and large hands. Long-jaw agreed with him, but
judging from the expressions a number of others didn't and were tired
of hearing him say it.

"—I say is, there's things mages are better at, and things the rest
of us are better at, and that's just the way it is, no use arguing with it,"
he concluded.

Long-jaw nodded. "You got it. That's it exactly. The mages, even if
there aren't as many as there used to be, they've been running things
this long, they should keep running things, no offense, Bielo. But you
see what I'm saying, the mages have the experience."

"No," said Broken-vein, who had bought another beer every time
he'd entered the tavern. "I'm not saying experience, you understand.
I'm saying nature. The mage is meant to be a ruler. It's the mage who
is naturally, naturally—"

"Naturally better at buggering other mages," said a swarthy man
whose apron was stained with something like chicken blood, and everybody laughed. "If we're talking nature, now, you have to admit I'm
right," he said with no glimmer of humor or apology, though Broken-
vein was glaring at him.

"Well, it don't have to be a bad thing, they keep it among themselves, is all. Besides, we haven't gone wrong depending on them before.
Look at all the things they've done for the city, they've—"

"I'm tired of looking at what they've done *to* the city, it's falling
apart—"

"And I'm tired of saying you've reached your limit once again, Seth," interjected Bielo amiably.

Seth—Broken-vein—glared at him, but the swarthy man pointed out, "You did start talking about the natural order of things," and he looked crestfallen.

"So I did, so I did. Won't do any good to say I'm sorry?"

"Won't have that kind of conversation in my tavern. People start talking about the natural order, my crockery always ends up broken," said Bielo, with a glimmer of Roder's expression, and Seth looked mournfully at the inch or so left in his mug.

"Well, isn't it the rest of us who've really been running things all along? The mages haven't done anything but argue and fight duels for the last hundred years," said the deep-voiced woman, returning to the argument, and three or four voices rose at once to argue with her.

"Running things? Who says anyone in particular is running things anymore?"

"Na, na, you've got to accept that there's laws, and there's the mages making the laws—"

"If you're talking about official, the kings are the ones that run things—"

"But who advises the kings? Their mages!"

"—Their queens!" triumphantly chimed in the deep-voiced woman, and everybody laughed.

But then what do we need mages for, anyway?" she continued.

"We don't need them," said the swarthy man. "They just happen to exist, and we have to put up with them, that's all." The laughter stopped and there was an uncertain pause.

Bielo, as he did every half an hour or so, remembered my existence, and glanced vaguely toward the counter that sheltered me, but it was much easier to distract him than it was to distract Roder. If Roder reminded me of the man with all the dogs on a leash, Bielo was lead dog of a loose pack, sniffing and running a few steps ahead of the rest, sniffing and running. A strong dog, a wise dog, but a dog nonetheless. He wasn't interested in what Enforcement was doing to the Web, just in the small doings of the local world that affected the operation of his inn.

Those doings, from the conversation, were small indeed. Though it was a planet run by witches, the witches were getting fewer and fewer, and none of them bothered themselves with the obvious uses of magic such as long-distance travel or communication.

The chatter seemed to go round and round, the complaints and assertions of people who had never had to decide anything important in their lives, people who believed the world should and could go on as it always had.

The argument about mages did one more slow lap and then slid off into a sustained complaint about an importer of foodstuffs whom everybody knew and disliked. Everybody had a different explanation for the man's nastiness even though they all agreed he was spiteful and petty, and they bickered about that for a while. Then they compared kings, and then they complained about mages again, and then they talked about a woman who had torn up the inn a few days before, apparently using magic. I acquired a basic working vocabularly and several interesting dirty words, and all of it ran around the inside of my head, squeaking and gibbering.

I would go mad from boredom if I had to stay on this world.

I had to figure out a way to get off, even if it meant going back to the Web, even if it meant my master could sniff me out again.

Suddenly I looked up, realizing the inside of my head was the only thing making any noise. The room was silent and half-empty, and the patrons who were left had mostly lapsed into morose reflection. It had never been festive, exactly. Bielo's patrons came to ease their needs rather than to entertain themselves. The ones who were left seemed to have no place else to go, and were merely delaying the inevitable rather than enjoying themselves. The same held for me, for that matter.

I slipped through the sour-smelling room and went up the back stairs.

"Girl," said a quiet voice from the bottom of the steps.

I turned.

"He will be fine," said Bielo.

I shrugged my shoulders and went into the room.

The armor didn't fit me as well as it had. Roder was right, I had grown again. The leather was tight between my shoulder blades and gripped my upper arms, the trousers barely fit over my thighs, and the overlap between the jacket and pants was much less. I struggled into it anyway, picked up my sword, and went to the window instead of the door. Bielo had seemed worried I would leave, as if it were any of his business, and I didn't want him to stop me.

I raised the sash as slowly and carefully as I could, hearing the rumbling vibrations and sure Bielo could hear them downstairs through the walls. Indeed, I heard a thud from downstairs, but it was only people coming out the front door and turning into the dark lane below us, some of Bielo's patrons leaving, still not talking. I waited a few minutes by the window but heard nothing more from downstairs.

I slid facefirst out the window and onto the low roof, squatted down, and swung myself down into the road, landing in a crouch with nothing more than a crunch of gravel to advertise my arrival. I sat down in the dirt to pull my boots on. I couldn't see any light through the cracks in Bielo's shutters.

The front door to the tavern opened only a few feet away, and a dark figure came out, turning to close and fasten the door. The figure passed close to me going toward the hill, head down in the unlit street. I didn't dare finish pulling up my second boot.

A few steps past me, the figure turned back and took a breath. "Well, all right, so maybe he won't be all right," said Bielo. "But that doesn't mean you would be of any help. You don't speak the language. You wouldn't know where to go or what to do. Go back up to bed."

The cat landed softly in the dirt behind me, and I finished pulling my boot up. "It is of no interest to me," I said. Unfortunately, I said it in my new language.

16
The Double Touch
(**Suicide's Victory,** Wound for Wound)

"**I**n that case," said Bielo with an unreadable expression in the darkness, "you are welcome to join me," and he turned and headed up the hill.

I watched him go until he was only a dark gray blur in the blackness, then surrendered. I got to my feet and followed after, silently.

The windows of the buildings on either side of us flickered dimly, if they showed any light at all. There were no streetlights. The buildings were black shadows against a black sky, and Bielo was barely visible a few feet in front of me. A backward world, indeed, though above us the stars shone stark and bright without the outside lighting. Now that I thought of it, I supposed the houses we passed had all been built by hand, with hammers and chisels and saws and sweat.

A pale light flickered up at the next corner, bobbing up and down.

Bielo shoved me in between two houses and fell down on top of me, wrapping his arms around me. "Hush, hush, hush," he whispered. "Pretend we're lovers. There's a curfew this far up the hill."

I struggled, but he was muscular despite his round hard stomach. He was warm, too. He muttered something to himself while I tried to get my hand to the hilt of my sword, but he wasn't breathing hard or straining to hold me down.

The pale light grew brighter, bobbing faster, then filled the space we were in with a milky glow.

"What's going on here?" In the light of the glowing sphere he held in his hand, the man nearly glowed in the dark himself. He was dressed in a jacket and kilt of pumpkin yellow and flame red in a diamond pattern.

Bielo answered guilelessly, scrambling to his feet and clutching his hands to his chest, "Sorry, sir, sorry, sir mage, my girl and I were just—"

I kicked his shin.

"There's a curfew, boy. Close your trousers and get inside," said the mage.

"Sorry, sir mage." It sounded incongruous in Bielo's weary voice.

The light bobbed away, but the mage called back, "Tell your flirtigiggs to wear a skirt, you won't have to go outdoors to get at her sit-upon."

"Sir," said Bielo. The light, moving the shadows up and down, faded. "Thought better of him," he muttered.

Don't touch me again, I thought, a little breathless.

"Sorry," he said, as if I had spoken aloud. "Had to be done."

He set off, walking more briskly now, and somehow I was walking beside him instead of skulking behind. We were climbing upward, toward the high horizon, which was growing brighter.

"You really resisted me," he said finally.

I didn't say anything.

"Humans don't generally resist the Massim model. We're too charming."

No comment.

"I'm not hurt. Just puzzled."

I didn't answer again.

"Huh. You don't find me in the least bit attractive? Don't happen to want to smile at me and spend time with me and trust me with your life?"

I sighed.

"Then what are you doing following Roder around?"

"He's following *me.*"

"Oh. That explains why you were going to go try to rescue him?"

Shut up.

He was a black figure in the black night, his breathing steady, watching me. The Monitor Massims were a custom model, then. I supposed you had to deal with the problem of crewing the ships with wild witches somehow. The witches gave up their freedom for love. Or maybe just strong affection. That would explain the pet-dog effect they had around him.

"You actually like the stiff-necked puritan for himself, don't you?" Bielo finally said.

I guessed I did. *Shut up,* I repeated.

He turned and walked away, and I followed.

We turned a corner into a fairyland, the amusement park I'd passed through earlier that day, but now even more astonishing. Everything was glowing in faint pastels. Every ornamental cornice, every porch roof, every piece of icing glowed in lavender, rose, and lime, and the odd-shaped windows shimmered lemon yellow. He glanced back at me. "They're mostly empty, don't worry." A muddy swath of water rippled down one side of the street, the only thing marring the picture.

We walked back into the square where we had landed earlier that day, and I realized the origin of the water flowing in the road, because a boggy spring still bubbled from the side of the earthen hummock our ship had made.

There were four buildings embracing the square. We passed the first, a pile that looked as if it had been assembled by a color-blind committee. A comfortable, elegant white mansion on the right side shone with a peaceful white light. Opposite it a black tower had only a few windows near its summit, from which cold blue rays thrust forth into the night, but otherwise it was only visible as a looming shadow across the dark sky. Beyond the two of them, a red building's windows glowed deep yellow and there were shadows of people moving about behind them. My steps slowed. Bielo glanced back at me.

"He's probably in the red building. That's where they have their court and their police, such as it is," he told me in a voice barely above the level of a thought.

"What are you going to do?"

He rubbed the top of his head. "What I have to do. It's in my nature, the contract he invoked. I have to aid him if he asks for my help, no matter what I said. Stay here." He trudged toward the front door, his shoulders down, looking less and less like Roder with every step. Roder wouldn't drag his feet on his way to an unwelcome task. He'd lift his head up and look around him with interest, accepting the job with fascination, pleased not to be bored for a change.

Bielo walked up to the front door and in, and it closed behind him. Stepping carefully and quietly, I walked across the square to the dark red building myself. There were no shadows walking across the yellow windows now. It was silent. I stood on my tiptoes to peer in a window. There didn't seem to be anybody inside, though the light illuminated every corner of the room. I dropped down again, looked down at my feet in the darkness, looked around me. No one on the broad front steps. I fit my toes in the grooves between the stones of the wall and, clutching the sill with my fingertips, pulled myself up again. I wriggled through the window. The light dimmed slightly. I slithered to the floor with a scraping noise and crouched, trying not to breathe loudly.

The light stayed dim but nobody called out, no doors opened, there were no footsteps. It was a meeting room with stepped rows of wood benches facing the center and windows in the outer wall. There was a door that led into another meeting room, this one much larger, a wide hall full of stone benches with a raised podium at one end. It was empty too, but it felt stuffy and I was uneasy, as if a large hand was pressing down on me. It smelled of smoke and the aging funk of people. The benches were littered with bits of clothing, books, and food.

There was a thump in the room I had just left, and I crouched next to the nearest bench. "Malka?" said a breathy voice. I stood up again.

Perhaps pets were not an unmixed blessing.

I worked my way between a row of benches. There were doors all along the walls, most opening into tiny meeting rooms, each one smelling of humans. The yellow light seemed to come from everywhere and nowhere, and every time I opened a door the room darkened slightly within.

A door in the corner, bigger than the rest, led into another small meeting hall. When I opened it and walked in, more stuffy pressure flowed over me from within. This room was like an amphitheater, with a balcony circling above and ranks of stalls below descending to a small round stage. In the center of the stage, on a tall stool, sat Roder, his hands folded in his lap. His eyes flickered at me and flickered away.

"Not such a good idea," he said vaguely to the air above him, and I heard a click. I turned back and saw that the door had closed behind me.

17

Redoublement (**Scolding Sharon,** Renewal of Failed Attack)

"**W**hat isn't such a good idea?" said an elderly voice from above.

"That question. You keep asking it, but I can't answer it. 'What mage made you?' is like asking 'When did you stop beating your wife?' "

"Mages aren't permitted to marry," said another voice, dry and light. It sounded as if they were sitting in the balcony directly above me. The stairs to the balcony were on the opposite side of the room next to another door, and they probably couldn't get there in time to catch me. I took another step back.

"That was probably his point," said the harsh elderly voice. "And I have not stopped beating my apprentice. You say no mage made you. Yet you are demonstrably a made thing, an automaton. Who then made you?"

I reached for the door handle and tried to turn it. It didn't move. I looked at Roder and found his face pinched with worry. He kept talking. "A company grew me. On another world."

"Are you uncomfortable answering that question?" inquired the old man.

"It is not the answer or the question which makes me uncomfortable," answered Roder awkwardly.

"He's resisting the truth spell, Master Prosper," said the young man.
The older mage, Prosper, said slowly, "What disturbs you?"

Something scratched on the outside of the door and made an inquiring meow. I rattled the door handle.

"What was that?" said the youth. I heard footsteps above me.

"My friend disturbs me," said Roder sadly, not moving his hands from his lap.

Feet appeared on the stairs, a slim, athletic body clad in soft rose, with a speckled rose neckring, and a young man's round face peering my way. "If that is your friend, she disturbs me also," said the face. "There's a grim little wench down here, master." He pulled at his neat little mustache and stepped down farther.

I pulled my sword out slowly and waded through the pressure of the room toward him. Roder rolled his eyes and then shut them.

"Wench?" said the older voice.

"Not a local girl, I think, unless the town maidens have taken to wearing entire cows and waving knives about," said the young man, jumping the last few steps and coming forward. He ran up the aisle between the rows of seats, watching me confidently and rubbing his hands together. I extended my arm and aimed the point at his viscera, advancing more slowly. He threw his hands at me as if spraying me with water. It made me itchy so I straightened my arm slightly. He stopped a fraction of an inch before he impaled himself, with a startled expression, and tried to sweep the blade aside with his arm. With a squeeze of my fingers, I pinked the arm neatly on the way past and returned the tip to his midsection.

"Yefim?" said the voice.

Yefim didn't say anything. He smiled tightly, his chest rising and falling. He revolved his hands on his wrists, said, *"Avert,"* and stepped forward confidently.

His thin little spell didn't even give me a hiccup. I was holding the blade out in the Jesup Line, something I learned and forgot early in my training. The Jesup is limited in sword-fighting, mostly used to break your opponent's rush so that you can take over the attack. Most sane people don't choose to stab themselves. The line is weak otherwise, because of the rigidity of the arm. It's too easy for your opponent to beat your blade aside. This was the first time I'd seen someone run himself onto the Jesup, and at walking speed too.

He stopped again when it had gone in a quarter inch, tried to take a breath, and realized that the rising of his chest would widen the slit.

"Yefim!" said the voice.

He opened his mouth to answer, and realized that speaking would do the same thing. His lips curved into an apprehensive smile.

Footsteps above. "Rot you for a clot of frog's eggs, Yefim! Answer me."

Yefim shuddered and stepped back smoothly, a stain darkening his rose tabard, but I pressed him, my arm still extended, and he moved back, step by step back down the aisle toward Roder.

The rose boy came to a stop at the edge of the small stage, looking as if he'd abruptly backed into a wall. With his chin shoved into his neck, he raised his hands and said, "No, please, lovely lady, I can go no farther."

"What are—" The man coming down the stairs in a sweep of silver robes had a curly mass of gray locks, heavy-lidded eyes, and a sharp-angled parrot nose. While I was looking up at him, Yefim inhaled sharply, slid sideways away from my point, scraped it across his chest, and leaped into the first row of seats, stepping over the backs to climb several ranks up. "How did you get this far?" said the old man to me.

"She walked," said Roder, his eyes still closed. "That's what she does. She walks into trouble."

With my eyes on both of them, I backed toward Roder.

"What are you doing?" inquired the old mage, cocking his head with baffled interest.

"Can you move?" I said to Roder.

"I'm tied up," he answered, wiggling his fingers as if it should be obvious to me.

"With what?" He didn't answer me. I lifted his right hand off his lap. It went up just fine. He watched it as if it belonged to someone else.

"Ah," said the old mage, sitting down on the stairs. "Armed and shielded from magic. Lovely. Are you someone's fetch? Whose?" He revolved one wrinkled hand in an irrelevant gesture that made my elbows itch, and Roder squinted in pain.

Yes, I was someone's fetch, but he wouldn't be acquainted with my master. I lifted Roder's other hand. They both stayed in the air.

"No, hm. Did you arrive with that exploding house, then?" Another gesture, this one requiring both hands. Roder averted his head from me. His shoulders tensed.

I put down my sword, grabbed both of Roder's hands, braced my foot on the lower rung of the stool, and pulled. Nothing.

"Are you a daemon? A conjuration? A clockwork monster like your friend?" The old man raised both hands into the air so that the sleeves of his robe slipped down to his elbows. Roder cried out, tipped forward, slipped off the stool, and landed on his feet, staggering. Then he crumpled to the floor. The old man leaned, pulling air with his fingers.

Roder began crawling toward him.

"Leave him alone," I muttered, grabbing his feet. I was getting very irritated. The room felt oppressive and close.

Master Prosper flinched, but kept kneading the air. "Inadequate, creature. He will come to me, and so will you."

"Leave him alone, I said."

No effect. Though I had his legs in the air, Roder was dragging himself along by his fingertips, and he was so strong I couldn't hold him back.

"No! Stop it!" I snapped.

The old man and the young man both winced and laughed.

I dropped Roder's feet and picked up my sword. "Stop her, Yefim!" barked the old man.

Yefim said, "She'll stop me."

I walked past Roder and toward the old man. He stopped making the pulling motions and held his palms up facing me. I could feel my brows pulling together in a scowl. It felt like the heavy air before a thunderstorm.

"Please don't annoy her," said Roder, collapsing onto his arms and panting.

I swung the sword around in the figure-eight motion of the mill, first past my left shoulder and then past my right, pivoting my wrist to make the hissing noises in the air essential for this attack. Its only purpose is to frighten unarmed and unskilled opponents, because anyone with weapon skill knows that wide actions are weak ones. I moved toward the old man, hiss-hiss-step, hiss-hiss-step, hiss-hiss-hiss-hiss-step, yet he still held his hands out, sure he could stop me somehow. I could feel the viscous thickness of the spells he was casting, and had to swallow several times, getting more and more enraged.

I felt the tip of my sword catch and drag, as if it had cut through a thread. A red line appeared across both palms and he flinched, his eyes widening. I continued the mill, making my steps smaller. He pulled his palms back, pulled himself back, and began hitching himself backward up the stairs.

"You—are—making me—kill you," I said between swoops. His foot slipped as he was pushing himself up another step. He lay sprawled on the stairs squinting at my hissing blade. Finally he closed his eyes, awaiting his death. He wasn't going to surrender. Stupid man.

I slapped him in the side of the head with the flat of the blade the way the Sefir Zul did, then kicked him as hard as I could in the easiest available target. He rolled into a ball, his face screwed up in pain, and bumped down several stairs. The other man laughed.

Roder, on all fours, was trying to get up. I grabbed his hand and pulled him to his feet.

"How do you propose to get through a locked door?" said Yefim, perched on the back of a chair and ignoring his master's struggles.

I stood on one foot and kicked like a mule with the other. It didn't budge. I heard something scrambling away on the other side. *Open.*

"The gnat strikes the first blow!" said Yefim, applauding. Master Prosper was still trying to get up.

I adjusted my angle and kicked again. *Open.*

"You are trying to make it angry? The door's enchanted, creature."

I slammed my heel into it a third time, thinking *open open open* until it shuddered free of its lock. Breaking down doors was one part of Zul's training I'd never been good at, that and fighting while hanging from a rope. I pulled Roder out into the big room and shoved the door closed behind me.

By the time we were halfway across, someone was kicking at the door, which seemed to be locked again. Roder was moving more easily, and he managed to scramble out the window after me without hurting himself or making a lot of noise. I crouched outside listening. I heard a distant sound, Yefim laughing, then a yelp of pain in the same voice. Not nice people, those two.

Roder moved farther into the square. "Come on, Malka," he said.

"Roder!" hissed another voice from the front door, and Bielo loped over to join him. "What are you doing? Now you'll really draw attention."

"Their attention was already well drawn," said Roder ruefully. "I'm afraid they saw through me."

"I'm ruined, then," said the innkeeper. "Ruined. We'd better run. They'll treat this as an emergency. They're actually efficient in an emergency." He drew the Monitor along by the arm, but Roder stopped him.

"Malka!" he said, turning.

I began to stand.

Then I began to rise in the air.

Someone was holding me by the collar and lifting me firmly back through the window.

18

Binding the Blade
(**Meeting Teeth,** Taking
Edge with Edge)

A droning chant was going on in the background and an argument in the foreground.

"It's an automaton like the other one."

"Nonsense. It's a dybbuk. Smell the necromantic odor it gives off."

"Don't smell too close, or it'll bite your nose off."

General laughter drowning out the chant.

"A very sylph. A lovely sprite from the legends." Young Yefim's voice.

Even more laughter, this time nervous. Many more than two mages were in the room with me this time.

There was some kind of tight bandage wrapped over my mouth, and a dark hood over my head. My hands were bound palm to palm behind my back, wrapped with the same kind of cloth, and my ankles were tied to the rungs of a stool like the one Roder had occupied. They hadn't made the mistake of using magic to capture me this time. Everything that held me captive here was from the material world, and they had used more than the normal restraints when I made the mistake of struggling with all my strength. That didn't mean they weren't using magic on me now. The hood was the least of my oppressions.

It hadn't just been Roder's two interrogators who caught me. They had gotten reinforcements, and it had taken all ten of them to subdue me. I could taste blood in my bound mouth.

"If it were a fetch, we couldn't have tied it up. It's a machine, you idiot. Look at it. Legs and arms and everything, it walks on the ground and breathes with a mouth. It's a material object. Has to be a machine."

The droning stopped and I breathed in a gasp through my nose. "Will you be silent?" said the peevish voice of Master Prosper. "How do you expect me to work if you keep yapping like that?"

"Pardon *me*," said the second voice, the one who thought I was a conjured spirit. "Perhaps you need more help after all."

"You'll just muddy up the works," grumbled Prosper, and my breathing slowed as he started the chant again from the beginning, while the others talked over him, more quietly now. The harsh language, in the mouths of these self-important bureaucrats, lacked the coarse cheer of Bielo's patrons. It crackled and bit, it sanded away at me as I sat muffled and bound in its center. That didn't bother me. What bothered me was what was going on inside me.

Silent and dark like this, frozen in one place, I had to put up with all the changes in me. Yes, I was coming apart at the seams. I wasn't meant to grow this big. But I knew that already, had known it for a long time. There wasn't anything I could do about it, though. If I was given food, I ate, and I grew, and one day I would burst, though I thought I could put it off for a while longer.

The thing that disturbed me more, the thing that indicated more deterioration in me than I'd thought, was a small and simple thing: Bielo and Roder had gotten away, and I was glad, and it was a complicated gladness. They hadn't caught the cat, either, but that pleasure was uncomplicated. Every familiar should have a chance to live free of its master. It was the thought of Roder's freedom, or rather the way I felt about it, and what I'd done about it, that made me upset.

What I had done was deliberately sacrifice my freedom, or at least my possibility of looking innocent, for their freedom. The two mages sent to recapture the two Massims had to be called back hastily to help with me, and I struggled even harder and bespoke them at the top of my voice, when I realized that, so the mages wouldn't be able to leave again. It was just the latest sign of rot, the decay that had started when

I apologized to the Sefir Zul. When I did not kill Roder. When I followed Bielo.

"Why is it rocking back and forth like that? Is it trying to escape again? Make it stop."

Hands grabbed my shoulders and tried to hold me in place. I twisted sharply, but that just meant more hands came.

My whole life, until the last few years, I hadn't properly been awake. I'd been no more conscious than my master's dog, and no less, like a very young child with emotions and intelligence but no particular awareness. I came awake on Caliban, but it didn't make me someone else. I was Malka still, just Malka no longer asleep. I had Malka's temper, Malka's cold sharpness, Malka's savage strength. The only thing I added on Caliban was a capacity for self-mockery that helped me pass the time when I was waiting.

This new feeling was different. Very annoying. It was as viscous as syrup, a sour sad feeling like warm vinegar. It was messy and blurred and it smelled as ugly as Bear smelled, before she met me. I regretted that Roder was free. I wanted him here in my place. I was sorry I had done anything to help him. I wished I was out there with him. I was glad he was free. I wanted him to think well of me. It wound around and around.

"Make the creature stay in one place. I can't focus the spell if she moves like that. And stop her making that noise."

Malka the Tragic, the beast whom the gods rewarded and made human but it wouldn't stop barking and scratching itself and it kept piddling in the corners and following strangers home. Or Malka the Buffoon instead, a god condemned to be a small but pompous human.

"Is she crying?"

"I think she's laughing."

"This conjuration is a complete abortion. I will take pleasure in dismembering the ball of dung that made her, whoever the idiot is."

Prosper's chanting voice rose to a creaky height, and they all fell silent, listening. It pushed on me from all sides, swirled around me, swathed me in layers. It was hard enough to breathe through my nose without all that pushing, and I couldn't concentrate.

Stop that.

Exclamations of annoyance. Prosper kept speaking. His spell was sticky and made me want to bite.

Stop it right now.

"What—"

"Great snakes, I never—"

STOP that.

"How can it bespeak with its mouth sealed?"

"Well, it's doing it," a grim rejoinder.

"Yes, I'd noticed, thank you for pointing that out."

"I'll put a protection shield up for us, then."

"You? You couldn't shield against a raindrop. I'll do it."

These mages couldn't open their mouths without arguing.

After that, they didn't notice anything I said. Prosper's voice got louder and more insistent. I couldn't make out any words, but it sounded as if he were repeating himself. Yes, he was repeating himself, and now he did it again, with even more volume, and his spell pushed and pushed at me, all over. It was very annoying, and I was tempted to push back.

Instead, I pulled. I sucked the spell in like a noodle.

He screamed.

So did I, or rather I squeaked through my nose. It had been just enough magic to make me grow again, and the bandages around my head and hands dug in sharply. So did my armor.

"Master? Master?" said worried voices, and there was scuffling.

"Is he dead?"

"No, worse luck," said the voice of the one who thought I was a conjured spirit. "Help me prop him up. He's breathing."

They applied damp rags and ice to Prosper, waved something under his nose, and babbled healing spells. They seemed far more interested in their ongoing arguments than in me. It gave me thought. I couldn't bespeak them directly with their shield up, and even if I could I couldn't get them to free me—I could never make people do anything completely against their will—but maybe I could get them to pay attention to something besides me.

I took a breath in through my nose, and let it out slowly. Gently now, let it seep out like water into a dry sponge. *There are more important things to worry about.*

"Well, this is all Council's fault anyway, if you ask me," said one of the more earnest voices. "They haven't been doing their job."

That apparently woke Prosper up, for he began to argue in a thin petulant voice that Council couldn't possibly have any effect on anything whatsoever because its members were charlatans, weaklings, libertines, and completely irrelevant. Council was beside the point. One of the others agreed that the point was to find out whether the captive was an automaton or a succubus.

Far more important things to worry about. Gently, gently. Lord, the bandage hurt.

The others laughed at him. "Don't be petty," said one.

I'll keep.

"The creature will keep," said Prosper grumpily, and I could hear him getting to his feet and swearing at the mages who were trying to help him up. "We need to be more systematic about this. The spells that protect this monster are strong. If we want to get inside it and find what it's made of, we have to plan better. And besides—"

Far more important things.

"—there are other more important things going on. There have been so many disturbances lately. Things falling out of the sky. Renegade mages seducing council members. Herb-wives getting mixed up with everything. Exploding houses. Strangers speaking nonsense. Ghosts. This creature is only a symptom. We need to get at the source . . ."

But they didn't leave the room. Instead, they sent out one of their number to bring more supplies. From the sounds, they were setting up some kind of circle on the other side of the room, wrangling and bickering, casting side spells whose overflow made me itch and wriggle. One of the side spells was particularly nasty.

"I caught that!" said one of them abruptly, and there was a frozen silence.

"My pardon," said Yefim politely.

The first voice said, "If you attempt to spell-afflict me again, I will permanently remove the skin on your buttocks and set you to spinning on them."

"But of course. My apologies," said Yefim. "Won't happen." The chatter and cursing rose again as if this were normal conversation. It probably was.

This was the kind of world my master wanted, a world where witches ran everything, where your influence depended on how good you were at persuading magic to do what you want. Where the government was an uneasy truce between individuals with power who were temporarily agreeing not to flay one another alive, and where people without power undoubtedly had no say in the matter. My little master would fit right in.

"Now," said Master Prosper finally. "We are agreed? The purpose is to find the origin of all the recent disturbances?"

"Not all, surely," objected another. "Some of it must be the usual stuff."

"All right, all right. This creature, then? And the falling house, and the mechanical man."

"The pale ghost."

"And the naked brown woman talking nonsense!"

"All those people talking nonsense. And slipping their containment spell."

They were Pegeen and the rest of Roder's crew. And who was the pale ghost? Then I remembered the thing that had been inside Tobiah, the hand inside the puppet. It must still be running around.

"We begin," said Prosper formally, and then spoiled it by saying, "You call this a seeing-vessel?" but eventually they all got down to business. It was a long chant. I concentrated on breathing through my nose. They were pushing on me hard. At the same time, though, they were creating a concentration of magic as big as an engine right there in the room. It was way too big for what they were trying to do, but I supposed they didn't know it. Even though I couldn't see anything, I could feel the warmth of the magic they were drawing to them with their incantation. It was like sitting at a fire.

My gag got tighter. The bands around my ankles and hands pulled harder.

"Something is messing this up," a peevish voice complained, interrupting the chant.

"Probably your incompetence," and they were all on their feet shouting at one another. Two of them, from the shouts, were trying to hit each other.

The captive is the problem. Remove the captive.

"It's the monster," said Prosper dryly, when the wranglers had been separated. "She's disturbing the flow. Remove her."

They carried me, stool and all, into another room and shut the door.

I was alone in the room, only the small sound of my breathing to accompany me. Now that I was by myself, I realized that to be tied up alone with my thoughts and the pain of my bonds wasn't necessarily the best alternative I could have chosen. I breathed for a long time, sometimes rocking back and forth, sometimes laughing through my nose.

Something warm landed in my lap and I nearly fell off the stool.

"Miiiiiiine," said Bear's comfortable voice, and she stood kneading my thighs with her paws.

Yours, small spirit, I agreed, and laughed, and laughed again.

What amused me was I found her presence consoling. I cared that somebody cared for me, even if she loved me because I was keeping her alive with my overflow. Yes, I was definitely falling apart. It had come to this. Malka, the Savage So Solitary in Splendor, taking comfort from a mangy artificial cat. Did humans feel this way all the time? I couldn't bear the thought. Why didn't they all just kill themselves and be done with it?

"Mine," she murmured, turned around, and lay down with her back against my belly.

[faded text at top of page, mostly illegible from previous page bleed-through]

19

Broken Time (**Carmichael Bah,** Change in Tempo Used to Fool Opponent)

The cat jumped out of my lap, a sudden jolt.

"Poor thing. Look what they did to her."

It wasn't a voice I'd expected to hear. Cully's.

Another voice, belonging to Fergus, annoyed. "Hold off. I have to undo the window wards."

"How could they do that to the poor little monkey?"

I am not a monkey.

"Stop being sentimental, Cully, or she'll hurt you again." Roder. They'd found him, then.

"You're all being too sentimental, if you ask me," said Electra bitterly. "Be quiet or the locals will come running. I can only muffle so much sound."

"Okay, you're in." Sounds of scrambling. Hands on my arms. The hood lifting off. Seven intent faces, and Cully trying to undo the bandage.

Idiot.

"Pick her up the way she is and let's get out of here. We can untie her later," said Roder calmly. I knew I could count on him.

Fergus took my feet and Cully went around behind me to lift me by the shoulders, and they loaded me and my stool out of the window to Electra and Pegeen, who were waiting outside, both looking entirely recovered and far more clothed than when I last saw them. The cat was washing herself in the middle of the square.

"Not here, either," Roder said impatiently, righting me when Electra and Pegeen tried to lay me down outside to undo me. "Can't you see she's got yards of the stuff around her? We'd be half an hour unwinding her here. Pegeen, can you cover our tracks?" Pegeen, pushing her glasses up her nose, nodded absentmindedly. She was wearing somebody's trousers, far too big for her, and a woven shirt that made her look like a stick.

"The poor thing is suffocating like that," objected Cully.

"Are you, Malka?"

I continue to breathe.

"Ouch. Fine, then," said Roder, and there were no more objections.

We were not returning to Bielo's tavern, but making our way through side streets nearer the top of the city-hill, where all the elaborate houses were. Bielo led the way, the set of his shoulders conveying how very frivolous and tedious it was of us to need his help.

"Here, I think. Yes, here," he said, stopping. "It was owned by a mage who died just last year, and his neighbors have been gone for decades."

The house didn't look abandoned. It was made of a sunny sandstone in chalky pastels of yellow and a soft, comfortable rose. Its lines were sturdy and worn, and the quiet light illuminating its facade seemed to come from everywhere and nowhere.

Fergus put down the bag he was carrying, kneeled, and put his fore-head against the stone door. His parrot waddled importantly back and forth from shoulder to shoulder. Something clicked.

The door swung open a crack and a dusty smell of pollen washed over us. There was birdsong, and even more glowing light.

Inside, there was the sound of running water. Waxed wood was warm beneath my bare feet as Roder undid the tight yards of fabric around my wrists. My hands, when I held them up to look at them, were creased and blue and without feeling. It was remarkable how human I was getting. I even had blood circulation to be impaired now.

Roder untucked the end of my gag and undid it by pulling it upward so it spiraled around my head. Everyone else except for Bielo was off exploring the house. Bielo sat on a wooden bench in the front room watching us.

"She doesn't find you attractive, you know, not in the usual way," the innkeeper said as Roder neared the end of the gag.

"Oh, I know," answered Roder with that sweet smile as he took the last of it off.

"Shtop zhat," I said, and had to stop myself because there was lint all over my tongue. This wouldn't do. It wouldn't do at all. I had to get out of this. Now I was free of the mages, I could get away on my own.

"Thank you, Malka, for rescuing me," answered Roder gravely, kissed my hand, and went into the other room.

Bielo didn't move from the bench.

You have better things to do with your time.

He looked blank for a moment, then said, "Won't wash. What is it you want to do that I can't watch?"

"I want to think."

He still didn't move.

"Alone."

"I don't agree," he said amiably. "From the condition of your face, it looks like you spent the last three hours thinking alone. If you're going to leave, you at least have to let Roder know. He went to great lengths to get you out. Now don't get all mad at me."

My sword wasn't in its scabbard. I whirled around, but it was nowhere in the room.

"The big fellow brought your scimitar along. It's in the other room," said Bielo. "You won't kill me, though. Roder said. You look like a goblin when you're angry, did you know that?"

I screamed at him.

"Malka," Roder said from the doorway, the others crowding behind.

"She wants to run away," said Bielo, in a complacent tattling tone.

"Let her," said Roder, crossing his arms and leaning against the jamb. "Cully, give her the sword."

Bielo glared at him in astonishment. Cully gave him a look of outrage too, but handed the weapon over.

"You want something to eat before you go?" Roder inquired. "Fergus stole quite a selection from the open-air market. There are some cheeses in here that smell positively ethereal."

"I am not a feral cat to be tempted with food," I said. "I am not a horse to be broken. I am not a monkey to be trained."

"No," agreed the Massim. The eyes were calm. "You are a great and powerful being. A noble hero. A mighty warrior."

I couldn't help it. I laughed. "Malka the Mighty," I agreed, and stamped my foot. Then I walked out of the front door of the house and stood in the lane outside, making a sort of humming noise that I couldn't stop making.

Nobody came out of the door after me. Nobody came down the road. I was all by myself. If I wanted to, I could walk away right now.

I stamped my foot again. A small foot. A small noise. I whirled.

"Aaaaaaaaaaah!" I shouted at the house.

Roder opened the door. "Yes?"

"I could blow up the world," I said. "I could kill you with a word. You do not know what I am. What is wrong with you?"

"I've never met anybody like you before," he said, with simple wonder.

"Aaaaaaah!" I shouted again, shaking my head back and forth, feeling like a wounded bear and undoubtedly looking like an annoyed parakeet.

"I'm sorry," he said. "I'm making it difficult. Go ahead and leave. I'll understand. Could you tell me something before you go?"

"What?" I growled, not sure I wanted him telling me to leave.

That sweet smile, and the river-colored eyes neither sad nor bored, and with no pity in them for me. "Do you like me? Because I like you, very much. Please stay. It would make me happy."

"Stop that."

"No. I want you to stay. I'll do whatever it takes."

He was leaning against the doorjamb again, his arms folded. He probably knew he looked good standing like that. I waited for him to go back inside. That was the next thing he'd do, pretend I was completely free, that he wasn't manipulating me.

He didn't go.

"Besides, Enforcement will undoubtedly find me eventually, and if they find me they'll go looking for you."

And if they found me, so would my master.

"I'm dangerous to you. To everyone," I said, feeling that I had already lost.

"I've marooned myself and blown up my engine on a low-tech renegade non-Web world. I've made the local administration very angry with me and very curious about my inner workings. There's a Web-wide government coup going on in my absence which I'm trying to stop single-handed. I've irritated Enforcement enough that they spent years setting you and your young friend up as my assassins and now they've got half their ships out trying to kill me. Meanwhile I'm trying to rescue an entire planet-load of Mennenkalt refugees, save the Web, and keep my crew alive. I'm more dangerous to myself than you could ever be."

He reached out his palms, but not as if he expected me to take them. It was more like the display of a sword-fight referee, showing he had no concealed weapons himself.

I stared at him.

The cat's heart-shaped face appeared between his legs, its whiskers brushing against his trousers. She rubbed her small head against him, marking him as her property, then sat down to give herself a thorough washing as if she had just had a hearty meal. Three houses down, I heard a door open and shut.

The android stood straight, stepped out of the door, making the cat jump away in annoyance, and he took my off hand, ignoring the half-raised sword and drawing me back into the house. "Come on back," he said. "You can always change your mind later."

I went with him. It was easier than standing in the street fighting with myself.

20

Body Parry (**Corps-à-Corps,** The Strategic Tackle)

The cheese was indeed very good, as was the thick-seeded rosemary-flavored bread Fergus had stolen to accompany it, and the tart crunchy pears. I sat cross-legged, feeling like a newly hatched chick, on a ledge at one end of a large back room while the others are more or less in the middle, sorting themselves into a chart of social dynamics.

The just-hatched feeling was because they'd had to cut me out of my armor before I could eat. It lay in a pile in the front room, stretched and sliced and torn, no longer usable for anything. There was no hope for it; I had grown so much I couldn't bend my elbows or knees while I was wearing the stuff. Roder had drawn me back into the house like a child's pull-toy, and when he saw how much I was hobbling he made me lie down on the floor right there so he could get it off. Bielo had a pocketknife, so he busily took over, complaining all the while, but he somehow managed not to cut the fabric of my black shirt and skins underneath while he ripped and muttered. Roder didn't bother to watch. He went into the other room.

"Are you older or younger than Roder?" I asked Bielo suddenly while he was slitting my left sleeve.

"Ha. Why do you ask? Because I didn't play martyr when I got stuck on this planet?"

"No."

"It's none of your business."

"Well, then, why do people like you and Roder so much? What did they put in the Massim to make you that way? Because the standard model was just an all-purpose diplomat."

"Hm. You know some interesting things." He was working the tip of the knife millimeter by millimeter over the crown of my shoulder, where the leather was stretched so tight my flesh bulged out through the opening he was making. I didn't think he was going to answer, but when he rounded the point he started talking again.

"You familiar with any cults?"

"Like the Mennenkalts?"

"No, that's an established religion. Anything that survives its prophet usually hangs together around its articles of faith, not because of the personality of its leader."

"Oh. Then the Disciples of the Light. And Mahwah Brethren, and the Blessed Flood."

"Right. Tell me about Brother Jonah of the Disciples."

I tried to remember. I'd seen pictures. "Blue eyes. Sort of dirty hair, medium long, and he had a deep voice."

"No, not his coloring or his hygiene. What impression did he give?"

"I don't know. Grimy and pompous. I never could figure out his appeal."

"Ah." Bielo tipped my head back and neatly slit the collar open, then began working his way down the other sleeve. I took a breath. My abdomen was still encased, but my throat was free. "I'll tell you. He gave an impression of inner certainty, of complete attention, and of calm. Also he had a great deal of physical presence, and he exuded sexual power."

"If you say so." Jonah was very dirty indeed, and he lived in a truck in a junkyard and I could never understand why his young followers believed anything he said.

"Well, then, Mahwah Brethren. Tell me about Mahwah Jebum."

I couldn't shrug. I wasn't following this line at all. "Dark skin. Sun goggles. Broad shoulders. Wore a hat all the time."

"You're missing the point. Certainty, attention, calm, presence, and sex. Doesn't hurt if they have brooding anger, too, like Mahwah did."

"Mahwah? Sex?" The man had looked like a tree trunk, thick and stiff. His people all wore hats and goggles too and burned themselves with acid under their tan-colored tunics.

"Yes, Mahwah. He exuded it. Though I heard he was limp as a

dumpling when it came down to the actual rough-bump. How about the Blessed Flood—Old Eoghan."

"Skinny man with pop eyes who looked like his Adam's apple was about to leap through the top of his head. Sexy as a celery stick."

"You're impossible," said Bielo, reaching the wrist. I took a deep breath and felt my shoulders rise above the ragged front. He stripped the remains of the jacket off and threw them to one side, then started at my right ankle, slitting neatly up toward my knee. "A ship's crew has to be made of witches, or the boat won't go, right? And a Monitor ship can't be crewed by Polytechnic graduates, so they have to be free witches. Free witches are dangerous and they want more than anything to get away. Can you see why the Monitor has to be very charismatic? When they designed the Monitor Massims, they threw in a dash of cult-leader personality. Certainty, attention, calm, presence, and sex. Stop laughing, I'm holding a knife to your kneecap."

"And humans get fooled by that?"

He gave me a puzzled look and kept cutting. "You try separating a Monitor's crew from their Monitor. In fact, the first run of Massims was so attractive they toned the later ones down. Caused too many troubles. Crushes, jealousy, suicides."

That answered my first question. "Then you're younger than Roder."

He pursed up his mouth and kept cutting up the casing over my thigh, efficiently sliding the point a centimeter forward and then ripping upward. Then he smiled.

"I'm not going to tell you," he said, and cut through my waistband to free one leg. "I'll just tell you they took out some of the need for power and control the earlier ones had when they toned the later ones down." Then he cut the other leg of my trousers off without saying any more.

When I went into the other room to get something to eat, I could see it laid out just as Bielo had said. Roder, though he sat silent against a wall separate from the others, was the center of the room's energy. They weren't looking at him, though. Fergust and Cully sat together to one side of him, not facing him, Fergus eating bread and leaning against the Calypsan's knee where the priest sat in his chair. The parrot was on the back of the chair. Pegeen and Octavian were sitting facing each other on the other side of him, and Octavian had his feet propped on the chair's seat either side of Pegeen's skinny thighs. Electra was against the opposite wall with her small furry familiar in her lap, alternately stroking and squeezing it, her head bent down. But even though they weren't looking at him, they had arranged themselves so he could see exactly what they were doing, as if they were children being good for Father Solstice.

I grabbed some cheese and bread and climbed into the ledge at the back of the room, and became part of the tableau: Malka the Household God, small, hot, savage, and ignored on the family altar. Roder glanced at me. I scowled at him. When I looked away, Electra was clutching her small animal and glaring at me herself.

Crushes, jealousy, suicides.

"I have to go back," said Bielo from the doorway. "I've done more than I said I would. I need to go home and get ready for the morning." I heard the front door closing quietly.

"Sleep, people, sleep," Roder said, leaning forward and rubbing his eyes. Pegeen was already leaning back with a piece of fruit in one dark hand, her eyes closed, and her opinionated mouth slack. Octavian put a toe in her belly and she snorted without opening her eyes. Cully and Fergus were already on their way up the stairs, Cully's arm slung across the engineer's shoulder, his beads clutched in the other hand. There must be beds up there.

I didn't move, myself. The ledge was warm and high off the ground and just because I had come back inside didn't mean I was one of Roder's tame dogs. But Electra didn't move, either. Nor did Roder.

"Go to bed," he said to her.

She gave her small animal a squeeze and it squeaked and struggled. She let it get out of her hands and then grabbed it by the tail as it scrabbled to get away. It squeaked again. Bear was watching it intently, her tail trembling at the tip.

"Let it go," I said.

The woman grabbed it around the middle instead, and shoved it head down into a pouch at her waist, not looking at me. The pouch squeaked and convulsed. She stood up too abruptly and left. I could hear her stamping up the stairs.

Roder stood up and came over to my ledge, leaning on it with both arms and looking up at me. "You say you're not a witch. The way you grow—you're not even human, are you, Malka?" he said. "You're a creature of magic yourself."

"Let it go," I said again. *Let it go let it go let it go.* I wouldn't explain anything to him.

He made that open-palm gesture again. "I have no pouch to put you in." He laid one of the palms down on my ankle. Warm and dry and light, as impersonal as ever. Something pale seemed to move outside in the street, but when I looked up it was gone.

"Go away," I told him, "I'd kill you." I opened my mouth wide, and breathed on him. When the heat of my breath hit him, he pulled his face back a half a centimeter, shocked. He got the point, all right.

"No wonder you wouldn't let me take your temperature," he said. "You could boil an egg in that mouth." He lifted his hand from me. "I went for a swim in the hot springs at Ahulani once," he told me gravely. "Very refreshing."

Then he went away too.

Certainty, attention, calm, presence, and never-you-mind, and the hot springs at Ahulani were boiling mud the natives used to cook entire cows. He was like a thoroughly civilized Sefir Zul, and about as dangerous to me as Zul was. Yes, I had become too human.

21

Indirect Attack (**Huong's Corkscrew,** Striking the Unexpected Target)

I wandered into the front room, rubbing my eyes. It was midmorning, and everyone was up again, most looking the worse for their sleep. Electra's elaborate hairdo wasn't meant to be slept upon, and the knot on the back of her head had partly unraveled. Her oval face, though smooth as ever, looked even more offended. Cully's face was puffy, and his wide-set eyes were small as those of a blinking child. Pegeen had gray scuffs on her brown skin, and thin-skinned Fergus looked crumpled up and unfolded like a piece of salvaged wastepaper. Only Octavian and the cat seemed unaffected, both of them grooming themselves, though Octavian seemed to be listening to something only he could hear, his eyes closed while he combed his long black hair and bound it neatly up.

They were trying to find magic so they could make a new engine.

"Any concentration of magic at all," said Roder, standing next to a low fountain and looking out the front window. A bird flew through the room, a swift flash of bright blue, but he ignored it.

"No, it has to be at least a certain size," said Octavian doggedly, not opening his eyes, and from the way Roder hunched his shoulders forward I realized Octavian was working and I'd come into an ongoing argument.

"I told you, we can merge them if they're not big enough."

"I'm not going to even *try* to talk to an engine with a split personality," said Octavian.

"Couldn't drive it," agreed Fergus.

Roder must be trying to make his own engine.

"Magic is not made up of personalities! You're anthropomorphizing," the android said to the window.

"Look who's talking," said Pegeen. "Bet you'd be plenty cranky if we said you didn't have a personality because you're manufactured."

Roder blew his breath out.

Octavian opened his eyes and tied the final knot in his ribbon. "It's beside the point, anyway. Even if you put all the magic from all the spells on all these houses together, you still wouldn't have enough to translate a mouse. I have to look farther away." He stretched himself out on the floor and folded his hands on his chest, like a decorative corpse.

"Shut up, Malka," said Octavian. "Like trying to thread beads in a hurricane." I hadn't said anything. Hadn't *said* anything either.

Roder kept looking out the window.

"Mages are looking for us," Octavian commented idly a little while later. "All-points bulletin about a mechanical man, a succubus, several assorted babbling idiots, and a ghost."

"We're the babbling idiots," said Pegeen. "We speak a foreign language, and they only know their own. Malka's the succubus. Roder's the windup toy."

"What's the ghost?" said Cully.

Something knocked on the door and everybody froze. Roder, unperturbed, had already seen the visitor coming and opened the door. Bielo walked in.

"You put me out of business," he said bitterly. "I didn't even make it inside; they'd boarded me up and plastered a sign on the door. Harboring fugitives. Suspicion of unauthorized conjuring. You put me out of business and out on the street. I told you. You can count on them to be inefficient as long as you don't get their attention, but you got their attention."

Roder shut the door behind him and went back to the window.

"And you don't care, either, do you?"

Roder shrugged, as if a shrug were a complete explanation. Maybe it was, because Bielo didn't seem to have anything more to say. He looked down at the witch on the floor.

"There's a big enough concentration of magic down that way," said Octavian, pointing from his prone position. Bielo stared the way he was pointing, which was near the corner of the back wall.

"He's looking for something we can use for an engine," said Roder.

"If he's looking the direction I think, that's the Beast and it's more likely to use *you*," said Bielo.

"Beast?"

"A local witch thing. An initiation ordeal, a spell sealed in a building. Mages go to the Beast when they're finished learning to be mages. All they have to do is walk through the building. They live, they pass. They die, they fail. You won't be able to do anything with it. It's hundreds of years old and set in its ways."

"We can try," said Roder. "It's big enough."

"You can't reuse a ready-made spell for an engine," I said. "Bielo's right. It won't work."

You could hear the sound of every eye in the room rolling.

"An opinion for every occasion," said Electra and flinched, though I hadn't actually done anything.

Roder said from the window, "Why not, Malka? No, I have my reasons for asking," he said mildly in answer to the expressions. "Why not, Malka?"

"You think magic is just . . . stuff. Clay."

"Well, yes, it is just stuff. Psicleons. Quasi-sentient, infinitely malleable, mentoid, nonbaryonic pseudomatter," said Fergus, meaning "what's your point."

"Stuff. Stuff that sort of thinks and you can make it do whatever you want if you just use the right words," I said. "That's what humans believe."

"And it isn't?" said Cully, bewildered.

Fergus said, closing his eyes, "No, all human beings don't think magic is just stuff. The Mennenkalts think magic is god. The Terps think it's the devil, the Hom Bulos refer to it as RGWG the Unnamable, and the Shoemaker Cabal call it life's heartblood and sacrifice chickens to it. The Polytechnic teaches that it's a virtual potentiality of a multidimensional partially collapsed universe. The Enforcement tech people think it's raw mathematical information. All right? Does that cover it? So?"

I was silent.

Roder leaned his elbows on the sill behind him.

I said to him, only to him, "A Web engine isn't a place or a thing. It's a condition. It contains its ship, not the other way around."

"What?" said Electra. "Roder—"

"Spatial inversion," said Fergus. "Well, yeah, of course, it involves a twist in space. The engine in a ship is inside out and bigger than its ship. Like ship scenery."

I nodded. He was completely wrong but in a useful way.

"I have no idea what you're all talking about," said Electra.

"You're saying we'd have to start from scratch?" said Roder. "None of my crew is powerful enough to make an engine from scratch, Malka."

I closed my mouth suddenly. What was I getting myself into? I wouldn't say any more. *Forget it.* The tides rose inside me, slowly, and subsided. Everybody in the room sat staring into space, quiet and content.

Roder said, "What were we talking about? Oh, yes, are there any of the local witches who could build an engine, Bielo? I don't need a big one."

Bielo looked down at his hands. "There's some mages who could, but no one who would. They're a provincial lot, don't know the stars are suns and don't care, and translation isn't something they're curious about. There's one of the mages who used to talk about the idea, but they all made fun of him. He's one who could make you an engine, too, very powerful witch, but he's out of town and I don't know when he'll be back, or even if he'll be back. Or you could scout around for a renegade, but they're even less trustworthy than the local bunch of bureaucrats."

"I need an engine," Roder repeated. "Find me someone who can build an engine and I'll take care of the persuading. Meanwhile we have to try everything we can. We'll go look at this Beast. Octavian and Fergus, you come with me." He opened the door and went out.

Bielo sighed.

"You're going with him, of course?" said Electra behind where I stood watching them.

"He didn't ask me," I said.

"I'm not going to try to stop you."

Pegeen said wearily, "Electra. Get over it."

Electra left the room smoothly, the effect marred only by the loops of hair sticking out behind.

"Not your fault, child," said Pegeen steadily. "Akamai's death upset her more than most."

"Upset's a good word," agreed Cully. "Like upsetting a stack of dishes. She was so sure she was next in line."

"Talk to your beads, priest," said Pegeen coldly, and Cully didn't say anything. It reminded me of the students in the Sefir Zul's school, the sideways glances, the disdainful expressions when you complimented the form of someone who was out of the room. "Next in line," indeed, like being next in line for one of Zul's lessons. A dubious honor.

The Sefir Zul, in his own way, was very much like the people Bielo had been talking about. Certainty, attention, calm, presence, a well-exercised capacity for anger, and heaven knows what the other female students saw—or smelled—in him because I certainly didn't.

Next in line.

I slipped out the door and saw the others up ahead. Roder, his shoulders relaxed, walked like a king with Octavian and Fergus attending him two steps behind. I followed farther back, thinking unuseful thoughts.

The others, when I caught up with them, were staring at a shabby stone building with an unfinished wooden door at the front and another at the back, standing alone on a hill overlooking the river. It looked abandoned, though there was a worn path leading up to the door from a gate in the stone wall surrounding it. I could smell the magic, warm and aromatic.

"Are you sure?" asked Roder, and Octavian nodded, not taking his eyes off the building.

"Big as the Ong's Hat Cybernal," the boy said. "Big as Malka."

"Too big," said Fergus, taking the second statement for a lame joke and looking worried.

"Be quiet, I'm trying to talk to it." Octavian sank down into a cross-legged squat and covered his eyes with his hands.

The morning wind rolled up from the harbor, carrying the sulfur reek of well-aged mud. A seagull angled overhead. The parrot on Fergus' shoulder bobbed its head at it and shifted from foot to foot. Out here, near the river harbor, you could see the way the city was built on the gently curved sides of a small, low mountain that dangled its feet in the water. You could see the weathered ranks of the lower-level buildings break into gaudy splendor like an orchid budding from tree bark about three-quarters of the way up the hill, and from here you couldn't see that the beautiful houses were, most of them, empty.

"Hst! Down!" said Roder, and I was flat on my belly.

A horseman came through the gate, a body with bound hands slung across his horse's withers in front of him. The rider was in grubby white robes, had a long white beard and a hooked nose. Another rider followed him, a young man.

The riders didn't see us. The old man stopped before the door of the building, and the young man dismounted and ran forward to help him slide his captive off the horse. Their prisoner seemed to be awake, though not completely. He staggered as they set him on his feet, and seemed to be asking something of the air. The younger man shoved him toward the door, opened it, and pushed the captive inside. They followed after him.

"A captured renegade," said Bielo.

Roder said to him, "They have to take the final exam whether they went through the training or not? Those are strict standards."

Bielo nodded, his face sideways on the ground.

Octavian hadn't moved from his sitting position, even though the rest of us were lying down. Now his shoulders were shaking.

"Whoa," he said, opening his eyes in surprise. "Waking up now. It's waking up. Watch out . . . Hello."

The building hadn't moved. The same spicy smell of magic came from it. Octavian, however, was watching it with complete surprise.

"Ow. No. No, I'm not. Ow," he said. Then there was a long, long pause. Abruptly he gave a long groan and began to get up. Fergus grabbed his ankle as he went past. Octavian looked down at him, said, "I know what I'm doing," shook it off, and kept going toward the shabby building.

"I think it's got him in its net," said Fergus. "They threw the native in and it started and it's taking Octavian too."

Roder went after him. He grabbed Octavian's shoulder and turned him around. They were arguing.

The front door of the building opened, and a startled face looked out. There was a shout.

Octavian turned as if to keep going, and Roder ducked down and stood up again with the boy over his shoulder. Another shout came, and the first face was joined by a second.

"Hup, let's go," said Roder, jogging past us.

"Oh-for-hea-ven's-sake-put-me-down," said Octavian in syllables jerked out by his bouncing.

"Not likely." They were pulling ahead, away from Fergus and me, and Fergus began to run in earnest. Bielo could run just as fast as Roder and was even with them. I could hear Octavian still arguing, but within a block I couldn't make out the words. I might have grown in the last few days, but I was still shorter than most humans and no stronger, and I couldn't keep up.

Someone behind me shouted again, and when I turned around the two locals were running after me. I took the first left turn, still plugging away. I heard their voices behind me, and I darted between two houses, then ran back the way I had come along a narrow alleyway. I turned right and chugged back down toward the house of the local Beast, glancing to one side to see my two pursuers heading away from me down the first street I'd taken. Intentionally or not, I'd thrown them off the trail of the others as well.

You can catch me if you just keep going, I said. Then I turned off and headed zigzag fashion toward my goal, thinking as I encountered other people, *not worth noticing, not worth noticing.* Nobody was dressed like me, though my black shirt and skins would have passed on a hundred worlds. The people wore yards and yards of fabric. The women wore long full skirts, the men trousers, full-sleeved shirts, and tunics. The children wore loose garments down to their knees and their hair was shorter than mine.

It was the first time I'd been alone since I ran from the Enforcer at Zul's. I liked being alone. Up until a few years before, I was always alone, because no one ever noticed me when I was small. If they saw me at all, I was a shadow just at the edge of eyesight. Just like the pale shadow I kept seeing out of the corner of my eye now.

I turned around and caught it slipping away. Skinny legs, skinny arms, and it turned steady blue eyes back toward me as it ran. It was the pale thing that had been inside Tobiah.

I still wasn't alone.

22

Passé (**Hayakutake,** Attack That Passes without Striking the Opponent)

"**T**he Beast wants to talk to me, and I want to talk to it," said Octavian doggedly. He was standing with his arms folded. Pegeen, still as a judge, sat on a bench watching him.

"That may be true, but can't you put it off until this is over?" Roder said patiently. "We can't risk exposing ourselves to the locals anymore. They're already looking for us."

When I came in the door, it seemed nobody had noticed I wasn't there. Nobody paid attention now I *was* there.

"I speak directly to magic," said Octavian, slowly and clearly. "It speaks directly to me. It's always saying crazy things to me and trying to get me to do things, because magic is insane. Every Cybernal and every engine in the Web is completely crazy because they're under so much pressure. This one is not insane. I know, because I am talking with it right now. It just wants to talk with me."

"If you're talking with it now, why do you have to go into that building?" asked Pegeen.

"It's made so you have to be inside it to talk properly. That's what it does when it examines witches. They go inside it."

"Why you? What's special about you?"

"I talk back to magic. It doesn't meet many people who can talk back."

"You are chosen because you are special. Only you. You go to a strange world, stop by the local temple, and the god speaks to only you," said Roder gently.

"It's not a fantasy!"

"No. It's a trap. It's a swindle."

"You would know, wouldn't you?" said Octavian.

Roder didn't say anything, just watched him with those eyes.

"I want to talk to it," repeated Octavian, not looking at him.

"Pegeen, would you take him upstairs and keep him safe until he gets a little more reasonable?" asked Roder.

"You mean until he agrees with you?" she said.

"I mean until he can see my side at all."

"Oh. In that case, yes."

I listened to their footsteps creaking on the wooden stairs, and the quiet thumps upstairs as they moved about. The sunny little house didn't seem so sunny in the daytime, though a peach-colored bird perched on a high molding was carefully running its beak through its feathers. The sound of trickling water still came from somewhere else in the house, but I found it irritating rather than soothing. It was my opinion Octavian knew what he was talking about. If the Beast thing was conscious and it had lived a long time inside that house, it was extremely bored.

I've never heard of that happening before," said Bielo. "The Beast just waits for its victims, generally. Have you considered—"

"The boy was raised to be easily led," Roder replied. "He's a human plaything."

"Doesn't look that easy to me."

"Malka was right. We're going to have to make an engine ourselves. And we can't." He paused. "Thought maybe you were intending to leave us, when you didn't choose to come back with us," said Roder to me, the first time he'd looked at me since I came in the front door panting.

Cully raised his eyes from his beads. Electra was already watching me. "Whoo," commented Fergus, the only person in the room who wasn't staring at me, but only because he was looking at the ceiling. "St. Stephen's perforated undershirt."

It took me off guard. I was not a member of Roder's crew. I was not his possession. He couldn't tell me what to do. I wasn't going to explain about how short I was and how hard it was to run fast. Besides, he had said I could leave if I felt like it.

"Child, you really should have stayed with the group," agreed Electra. "You could have gotten lost." She had repaired her hairdo since we went out. She looked smooth, sleek, perfect, and utterly forlorn, and she was petting her small furry familiar with short rapid strokes. Its blinking eyes looked pinker than usual.

Leave me alone.

Roder winced, but Electra, still staring at me, stroked her familiar so hard it whined. She frowned at it and gave it a shake. It closed its eyes.

"Let it go."

"What?"

"Let go of your familiar. You're hurting it."

"It's not even a real animal, child," she said. "I made it myself. I can do what I want with it."

"It made itself. You asked it, and it made itself. It does you a favor by existing. Now let go of it."

She squeezed the small furry thing harder, maybe not deliberately, and the animal shrieked. So I jumped on her.

Roder pried my hands off her while Bielo dealt with her. Roder carried me by my arms up the stairs, ignoring my heels on his thighs and the attempts I was making to bite him. Once we were inside the upstairs room and the door was closed, I backed against the far wall and glared at him.

I showed my teeth.

He shrugged. "So you're not human. I'm not human either."

I opened my mouth to scream at him and closed it again.

"We're going to have to make this up as we go along," he said. He had been leaning with his back against the door waiting for me to finish, and now he straightened and moved forward, the door opening a crack behind him as he released the pressure.

"You're the one making things up," I said fiercely, and didn't know what to do with my hands, so I put them behind my back. My sword was somewhere downstairs on the floor. He took another step forward, and I backed up until I was up against the far wall. The window next to me was open, and I briefly thought about jumping through it and climbing down the tree outside.

"Well, if I'm making things up, then once upon a time there was an android and he met a fallen angel . . ." he said, shrugged again, and kneeled in front of me.

"Fallen angel my elbow. Fallen squirrel from a tree," I said. He didn't smile, just stayed there looking up at me, the sun from the window slanting across his face so that his eyes shone.

I had to lean down just a little bit to kiss his mouth, which I did eventually, very carefully. His skin was very dry, and nearly as warm as mine. I brushed my lips against his, and pulled my head away to consider the encounter. He had his hands behind his back, too, I saw.

He kneeled looking at me for what seemed far too long, so eventually I kissed him again, more firmly. Nothing broke. He didn't grab me or push at me. He just kissed me back, and when I parted my lips he did too, and turned his head slightly.

I wasn't giving him any steam burns. I was getting a crick in my neck, though. I didn't understand any of this. I never had. When I was little, it was irrelevant to me how humans justified their instincts to themselves, and when I got bigger, it was of no interest.

My master's pleasures almost made more sense to me. There was a grand fascination to the idea of death and ending, much more extraordinary than the mechanics involved in starting new life.

Kissing was better than it looked, though, I was finding. *Yes.* That was because he kissed me only when I wanted him to. It was frightening to have anyone paying such complete attention to me. Roder did that. He paid attention. He didn't touch me when I didn't want him to, but when I wanted him to, there he was. And there he was, and there. *Yes.* It was astonishing, and I thought I might understand it better if we kept going like this. *Yes.* His hands felt hot and dry too, when he slid them under my shirt. My very human skin shivered and drew itself tighter as he touched me.

"You are nothing but a child molester," said Electra fiercely from the open door. Roder jerked his head up to look at her, rolling to his feet.

The thing from inside Tobiah that must have been crouching outside on the tree leapt through the window anyway, even though the android was no longer completely distracted with his back to the window. So it missed him and landed on me first, and had to scramble to get at Roder.

It tried to slide its arms under his armpits, and it wrapped its long pale legs around his middle as he rose. Roder grabbed one of its long-fingered hands and peeled it away from his shoulder, ramming the thing against the wall with his back. Electra screamed, "Help him! Where are you going? Help him!" as I ran past her, down the stairs, past Bielo who was coming up and flattened himself to let me past. There it was.

I snatched my sword up from where it leaned against the wall. Fergus and Cully began to stand up as I raced out again.

When I got back, Bielo, expressionless, had the thing by the head and was bending its neck backward while Roder kept it from getting away. There was a long, rubbery crunch and then the head was dangling, but the arms and legs were still clutching Roder. Electra made a little clicking noise, half of a retch.

"Roder wasn't molesting a child, he was molesting an animal," I said to her, and her lips pulled back from her teeth as if I smelled bad.

Bielo brought his fists apart and clapped them either side of the head, which caved in. "It's dead, I think," he said.

"If it is, it's locked in position," grunted Roder. They had to break the arms and legs to loosen its grip. All the while its milky blue eyes regarded some spot in the nonexistent distance.

"What is it?" said Roder, looking at it on the floor. "Something the mages sent after me?"

"It was the thing inside Tobiah."

"What?"

"Didn't you see it? It was inside Tobiah—the witch who blew up the engine," I explained when they both looked at me. "That came out of him when he was in there."

Roder sighed. "Anything else you haven't told me?"

I shook my head. I didn't know. I knew it was a beautifully layered attack, but I didn't know if it was over yet. If Electra hadn't interrupted us, it would have worked. Any of the layers could have worked—that was the beauty of a layered strategy. If I didn't kill Roder when I first met him, if Tobiah didn't kill him on his first attack, if Zul's attack didn't work, if Tobiah didn't manage to take him out when he took out the drive—each incident led Roder to believe he was invulnerable and that he could both trust me and outfight me. Zul knew the android was a sensual being, intrigued by puzzles, and obsessed with Foresters, so he gave him a tidy little Forester puzzle package, then when the android was otherwise occupied, Tobiah made his third attack.

Had he intended another layer after this one? I didn't know. I didn't think so, but I couldn't be sure.

"Just that I am dangerous to you," I repeated, as I had said to him the night before.

He nodded and ran his fingers through his hair. "And you can't tell me just how you are dangerous. I understand," he said. It was acceptance, and it made me feel as I had when the broken engine had poured into me, but it wasn't magic and I wasn't going to get any bigger this time. If anything, I felt smaller.

"So he's your younger brother then," I said to Bielo after Roder had gone downstairs, and he gave an involuntary laugh.

"Makes me an excellent innkeeper and a lousy Monitor, having such a big need for power and control," he said, and "Come on, pretty girl," to Electra, who was still standing ramrod-straight and furious by the door. She took her eyes off me and met his level gaze with surprise. She opened her mouth, looking flustered, then he took her arm and started down the stairs before she could say anything.

It was the only comfort I had, the only assurance that I hadn't gone completely human: that I wasn't smitten with Bielo too.

23

Disengage
(Clammy Handshake, To Take Blades out of Engagement)

In honor of the argument, Octavian had washed his face and combed his hair again. Pegeen had pulled a chair out from the wall and was sitting to one side, looking down over her glasses with one hard brown hand stacked on the other in her lap. It was just before dinner.

While I listened to him state his case, part of my mind was busy wondering what Pegeen and Octavian saw in each other. If I could figure that out, I could settle the puzzle I'd been meditating on all afternoon.

Octavian wasn't the puzzle. Yes, he was way past the age when the Alcibiadan agents usually threw a suicide celebration for their party favors. His bones had thickened slightly, his dark skin didn't have the tender glow it once had, and no matter how carefully he combed his hair, it wasn't silk anymore, just hair. He was still beautiful, still a living, breathing plaything, and yet, free from his agents, free to live, free to make his own choice, he chose the sarcastic dark Pegeen for his partner, and she chose him. That didn't make any sense, but then human beings didn't make sense, and I already knew that.

No, the puzzle was seated facing Octavian, leaning on his knees and listening carefully. He wasn't human, so he ought to make sense. Well, he was sort of human, modeled on a human being but designed and grown from the cell level all the way up, far too expensive for most purposes, but surely he'd been designed to make more sense than humans did.

Octavian was saying, "I do see your point. I really do. I think you need to listen to mine."

"I'm listening," said Roder.

"When I communicate with a Cybernal or an engine, I'm not just talking. My Talent isn't talking. It's more like I go inside the skin of the thing and think with it."

"Well put," muttered Pegeen austerely. He gave her a sideways glance and continued. I suspected an inside joke.

"I can only do that with magic that has a skin, some kind of a container, because otherwise I can't stay inside long enough, I slip out."

Pegeen pushed her glasses up her nose, and Octavian glanced at her again.

"Pegeen, shut up," said Roder.

Octavian continued, "That's what a Mind is. Polytechnic engineers have scooped up a certain amount of magic, and then they force the magic to make a skin for itself, a skin much smaller than it should be. It's not like a familiar, it doesn't have any real matter mixed in, it doesn't have a physical skin that holds the power in." He stopped, searching for words.

Roder waited and paid attention, though he must know all this. Everybody in the room knew it.

Bielo leaned over and said in my ear, "What's confusing you?"

I shook my head. I didn't want to ask him because he was part of the same puzzle.

Octavian said, "I know I complain a lot when you ask me to communicate, but there's a reason. Because of the way they're made, all the Cybernals, every one of them, is crazy. The NeverMind is the worst, but they're all bad. Magic doesn't like being confined to begin with, and the skin on a Mind is too tight. They're like tortured prisoners. You can't imagine. If they weren't all so fascinating to talk to, I wouldn't do it."

"I sympathize. And what's your point?"

Octavian sighed. "That Beast down there is different. It's healthy. Somebody, some human witch, has to have made it, because magic doesn't concentrate itself like that. Whoever made it was a master, though. It's not a sealed system. It's more like a whirlpool, or a tornado, and yet it's a Mind. It's conscious. It thinks, yet it's free."

"And?"

"And it's really interesting, and it wants to talk to me, and it's not like an engine, you can go right inside it and not get burned up, and I want to go into it," finished Octavian, looking down at his hands. "That's what I do. That's my Talent."

"So we come back to what we started with," said Roder, but he was still waiting.

"Well," Octavian said, looking up at him hopefully, "it's rational, as rational as magic gets, and it's big enough to reach the Web. What if I could use it to get in touch with the NeverMind? What if I could get it to send a ship for us?"

Roder laughed. Octavian seemed to freeze, and Pegeen to turn to petrified wood, but the android leaned back and stretched. "Oh, Octavian. All right, you convinced me."

The boy relaxed. "You think it's a good idea?"

"No. It's a bad idea. You convinced me it's your own bad idea, not the Beast's. I thought you might have been taken over."

"Then I can't do it?"

"What am I, your keeper?" said Roder austerely. Now that he put it that way, I had thought he was.

"Now?"

"After dinner, for heaven's sake," said Pegeen.

We weren't in the same house anymore, or even on the same side of the city. After the Tobiah-ghost's attack, Roder and Bielo had stood together arguing quietly. Bielo had decided the encounters with the Beast and the ghost made us too conspicuous. In a discontented gaggle, we left the sunny house with the birds and slipped through the streets, invisible to spying eyes by grace of Pegeen's skill, Bear slipping along behind us. We'd seen no evidence of human beings, not even the patrolling mages who had stopped Bielo and me my first night here.

This new hiding place was a house like an explosion at a carnival. The outside was decorated with an elaborate swirling mosaic made of glass bottle bottoms, mirror pieces, buttons, dice, and small kitchen tools, but it was sedate compared to the interior. Every wall, painted and encrusted with small objects, bellied and swelled. The ceilings swooped and curled above, dribbling crystals and satin cords down to just above Cully's head.

"Don't go into the attic, it's not exactly empty," said Bielo when we came in. "Mage who owned this place incorporated himself into the decor up there a couple of years ago. He's not exactly alive anymore, but it's a little unnerving." Then he took Pegeen out to get some more food, and returned with two full coarse-woven bags. They'd walked concealed by Pegeen's skill and then bought the food openly in the market, said Bielo, because none of the vendors cared that the mages were looking for him.

Now we sat down to dinner in a large room that was an optical illusion. The walls were painted with a humid jungle scene so realistic it looked as if you could walk between the dripping boles of the nearest trees into the permanent twilight beyond. In several cases, you could, because the painting merged into sculptures of tree trunks that bordered deep alcoves set into the walls and lead nowhere. Bear was sitting on the sill of one of the alcoves, folded in around herself.

The tree branches reached to the top of the building, and the light that flickered dimly far above us was the real sky seen through the canopy of painted leaves, because the walls of this room went the whole height of the house. I had never seen trees like this on any world I'd visited, and I suspected the artist hadn't either.

We were seated at a huge stone slab the size of a boulder, encrusted with lichen and surrounded by benches that looked as if they were roughly hewn from the wood of the imaginary trees around us, eating Bielo's heavenly stew from coarse stone bowls. The decor was indeed a bit much.

"What is wrong with these people?" said Pegeen, trying to find a level spot on the boulder to balance her drinking cup, which was a glass container made to look like folded leaves. "At least the last place had flat walls and ordinary furniture, even if it was infested with conjured birds."

"This is a renegade world gone to seed," said Bielo.

"Aren't they all?" said Pegeen. "Who were the settlers?"

"I don't know. I think they ran away during the Thaumaturgic Period, after the Web was established and right around the time Enforcement got going. Five hundred years or so. After they got here, they had the usual sorcerous power struggles."

"Standard stuff?" asked Roder.

"Fire, pestilence, plague, rot, drought, mutations, the lot, from what the histories say. The witches nearly did themselves in, and I wish they had, but they were taking all the normals with them too. Sorry, present company excepted," he said when he realized why nobody else at the table was nodding. "The fighting was bad enough that they lost all their technology, magic and material alike. They were down to sympathetic magic and hoodoo spells. They pulled themselves out of it, made a magician's guild and a sort of Polytechnic, they conjured the Beast as a kind of backup filter, but they're still old-fashioned superstitious magicians, and they're loopy as drunken cats." He gestured at the room around him.

"So why are they disappearing?" said Pegeen. "Surely not a fatal addiction to interior decorating."

They're being replaced by something else a little more sensible," said Bielo. "Mostly out in the countryside. Cottage magic, herb-lore. They don't know it yet, but most witches don't make it into the mage brotherhood anymore, they're trained at home by the herb-wives. Meanwhile, we have this grand city to maintain."

Roder's face came alive. "Could the herb-wives help us make an engine?"

Bielo laughed. "I would have told you. No, they're far too sensible to bother with big stuff. You need a mage for that."

"Can't we just stay here, Roder?" asked Electra. "It's primitive, of course, but you could change that."

Roder shook his head. "I have to find or make an engine—or get a ride out, if Octavian's Beast can send a message. I can't just give up and let Enforcement take over the Web. If Enforcement doesn't need witches anymore, you think they'll let you live?" There was silence.

"I think we're stuck here, Roder," said Fergus.

Cully said, "Bielo, how unfriendly are they to strangers in the countryside?"

"Depends," said the android. "You'd be better off looking for a home across the sea in Deistel Dom."

There was an apprehensive silence.

"Well, if we're stuck, I'm going to lose you all, aren't I?" said Roder. "It's just a matter of time."

It wasn't exactly a silence that followed. Instead, everybody decided it was time to take a sip or put a forkful in their mouths.

"Lost my crew the moment they found better jobs than the ones I could give them," said Bielo.

Pegeen said, "There aren't exactly any Forcers standing outside the door to keep us from leaving, Roder."

"I'm the last active Monitor. You are the last active crew," said

Roder. "It's been over a year since I heard from any of the others. I didn't tell you that because I didn't want to put any pressure on you. But we're the only ones left to stop Enforcement."

Pegeen pushed her glasses up her nose again. Cully looked around the room.

"I'll stay with you, of course," said Electra.

There was a silence that went on too long, and she looked from face to face. Then everybody started talking at once.

24

The Forward Cross Step (**Bullet Train,** To Run at Your Opponent)

After Electra began screaming at us all and ran out into the street, the discussion went back to being civilized. She returned half an hour later when it became clear nobody was going after her, least of all Roder, who seemed to take her action personally and wouldn't say a word to her for the rest of the evening. I watched from a position behind the cat in one of the alcoves. That didn't keep me completely safe. At one point, Electra turned and demanded of me, in a tone she obviously meant to sound sarcastic instead of wounded, "Well, what does the doll-baby want to do? Let's find out what she wants to do, why don't we? Are you staying with Roder or not, doll-baby?"

The cat drew its whiskers back and hissed at her. I thought that was a completely adequate response.

Bielo, who had dropped out of the discussion early, came and looked in at me in my alcove. "What was making you look so confused earlier?" he asked, ignoring the voices going on behind him.

I wasn't going to talk to him, either, but unlike Electra he seemed prepared to wait for an answer. Also unlike Electra, he could probably answer my question, even though he was just as likely to understand my motives.

"Why do they make you androids so human?" I said.

"Human? You say that like it's a dirty word."

"It's a messy word. Why do you and Roder have emotions? Why do you have to eat regular food, why do you have to sleep?"

"And?"

"And what?"

"And why are we made so we can fancy a pretty girl, and why did they include the equipment for dancing the old daggle-tail jig? They did, in case you were worried."

I knew I shouldn't have asked him. That last part was part of what I had been puzzled about.

"Well, early on they used to try to leave all that stuff out, and you know what happened?"

I wasn't talking to him anymore.

"Mass murderers, that's what happened. The response of a perfectly rational superhuman when faced with human behavior is homicide. We're better off irrational."

I had to agree, even though he was joking. Probably joking. The more human I became, the harder it was for me to kill. I still wasn't talking to him. He grinned and went back to watching the argument. But that wasn't my real question. My real question was, why had my master made *me* so human?

I remembered my master talking about human emotions once. "So basic, so pure," he said. "So simple when you think about it. Like any other animal. A person wants to survive. Just survive. The organism itself exists only to keep on existing. All the rest, all the technology and philosophy and social grease, all of that is only layer upon layer of elaborate justification, quite beautiful but utterly unnecessary."

My little master entertained himself in the evenings unraveling the layers of selected people he said wouldn't be missed. Sometimes he peeled away a layer or two of me when there wasn't anyone else available, but I didn't have many more layers than the dog back then so he always lost interest. Besides, he needed me.

He considered himself a perfectly rational superhuman, my little master, with his neat ringlets and his interested blue marble eyes. The room felt cold and I wrapped my arms around myself.

The discussion went in circles. "I cannot make you stay with me, and I cannot stop being a Monitor," Roder said patiently for the tenth time. "I have no choice. It's you who have to choose, but I would rather you didn't choose right away. You're assuming we are trapped here, but we haven't even tried yet. Whatever you decide to do, I am going to keep trying to contact the NeverMind and get back to the Web."

"We're on a renegade world. They don't have engines, Roder. They don't even have astronomy. We tried to hijack their Beast and it nearly ate Octavian," said Cully. Octavian frowned at him but he kept going. "Besides, what's the point? If you're the last Monitor, if Enforcement has taken over the Web, what's the point? What do we have to go back to? Enforcement doesn't need witches. Why don't you give it up?"

"You're acting as if I'm human and could choose my fate," said Roder.

Pegeen took off her glasses and squeezed the bridge of her nose, her brown fingers stiff. "You've made a lot of choices since I've known you," she said.

He smiled at her, the light eyes calm. "I was made for one thing, but I have many choices in how I go about it."

They were trying to quit their jobs and take their boss along with them, along with his reason for existing.

"Let him be," I said from the alcove and everybody jumped. They'd forgotten I existed.

"Let him be yours, you mean," said Electra, and Roder closed his eyes.

Blessed–Spirit's–stinking–pus–stained–longjohns," said Fergus deliberately.

"I swear, Electra." Pegeen looked furious.

Electra set her mouth.

I started again, "You want to find an engine to get back in the Web. If you want, if you want, I, I can—"

"I can at least use the Beast to contact the NeverMind, for a start," interrupted Octavian, glaring at me.

"Oh, all right, all right," said Roder, laughing.

I was colder than before, shaking. I had almost done it. I had almost done it, and Octavian wouldn't let me.

"Bed," said Pegeen in a practical tone.

When everyone had left the room, Roder leaned into the alcove, pushing a sleepily complaining Bear to one side, and putting his arms under my shoulders he pulled me out. My knees were stiff.

"I appreciate your offer, whatever it was, but I will never ask you to give up your freedom," he said. "I will never ask you to be anything but what you are."

That's what I was afraid of.

He led me to the back of the house, opened the door into a dark room, and stood leaning against the jamb after I went in.

"They don't want to leave you," I said. My voice sounded muffled. There were tapestries on the walls and curtains over the window, and the room was small and very brown.

He folded his arms and leaned his head back, tired. "They will, and just as well. I give them something to do with themselves temporarily, but it's better for them to head out on their own. They don't know what it's like to have a real purpose. The first day I was squirted out of the tank, I knew what I was supposed to do with my life, and I've never done anything else. I suppose it's easier for me."

"Could you go against your nature?"

He laughed.

"Now that would be hard. Bielo managed it, so I suppose I could. I don't want to, though . . . Can I stay with you tonight?"

He watched me.

"Where is Electra?" I said.

He walked away down the hall and I heard him rummaging in the kitchen, then he returned with a wooden spoon, a plate, and something that looked like a spatula. Kneeling down and pushing the door shut, he managed to wedge the spatula and plate together under the door so that it wouldn't open easily. "There," he said. "That answer your question?"

I nodded.

There was a small rug on the floor, but he yanked the curtains out of the window and the tapestries off the walls, making me lie down and tugging and tidying the folds of fabric over me as if I were a package to be mailed or a corpse being arranged for a funeral. Shrouded, only my head peeking out, I started to giggle. "That's better," he said, and kicking his shoes off he slid into the wrappings himself. It got very hot in there, very quickly.

Yes.

In the middle of the night someone walked up to the door and tried the handle. Whoever it was, when the door wouldn't open, got down and tried to shove the utensils out from under it. I felt Roder shift position, reach out with his leg, and brace his foot against the end of the spatula, holding it in place. After a few minutes the noise stopped, but I didn't think the intruder went away for a while. Roder went back to sleep with his foot braced like that and his head tucked just above my collarbone. The cat was sleeping against my back. I don't know how she got in.

Electra looked ill in the morning, and she was ferociously polite to me all through breakfast. I wasn't sorry to leave her when Roder, Pegeen, Octavian, and I went out to try sending a message through the Beast.

Now we were outside the shabby building where the local mages kept their monster, and Octavian, trembling slightly, was murmuring under his breath, talking to the captive inside. Pegeen was looking even more egglike than usual.

"It says just come in the front door," said Octavian, leaning back on his heels with his eyes half-shut in pleasure.

"It does, does it?" said Pegeen.

He glanced at her with a half smile. She slapped him with her weathered hand, a blunt, quiet sound. It didn't look very satisfying for either of them.

He didn't move. "I am sorry," he said.

"But you're going in anyway."

"Yes."

She turned her back on him.

"Here goes," he said, stood up, and walked up the path to the unfinished wooden door. He put his hand up, it opened, and he stepped in. Pegeen closed her eyes.

We waited, crouched down. It was chilly this close to the river. A dank breeze wiped across us, and the rising pale gleam of dawn at the horizon made it feel even colder. Pegeen opened her eyes again and shoved her glasses up firmly.

"Can you tell if anything's happening?" said Roder.

"It's not my Talent," she said. "I can see what's obvious and I can hide what needs to be hidden, and that's all." She had her tight mouth even tighter and was staring at the scene before us.

The walls of the building rippled like the air above a summer road, but nothing happened.

"He likes it so much he'd risk death, and never mind me," she said, though nobody had asked.

"Well, yes," said Roder.

She shrugged and adjusted her glasses. "Forgot who I was talking to. Sounds rational to you too, doesn't it?"

A whiff of rotting mud came up from the harbor. Roder and Pegeen both wrinkled their noses. "Plenty of rustic charm here," she said.

Roder looked down at a patch of river just visible below, an olive triangle between two buildings. "They don't have much technology here, physical or magical."

"It's pathetic. This kind of thing is what Enforcement was designed to prevent, isn't it?" said Pegeen.

No, it wasn't what Enforcement was designed to prevent. This place was just a world like most human worlds, illogical, messy, and complex. Enforcement was designed to stop someone like my logical, tidy, straightforward, reasonable little master. He didn't waste energy on things like palaces and rituals, robes and spells, my master. He went right to the point. "The point, Malka, is to survive. For that, I need power, Malka. Power. Not fame, not possessions, not followers. I am no different than any other human being; my first need is to stay alive, and my second is to have power so I can stay alive comfortably."

I couldn't nod at the time, being tied to a board with some of my loose bits pinned down, but he wasn't exactly talking to me. My master's idea of survival involved moving an entire world off the Web, taking it over, and dumping his partners once they had served their purpose. His idea of surviving comfortably probably involved the slow, carefully examined death of any number of interesting people, probably starting with those partners. No, probably starting with me, once I'd stopped being useful. He had designed me to want to keep on living, after all, and nothing fascinated him more than the will to live.

Maybe that was what kept him following me all these years, instead of just making a replacement.

The back door of the Beast's building slammed open with no notice, and I jumped to my feet. A slim figure fell out of the door, but it wasn't my master, not this time.

"Whooo!" shouted Octavian happily as Pegeen ran up to him. "Ahhh!" He got to his feet and grabbed her as she reached him, dancing her around. Two men who had been in the building behind him started toward them, and he whirled her around one more time, took her hand, and raced toward us. We all ran.

"What happened? Slow down, I think they gave up chasing us. What happened, Octavian?" demanded Roder halfway back. In the growing light Octavian's eyes were sparkling, and he was wearing a new piece of jewelry, three seamless silver rings around his neck, interwoven with the chain of his pendant.

"What didn't happen?" he replied. "It was everything I hoped."

"Did you reach the NeverMind?"

"Oh, the NeverMind knows," said Octavian. "The NeverMind knew all along. It's all one thing. Magic's all one thing in one place. All one thing."

"Is the NeverMind sending a rescue ship?"

"You already have a rescue ship," said Octavian, smiling brightly at me.

I dropped a step behind.

"Everything's ready," he went on. "This was all meant to happen. Everything's coming to you, Roder. We don't have to decide to go anywhere. Right, Malka?"

"Oh," said Pegeen, paused, and said again, "Oh." Roder put his hand on her arm. She shook it off.

Octavian jumped up into the air from sheer joy. Pegeen followed after him, her head down.

I unfroze, joint by joint. They didn't believe him.

25

The Cripple's Blow
(**Second Intention,**
Pretense of Failed Attack)

It was an hour later, and Octavian still glared at us from a twisted chair in the jungle dining room. "I didn't just speak to it, I merged with it. It couldn't lie to me, I was part of it."

"Fine," said Pegeen. "You merged with magic and became one with the Web, and discovered it had a purpose and a meaning. Did you see a white light and a few dead relatives, while you were at it?"

"I didn't say I knew the meaning of the universe," said the boy. "I said magic was all one thing, and it thinks, and it has a plan."

"A cosmic plan?" said Cully carefully, fingering his beads.

"No. A backup plan. An emergency plan. A battle plan."

"You're not making sense," said Electra sternly. Fergus, his chin on his arms and his parrot shifting from foot to foot on top of his head, stared from the other side of the room. Roder stood behind him, face still.

Octavian closed his eyes and leaned back. "You don't have to believe me. But we didn't just land here by accident. We were brought here. Everything we've been looking for, it's coming here."

"We're in heaven, in other words."

"No. We're in the path of an accident about to happen. Like those

Mennenkalts we were chasing after? They're coming here. We just got here ahead of them," said Octavian with irritation as if they were the ones talking vaporous nonsense.

Roder said. "Why?"

We're in the middle of a war between Enforcement and magic," said Octavian. "The black-matter drive kills magic. Magic is fighting back." He made a sudden screaming face so graphic, so cold, so evocative of black-matter it made me shiver in agreement, but it was the final straw for the others.

"Oh, Octavian."

Octavian made a rude noise. "Soon," he said. "It's coming soon."

"Everything's falling apart. This isn't . . . it shouldn't . . . I won't have it," said Electra, and she stood up and walked out.

Bielo stood up and began to follow her.

"Stay, Bielo," said Roder. "She'll be all right. We have to plan."

Bielo kept going, Pegeen went over to Octavian and started talking to him in a lowered voice, and Fergus and Cully pushed their chairs in and left, not looking at Roder.

Roder raised an eyebrow at me. "Don't suppose you have any ideas?"

Forget it, I said, loud and messy, and the room shimmered the way the Beast's building had. Bear jumped into my lap and started kneading my thigh with her paws, staring up at me in possessive bliss. The house was silent and calm. Pegeen's face was blank, her eyes turned to the side trying to remember, Octavian's mouth drooped with disappointment in me, and Roder stared like a mannequin into space.

My master said every living thing existed only to survive, but I existed to grow louder and messier until I blew up and took my friends with me. How long did I have? Was Malka pushed or did she jump? I was full, full to bursting, and the roar of the sea pressed against the inside of my eardrums.

Something else was inside there. *"Malka?"* said Octavian from within my head. I looked up, and saw him shaking with his eyes closed, exactly as he did when he talked to the NeverMind.

"No," I answered, and he shook harder but didn't go away.

"They're coming. You have to—" he said.

Then he opened his eyes in surprise, still trembling, and said to Pegeen, "They're coming *now*. Not the Mennenkalts we were chasing, but the ones Enforcement took captive three years ago."

She looked annoyed. "What? Oh, Octavian."

Roder leaned over to put his hand on Octavian's shoulder.

"Now!" repeated Octavian in that deep wild voice, the NeverMind's voice, but in the local language. "We must defend ourselves now! Wizards, Sorcerers, Magicians, to me! Join with me!"

As he said it, he stood up. So did Pegeen, in a jerky unison, both of them startled. "Yes," said Octavian, looking at the door, and Pegeen nodded in agreement.

"Come now," said Pegeen in the local language. She looked as if she were listening to something, and when I looked at Octavian he had the same expression. They both started walking toward the door.

"Octavian," said Roder.

I leaned back, away from the door. I was in a whirlpool. Something was clawing at me.

"Octavian," repeated Roder.

Neither one answered.

"Octavian. Pegeen."

Octavian began to giggle as if somebody had told a wonderful joke, and he and Pegeen paused in the doorway, clutched each other, and laughed helplessly.

"Are you possessed?" Roder demanded. They didn't answer. In a minute, they stopped laughing, let go of each other, and started walking. He ran after them and grabbed Octavian, who didn't protest, just started trying to get loose like a cat in a net. Pegeen kept going, and Roder started after her into the street still holding Octavian.

A man in a saffron tailcoat, wearing amber jewelry and a high-domed hat, walked past without looking at them.

"I think it's something else," I said. "There's something big going on."

Roder, annoyed, was holding Pegeen by the middle, but she was walking in place. Octavian had twisted himself over so that his head stuck out from under the android's elbow. The saffron man went past them without a glance.

"It's like holding oil with your fingers," Roder complained. "Help me." Pegeen was trying to peel his arm off her, picking away with her strong fingers. Another mage, wearing only a shirt and his neckrings, passed us without a glance.

"I'll go get Bielo," I said, and Roder nodded. But when I turned, Electra and Cully were forcing themselves past me, Cully muttering, "now" in the local language and fingering his beads. Fergus popped out after them, cheerful and oblivious with the parrot on his shoulder, but when I put a hand to his chest he walked past it. I peered into the house, and saw Bielo. He stood in the middle of the room with his hands in his trouser pockets.

"You have anything to do with the sudden urge people had to walk out on a perfectly good breakfast?" he asked me.

I looked around. Three mages in nightclothes bustled past at the end of the block, not one of them sparing me a glance. They were heading up the hill along with the current of magic, walking with the same purposeful speed as Octavian and Pegeen had. Bielo stepped into the street to stand beside Roder and stare after them. Roder was still holding Octavian, who was picking at the android's grasp and walking in place, but Pegeen had gotten away and was rounding the corner. I leaned back against the pull myself, though it wasn't pulling on me exactly. I was just a boulder in the river, not a floating leaf.

"You're not going anywhere," said Roder to me, grabbing Octavian's arm when the boy managed to worm free. "Why aren't you going with them?"

"I am not a witch," I said. "This is for witches."

"It's a spell for witches?" he said.

I nodded.

Octavian was a pretzel. He looked as if he'd willingly break a bone to get free. Roder let go. The boy began walking again and disappeared around the corner.

We started walking after them. It was still early morning, though the sun was beginning to warm the city. People forged their way past us, most of them local mages with the neck jewelry and the awful clothing. The occasional nonwitch peered from doorways and windows as we went past.

"What do you think it is? You think the boy triggered some kind of local emergency alert when he went into the Beast?" said Roder. "Is this their version of a burglar alarm?"

"Never heard of anything like it," said Bielo.

"What a mess," said Roder wearily. "I shouldn't have let him go in."

The sun shone, but I shivered. It wasn't nerves, and it wasn't cold air. It was a more familiar, bone-chilling kind of coldness, and it was somewhere near. I looked up. There was a small orange speck, a ball, in the sky above the harbor, and that was where the coldness was coming from.

"Octavian didn't set it off. I know what the emergency is," I said. "He was right. Enforcement's here."

Roder laughed.

"Really," I said, and pointed. He peered along the line of my finger and raised his eyebrows, watching it approach.

I craned my neck and the Enforcement ship was close enough to see now. It was an old sanction transport, a refit, not one of their new little bulbous arrows, and it was meant to spend long periods in open space and free fall. The orange skin of the ship was broken at intervals by hatches, portholes, access bays, and patches where the skin had worn away and been replaced by other material. The drive end was aimed toward us, like an axle, keeping still while the rest of the ship revolved. In the center of it was the viewing port of an iris door in the center of that. Around the axle, the words *Hilma K. Lewis* revolved, around and around, and it gave off an aura of bitter cold.

Class Three sanction on Mennenkaltenei, three years ago. Twelve thousand Mennenkalts aboard the *Hilma K. Lewis*. Last heard off the Web chasing an escaped prisoner. We might be off the Web, but we hadn't escaped.

"That's the emergency, then," said Roder. Bielo nodded. They both sighed in unison. "Too bad," said Roder. "We're dead."

There was a huge surge in the flow of magic up the hill, and the people passing us began to run full speed. The whole world seemed to pause, and a dark column of smoke rose above the center of the city, a twisting shape like the body of a tornado. It loomed over us.

In the pause, in the stillness, the column of smoke took on the form of a giant. It had a head, and arms, and enormous legs. It reached back with one incredibly long arm and made a throwing motion that seemed to last forever and to cover the whole sky.

Then it finished the throw, and the world began to move again.

Several small things shot out of the iris door of the Enforcement ship and fell, and at the same time the axle slowly began to turn along with the rest of the craft. The ship too fell, for one breathless second, as if it were going to crack like an egg on the city below. Then the spinning sphere halted in midair, took a sprightly hop, and after a single swooping pass to the hills north of the city it landed like a bird.

Roder stood with his mouth open. "They did it," he said. "That's not normal flight. The locals did it."

"They can't have," said Bielo. "Enforcement engines are impervious to spells. They can't have."

Silence. They both stared.

"Now we're really in trouble," said Bielo, and Roder nodded.

People were still walking up and heading blindly toward the top of the hill, and magic was still pouring past me.

The twisting column of smoke above the center of the city folded in half and vanished like dust in the wind.

There was a blinding fountain of magic pouring back down the hill. I heard far-off yelling, and two people who had just passed us going up turned around in bewilderment, stared at each other, and began to run back down the hill. More people began running past us, though others were walking and talking.

"We're in for it," said Roder. "They're sure to notice us."

"No," said Bielo and chuckled. "They won't notice a thing. I'll bet they're all holding their bowels shut with knees and elbows right now."

A man in gray and blue stripes, as if to contradict Bielo, glanced at me. *Not here, not now.* His legs buckled and he sat down. Too loud. I couldn't control it anymore. But at least he forgot me as he staggered back to his feet and ran on. Roder and Bielo hadn't noticed. We kept going up the hill against the flow.

When we reached the square at the top, it was almost empty. All the witches had scattered, and Octavian and Pegeen, with their arms around each other, were walking toward us. There were two natives likewise embracing in the small garden at the center, a bald man and a long-haired woman, and beyond them in the red building the sound of many voices raised in far-off fury.

"I told you," said Octavian severely as he and Pegeen came close enough to be heard.

"You told me, Octavian," said Roder. "You were right."

"Hah. Kaihan's back in town. I should have known," said Bielo, not listening to them. He pointed.

"What?"

"The bald man over there. He's the mage I told you about. The local witch who might be able to build you a drive. The one who might be willing to do it."

Maybe I was safe after all.

"Who's that?" said the bald man when Bielo called his name. He shaded his eyes against the early-morning sun. The black-haired woman he was embracing turned to face us too. She saw me, and I saw what she was in the same moment.

Maybe I wasn't safe after all.

Octavian had been right. It was all happening at once, and all in the same place. I started backing away.

"Ekestverte yer andanfellter, lle perfent kamm!" she started in amazement, her insane green eyes widening. "Lle kurfurst? Lle kurfurst zhatter?" The power glowed from her. She was speaking directly to me, directly to the ocean inside me. She saw me. She saw all of me.

"NO," I said, still backing away. "Thank you, no. I like it this way." We had found the escaped prisoner the Hilma K. had been chasing. She was a Mennenkalt, but worse, she was one of the Mennenkalt gods, one of the ones they bred for the Power. I could smell it, glowing from her like a loaf fresh from the oven.

Like every other Mennenkalt I met, she wanted to break me open like a penny bank, and unlike every other one I'd met she could do it without my permission.

26

The Counterattack (**Screaming Geek,** Against Attack Already in Progress)

We were inside the black tower, the ugly tall one on the square with the blue lights coming out of the top. It was just as ugly inside, and even darker, and it belonged to the imperious bald gentleman, Kaihan, who sat cross-legged on the floor as if he were above us on a throne. He was listening to Roder, had been listening to him for ten minutes without saying anything and without moving. In spite of his torn and grubby shirt, in spite of the long red scratch and the scum of grime on his face, in spite of the weariness that gave a squint to the hard black eyes, he was almost as frightening a character as his girlfriend, for the power in him was like a knife.

Bielo was right. The natives couldn't have downed the Enforcement transport without somebody like this. The other local witches had all been merely people with a little Talent. This man was an elemental, more of a spirit than a human witch.

The reason I was sitting as far from the others as I could wasn't the powerful Kaihan, though. The reason I had my back to the wall and an eye on the door was squatting on her haunches beside him, rebraiding her long hair. She was almost as dirty as he was, as if the two of them had been rolling around on the ground. I didn't trust her, even if she *had* apologized.

I didn't trust her because every time she looked at me, and she looked at me often, her pupils contracted as if she were looking at the sun. She wasn't trying to crack me open anymore, but I was making her ill, and that was quite an accomplishment. She was one of the highest of the human deities of the Mennenkalts. Kaihan called her "Lisane," which was a Mennenkalt word, but he obviously didn't know what it meant. It meant "nameless," the same way the Hom Bulos called magic "RGWG the Unnamable."

Roder stopped talking. Neither of our new acquaintances jumped in to fill the silence. Kaihan's black eyes didn't waver. He was as much like the other mages I'd seen as an alligator was like a poodle.

"Please—" Electra started, and Bielo put his hand over her mouth. She had been crouching on the porch of the white building and ran to Roder when we reappeared, but Bielo had intercepted her then, too. Pegeen, cloaked, had gone out to find where Fergus and Cully were.

The man didn't move. I wasn't even sure he was breathing. In the last half hour Roder had given him a brief history of the Web and of the technical development of witchcraft, explained what Enforcement was, outlined the job of Monitor, laid out the present situation, and asked him if he would consider making us an engine, while giving him a crash course in cosmology that had some rather large holes. Kaihan's only question so far had been one about how stars made their light, which he quickly retracted with an apology for wasting time.

Now he said in his deep voice, "Instantaneous travel and speech over vast distance?"

Roder nodded.

"And these Enforcers of yours, when their control is even slightly threatened, they retaliate immediately by destroying whole worlds."

"Lately, yes, they have been."

He still didn't move. Austere bugger. "I have no idea how to make this thing you want."

"Well, I do," said the nameless Mennenkalt goddess, and my stomach clenched, but she continued: "I made a little one when I ran away."

She made it sound trivial. She had gotten herself off an interstellar transport in midtranslation, all by herself. She had escaped a platoon of Enforcers, all by herself. She had stolen a little rocket lifeboat and made an engine all by herself, and landed on a strange planet, and made nice with the most powerful magician around, all by herself. The Mennenkalt gods were fearsome creatures.

"Ah, yes," said Kaihan, regarding her.

She tucked her black hair behind her ear.

He turned back to Roder. "If I make you one and let you go away, can you keep them from destroying us all after you're gone?" said Kaihan. "Ah. I see that's the question. These Enforcers will kill us, won't they? No matter what we do."

The inside of this tower was a sink of silence. When nobody was moving or speaking, you couldn't hear anything at all except a kind of deep heaviness in the air.

Roder sighed, finally. "If you had enough power and enough magic and enough time, you could make an engine big enough to move the whole world. I knew of a man who did it once."

I wasn't going to say anything. Wasn't going to volunteer, if there were a chance, if there was any other way. The woman stared at me as if she could see what I was thinking. Her pupils were tiny holes in the green sea of her eyes.

"But we do not have enough time," said Kaihan.

"Time is relative. Time is just an idea. We have enough power, and we have enough magic," said Lisane.

I pressed my back against the wall, hard, feeling the rough coldness of the black stone against my shoulder blades. *No.*

Everybody flinched. "Would you just stop that, child? You're hurting everybody," said Electra. She turned her face against Bielo's hand.

"Child?" said Lisane. "She's as old as the ages, as big as the sky, and she knows what's good for her, which is more than I can say for you. No, spirit of anger," she said to me respectfully in Mennenkalt, "I do not question thy will or thy vision, and I will seek thy help elsewhere." Once again, she seemed to be talking to all of me, in a spooky way.

She stood up. "You want to try?" she said to Kaihan.

He regarded her with those cold black eyes, not looking any more convinced than he had a moment before. "Why do you even ask me?" he said. "You will do as you wish." She leaned down, said something in his ear, and strode to the front door. He watched her go, and there was a crease at the corner of his mouth that told me the basilisk was smiling.

"Then we must make a world engine, not a little boat that will hold only you," he said to Roder, and that was that. He was no trusting savage.

He knew what was involved. It took tremendous arrogance to make such a decision for a whole world.

Roder took it for the ultimatum it was, though Electra, looking from face to face, was ready to jump in and fight until Bielo took her off to one side and talked face-to-face for a long time. By the time he was done, she was looking as complacent as ever, especially after he kissed her hand.

Outside Kaihan's coal-colored tower the rest of the country was going to hell in a number of creative ways, Pegeen reported when she came back with the others. The moment the transport ship landed, all its prisoners poured out and began to settle in, causing interesting interactions with the natives. Some of the refugees, determined to straighten things out, had already reached the fringes of the city. Mennenkalts were peaceful people, but opinionated and persistent, and there were twelve thousand of them.

Meanwhile, the local government was too wounded to cope. The creation of the spell had required the power of all the witches in the world, most of whom had not been volunteers, and the resulting quarrels were fierce.

Kaihan listened to this with his hand over his eyes and decided to ignore the political turmoil his world was in. He called in a colleague to help, a surly gentleman with a long white beard by the name of Gelmas who looked vaguely familiar to me, and I puzzled over that until I realized he'd been the elderly gent with the prisoner and the horse the day before. While Kaihan explained things to his annoyed friend, Lisane stood in the doorway and spoke in Mennenkalt to the air outside, saying things that made my insides crawl.

Fergus said, "She's sending out an invitation to a party?" I'd forgotten how poorly he understood Mennenkalt.

Cully answered patiently, "The pronoun makes a difference, Fergus."

Then endless rivers of magic began surging in, flooding the chamber. The others looked as pale and ill as when they were in translation. I, on the other hand, grew hot, dizzy, and replete.

After that, creating a living drive seemed to require much arguing and plenty of chalk. Kaihan's friend Master Gelmas was squatting in his white robes scribing geometric shapes on Kaihan's clean black floor. "It's not just the motion of the wandering stars which must be taken into account," he said authoritatively, drawing a precise arc between two of the points of a nine-pointed star. "The fixed stars have a proper motion as well."

Kaihan perched on the bottom step of his black throne rubbing his shoulders. He's wiped his face clean and changed into austere black clothing. "Balderdash," he said. "The fixed stars haven't got a thing to do with it. This fellow says they're big suns and not even close to one another."

"You can't deny that my methods work," said the other man, picking up a different color and drawing a straight line by putting the chalk to the floor and shuffling backward.

"Your methods work because they amuse the spirits," said the Lisane, standing in the doorway. "I find them pretty funny myself." Glemas glared at her.

"It's just the . . . genetics . . . of . . . brain chemistry," said Fergus, using Standard words for half the sentence because there weren't any words in the local language.

"Just the gobbledygook?" mocked Master Gelmas, not understanding most of what Fergus had said. "Is that all?"

Fergus rolled his eyes, and groped for words. "People are either born with brains that can interact with magic, or they're not. Spells are just a way of focusing the mind. They're not necessary."

Master Gelmas finished the line with a neatly drawn interlocking knot. "Of course. That's obvious. But without carefully crafted spells, you don't have focus and all you get is nonsense." He went back to the center and started drawing another straight line in a third color. The line passed under Kaihan's feet, which he lifted up while the old man shuffled past.

I watched from one of the stairways that wound up the inside of Kaihan's vast tower while they moved around and squabbled. The room was bulging with magic. The heated pressure was steady, pushing on all of me, burying my outer layers, but it wasn't unpleasant, and it wasn't just caused by Lisane's bespeaking or the scribblings of Master Gelmas. Somehow or another, Roder's witches, the Lisane, and the local mages were weaving something intricate together. Master Gelmas created an interlocking diagram that covered the whole circular floor, around the nine-pointed star in the center. Octavian straddled it, his black-fringed eyes half-closed. He still seemed elated from his morning's encounter with the Beast, though he wouldn't say anything about it and he wouldn't look at me. "The flow in the north is weak," he would say with a smile, and Pegeen would walk to that end of the diagram and stare at the floor.

Fergus, following her, would stoop when she pointed and draw patterns in the air with his fingers.

With each layer Master Gelmas scribed, Kaihan moved a step higher on his throne, occasionally holding his broad hands out as if warming himself at a fire. The Lisane walked and watched, moving from one end of the diagram to another, talking and talking, seeing things none of the rest of us could see, staring at me from time to time, and her face was the color of skim milk.

Just outside the design, Cully and Electra stood against opposite walls, Cully sliding beads through his fingers and Electra fluttering her hands over her small animal, and every once in a while one of them would say something quiet to another one of the participants. Only Roder and I had nothing to do. The air was heavy and hot, and I was restless and confused, but the others seemed unaffected by the heat so I said nothing.

"Have you thought what form it should take?" inquired Kaihan. "Animal? Human? Abstract?"

"It will take what form it happens to take," grunted the old man, holding the front of his robe bunched in one hand so he wouldn't sweep out the marks he was making with the other hand. "If we had time to make this a year-project I would bother with aesthetics."

The Lisane stopped, balancing on one foot. "Not aesthetics. Function follows form. The tool shapes the task."

"Crude sympathetic magic," said Electra in Standard to Cully. "I guess they believe the charm should look like the thing it's supposed to affect."

The Lisane caught the condescending tone, if not the meaning. "I am talking about the natural form of a being. Things are true to their natures, and form is part of nature."

"Wouldn't human be easiest?" Kaihan moved another step upward.

"No. Human form is the most difficult and the most dangerous." She met my eyes and balanced on the other foot. "When you make a living thing, it should be like enough to you that you can speak with it, but unlike enough that you don't expect to understand it. Unless you have a compelling reason otherwise." She hopped to the next open space.

"Only the novice speaks of what should be, not what is," muttered Gelmas.

Electra wasn't convinced. In Standard, she said to Cully, "Why does it have to have a shape at all? Drives don't have a shape, minds don't have a shape. Seems to me these primitives are making a lot of fuss over window dressing."

"It's good basic engineering, and you're being rude," said Pegeen acerbically from across the room. "Why do you think every witch's familiar has a different shape? It's not just because they feel like it."

Electra rolled her eyes.

"It's lopsided again on that side," called Octavian to Pegeen, waving toward our end of the hall.

Somebody hammered on Kaihan's door. He ignored it.

"Still lopsided," called Octavian.

Fergus sat back on his heels. "I've retied this intersection three times already. What's going on?"

"I don't know. It feels like the floor's on a slant and everything's rolling downhill."

The hammering came again. "Somebody please get that," said Kaihan.

I stepped where Roder did, in between the lines, carefully skipping the blank spots he skipped. Master Gelmas had a hand that was supernaturally steady. The lines looked as if they had been ruled, or grown, or poured across the floor from an enormous bucket. Some were wide and straight, others thin and curved, while others were made of stripes that flowed and wove around one another. If I looked too closely at the floor I felt as if I were walking on hot water with a lace of sunlight reflecting off its ripples.

"Whoa," said Octavian, rocking unsteadily on his feet as I passed him in the middle. I gave him a look, but he wasn't making fun of me.

"What?" Pegeen straightened up.

"Now it's not tipping anymore."

"Hmf."

Octavian looked ghostly. So did the others. The light by which I was seeing everyone came only partly from the oil lamp Kaihan had casually hung from a railing. The rest of the light came from beneath them, from the pale lines on the floor. The dark floor, which did not show the dust, seemed to drop away from beneath the network and now I was walking on hot rising air in the spaces between the mesh of a net of pale light. It was all I could do to keep from stepping on the lines instead, so the web would hold me from falling.

Whoever it was knocked on the door again, slow measured persistent thuds, and Roder quickened his pace. As he reached the door, Octavian said, "It's her."

Fergus, who had been resting with his legs wide, said, "What?"

"Malka's doing it. Now everything's falling off in the other direction."

I twisted around to look at them, leaving my feet where they were, and even Gelmas was peering up at me.

Pegeen shook her head impatiently. "Of course. I forgot. You create a blank space on the scans. You must do it with a small steady draw of power from the space you're in."

That made me sound like a bathtub drain.

The hammering came again. Roder opened the door. A man stood outside with his fist raised to pound again. When he saw Roder and me he looked offended. He was fairly offensive himself, being fitted out in a kind of rumpled toga in magenta and turquoise.

All the pressure was from behind me now.

Roder merely looked inquiring.

"Master—" The man cleared his throat and began again; "Master Kaihan is commanded as an observer to a meeting of full Sassevin Council, to be held an hour from now in Chancery. Where is he? I am to deliver the message in person."

"Go away, Ferris, I got your message," called Kaihan. Roder shut the door in the man's face.

"Then we either have to adjust for the drain or make it stop," said Octavian as if there hadn't been any interruption. The motionless hub of the wheel of lines, he stood with his legs straight and his face grave, all the others looking to him.

I had seen witches working together once like this, only then I was in the center and my master drew the lines. He drew them with blood in a jar and a steel dip pen, not chalk, and the blood he used was the vinegar that ran through his veins. He drew me all over with red and I reeled in the lines.

"You won't make it stop," said the Lisane. "You can't adjust for the drain. She is what she is. Right, Malka?"

All the eyes were on me. I felt intoxicated and full, now that she mentioned it. Reeling in the lines, like a fisher at her net. "Right," I said.

I opened the door again. The mage was gone. It was simple enough for me to leave. Or maybe not so simple. Outside, the air was thin and cold, and yet it was blazing hot and bright, and the buildings wouldn't stay in one place. I tried to make them stop with my fingers, but they wouldn't.

27

Exchange of Feints
(**Fast Eddie,** Against a
Skilled Opponent)

"**M**alka, wait," Roder said, and stepped out into the square behind me. He was standing in a pool of shadow not much bigger than his feet, and I looked up, still spinning, to see that the sun was directly overhead. I'd lost half a day to the midnight inside, and now the tip of the tower high above him seemed to be rotating around the sun like a clock hand. Roder's arms were under my shoulders, my face was buried in his shirt, and my knees and feet were going in different directions. "Hold on, hold on," he was saying from somewhere near my left ear, and I dutifully grabbed a handful of his shirt.

I was sinking down anyway, but he helped me sit when I got to the ground, and then put a palm between my shoulder blades to make me put my head between my knees.

"Stuffy in there, wasn't it," he said, taking the hand away though I didn't want him to. Stuffy was a good word for it. The air out here was empty.

I was looking at the tops of my feet, which felt explosive. "I have to take my shoes off," I announced, and started to fumble at the joins. He came around, kneeled, and undid them for me, but then he couldn't get them off, even with my help. I started panting with the pain, and he rose and went away and left me sitting there with my feet the size of melons in cherry-sized shoes.

A moment later Bear drifted against my left side, came around me, and crouched down with her back to me, looking across the square. Every hair in her thick pelt caught the light and glowed in the noon sun, and her sides sparkled and vibrated as they moved in and out with her purr. She was bigger too. *Vampire,* I said to her, and her sides rippled in a comfortable twitch but she didn't go anywhere.

Roder kneeled down with a small knife and cut into my left shoe, removing it like the skin of an orange, then moving to the other foot.

"You should be inside," I said, dribbling magic out of my nose as I said it. I was sitting in a radiating pool of magic that was flowing gently down the steps, like a leaky steam boiler but much more dangerous.

"Doing what? I'm not a witch."

"No."

"And you got taller again, Malka, and you were wearing shoes that you couldn't possibly wear."

"I don't want to die," I said. I didn't intend it to sound that stupid.

"No?" he said finally, sitting down next to me.

"I wasn't meant to get this big." Everything was leaking out, not just the magic. I closed my mouth and rubbed my right foot, trying to make the throbbing go away. It was swelling already, and the heat of the sun was making me feel worse.

"How big were you when you started?" he said, which somehow seemed a reasonable thing to ask, so I pointed at the cat.

"Smaller than that."

"Ah, Malka," he said, and he put his arm around me, and I leaned against his side. "Were you somebody's familiar?" he said. I moved my head yes against him. He put his hand on my cheek, moved my chin up, and kissed me carefully. "Bet you weren't nearly as pretty then, he said, moving his face back an inch and talking almost silently.

"I had big furry ears," I said, and he laughed, and somehow I was laughing up at him. I closed my mouth and pulled away. He'd done it to me, gotten me to trust him.

"Don't," he said, "Please don't." Big clear eyes, long lashes, sculpted face, sincere.

So I pulled away some more, and he tried to hold on, and it was exactly the wrong thing for him to do right then, so I jerked myself free.

I looked down at my feet again. They were little red pillows, and I could barely wiggle my toes. He had just done exactly the wrong thing, I thought again. There was a first time for everything. He'd never done the wrong thing with me before. What a nice thing for him to do. I stood up, conscious that I wasn't thinking right.

"What are we doing?"

"We are walking," I said.

I made it to the little garden in the center of the square and then he made me stop. I didn't know if it was far enough away from Kaihan's tower, but it would have to do. I sat down on the bench and the cat jumped up beside me. My feet were itching now, and it was all I could do not to scratch them. Reminded by Bear's presence, I decided to scratch another itch instead.

"What happened to Akamai? Why did she go out of the ship unprotected?"

He didn't seem to hear me. Just when I had decided to ask again, he said something that I couldn't quite make out.

"What?"

"It was a test, I said. She was testing me. I suppose I failed."

"You were supposed to come rescue her from her own stupidity?"

"I always had before."

We sat there. The blazing sun didn't seem to affect the black building, which still looked like a midnight shadow. A few dark birds wheeled way overhead.

"We were partners for a while. She wanted me to care more for her than for my job. But I *am* a Monitor. That's not just my job: I *am* a Monitor, I was made to do that. I watch things, and I make sure they keep going. She wouldn't accept that."

"Huh. Humans."

"Yes," he said with feeling. "I will never understand. Never."

"Here," he said presently, "sit sideways and put your feet up. It will help with the swelling."

I put my legs across his. He slid his arm around my back to make me comfortable, and it seemed entirely reasonable to kiss him, so I did. He put his other arm around me, and kissed me back, and the boiling waves of the ocean inside me slowly tumbled in on themselves and melted down into smaller rolling breakers for a while.

"She called you the god of rage," he said. The bench had a longer shadow now and I hadn't thought about my feet for quite a while.

"Spirit of anger."

" 'Deihelmalkha,' " he said, quoting the Lisane's Mennenkalt word. "Translates as rage." He sounded charmed.

I didn't like that as much as he did. I preferred anger. Anger sounded controlled, dignified. Rage was what a monkey did when it was punished, what a squirrel did from the safety of a tree, what my master's dog did when he cornered it and beat it, all that snarling and biting and screaming. Rage was frightening from a big person, funny from a small one.

Roder cocked his head. "Malka," he said, "I have to ask. Where are you really from? The description I gave you of Forest was completely wrong, and you didn't correct me."

"Yes, it was a desert world, the whole thing, dry and hot," I said. "That's why he wanted to move it."

"He?"

It was too late to take it back. "My master."

"Your master. The one who made you. *Your* master was the witch who built the world-moving engine."

I didn't say anything.

"*You're* the Forest engine?" he said, drawing back. I swung my legs off his lap. "You're the Forest engine and you didn't tell us? They're in there trying to make you from scratch in half a day."

I stood up and backed away.

"Would it kill you to offer to help?" he demanded. "Do you have to be so mistrustful?"

The door of the black tower was sliding open finally.

"Yes, I do," I said. He stared at me. "Yes, it would kill me."

Electra and Bielo emerged, followed by the others, blinking in the light. They were coming toward us, looking cold and pale. "It will take another day, if it works," called Kaihan, his voice hoarse. "It's dangerous in there, now. You'll have to wait somewhere else."

"I don't think we have another day," said Roder urgently, walking to meet them. "There's another possibility."

There is no other possibility.

They staggered, all of them, as if they'd been hit by a breaking wave.

"Malka, at least consider it."

No. Kaihan put his hand to his head, wincing. I backed away some more.

"You're being unreasonable," Roder said.

I am what I am. Leave me alone. They swayed again.

"What is going on?" said Electra. "Would somebody please explain why we have to put up with this, this animal screaming at us all the time? This is dreadful."

"Malka," said Roder. "You could save the whole world if we could find a way to do this."

There is no way to do this. I couldn't seem to say it softly or gently. It came out in a rush, a torrent, and it was blistering hot and insistent. They were all looking ill and unsteady. Only Lisane stood unmoved in the tide flowing over them, watching me with her pinpoint pupils. *You tell them,* I said, not knowing why I was appealing to her except that she hadn't destroyed me yet.

"I will," she said.

"Malka," began Roder, and I interrupted whatever kind and reasonable and sensible thing he was going to tell me, saying, *I am not here. I am not here. Not here.* Repeating it with the voice of the storm, I walked away from them all and they couldn't find me anywhere all the time I was doing it.

The street, all cobblestones, was hot and rough under my feet and I soon began to walk more carefully. I passed by people standing in worried groups talking, but I was *not here* and they obliged me by not noticing.

Once I stood still where I was and turned around, sighting up at the top of the city and thinking. Then I turned around and kept working my way around and down, using none of the lanes I knew.

It was not my choice. It was not my choice.

My master made me, with pins and spells and razors and a hank of his own curly hair. I was the container for the Forest engine, but not a blank room like the one on Roder's ship, not a smooth planet-sized sphere like the NeverMind, not a plain box or a metal locker or a translucent dome. I was a container with a life of my own, a container with a face and emotions. He'd spent a lifetime making the engine inside me, and as one last touch he stuffed his world-sized engine into a small furry Malka with big ears and a bad temper. He gave me a craving for life that would make me entertaining as long as I lived, and he ensured that I would not be able to keep going, would not be able to keep from exploding, without using the engine inside me. And every time the engine inside me went into drive, he promised me, I would die, and every time I died, he would give me his complete attention while I did it.

I did not want to die, and I could not keep on living, not for long. That was how he made me.

He was a small man. Nobody looked at him twice, or if they did, they underestimated him, and he liked it that way.

In late afternoon I stole a pair of shoes someone had left next to their front steps. A little later I walked into somebody's house while *absolutely elsewhere* and took some food out of the cupboard. I was used to living like this, I'd done it all my life. No one ever noticed I was there unless I wanted them to. It had been a mistake to let the Sefire Zul notice me, or Roder, and I wouldn't do that anymore.

An old man was standing in my way when I came out of the house and I began to walk around him. "Ekestverte yer andanfellter, kavelnes," he said urgently. It was an elderly Mennenkalt, pale and thin as a leaf but imperious.

Go away! I said, surrounding him, and he disappeared, reappearing in midair a block away and landing on the street with a thud. I ran the other direction. I'd never done that before. My heart pounding, I stood with my back to the side wall of somebody's house. I'd forgotten the Mennenkalts in the *Hilma K. Lewis.* I'd forgotten them completely.

I was down between big buildings near the river. Here was an abandoned warehouse, walls stained green with rot, smelling of fish and weed. I slipped through a crack between shutter and door and came into a huge dark space with a shaft of light slanting down from a roof-high window. There were planked bins either side of me, with encrusted fish remains smeared dry on their floors, and a long dank aisle between the bins. I sat down and put my legs in front of me.

I did not want to die. I could not keep on living, not for long. And if Enforcement came to find who knocked the *Hilma K. Lewis* out of the sky, my master would be right behind.

The floor beneath me was damp as if the river was rising up from below, but I held an entire ocean the size of a world within me, rolling from seam to seam and trying to escape.

A soft "Brrr?" came from the door, and Bear wormed her way into the building.

"I don't know how to do this," I said to her.

"Malka," she agreed with distaste, shaking a paw.

"You don't have much of a vocabulary, do you?" I said.

She hauled her head back, stuck out a long pink tongue, and began awkwardly washing her shoulder.

"How can you go with me when you're part of Akamai?"

She gave me a blank look.

"A familiar is part of the witch that made it," I said. "You chose not to be part of yourself?"

"Kitten part of mother cat too, still can get born," she enunciated carefully, turned around, and washed her front paw with her back to me.

"Big help. You're a big help."

I put my head down on my knees. When I lifted it again, the shaft of light above was horizontal and the color of glowing honey. The sun was setting. I put my head back down on my knees again.

In Kaihan's dark tower, something like me was growing, an engine that could carry the whole world away. It would take less than a day to finish growing. There was a chance I wouldn't have to do anything. I would wait and see what happened.

Bear came and settled against me. I lay down on my side with her warm body against my stomach. I waited and thought for a long time, until the light was gone and was starting to come back again.

The air was gray when I slipped back outside between the shutter and the door. I turned in a circle. If I wanted to find Roder, I would have to go toward the center of the city. If I wanted to find him. I started up the alley between my night's shelter and the next building.

A huge shadow the size of a pond suddenly blinked into being overhead, as if a cloud had condensed in the sky in an instant, and then it began to shrink and grow darker. I looked up. I was looking at the underside of a well-used spaceship, its belly hammered and dented and smeared with grass stains and dirt, which was sinking slowly toward the next street like a balloon that had lost its air. All over the sky and in every direction, other battered, dirty ships were appearing, and as they sank slowly toward the city others appeared and followed.

The rest of the Mennenkalts had somehow found their way here, a whole planet's worth of them.

At least now Roder would have his pick of ships. He could take one of the Lazarus junkers and we could escape. I could change my mind again, if I could avoid the attention of the Mennenkalts. I broke into a run in my borrowed shoes, heading up the hill.

28
The Failed Attack
(**Wallenda,** Theatrical Fall)

It would be harder than I'd thought to stay away from Mennenkalts. There were secondhand Lazarus ships popping into existence all over the sky, around every corner, past the rooftops in the next street. I turned into a lane and found my way half-blocked by a descending vessel. The ship sank slowly to the pavement, jerked as we approached, and landed off-kilter. A door began to open in its side with a ladder unfolding from it. The face of a Mennenkalt, a woman's face, round and red-cheeked, peered from the door. She saw me and said, with an expression of dawning delight, "Hello there, spirit!"

I skittered away and darted back and forth between the settling ships and the scattering people, but I wasn't fast enough. Rounding one of the ships, I cannoned into a Mennenkalt man who fell backward and sat down, shouting after me, saying, "No! Spirit! Stay!" A moment later, a tall Mennenkalt man with a mustache snatched at me, and behind me somebody's hands grabbed the back of my shirt, but I pulled free.

They were worse than they'd ever been. I didn't like what that implied. Mennenkalts couldn't exactly predict the future, but they knew far more about the present than they should have. Right now I was a birthday present and they wanted to open me.

Meanwhile, a small ship, trying to land on the sloping roof of a house next to me, jiggled suddenly and began instead to slide down the incline and out into the street, landing with a rumbling bounce two stories below. The hatch began to open and stuck halfway. Fingers appeared under the bottom edge and inched it upward. I ran faster and rounded a corner out of sight before it was wide enough to let the occupants out.

Something heavy and sharp landed on my shoulders, and I whirled around, dislodging it. I realized it was Bear as she flew off with a squeal, twisting in midair to land on her feet. She glared at me, her head down, sides pumping in and out.

"I'm sorry," I said, scooped her up, and ran with her.

Another ship, this one in even worse condition than the ones I'd seen before, landed like a dropped egg in the street. There was a gaping hole in one side, and rust at the joints. A hatch flew open, and a boy of six or so poked his head out, followed by an annoyed woman who grabbed his collar from behind. "Wait, wait," she said in Mennenkalt, and climbed out, then helped him down. He danced impatiently in the street while she helped another dozen children out. "Everybody hold hands," she said, and they set off downhill. Another adult head, that of a man, rose out of the hatch. "Oh, right in the middle of a city, how stupid," he said, and climbed out. He turned and helped another group of children get down to the street. "Wait, wait, I have to let the engine out," he said to them, and went back inside. Neither of them noticed me plastered in the doorway of the house opposite.

As he climbed back out, a hot wind of magic blew out past him, and I gulped it involuntarily, feeling my knuckles swell and my jaw lengthen. He had literally released the engine's magic, let it out of its casing. He felt me drinking it up. "What?" he said, turning to stare. "Are you the spirit foretold?" he said to me, starting forward, his eyes wide.

No. Don't touch me.

He jumped back, shaking his hands as if they were burned. They probably were.

I ran again, holding the cat tightly, trying not to be noticed.

It was hard. Most of the people streaming past me were indifferent. Even Mennenkalts could be born without any magical abilities, and most of the people were trying to keep their children from getting too far ahead, or concentrating on helping older people and invalids keep up. They were joking, or snapping at one another, or speculating about the fertility of the land on their new planet. In between the small family groups, though, were people with anxious eyes, the Mennenkalt version of witches, scanning the houses, staring at the sky, looking in the faces of everybody going the opposite direction, and whenever their eyes caught on me they started to glow like matches too close to the flame and I had to lash out at them.

The driver of every ship, as it landed, freed the engine. It made sense in a twisted way, even though they were leaving themselves without escape from this nameless planet. The Mennenkalts disapproved of translation engines because they were so cruel to magic.

In freeing their engines, though, they were being cruel to me, not just because it meant there wouldn't be any working ships for Roder to steal. If I was anywhere near, the power of every engine they let loose was drawn to me and into me. I couldn't stop it, it wasn't in me to stop drawing it in, but my physical body could only grow so much and my skin was spouting magic from every pore. When I opened my mouth to speak, it gushed out in a flood, and soon every person I had to bespeak I left kneeling, blurry with pain.

The cat in my arms seemed to grow heavier and heavier, and finally I began to lose hold of her. She slid from my grip and landed on all fours, but her head was level with my thigh. She was as big as a dog and her fur was dense as a beaver's. "You can carry yourself, you leech," I said, and kept running. I heard her feet thumping behind me.

There was no one in the mosaic house with the jungle room where we had taken shelter the night before.

There was no one in the house with the birds, either.

There were scores of people in the square at the height of the city, but they were all Mennenkalts who had just landed and were letting their engines out, and there was no one and nothing inside Kaihan's tower except a blinding heat and pressure that I ran from, leaving the door open. Roder had gone elsewhere. There was no time. I had to find him.

There was even less time than I thought. As I jogged through the square, when I was halfway across, a shadow swept across the crowd, and a cold, cold, wind, and the Mennenkalts began to run, scooping up children and supporting the elderly between them. Knowing what I would see, I looked up. An orange-painted belly rotated two hundred feet above us, like a ball thrown into the air at the crest of its arc, but it hung and hung, never falling. Just above the tops of the buildings to our right, another orange bulb floated, and another one off to our left.

"Class Two violation of Control Act detected," said a recorded voice from everywhere in Standard. "You are hereby notified that a Class Two sanction will commence in ten hours. Web travel privileges are temporarily suspended. Legal visitors and those wishing to file official protest may present themselves at any Enforcement vehicle until one hour before deadline." It was a recording I'd heard before, when I was very small, but it was in a language most of the people on this world had never heard.

This time the ships didn't stay hanging for ten hours the way they did then. They all began dropping at the same moment, sinking down into the city like balloons going backward. The ship directly above me got larger and larger and began to settle no more than thirty feet away from me, cold as winter, cold as starvation, cold. I backed away from it.

After it landed, a door gaped open at the base, with a ramp slithering tonguelike out of it, making the whole thing look like an eyeless head, and a huge man all dressed in rumpled, grimy orange strolled out on the ramp, his quill-like hair standing on end. He had a short, untidy beard, his neck was dirty, his face was red, and he had the engraved hilt of a scabbarded sword extending up past his left shoulder. He saw me and blinked his small eyes.

I drew my sword. He turned and yelled up the ramp, "Throw me a communicator."

Somebody said something in reply, and he said, "You ask me a question?" in a tone sufficiently contemptuous that a small silvery sphere lofted through the air without further talk. The sphere was swallowed by his large palm. He turned back to me and stepped off the ramp, drawing his own sword smoothly.

I saluted the Sefir Zul, and instead of saluting me back, he came forward slowly and implacably, bringing a whiff of coldness with him as if he were made of the black-matter that powered his engines.

No. He didn't flinch. He kept coming. It was colder and colder the closer he got.

Stop. He didn't stop. He was ten feet away, and now the cold was biting at me. It was as cold as the thin wind from the small silver sphere Tobiah had used to kill Roder's ship. His sword wasn't the weapon he was using against me. The communicator he had asked for was sword and shield enough. It was made of black-matter, a tiny chilly killer all by itself, and he knew it could destroy me.

I turned and ran like a cockroach surprised by the light, darting into the nearest building, the red hall of the mages, scurrying down the corridor, taking the first left, then the next right, then scurrying through a door that looked inconspicuous.

I was in the small theater, the room where the mages had held Roder, and there was no other way out. I stood in the small stage at the center, circling around. In the daytime, I could see that the upper balcony had tall windows across one wall, facing only the sky. Maybe I could climb out one of those and drop to the ground. A broken ankle was preferable to being eaten up alive.

As I started toward the stair, the door rattled, and I dived behind one of the benches, but it was too late. The Sefir Zul ducked his head beneath the top of the doorframe and came in, his drawn sword reflecting the light from the windows and sending liquid bugs of light scattering over the walls. He came toward me smoothly. I stood on the bench, my knees locked, gripping my hilt too tightly, and when he angled the blade toward me, the only thing I could do was leap over the back of the bench to the next bench, run down to the end of the bench, and scurry into the aisle.

He didn't try to pursue me, just looked annoyed and moved to a place where he could reach the stairs or the door with equal ease. He dropped his hand negligently, the blade twisting in his grip. "A lesson, troll? You wish a lesson?"

"I am not fooled," I said.

"You are fooled, and fooled, and fooled again, but you made an excellent weapon. I salute you, troll. You help me rid myself of three enemies."

Three? He was shifting his weight. I remembered to bend my knees and relax my grip. He strode forward abruptly, and when I tried to climb across the benches to get away he just raised his foot and walked the benches himself. I ran to the back wall of the room and scurried along the narrow space behind the last row of benches, but he cut across the rows of benches diagonally and arrived at the door before I could get anywhere near it.

"Nice puzzle for the Monitor, nice smelly bait for the Mennenkalts, nice worm on a hook for the Forest witch," he said, hefting the communicator in his left hand while he moved toward me with the sword. "All in one place, troll, very good."

All in one place? I was bait, was I? Bait for Roder, bait for the Mennenkalts, and the "Forest witch" could only be my master. I was bait for my master. He was on his way, then.

I was breathing hard, crouched on the seat of one of the benches, where I had leapt when he cut off my escape. My short legs in their tight trousers were not enough for this. He could cover the width of the room in five steps. The room? He could cover the Web itself in five steps, and erase a planet with a screw of his thumb. He had taught me everything I knew about sword-fighting, and I was a small Malka troll, and he had used me from the moment he saw me and probably long before that. The Mennenkalts were here chasing me, I had brought Roder here myself, and Zul had planned it all. There were layers within the layers, like Tobiah's inlaid clock, and I couldn't see all the layers.

I was Malka troll against the all-knowing, all-powerful Sefir Zul, and there was no help for it. I jumped over the benches and ran to the small flat stage. It was no bigger than the bouting circle where Zul gave his lessons. Once again, I raised my sword to my brow and swept it aside with a hiss of divided air, deliberately letting my swing go a little wild, not too wild. "You will have to kill me, honored sir," I said, and bent my knees a little too deep, and raised my chin too high, and gripped my hilt so hard the tip trembled.

He looked disgusted. He walked down the aisle without even raising his sword, without even bothering to drop into the fighter's crouch. He hadn't washed since I saw him last, and I could smell him coming a few yards away.

Something fell up above us, something in the balcony. There must be someone there. His eyes flickered, but he decided not to worry about it. As he came into distance, he abruptly moved his feet faster and swung his blade up, as unstoppable as a rolling boulder.

I screeched, sucked my gut in, and swung my sword at him when he was just out of distance, and jerked my elbow back at the end of the swing so that my flailing blade cut down on his, knocking it into the floor. "Aaaaah!" I yelled, and ran backward instead of slicing at him again. I hoped he wouldn't recognize the classic Slap I had just executed, hoped it was messy-looking enough.

No, he hadn't recognized it. He thought too poorly of me. Ready to take my second blow, which would have been the right thing to do if I'd meant the Takagi I had pretended it was, he stood annoyed and then started after me again. I retreated, practically falling down as I moved away, and he obliged by moving forward steadily, his blade held in reserve. I stabbed at him and fell backward off the stage, landing on my back. I planned to regret that action deeply, later on.

Instead of following, instead of jumping down on me and finishing me off as I wanted him to think he could, he stopped and stood at the edge of the stage, radiating cold, looking down at me where I was lying with my blade ready to take him.

"No," he said. "No good, troll."

I began to roll left, then rolled right instead and heard him striking the floor behind me while I crawled away. I wriggled under the next row of benches, jumped over the one behind it, and then scooted myself the length of the next row between the legs, collecting a mat of gray dust on my chest. I emerged barely in time to run out of his way, and stood panting again at the back wall, still shivering with the chill his communicator had cast on me. Something else thumped softly above us. There was definitely someone in the balcony, someone furtive. Neither one of us looked up this time.

Zul walked slowly up the center aisle from the stage, and stopped halfway up, leaving room for me to break for the door. I raised my sword and didn't move. If he wanted me to think I could escape, he had something planned. I didn't dare.

"Coward," he said, and tossed something at me with his left hand.

The silver ball spun toward me. I screamed with pain, and batted the communicator away from me with my beautiful shiny weapon, closing my eyes, feeling the cold down through the blade, feeling the sea inside me freezing and cracking, feeling my muscles cramp and fail.

No, I was still breathing, I heard the ball land and roll out the door. I opened my eyes and jerked my hand up to defend myself, but Zul hadn't attacked after all. He was staggering backward, his face hidden.

He had a cat the size of a dog on his head. Bear had his head between her front paws and was kicking his face with her powerful hind legs as if he were a catnip toy. She must have dropped on him from the balcony railing.

With his hand, Zul was trying to pry her off, but with his right hand, he was weaving his blade before him as if he were fighting another imaginary opponent. He kept walking backward, making no sound himself, while she screamed and kicked, dark spots of blood spotting his orange uniform. When he felt the back of the stage with his legs, he sat carefully down, still keeping the blade in front of him, now feeling the cat as if looking for something.

I ran down the aisle toward him and danced before him, looking for an opening to hit him. There was none. His edge, in the intricate nonrepeating pattern he was making, cut across every open target. I ran to one side, climbed over the bench backs, and got up onto the stage on one side of him, praying he couldn't see me. He found something in the cat's hunching back and squeezed. Bear wailed. I dove at the back of the man while he was still parrying the empty room. I fell on him with my sword extended, and drove it right through.

He stood up, and I barely managed to yank it back out of him. Bear gave one last frantic kick and sprang away, crashing onto the floor as if she were crippled. He turned around, his face a red mask, with a red wet beard and rows of claw marks ripped across his eyes and fanning out across his cheeks. He put his left hand on the stage, lifted his right foot to come after me—

—and fell backward, barely missing Bear as he landed.

His chest was still moving and he was still holding his blade.

I wasn't going to go near him. I didn't believe him. It was the same action I had tried to do to him, the theatrical fall. I inched over to the other end of the stage and carefully got down, sliding along between the benches. Bear was staggering up the aisle toward the open door, lurching as if she were drunk.

"Are you all right?" I said to her.

She gave me a cat look. "You are mine," she said firmly and wobbled out the door.

I looked around at the Sefir Zul. Now his chest wasn't moving anymore, but I would wait. I wouldn't move until I was sure this wasn't another layer of strategy. Zul was capable of anything. Anything.

Or maybe not.

I wiped my blade on my trousers and sheathed it.

"Well, bravo, monkey," said a quiet voice I didn't want to recognize. The voice came from directly above me.

29

Pretended Stumble (**Wounded Bird,** Easy Prey)

I looked up, and there he was. He was leaning over the balcony rail staring down at me, no older than he was when I left him, my master. He still wore his hair the same way, careful ringlets that framed his dry little face and took him an hour to do properly, most of it pulled back into an elaborate tail and the rest draping neatly.

"Look at you. Too big," he said. "Much more elegant the way I made you."

I opened my mouth and shut it again. Something the size of a squirrel monkey with a doll-baby face was not elegant, but I wasn't going to argue with him. I always lost, because he never stopped until I lost my temper, and then he hit me.

An expression of impatience passed across his face, and he shifted his eyes to Zul's splayed body. "That was very messy."

"It worked," I said. Don't talk.

He chuckled, a low and deliberately musical sound. He always pitched his voice a little lower than it really was. I realized he wasn't much bigger than I was now. He was a pocket-sized man himself, small even for a Forester.

"Malka monkey, so alive and so savage. Yes, it worked. You made a mess. It must have annoyed him. He had a file on you the size of a library, nearly the size of the file he had on me. I did a little research on Caliban before I left. He didn't figure out how well I made you, though."

Very well indeed, I didn't say, though that was what I was supposed to say. He used to stand me on a table in front of friends and prompt me, "How well is the Malka monkey made?" and I would perform in my high baby voice like the talking animal I'd been, so his friends would underestimate him.

Leave me alone.

He winced. "Not so loud, not so loud," making shushing motions with the small neat hands. "You're loose at the seams, it's spraying out all over you. I can take care of that. You shouldn't have run away, monkey mine. I'm the only one who knows how to fix you."

He was the only one who knew how to break me, too. "I don't want to be fixed."

He laughed and stood up from the railing. "You'd rather keep sucking the magic in until you blow up? Greedy, greedy monkey. Come on, come here." He strolled along the edge of the balcony.

"I don't think so. I don't think that's a good idea."

"I think it's a very good idea," my master said. "I gave you most of my power when I made you. I have been traveling by commercial ship from world to world, stopping here and there to make enough money to buy a ticket and using all the ability I had left over to keep myself alive. A ticket, Malka, you made me buy a *ticket* when I'd given twenty years and most of my power to make my amusing little familiar into an engine that could move a *world*. I think it's a *very* good idea. *No,* you are not going out that door. *Stay, Malka.*"

I stayed, unable to move for the moment.

My master posed at the top of the stairs, one trim little leg bent to one side, the other pointed toe forward, his fine small hands braced neatly on the banisters either side of him, the curly locks falling just so over the tailored shoulders of his jacket, just the kind of witch who would think it funny to make his familiar an elegant-looking little creature with a foul temper, a tendency to bite, and a greedy appetite for loose magic.

"Let me look at you. Just let me look at you. You've made some adjustments in proportion, haven't you? I don't know whether I agree. I think larger hands and feet. And those very entertaining breasts will have to go." He came down one step and paused, considering.

"The ears go back on. Pink inside, weren't they? With fringe on the edges."

No ears. It had taken me years to get rid of them. I didn't want the ears back.

"And I'm putting the whiskers back over your eyes." Another step, another pause. "After we get out of here, of course. I took a gamble getting here at all. You can't buy a front-row ticket to attend a Class Two sanction. So I had to piggyback on an Enforcement ship while they were searching for me, and put up with their hideous idea of translation to get here," he said, pitching his voice even deeper. "And I never want to, and I never *will*, Malka, I never will do that again. I am not happy with you."

"Make yourself another familiar, then," I said.

"Don't you think I would if I could?" He skirted around the body of the Sefir Zul. "No, a witch gets one chance when it comes to familiars. I gave you part of my self when I made you, Malka mine, and I can't take it back. I have to remake you instead, after I've put you to your proper work. Why did you run away from me?"

"You said to stay away from anyone who would hurt me," said Malka the stupid monkey, already back inside her cage but pulling hopefully at the latch of the locked door.

"Did I?" He tapped me with his short finger. "So you thought you'd be a lawyer and play with the words I gave you?" This close, he smelled dry and tired. I could move now. He liked me to run a little, not so far I got out of reach, but enough to make it entertaining.

He wasn't all-powerful. He could tell me what to do, but he wasn't all-powerful. He wasn't even very big. I'd been running away for half a century from a small, vain, mean man with a fondness for cruelty and self-important clichés.

The foot of the Sefir Zul moved. There was another layer. There was another layer.

"Leave me alone," I said again, louder this time.

My master staggered and rippled, but he said, in his most mellow voice, "Leave me alone? Malka, you can't be alone. You're part of me. Even if you killed me, you'd have to go with me. Familiars don't survive their makers. I gave you part of my brain and part of my body when I made you. Go ahead, shout at me, try to kill me, but you love being alive, don't you, Malka? I made you that way. So it's life *with* me or no life at all without me."

For a moment I almost believed him. Though I knew differently, I couldn't stand the idea of going back to being nothing but magic, drifting and dreaming and outside time and space. I couldn't give up this small, intense material life for that.

Zul's other foot moved. He bent his elbows and felt around on the floor, put one hand on his belly, and sat up. He belched and spat blood. "Fah," he said distinctly, and opened his small black eyes. His face wasn't all red. Some of it was pale, almost blue, but I hadn't killed him after all, not yet.

My master turned around to look for the source of the noise, and so I abandoned all my rational arguments, made a wordless snarl, and kicked him as hard as I could in the back of the knee. I used to do that all the time, but then it was in the back of the ankle and he just laughed at me.

"Hey!" he yelped. "You little bitch!" and he swung around and backhanded me, then leaned down and massaged his knee.

"Bigger bitch now," I said, and kicked him in the other knee with all the force I could muster.

"You want to get beaten bloody?" he yelled in his natural voice, which was about an octave higher, and came after me, limping in his fine tight beige trousers.

Zul felt around on the floor beside him and came up with his sword. He braced his other hand on the floor and got up to one knee, using the sword as a prop.

I backed away, defending myself from my master's blows with my hands, not very effectively, not nearly as effectively as I could. I had my sword in its sheath, but I ignored it and hoped he would too. "I don't care!" I screamed. "You're going to hurt me anyway, you always do!"

He smacked me in the face again, and again. Step by step I backed up the aisle between the benches. With each step, he followed me and hit me again. He loved to hit, loved to make me yelp, loved to throw things at me while I scampered around the room and whined and screamed and raged. It was why he designed me to be as angry as I was, because it made such good sport. Oh, he was happy now that he had me back.

Zul was on both feet now, his hair standing on end, his black eyes staring at me over my master's shoulder. The whole front of his grimy shirt was smeared with blood. He lurched forward, and coughed wetly.

To cover the noise, I started making squeaking noises, flapping my hands, and twisting away from my master's blows, so he narrowed his eyes and chose his targets more carefully. I took another step back, and another, and my master followed me, steering me with blows away from the open door, until I had my back to the wall, right next to the door.

"Stop! Stop!" I squealed, and so of course he hit me again, harder, and then he paused and kicked me in the knee, and then as I wailed at the top of my voice, he lifted his foot again and raised it for a kick to my belly.

The Sefir Zul, right behind him, had a much more controlled swing even if he was standing at an angle and drooling blood. He sliced right through my master's neck to clear him out of his way.

Then he checked the motion gracefully, used the force to angle it around, and cut straight through my neck with the backswing as my master's body fell from between us.

Or he would have, if I had been there. He was sure I would be. He had contempt for me, just as he always had, just as I had told him I should with my squealing and flapping and furious kicking when I was fighting someone besides him. He misjudged me. So he missed me, because I wasn't there. Malka had her layers too. I was out the door and running through the halls, as fast as I could, not waiting to see how long it would be before I disappeared into thin air because my master was dead.

I scrambled through the window to the outside and fell with a painful thud to the ground below. For a minute I couldn't catch my breath. Was this it? Was this what my end would feel like now he was dead, a painful suffocation? I got to my hands and knees anyway, stood up, kept walking, and broke into a shuffling trot without any breath.

About ten feet farther, I gasped some air in. Halfway across the square, I was wheezing, but I could breathe. I was still alive, then, even if he was really dead. I didn't think even my master could keep going with his curly head separated from his tidy square shoulders. Yes, my master was dead, definitely. I felt something hauling at me, tugging at me. Something was sucking the spirit out of me. A whirlpool of magic, pouring away from me and back to the building I had just left, but I had a million whirlpools inside me to replace every ounce I lost.

Dead, he had to be dead. Even though I was breathing more or less steadily now, I sat down right where I was, right there in front of the steps to Kaihan's black tower. I drew my knees up, wrapped my arms around them, and rocked back and forth, silently, hoping I was mourning the little bastard who gave me birth, and mourning even more the fact that part of him lived on in me. Part of his brain, part of his body, part of his power.

I wanted to rip those parts out, whatever they were. Did he give me my permanently lost temper, while he got to keep the mean, controlled nastiness? Did I get the wordless screams, while he got the mellow, supercilious flow of words? Did he give me the part of him that his dog loved before, or did the dog ever love him at all? Whatever it was, I didn't want to give it room. I wanted it dead in that room with him, even if that meant I was dead too. I assured myself I meant every word, and rocked back and forth some more, because I suspected if I gave it some time I might change my mind, but no wonder familiars died too when they killed their masters. They had to, if they wanted to get rid of them completely. The magic inside me was pouring out as if I'd been punctured.

There was a footstep, and I froze, afraid I'd somehow resurrected him with my thoughts, half laughing at myself for the superstition, already recovering from his loss.

"Malka monkey," said a slightly slurred, quiet, musical voice. "Bad monkey," and it laughed.

I jerked my head up. My little master was staggering toward me, the tailored jacket a sodden mass of dark red, the ends of his hair limp with blood, his hands holding his head up, his neck crawling where his head and shoulders were knitting back together. The magic that was pouring out of me was pouring into him.

"To kill me you'd have to kill yourself," he said, letting go of his head with one hand. "You can't do that, can you? You're as eager to live as any collection of biochemicals, aren't you? Remarkable. Like a fish in a net, breathing in the thing that kills it, because it can't stop breathing, because that would kill it." He sounded almost happy.

I rocked back on my heels and stood up.

"I love life," he said, shaking his head in wonder, wincing at the motion, but still walking toward me. "Living things, random clots of cells, rolling along in the mud, breathing, eating, thinking, building houses, writing books and having babies, all for what? So they can keep on living."

"You don't love life, you love death," I said, backing up.

"Of course. Who in his right mind wouldn't? Purity. Simplicity. Conclusion. Happy endings." He took the other hand off his head and wiped it on his beige trousers, leaving a smear of blood.

"So why don't you die, if you love death that much?" I took another step back.

"When I'm having so much fun? I can keep following you forever, sucking the life out of you. Can you feel it, Malka? I can take as much from you as I want, whenever I want, as long as I'm near."

I turned and ran, but I could feel the trail of magic like a leash, like a tail of string from my center unraveling behind me, and when I turned around there he was, only a few feet away.

"I can kill you, and I can bring you back to life, and I can take as much from you as I want, whenever I choose," he said contentedly. The blood was drying and disappearing from his clothing and his hair. His neck was smooth, with no trace of a scar.

Too smooth. He was too smooth all over. He only acted this way, only acted the serene all-knowing devil, when he was risking it all. He loved to risk his life. What was he afraid of?

"You can take as much from me as you want," I said, stretching the moment, casting about for any escape. The ocean inside me was unsettled and, though he looked completely healed, I could still feel my power flowing to him. He had opened a channel between us, and hadn't closed it back up. If I didn't fight the channel . . . I could feel the flood speed up.

His eyes widened slightly, and his mouth curled. "As much as I want, any time," he repeated.

"How much do you want, and when?" I asked him, letting go a little more. Bespeaking as *loud* as I could so he wouldn't notice what I was doing with the channel, said, *"This much? Now?"*

He laughed, with an edge to it that was unfamiliar.

"Or this much? Or this?" It wasn't enough, though the pavement seemed to flow and puddle beneath his feet. I let the channel widen, let the surge increase.

"Such vitality," he said, stepping closer, his face smoothing even more, blandly supercilious. He didn't know how much I'd grown since I'd left him. He was fooled by my size. He had no idea how much was contained within me, and he had left the channel open.

"This? Is this as much as you WANT?" I said. *"You can have as much of me as you WANT, any time you WANT, can't you?"* I could add to the outpouring just a little, I found.

He shook his head. "Settle down." But now his face was glowing with a yellow light, his curls lifting away from his head, his tailored jacket sparkling with hundreds of tiny glints. "Let's go before these Enforcement people get overexcited." He began to make motions with his fingers, closing motions.

"You want all my power?" I repeated hoarsely. *"You want me to empty myself? Is that what you want?"*

"Malka, down," he said, backing away, his little jacket tight as a sausage, his beige trousers stiff, the tiny glints becoming sparks. I could smell burning hair.

"You want my death so you can have life? You want life? I give you my life! You can have it. NOW!" I yelled, and, finding the control to do it, let the channel between us open completely. I gave him my life.

In the moment before the connection between us winked out, I saw him expand to twice his size. His hair stood out from his head, his cheeks filled up, and his beautiful jacket and trousers exploded. Then he was gone and there was a falling cloud of tiny sizzling sparks that burned out before they hit the ground.

I still could not kill, but what made me alive was more than he could take.

A voice said, in Mennenkalt, "Spirit . . . ?"

I jerked my head up and there was somebody already standing over me, somebody no less dangerous to me though much better intentioned. It was yet another Mennenkalt elder, this one an elderly woman in weathered green, with dumpling chin and dismayed blue eyes, appalled—no, saddened—by what she had just seen, but bravely venturing on.

"Kavelnes peder lle yer peder. Kurfurst lle zhatter, ekestverte yer andanfellter." Shackled spirit, the time is now, and the time is past.

The Sefir Zul's voice yelled, "Over there! That's her!" and broke into wet coughs. I looked up and he was coming out of the building. They wouldn't stay dead, either of them. Any moment now, my master would be back too.

"No, no, no," I said, and as the woman staggered back and raised her hands, I ran into Kaihan's tower, slammed the door behind me, and stood in the dark.

So my decision was made. As usual with my decisions, it was made when I wasn't paying attention. I did not wish to be released back into Nothing, thank you very much, I did not wish to be a Mennenkalt deity. I liked the game of being Malka very much, and probably even more now that my master was dead, but I had to move this planet out of danger.

30

Attack with Opposition (Grizzly's Kiss, Overpowering the Blade)

It wasn't going to be easy. Since I had killed my master, I wasn't holding together as well as I'd thought I could. Here in the dark, I could feel the surge and flow of the immense sea of magic inside me, whirling around. It sprayed out whenever I did anything, not a controlled act but a pressure leak. At some point, I wasn't going to be able to stop it. It was going to keep going, and then all my insides would come out all at once, just like Roder's ship when the drive collapsed. The Mennenkalts had almost the right idea, but even if I could stand the idea of letting them kill me, I couldn't let them do it. It wasn't my nature. Not the natural order of Malka. Malka was fierce and independent, a creature who bit and ran away and kept biting and running away.

It was dark and empty and incredibly hot inside the tower. When I looked up, all I could see was blackness, and it made me seasick, because inside I was swinging wider and wilder, diving through the heavy waves of the ocean inside me, being thrown to the top. I had to hurry. Time and space might be only metaphors, but my body was made of normal matter. It would not survive long enough to do the job if I ignored the philosophy of reality. What a strange thing it was to be human, to be bound to the here and now. A very intense experience, very focused. "Small but intense," I said, and felt myself spill over, as if I were a bowl so full of water every movement made it overflow.

"Who is it?" said a blurry voice from the circle at the middle, inside the nine-pointed star. "Who's there?" It sounded like an elderly person without teeth, just waking up.

I squatted down, peering. "Hello."

Something unfolded slowly in the circle, sitting up, then standing. It wasn't very big, and it was on four legs, but I couldn't see much more than that. It seemed to be turning around. I caught a silhouette of a low head, and a long nose. Was this the engine they'd made? It was smaller than Bear.

"What you want?" the mushy voice came again, growling.

"I want to help you send the world away," I said.

"I'm not ready." It turned around again, and laid itself down.

After thirty seconds or so, I realized that was all it was going to say. I reached over the chalk lines and poked it in the side. It was rough, thick, and nappy like a carpet. "Wake up."

It grunted and shifted. No answer. I sat back on my heels. *Wake up.*

It yelped and jumped to its feet, snapping at its own side as if a bee had stung it. "Not *ready*," it said. "Stop. You're interrupting my life." It turned around and around four times in its little circle, then lay down again with a thump. I couldn't quite see, but I thought its head was buried under its forelegs.

I hadn't figured on this. I had just assumed the drive would know what to do, would feed on the magic I was leaking so lavishly and then follow its own nature. *Wake up.* No answer. The dark blur in the center of the diagram was busy with its dreams.

Wake up. I showered the immense chamber, made its walls crawl, when I spoke, but I didn't have any effect on the drowsy engine. *Wake up wake up wake UP.* The dark rounded back shook like gelatin, and I heard a moan, but no response.

Boom.

I jumped and turned around, and the door was still vibrating.

Boom.

The door shook and clattered.

Boom. An Enforcement shock cannon aimed at Kaihan's front door. Zul's call for help had been heard. Boom. Boom. Shuddering waves of air blew past me.

I turned back to the thing in the circle. *Help,* I shouted, and felt the force of the stuff inside me pour out on the creature, a jet of escaping ectoplasm as remorseless as a fire hose. *Help,* I repeated, and it flinched; *help,* I repeated, and it screamed, and so I said *help help help help HELP* and then something like a wisp of brown smoke lifted from its blurry body.

Boom.

I was afraid I had killed it. Then the smoke curled up more thickly from its flank, turned a questing head, and spiraled directly toward me and into me as if I were an exhaust fan.

Stop.

"No," it said grumpily, and finished pouring its whole self into me.

Boom.

You wanted help. Here I am, it said. My shirt drew more tightly across my breasts, and the lower hem lifted above my navel. My arms were locked in the tight hug of the sleeves. I could feel my thighs spreading out my trousers, and the bottoms of the trousers crawling up past my ankles. Instead of drawing power from me to power itself, as I had planned, it had crowded itself into me, and my already crammed interior was distended beyond the ability of my skin or my clothes to contain it. Like my master, I was going to explode.

Boom.

I ran along the inside of the wall, looking for doors. No secret catches. No hidden passages. No concealed instructions.

Boom, and a crunch. Kaihan's front door was as well defended as Roder's had been, but it wasn't enough here either. I turned and faced the doors, my sword in my hand. Malka the Defender. Malka the Warrior. Malka the . . . Malka the Malka. That was all.

So I did what Malka would do in a situation like this. I glared at the door as it splintered again, and I smacked that door with my sword, as hard as I could, and I stamped my small foot, and I screamed at the top of my voice. Then, because it was an extremely bad situation, I threw the sword on the ground and I jumped on it, no matter how pretty it was, and I screamed again. A big loud scream with my mouth as open as it could get. I opened it wider and wider, and like the rest of me, it had gotten bigger.

It was wonderful. I could scream so loudly with this mouth that the whole black chamber of the tower filled with the noise. I could scream so loudly the walls shook and drowned out the shock cannon.

It was just like scratching an itch, an itch so intense that I'd cheerfully scratch a hole in my skin, scratch straight through to the bone if it meant the itch would stop. I screamed and screamed.

I found I could scream so loudly, with my mouth so large, that my mouth began to slide back over the rest of my head, like a sock turning inside out, like taking your shirt off by rolling it off, and the scream kept getting louder, and my mouth got bigger, but it felt good. It felt like loosening a tight belt, and I was screaming louder and louder the more I did it, so I kept rolling me inside out until that Malka body was right off, sitting on the floor with its legs stuck out and the most astonished expression on its face, and I have no idea how all of me fit into that little thing when I was as big as I was. Big as the world. Bigger.

Boom.

Slow time, I said with my enormous mouth, and looked around to see what was going on. What should I be doing?

The Malka part of me said *getting us out of here.*

Oh, well. That. I surrounded the whole world and knew it for what it was, as simple as that, as complicated as that, and it took forever and no time at all.

I don't remember it all. Much of it was mathematics, but a lot of it was poetry, and every bit of it was revenge against the Sefir Zul. I remember looking down from the sky, through the clouds. I think they were like drifts of powder, like white treetops, like underwater explosions, like frayed quilts, but each one was different so I explained them all differently, at the top of my voice. I was looking up, too, through the spinning currents of red iron and layers of folded rock, but every fold and current contained meaning and had a name, names I yelled as hard as I could. Every river on the world rolled in its channels between eccentric patchworks of human property, and thin determined roads wriggled along, but every river and every road was itself, and each stream and lane that fed them had their own arguments. I wish I remembered even one of those arguments. They were elegant and really nasty. Argumentative arguments. I remember mountain ranges, deserts, oceans flat on top and jagged on the bottom, and I remember life. Life had its own premises and equations, and each species and individual had them too, and every one of them was annoying Zul, and I explained them to Zul in a happy shout, and outside the tower he swore at me in slow motion, bleeding.

Soft-bodied invertebrates clung to rocks, squeezed themselves through the water, snaked through mud. Animals so small they couldn't be seen hunted and ate other tiny animals, or grazed on plants that were even smaller. Single-celled organisms floated on every surface, flowed with the water, drifted in the air. Animals bored the Sefir Zul, so I told him about them at length. Birds, cattle, sheep, furry things like rats, and austere, grimly smiling reptiles moved in every direction. I surrounded them, and knew each of them for what it was, and flung them at him one by one.

Hurry up, I said to myself.

Time is slow, time is now, I answered. I was savoring the revenge in every detail.

Everywhere there were human begins, even in the most desolate places. In a deep shadowed canyon carved into a flat-land a woman was sitting on a doorstep carved into the vertical rock, trying to get a piece of corn out of her front teeth. Too bad, Zul. In the middle of a sea flecked with bursts of light shooting back up at the sun, a boat rocked, and a dark man with naked limbs no bigger around than my wrist squatted staring down at the water. Around bays, across plains, along brooks and above the frost line, there were human beings, each one an entire person unto himself with a lifetime of memories and a stubborn, implacable difference of character from every other person, and none of them liked the Sefir Zul, none of them would ever have to obey him, and he couldn't do anything about it.

Something went boom. *Hurry, hurry,* I said, and stamped my small foot. I laughed at how small I was. Something so small as Malka could stick a pin in the Sefir Zul and shove it right through.

In the city that wound itself around a hill at the bed of a great river, people lived too. They lived in the silted banks, in the strong-smelling streets that wound up from the river, in the close-built homes banding the belly of the city, and even in some of the mansions still left standing near the crown. People were alive at the flat top of the hill, some of them dressed in orange and operating a shock cannon while a bleeding man, listening to everything I said, leaned sideways and raged at them.

I swallowed them all, all the people, and knew them for what they were, right then, right there, and I let their arguments continue inside me, and I thumbed my nose at the Sefir Zul. Swallowed them whole, tipped the cup and drank them up and their city and their country and their world, and then I spat out Zul.

Another boom, and that human Malka inside me shouted *Now! Go now!* She was a cranky little sprat, but she was right.

So I did. I turned myself inside out and translated everything I knew about everything inside me, except for those orange people with the shock cannon, especially that Zul fellow who smelled so bad, and all his ships. They got lost in the translation.

And then, being already inside out, I stepped outside myself, left myself brooding and immense, and I blinked and sneezed and forgot most of it. The chalk dust had gotten up my nose. The front door was completely shattered, and daylight showed through, but there was no-body outside at all.

I stepped through, and went out to see what had happened.

31

The Salute
(**Malka,** Her Salute)

I looked up. There was Nothing up there. No Enforcement ships, no sun, just a sweep of porcelain sky. There was me down here, though. I was in translation along with every other human being in the world, temporarily a memory in the mind of the enormous, very cranky engine containing us all, an engine that didn't have anything to do with me anymore and had forgotten completely about the Sefir Zul, so there.

I sat down on the front steps and stuck my legs out in front of me. They were short legs for a human woman, and now they probably wouldn't get any longer. At least they were in proportion to the rest of me. I reached down, took my shoes off, and stretched out in the sun, leaning back on my elbows and wiggling my damp toes.

I sniffed. Something smelled funky, like sweat or hair, human. I sat up. Nobody around. I lay back down. I would have to bathe more often if I was entirely material now.

Someone was at the other end of the square, coming toward me, a man of medium height, wearing a loose shirt and trousers in a weathered woven fabric. As he came closer, I saw he was good-looking in a serious dark way, and very lifelike. His eyes, fringed with astonished black lashes, were the color of river water flowing over pebbles. I recognized the model.

I sat up, fumbled at my back, found the hilt of my sword, brought it to my forehead, and swept it aside grandly, with a hiss of divided air.

"Where are we going?" he called, pointing at the sky.

I shrugged and laid the sword down, off to one side. "The Never-Mind. You can give it your message directly."

He came up, and stood and looked down into my face. He smiled, a sweet smile. And he knew it, too.

A thin ripple, a memory of an ocean wave, washed across the space inside me, saying *Stop that*, but it was a very small voice. He ignored it with a flicker of his eyes. So did I, though I knew it meant I wasn't completely human after all.

He sat down on the black step with me, and I leaned my shoulder against him, but not too hard, just hard enough.

"It didn't kill you, then."

"I'm not admitting anything," I snapped, sitting back upright.

There were other people coming too, and I wished they wouldn't, and they did what I was afraid they would do, which was fuss and exclaim and celebrate. Well, most of them did. Octavian, for instance, told me, smiling contentedly, "I knew it was going to happen. The Beast knew." Electra gave me a huge hug and I managed not to bite her while she was doing it, though I did growl low in my throat so she pulled away quickly. Cully wanted to hug me too and I let him, and Fergus nodded his head at me and blushed.

Not everybody fussed. Master Kaihan stood back and watched me with his black eyes. Bear staggered up from somewhere, as big as a jaguar, and sat in my lap, taking up the whole thing, purring and making my thighs hurt. The Lisane, her pupils back to normal when she looked at me, said in Mennenkalt, "Thank you, god of rage."

"I'm not. That is," I said gesturing back at the black building behind us.

"No," she said firmly. "You are the small god of rage. That back there is a big engine for making worlds move."

You can't change who you are, not really. I believe that. But identity is a big place, with attics, bedrooms, back stairs, rear doors, and basements. You don't have to spend all your time in the front room. You don't have to go in there at all if you don't want to, and maybe I would get to grow another couple of inches after all, in a while.

Delia Marshall Turner is an educator who lives in
Philadelphia with her husband and daughter. She is
a nationally ranked saber fencer.